someone else's life

someone else's life

KATIE DALE

EMBER

This is a work of fiction. Names, characters, places, and incidents either
are the product of the author's imagination or are used fictitiously. Any resemblance
to actual persons, living or dead, events, or locales is entirely coincidental.

Text copyright © 2012 by Katie Dale
Cover art copyright © 2012 by Dimitri Caceaune

All rights reserved. Published in the United States by Ember, an imprint of
Random House Children's Books, a division of Random House, Inc., New York.
Originally published in hardcover in the United States by Delacorte Press,
an imprint of Random House Children's Books, New York, in 2012.

Ember and the E colophon are registered trademarks of Random House, Inc.

Visit us on the Web! randomhouse.com/kids

Educators and librarians, for a variety of teaching tools,
visit us at RHTeachersLibrarians.com

The Library of Congress has cataloged the hardcover edition of this work as follows:
Dale, Katie.
Someone else's life / Katie Dale. — 1st ed.
p. cm.
Summary: When seventeen-year-old Rosie's mother dies from Huntington's Disease,
a devastating secret is revealed that sends Rosie on a journey from England to the United States
with her ex-boyfriend, where she discovers yet more deeply buried and troubling secrets and lies.
ISBN 978-0-385-74065-4 (hc) — ISBN 978-0-375-98959-9 (glb)
ISBN 978-0-375-89972-0 (ebook)
[1. Family problems—Fiction. 2. Secrets—Fiction. 3. Identity—Fiction.] I. Title.
PZ7.D15244So 2012
[Fic]—dc22
2011005407

ISBN 978-0-385-74066-1 (pbk.)

RL: 6.0

Printed in the United States of America

10 9 8 7 6 5 4 3 2 1

First Ember Edition 2013

Random House Children's Books supports the First Amendment
and celebrates the right to read.

For my wonderful parents.
Thank you so much, for everything.

And for all those whose lives have been touched by
the shadow of Huntington's disease. Your courage
and strength are humbling and truly inspirational.
May a cure be found soon.

Prologue

"Are you turned on?" Josh whispers, his breath tickling my ear in the dark.

"Shh," I chide, my eyes glued to the screen as Patrick Swayze and Demi Moore sit at the potter's wheel, their hands sliding over each other in the slippery clay. "It's romantic."

"And very suggestive . . . ," he says, a delicious shiver thrilling down my spine at his touch in the dark—secret and sensual.

Is this how it feels?

I gaze at the screen as the lovers' kisses get stronger, deeper, the pot long forgotten, goose bumps tingling all over my body as Josh's skin strokes mine.

I bite my lip. *Is this what I've been waiting for?*

I watch as the lovers come together for the last time in this life—their love for each other real and passionate and achingly visible.

Is that what we have? True love?

I look at Josh.

A love that will last forever, no matter what . . . ?

He smiles, his deep brown eyes sparkling in the dark as he gently cups my face.

"God, I love you," he whispers, his gaze deep in mine.

I stare at him, my heart thrumming madly against my chest. He's never said it before—neither of us has.

This is it . . .

"I love you too." I smile, my grin splitting my face, my stomach erupting with butterflies as I dissolve in his arms, pulling him closer than ever before . . .

This is really it . . .

PART ONE

Someone Else's Footprints

What's in a name?
That which we call a rose by any other
name would smell as sweet.
—William Shakespeare,
Romeo and Juliet

Chapter One

Sunlight dances over the little girl's dark curls as she toddles clumsily through the dry grass. Her rosy cheeks dimple as she grins, her green eyes sparkling as she lunges sticky fingers toward the camera. Suddenly she trips.

The picture immediately jolts and twists into the grass, continuing at a skewed angle as a chestnut-haired woman rushes over to the child. But she is not crying. The screen fills with silent giggles as her mother scoops her up, her beautiful face filled with tenderness as she cuddles her daughter tightly, protectively, holding her so close it seems she'll never let go . . . The picture begins to blur . . .

I click the remote and the image flicks off, plunging the room into darkness. I stare at the blank screen. It's weird watching your memories on TV, like watching a movie. It's like somewhere, in some wonderful world, those moments are trapped, bottled, to be enjoyed again. I wonder if heaven's like that—if you get to choose the best moments of your life and just relive them over and over. I hope so.

The world outside looks different already. A desert of white—the first white Christmas Eve in Sussex in years. The snow hides everything, glossing over the lumps and dips and tufts to leave a perfect, smooth surface. Like icing on a Christmas cake. It's all still there, though. The dirty gravel that hisses and spits as you drive over it, the jagged rocks in the garden, the muddy patch where nothing grows—they're all still there, hidden, sleeping, beneath the mask of snow.

Like my mother.

Nothing on the *inside* changed, the doctors said. She could still understand what we were saying, she just couldn't respond like she used to. Couldn't hug me and tell me everything was going to be all right, like she always had. Like I needed her to. Because everything was not all right.

I pull the blanket tighter, but it makes no difference. I'm already wearing three sweaters. Ever since Mum got ill I'm always too hot or too cold—I can't explain it. Yesterday was one of the hot days, even though it snowed practically nonstop. Everyone looked at me like I was crazy, standing in the snowy graveyard in Mum's strappy stilettos and my red velvet dress among the whispering sea of black, disapproving sighs rising like smoke signals in the frosty air. But I didn't care—the biddies could tut all they liked—she was *my* mother and the dress was her favorite on me. She called me her Rose Red.

The shoes were her favorites too—I remember her dancing in them at my cousin Lucy's wedding. I was about four or five at the time, hiding beneath the buffet table in protest at the fuchsia meringue I'd been forced to wear as flower girl. But when Mum started dancing I forgot all about that. I

2

crawled out and just stared at her, mesmerized. God, she was graceful. Everyone stopped to watch her whirling, swirling form as she glided around the room, those heels clacking like castanets.

When the song ended she stopped, breathless and slightly dizzy, and looked around as if unsure where she was. Then someone started to clap. Embarrassment flushing her cheeks, she ran a hand through her hair and scooped me up into a tight hug, her eyes shining with tears. It was only later that I discovered it was the first song she and Daddy had danced to at their wedding.

The stilettos were one of the first heartbreaks of the diagnosis. I remember hearing Mum crying in her room one day and padding up to find her sitting on her bed, placing them carefully into a silver box like a coffin, shrouded with beautiful rose-colored tissue paper. The doctors said high heels were just an accident waiting to happen, and that, with everything else, was something she really didn't need. I watched as she kissed each shoe before pressing the lid down gently and tying the whole precious package together with a blue ribbon. The first of many sacrifices to Huntington's.

That was a long time ago, though. That Mum died long before her heart stopped beating last Tuesday. The real Mum. The way I'll always remember her, wearing those precious shoes and swirling and whirling away to her heart's content. Not lying alone, small and frail and empty, in a hospital bed.

The sharp ringing of the telephone makes me jump. I count the rings—one, two, three—and the machine kicks in.

"Hello!" Mum's voice sings, and my heart leaps. "You have reached the Kenning residence. Trudie and Rosie are

3

out at the mo, but if you'd like to leave a message—you know what to do!"

I swallow painfully. Aunt Sarah's been on at me to change it—and I know I should—but I just can't bring myself to erase her voice. She sounds so happy. So alive.

The caller clears his throat uncertainly. A familiar trait, no matter how much time's passed. My eyes flick to the phone.

"Um, hi—Rosie? It's Andy. It's uh, it's been a while, huh?" Awkward pause. "Listen, I'm—I'm sorry about your mum, it must be . . ." Another pause. "Shit. Look, I'd really like to see you—call me, okay? No pressure. Just as friends. Okay? You know I'm always here if . . . You know where I am. Bye."

Wow. Andy. He's right, it has been a long time.

"You should call him, you know."

I twist to see Aunt Sarah in the doorway. Is it that time already? Sarah works long hours at the local hospital, but that hasn't stopped her checking up on me whenever she can—to make sure I haven't slit my wrists or burned the house down or anything.

I shrug. "Maybe." *No*, I think. *No, no, no.*

"And why not?" She leans accusatorially in the doorway.

"I didn't say *no*, I said *maybe*," I protest.

"Same thing," she replies. "I know you."

It's true, she does. She's known me my whole life— literally. I was my mother's last hope for a child, at the age of forty-two—the miracle baby—and Sarah was the midwife who delivered me that night. The night my father never came back.

4

She's not really my aunt, or even a relative at all, but she's Mum's best friend and our next-door neighbor, and she's been there at every major event of our lives. Our guardian angel—younger than Mum, but older and wiser than me. A fact I'm never allowed to forget.

"Seriously, Rosie, you should go out, see people—enjoy the snow! God knows it won't last long!"

"I'm fine," I tell her.

"I know you are, sweetie . . . but it would be good for you, you know?"

I hate it when people tell me what's good for me—*Have a nice cup of tea, it'll make you feel better. Go on, Rosie, have a good cry, it's good for you.* Yeah, coz *that*'ll bring my mother back.

I get up and cross to the stereo.

"Look, Rosie, this isn't easy for any of us, you know?" Sarah sighs, smoothing a hand over her frazzled ponytail. "But you shouldn't hide away like this—it's Christmas Eve. You should be with people—family. I know you're going to your nana's tomorrow, but she'd *love* to have you to stay with her, not just for the holidays—"

I flick through the noisy radio stations.

"Rosie . . ."

I can see Sarah's reflection in the glass cabinet. She looks tired, drained—and old. Sarah's never been old. But I don't care. How can she be like the rest of them? Patronizing and clichéd and telling me what to do? I turn the volume up high, and a choir belts out "Joy to the World."

"Rosie!" She battles with the racket. "Rosie, turn it down!"

"I don't like that one either!" I yell back. "How's this?" "Rockin' Around the Christmas Tree" replaces the choir. I turn the volume higher. *"Have a happy ho-o-liday!"*

"ROSIE! Turn it *down!*"

"What?!" I yell back, cupping my hand to my ear. Maybe now she'll know how it feels.

"ROSALIND KENNING, YOU LISTEN TO ME!" Sarah yells, and I flick the radio off, her voice echoing in the sudden silence as I turn round. She is flushed and breathless, the light from the hallway behind her showing up every frizzed hair like a frenzied halo.

"I've come to a decision," I say. Calmly, rationally. "I need to know." I take a deep breath. "I need to know if I've got Huntington's."

There it is. Out in the open.

The color in Sarah's cheeks melts away, leaving her pale and serious. "Rosie . . ."

"I've made up my mind," I say, swallowing hard. "I can't live like this, not knowing. I need to know if I'm going to get it too, if I'm going to . . ." The words stick in my throat. "I need to know the truth."

"Rosie." Sarah swallows, steps closer. "You have to think about this, take some time . . ."

"I have." I round on her. "Don't you think I *have?*"

"Look, I know that with your mum gone everything's strange and scary—"

"You don't know anything!" I scream at her, my legs trembling. I've never shouted at Sarah, never yelled, never . . . but suddenly all the feelings that have been bottled up for too

6

long gush out in one big mess. "You *don't* know." I shake my head. "You don't—you can't . . ." I look away.

Sarah sighs. "All I'm saying is that it's too soon to be making choices like this, to take the test—"

"Too *soon*? When do you *want* me to find out? When I've got kids too? I'm not a child anymore, Sarah—I'm nearly eighteen!"

"I know, Rosie, but this is a life-changing decision we're talking about here. There's no cure, and once you know, you can't go back . . ."

"I can't go back anyway!" I choke on the words. "And no, actually. It's not a life-changing decision because nothing *actually* changes, does it? It's already decided whether I live or die—I'd just quite like to know which it's going to be, okay?"

Sarah looks beaten, hopeless.

"What kind of a life can I have otherwise?" I ask quietly. "Not knowing? Not knowing if one day *I'll* end up like—"

"You won't."

"Sarah, it's hereditary." I sigh. "It hangs on the toss of a coin."

"No." She takes my shoulders gently, her eyes so sad. "Rosie, sweetheart, you don't have Huntington's. You don't need the test."

"I'm not asking your permission, Sarah," I tell her quietly. "I've got an appointment at the clinic on Wednesday, and—"

"No," she says. "You don't understand." She takes a deep breath. "Rosie, you don't have the disease."

"Sarah," I say gently, as if to a child. "There's a fifty percent chance that I do—it's a genetic fact."

"That's what I mean," Sarah says slowly, not looking at me. "There is no chance."

"I—" I blink. "I don't understand . . ."

"Rosie . . ." She sighs, rubs her hand over her brow. "Oh, God!"

I don't move. Don't dare breathe.

"Rosie, you don't have the disease—you can't possibly, because—" Desperate pause. Swallow. Breath. "Because Trudie wasn't your mother."

Her eyes meet mine at last and I flick mine away.

There's a red stain on the carpet by the door, where Mum spilled red wine as she was handing it round one New Year's Eve. She'd said she was just a bit tipsy, but I knew she hadn't had a drop to drink all night.

Now it looks like blood.

"Rosie, I've wanted to tell you for such a long time, especially with Trudie getting worse and worse, to put your mind at rest, give you one less thing to worry about, and because you deserved—*deserve*—to know. But I couldn't while she was alive, don't you see? You were everything to her."

I tug at my sweater. It's hot again. Insufferably hot.

"God, this is awful! I'm so sorry, sweetie—this isn't how I wanted to tell you at all. But if you take the test they might compare your DNA, and I just . . . I didn't want you to find out from someone else. I had to tell you—to explain . . ." She trails off. "Rosie?"

I blink hard, trying to concentrate, focus.

She sighs. "Rosie, you had to know—you *have* to know— because it's the only way you can move on with your life— your own long and healthy life!"

The room whirls faster and faster.

"I don't understand."

Another sigh. The same gentle voice. "Rosie, you haven't inherited the disease. She wasn't your mother—"

"NO!" I scream, the loudness of my voice startling me. "She was—she is!"

"Rosie—" Sarah reaches for me.

"No! You were there!" I accuse her, wrenching away. "You were there when I was born, you *delivered* me—how can you . . . ?" I gasp for breath.

She nods. That weak smile again.

"Yes, yes, I was, which is why I know that Trudie wasn't—"

"Stop it! Stop *lying* to me!" I yell. "This is sick! This is just some sick way to stop me taking the test—admit it!" My eyes search hers, desperate for some sign that it's not true, that she's made it all up, but she just looks sad, tired.

I feel faint, giddy. *She was! She was my mother. Wasn't she? I close my eyes. She would have told me—she would have told me if I was adopted. Wouldn't she . . . ?*

"Rosie, sit down, you're swaying. Let's talk about this— please, let me explain . . ." Sarah reaches out, guiding, helpful.

I swipe her away and run, just run. Out of the back door, through the gate, the woods, hurtling down the hill toward the fields, yanking off the sweaters and sprinting blindly through the snow. I can't breathe. The flakes swirl faster and faster, dancing and whirling and twirling with my lost mother in my mind.

I've lost her, and she wasn't even mine.

The words tumble clumsily into the dance, cold and hard and heavy.

She wasn't even my mother to lose.

I'm losing him.

Josh's words tumble painfully around and around my head:

"We need to talk."

I know what that means.

Ever since he started college I've been expecting, dreading, fearing those words.

"Coming for a swim?" Melissa grins, running up beside me. "I'll race you fifty lengths!"

"Not today." I shake my head. "I'm not in the mood."

She sighs. "You've been *moody* for days now—this must be a record!"

I hug myself tightly.

Her face softens and she hooks her arm through mine. "Have you tried a hot water bottle?"

"What?"

"That works for me—or camomile tea?"

I stare at her. Why does everyone think anything can be solved with a cup of tea?

"Or I read that lavender oil can really help, if you rub it in."

"Where?" I ask, totally bemused.

"Your stomach, silly—it's supposed to help ease the cramps."

Cramps? Suddenly I understand.

"No, I haven't got—" The words stick like thorns in my throat as I calculate quickly.

"Oh, I get it!" Melissa grins. "You're just scared I'll beat you, huh? Frightened of a little competition?"

I smile weakly, my head pounding painfully.

Five weeks . . . nearly six . . .

"Come on," she laughs. "Don't be a baby!"

She drags me numbly down the street, my legs threatening to buckle any second as my blood rushes deafeningly in my ears.

Don't be a baby . . .

Chapter Two

The ground rushes up to meet me, and it's only now, collapsed in the snow, that I realize where I am.

Stark silhouettes of skeleton trees clutch at the first evening stars, and the vast expanse of snow is littered with row upon row of cold black headstones.

And there she is.

GERTRUDE KENNING

BELOVED DAUGHTER, WIFE, AND MOTHER

"*Liar!*" The scream rips from my throat, Sarah's words stabbing my brain as I screw my eyes shut, trying to drown out her voice, her pitying face. Her expression shifts into a smile, and now the face I see is my mother's, her brown eyes shining with warmth and love and life.

"*Liar!*" I sob, clawing at the snow, hurling the lumps of ice and mud at the grave—at the lies set in stone—flinging them harder and harder, my fingers bleeding, my eyes blurring, until finally my legs buckle beneath me, hot tears streaking down my cheeks. "You weren't my mother!"

But she was! She *was* my mother. The only one I had. And now this . . . this is all that's left.

I crumple into the snow, the crisp pain stinging my skin as my tears mingle with the ice.

I miss you, I miss you so much . . .

I close my eyes, remembering how we used to lie like this, making figures in the snow—a mummy angel and a baby angel. . . .

Tears flood the memory.

She was never my mother, never mine. My whole life—my whole life—is one big lie . . .

I struggle to my feet, bombarded with a kaleidoscope of memories—bright, garish, fake memories.

All fake—all lies.

My throat burns with tears.

Why didn't she tell me? Why did she lie? I had a right—I have a right to know who I am . . .

The graveyard spins around me.

Who am I . . . ?

I close my eyes.

"Rosie?"

I whirl round, my breath caught in my throat.

He looks different, older, his chin spattered with stubble, his hair longer, but I'd still know him anywhere.

"I thought it was you." Andy smiles hesitantly. "Are you okay? Did you get my message?"

I nod silently, glad of the dark hiding my tears.

"I was going to call round, but . . ." He shuffles his feet. "I wasn't sure whether . . . if you . . ." He swallows, his shoulders hunched, his hands deep in his pockets.

I hug my arms against the icy breeze, staring at my shoes.

"Besides, I've been under house arrest—Gran's visiting." Andy clears his throat. "We've just been to the Christingle."

I follow his gaze to the brightly lit church, its stained-glass windows spilling colored light over the chattering families huddling together outside.

Suddenly I shiver.

"Bloody hell, Rose, you're freezing. Here." He pulls off his jacket, and as he wraps it round me a bottle falls out. Vodka.

"That'll help too!" He laughs nervously, picking it up.

I stare at it, surprised.

"Well, you know." He shrugs. "Sermons can get a little dull . . ." He grins that familiar lopsided grin and my heart flips. "Not really—I'm off to a party. This big family Christmas thing is driving me crazy, and—" A frown flashes over his features. "I mean . . ."

I take the bottle and tip it skyward, the liquid burning my throat and making me feel sick. I take another swig.

"Easy!" Andy laughs. "I know you—two glasses of wine and you're a goner."

I look at him. *I know you.* My chest aches.

"Well, it's . . . it's good to see you, Rose." He smiles, those incredible blue eyes making my insides twist, my head rushing with memories. Real, bright, happy memories. "It's been a long time."

It has, but suddenly it feels like yesterday.

"Can I give you a ride home?" he offers.

14

Home. I wince, thinking of the dark, empty house filled with lies. I shake my head. It's not my home. Not anymore.

"Okay." He shuffles his feet, turns to go. "Well . . ."

"Wait," I say quickly. He turns.

I hesitate, the night dark and cold around us, his jacket warm on my shoulders, the sharp vodka racing through my veins.

"Did you say something about a party?"

The door opens, and I surrender to the music. The whole place is throbbing with it—*thud thud thud thud*—consuming and obliterating all thoughts, all conversation. I welcome it. Dropping the empty bottle by the door, I step into the throng.

Anonymous faces crowd in as Andy weaves us through the room, past flashes of blond hair and glittering earrings; heavy-lidded goths and pouting lip gloss; flesh, piercings, bottles, lines of shots, shrieks of laughter and, permeating it all, the unmistakable smell of weed.

"You want something to eat?" Andy mouths.

I shake my head, reaching instead for one of the shots. I down it easily, barely feeling the sting as it slides down my throat. I reach for another, but Andy catches my arm, pointing over my shoulder. "Hey, there's Bex!"

I turn and squint into the crowd, but the dark mass of writhing bodies twine into each other anonymously. I turn back to Andy, confused, and am suddenly shoved headfirst into his shoulder, beer slopping over my back.

"Hey!" Andy pushes the guy who knocked me. "Watch it, okay?"

The guy staggers away and collapses on a sofa.

"Ow . . . ," I moan quietly, the taste of fresh blood salty on my tongue, the scent of Andy's aftershave tickling my nose.

Andy looks down at me, concerned. "You okay?" He brushes my lips carefully with his thumb, and my head swims with more memories.

"You're soaked!" He grins, wiping beer from my hair. "Come on, let's get you cleaned up."

Apart from a pile of jackets, the bathroom is empty, the faint *thud thud thud* pulsing distantly through the floorboards. Andy grabs a damp cloth and starts to gently clean my cut, his brow furrowed in concentration as he leans closer, making me dizzy. He cups my cheek and my skin blazes, my heart pounding as his eyes meet mine.

Without thinking, I lean forward and press my lips against his.

He pulls back, surprised. "Rosie—" I search his eyes anxiously, his gaze deep in mine.

Then suddenly we're kissing, the taste of his soft lips so sweet and familiar, my heart thumping frantically against my ribs.

God, I haven't been kissed—haven't been touched—in so, so long . . .

I press closer, the kisses deepening, lengthening, as my mind spins into oblivion, my body on fire.

This is it. This is what I need. To escape. To just lose myself completely. To forget . . .

I kiss him harder, pushing my chest against his, my hand moving to his zip.

"Mm . . . ," Andy groans.

I tug at the little metal pull.

"Rosie . . ."

I push closer, my tongue sliding against his as I slip my hand inside . . .

"Rose, no—Rosie!" He pushes me away, my lips stinging in the empty air.

"I'm sorry," he sighs, running his hands through his hair. "I'm sorry, I can't . . . I can't do this."

"What?" I blink, his face swimming in front of mine. "Why? What's wrong?"

He looks away and I frown, trying to search his eyes, but they won't keep still, won't focus.

"Andy?"

"Rosie, I just . . . I can't." He looks at me, his eyes pained, then looks away, sighs.

Then I realize.

"You don't want me." I swallow painfully, my throat sour as I shiver, cold suddenly. "You never did."

"Rosie, no, that's not what I—"

I push past him, my chest tight, the room blurring as I stagger for the door.

"Rose, wait—" He reaches for me

"*Get off me!*" I wrench away, reeling as I lurch into the corridor.

There are bodies everywhere—leaning against walls and sprawled over the floor, yelling at me as I stumble over their limbs, my own legs threatening to buckle at any moment. I clutch at the wall, feeling my way along, trying to keep going, stay upright, get out of here, *breathe.*

Suddenly the wall ends. I feel myself falling and can't stop. I wince, ready for the slamming pain. But it never comes.

"Whoa there, tiger." A guy's face swims in front of mine as he pulls me upright and he leans me back against the wall.

"You okay? Nearly had a little fall there."

"Another one falling for you, Kyle?" his friend jokes.

Kyle laughs, and I hear myself join in. He takes a swig of beer, then offers me the bottle. I take it eagerly—too fast— the glass crashing against my teeth as the cool liquid slops down my front. Kyle laughs, and I smile up at him, licking my lips, the taste of beer bitter and cool in my mouth.

"What's your name, anyway?" he asks, brushing my hair out of my eyes. "Do I know you?"

"I . . ." I try to concentrate, but his face keeps swimming out of focus. "Um . . . Ro . . ."

"Ro?" He has dimples when he smiles. "Well, Ro," he says, leaning in closer, "you've got very pretty eyes."

He moves to tuck my hair behind my ear, and suddenly I'm kissing him, hard. He smiles in surprise, then kisses me back hungrily, pressing his body against mine. My head bangs violently against the wall, but the pain is welcome, the kisses rough, desperate, his stubble scratching my cheeks, his tongue writhing in my mouth. His grip tightens, and I clutch fiercely at his back, my eyes screwed shut, blotting out everything else.

Suddenly he's ripped away, my lips burning as I gasp for air.

18

"Hey! What's your problem, Andy?" Kyle snarls.

Andy. *Shit.*

"Leave her alone, Kyle."

"It was her! Couldn't keep her hands off me."

Andy grabs my arm. "Come on."

"Hey." Kyle stops him. "She's a big girl, Hunter, she can do what she wants." He winks at Andy. "And she wants me."

"She's had too much to drink."

"What are you, her mother?"

I wince.

"Just . . . Leave her alone, okay?" Andy says.

"What's it to you?" Kyle challenges.

"I said"—Andy steps closer—"leave her—"

"Yeah, Andy," I hear myself slur. "What's it to you?"

Andy stops. He's looking at me, but I can't see his eyes.

Kyle laughs. "Oh, dear, Hunter. Seems you're not needed after all. Do us all a favor, eh, mate? Get a life." Kyle drapes his arm round my shoulders. "Come on, sweetheart, let's find somewhere we won't be disturbed." He pushes past Andy.

"Wait." Andy catches my arm.

"Back off, Hunter!"

"Rose," Andy says. "Rose, look at me."

I stare at the floor.

"Rosie!"

"Whoa—hold on a minute." Kyle's arm drops from my shoulder. "Rosie? Wait, you're Rosie *Kenning*?" He swipes my hair from my eyes and peers down at me. "Jeezus Christ." He smirks. "Now, what's Crazy Kenning's daughter doing on the loose?"

What? My face burns.

19

"Hey everyone! It's Crrrazy Kenning's kid!"

"Kyle!" Andy grabs him, and Kyle holds up his hands in mock surrender.

"Hey, she's all yours, Hunter. My mistake, mate." He staggers off along the corridor, drunkenly toppling from one wall to the other. "Should've recognized her by her walk, eh, lads? Just like her old lady—remember the prom?" They laugh and whoop appreciatively. "Whoaoaoa! And as for that fall—whoops!" Kyle falls into a chubby guy's waiting arms. "Classic trademark."

"I . . ." I can't think. Can't breathe.

"Sorry, sweetheart." He dances over and slings his arm round my neck. "Nothing personal. You're very cute, really. Just crrrrazy genes."

Hot. Too hot.

"Yeah?" Andy growls. "Why don't you come over *here* and say that?"

"Look," Kyle coos, "Hunter. *Mate.* No hard feelings, okay? She's yours, and I respect that." He slaps Andy on the shoulder. "In fact, I owe you one, mate—any longer and I might've caught something!"

Andy swings at him, but Kyle ducks just in time, laughing. "Uh-oh, looks like we might have another one for the loony bin, eh, lads? And don't they make a lovely couple? Him all macho honor and her— Oof!"

My knuckles sting like mad and the room spins crazily as my back slams against the wall and I slump to the floor as Kyle crashes headfirst into the drinks table.

Merry Christmas, I think as everything fades to black.

I slump to the floor as Melissa locks the bathroom door behind us.

"Okay," she says. "Spill."

I chew my cookie, tasting nothing as it crumbles dryly in my mouth, buying time.

"Sweetie, what is it?" She wraps her arm around my shoulders. "You've been quiet all day. This isn't like you."

I close my eyes. *How can I tell her?*

She sighs. "As if I don't know."

My eyes fly open.

"I know you." She smiles sadly. "And you're going about this all wrong—you need to pick yourself up, get back to the party, drink some punch and have some *fun!*"

I stare at her.

"You need to show my idiot brother just how lucky he is to have you!"

I look away, exhale. *She doesn't know . . .*

Someone knocks on the door.

"Just a minute!" Melissa calls. "Sweetie, trust me, hiding away up here piling on the pounds is seriously not going to help *any-thing.*"

She snatches the cookies and I pull my top down over my belly self-consciously.

"Yes, Josh is going to meet college girls—that's a given. He's at college."

I nod miserably, flinching as the knocking turns to a battering.

College girls. Older, more sophisticated, *uncomplicated* . . .

"I said, just a freaking minute!" Melissa hollers, slamming her own fist against the door. "But sweetie, you have absolutely nothing to worry about." Melissa squeezes me tight. "Because there's another, much more important, given." She smiles. "Josh *loves* you. Just the way you are."

No, I think, closing my eyes as the hammering continues inside my head.

Just the way I *was* . . .

Chapter Three

My eyes fly open as someone hammers violently against my skull.

Aaah! What? Shit! Oww!

I clutch my head and squint around tentatively, trying to focus.

What is that?

Suddenly, the door bursts open and slams against the wall.

Owwwoohhhhh—shit!

"*Andy!*" I clutch the duvet against me as my head implodes. "What are you . . . How . . . ?"

"I knocked. About five times. Your coffee's getting cold."

"But—but what are you *doing* here?!"

"I *live* here." He dumps a pile of stuff in the corner and wrenches the curtains back, harsh daylight burning my eyes as I shrink beneath the duvet. A blue duvet. Andy's duvet. Andy's bed. *Shit!* I glance down quickly at my crumpled top and jeans—at least that's something.

A mug bangs down next to my head. *Ow.*

"Coffee."

"Um. Thanks," I mumble, peeking out.

"Thank Mum. She made it."

"I will."

He stands there for a moment, tall and shadowy against the bright window. I can't see his face.

"Listen, Andy, I—" I rasp, then clear my throat. "What am I—I mean, how . . . ?"

"You don't remember?" he asks incredulously. "You don't remember last night?"

"I—" I hesitate, then shake my head helplessly.

He looks at me for a moment, then sighs heavily and crouches down next to the bed. He brushes a hair from my face.

"You were very drunk," he says gently.

I can believe it. I can barely focus, and my whole body aches like hell. Especially my head.

"You don't remember anything?" he asks, his eyes searching mine. Those eyes. Those blue, blue eyes.

"Did—" I begin, the duvet warm around my body.

"Yes?"

"Did I . . . ?" I look into his eyes. "Did we . . . ?"

The softness in his face disappears. "No," he says. "We didn't."

He stands up briskly and checks his watch.

"Shit—Gran'll kill me. Look, drink your coffee and I'll meet you in the car." He tosses me my mobile. "You've had about eight missed calls."

24

The phone blinks at me accusingly. *Nana.* I close my eyes, flooded with guilt.

"I told her I'd drop you off on the way."

I look up. "The way?"

"To church. It's Christmas Day." He gestures at the pile of opened presents he brought in—a stack of travel books, a camera, and a large backpack.

"Going on holiday?" I venture.

"No—my gap year—any more questions?" he snaps.

I look up, surprised. *His gap year?*

"You've got five minutes."

He slams the door, and my skull splinters.

What happened?

My eyes wander round the room, over the old Arctic Monkeys poster and his beloved Wii, past the basketball laundry-hoop and up his snaking CD collection to the photo montage I'd helped him Blu-Tack round the mirror over his sink. Not much has changed, really. Not in the eighteen months since I was last here.

I pull the duvet over my face, the musky scent of Andy's aftershave tickling my nose, and suddenly I remember kissing him last night, the smell of his skin, his hair, as he held me close, the taste of his lips so familiar, so *right* against mine. My head spins as I close my eyes, intoxicated. *God, I've missed him.* Andy. Andy's room, Andy's bed. Snug and warm and comfortable, just as I remember.

Not that we'd ever . . . we'd never— Not that we hadn't *wanted* to, just . . . I didn't want it to be just some clumsy fumble after school, listening for the front door and scrambling back into my uniform if anyone came home. It had to be special. Perfect. And we'd planned the perfect occasion.

After my GCSE exams, the school arranged a prom, a great formal farewell before we headed out into the big wide world: some of us going straight into jobs or apprenticeships; some, like me, destined for a glorious six-week summer holiday—six whole wonderful weeks that Andy and I were going to spend discovering Europe with our Eurail passes—before I finally joined him at Maybridge Sixth Form College to knuckle down to my A levels for two years before heading on to uni.

That's what got me through my exams, to tell the truth. All those long dismal hours of revision, the arguments with Mum over anything and everything, just knowing I could look forward to this amazing adventure, to the prom the night before—a magical evening when I'd wear my ball gown and dance with Andy, and then . . . well, his parents were away for the weekend . . .

And it was everything I could have wished for. Gone were the desks that regimented the exams, and instead a lazy disco ball sent glittery stars spinning round the school hall as we swayed to the band, our secret lighting us from inside and sparkling in our eyes.

We left early.

Andy's house was dark and empty as we tiptoed upstairs in the moonlight, my senses on overdrive, aware of every touch, every sound, my heart beating madly as we stepped into his bedroom. Suddenly he flicked a switch, and I gasped as a hundred tiny fairy-lights flickered to life, twinkling over the mirror, looping around the window, and circling

26

his bed, which was scattered with rose petals. It was beautiful. Perfect.

He turned to me, his eyes sparkling, and kissed me, a long, lingering kiss that sent shivers down my spine and my head spinning into orbit as we fell onto the bed. I kissed him harder, enjoying the weight of his body on mine as his fingers slid down my back, my waist, my hip, and finally I gasped as they slipped inside my knickers, smooth and warm and so, so gentle.

He began to tug them down, down . . . but suddenly I grabbed his hand, stopping him.

"I'm sorry," I gasped, struggling for breath, "I'm sorry."

"Hey." He smiled, kissing me. "Shh, don't be." He brushed a hair from my forehead, his eyes deep in mine. "You call the shots. Okay?"

I nodded, and we struggled up into a sitting position. I pulled my dress back down and hugged my knees, my cheeks blazing.

What now?

Andy leapt up. "Some chocolates, Mademoiselle?" he asked in a French accent, grabbing a pretty box from his bedside table and presenting it with a flourish. "Decadently dark, dreamily creamy, finest Belgian chocolates, fresh from the expert chocolatiers of, um, Tesco's."

"Magnifique," I giggled, watching him as he tore off the wrapping, his cheeks glowing in the soft light, his blond hair deliciously ruffled next to his crumpled shirt. He was so gorgeous, so sexy, so Andy.

"Voilà!" he announced, opening the box. "Now, would Mademoiselle care for a truffle delight? A caramel sensation?

Or perhaps that most controversial of delicacies, a strawberry creme?"

A tiny, puzzled smile flickered over his face as I took the whole box from his hands and pushed it aside.

"You're wonderful," I told him.

He smiled. "You too."

Then I kissed him, deep and meaningfully, my fingers traveling down to his shirt buttons.

"Rosie." Andy broke away suddenly, his eyes searching mine. "Rose, you don't have to—"

I placed a finger over his lips, and smiled.

"I want to."

I climbed onto his lap and kissed him again, undoing one button after another, tugging the shirt free from his warm, smooth, firm body, lifting my arms as he pulled my dress up over my head and dropped it in a lilac pool on the floor, shivering as his fingers trailed gently down my bare back. Finally, his eyes found mine.

"You are so, so beautiful," he told me, kissing me. "I love you." He stroked my face. "But are you sure—"

I kissed him in answer, placing his hand on my breast, then reaching for his buckle. He didn't need telling twice. He pulled me to him, the warmth of his skin against mine making me shiver uncontrollably, his kisses hot and breathy as I pulled him ever closer, wanting him so desperately. His hands were everywhere—my hair, my back, my breasts, my legs—then suddenly, he stopped.

"Did you hear that?"

"No," I panted, pulling him closer.

He kissed me, then stopped again. "Listen."

There was a faint humming sound from my bag. My mobile.

"Ignore it," I whispered, my fingers tangling in his hair. "They'll leave a message."

"But it's the middle of the night—it could be important—"

The ringing stopped.

"See?" I smiled. "Can't have been that important."

"I suppose not." Andy grinned, rolling me underneath him as I shrieked happily. "Now, where were we?" His mouth found mine.

Suddenly the humming started again.

Andy looked at me.

"Okay," I groaned, fumbling for my phone.

It glowed green in the darkness: *Bex*.

"Typical." I grinned, flicking it off. "Wanting a progress report, no doubt."

"Well, we'd better give you something to tell her, then," Andy growled, nibbling at my neck and making me giggle.

Suddenly, the shrill ring of the house phone made us both jump.

"What the . . ." Andy frowned, checking his watch. "It's one o'clock in the morning!"

"Ignore it," I pleaded, kissing his ear. "No one's here."

He kissed me absently, still listening to the phone. "I'd better go."

"Andy . . ." Another kiss.

"I'll be right back, I *promise*." He smiled, gently disentangling himself from my arms. "Okay?"

I pouted, and he kissed my lips. "Okay?"

"Okay." I smiled. "But hurry!"

The ringing stopped, and I lay there, listening, but couldn't hear anything. I picked up Andy's shirt, which was still warm, still filled with that same delicious Andy smell, and pulled it on, draping myself seductively on the bed just as he returned.

"Well?" I purred. "What do you think . . . ?"

Andy handed me the phone. "It's for you."

"For *me?*"

"Bex." He rolled his eyes.

"No. Way. She rang your *house?*" I scrambled up from the bed to take the handset. "Bex, this'd better be good . . ."

"Rosie—finally! I called your mobile five times!"

"Sorry, I didn't hear it—I was busy . . ." I grinned at Andy. "What's so important?"

"It's your mum," Bex said. "She's here."

"Shit!" I sighed crossly. "Does she want me to come home? Well, tough, I'm sixteen years old, and I'll do what I—"

"No, Rosie," Bex interrupted, her voice urgent. "She's had an accident."

I jump at the sound of Andy's car horn. Shit. I wrench the covers off and jump out of bed—too quickly. The room spins, and I grab on to the sink for support, shutting my eyes and praying not to throw up. I wait for a second.

Nothing. Gingerly, I open an eye and am greeted by a sullen, ashen-faced reflection. I stare.

Gone is the rosy-cheeked schoolgirl who last looked in this mirror. The girl with all the friends and the amazing

30

boyfriend, the girl looking forward to a carefree summer of traveling—to the rest of her life. She disappeared eighteen months ago.

My eyes flick to the photos surrounding the mirror, searching for her, but though dozens of smiling faces beam back at me, there's no one I know. I stare at them. Gone are the photos we'd tacked up of our school friends, our dates, our memories—replaced with strangers: out clubbing, on holidays, in the park—Andy grinning and laughing with people I've never even met, having the time of his life. *Having* a life. *Going traveling*, I remember, my heart sinking.

But not with me.

My chest aches. Suddenly he feels a million miles away. I was wrong. Things *have* changed. *We've* changed. Everything changed that night. The last night I was here.

But he kissed me last night, I remind myself desperately—*that must mean something?*

My eyes dart frantically over the photos, desperate to find a picture of me, of us—a party, a date—*something*—some sign that he's thought about me in all this time, that he's missed me as much as I've missed him. Suddenly my heart stops, my eyes frozen on a picture of Andy, his arms wrapped tightly around a girl, grinning at the camera as she kisses him tenderly.

A pretty *blond* girl.

I pluck the photo from the wall, my fingers trembling as I stare at their interlocked fingers, their matching UEFA football shirts, the stadium behind them where the Euro championships were held two summers ago . . .

Something hits me in the chest. Hard.

Two summers ago. Just after we broke up. *The summer we were going to go traveling.*

The summer he went without me . . .

I can't breathe. My chest tightens as all the pain of his leaving floods back—the burning insecurity that I wasn't good enough, that I'd never been good enough, that he'd finally got tired of waiting for me to be ready—or worse, that now he'd seen me naked he didn't want me after all.

"You don't want me." My voice echoes suddenly in my ears, my cheeks blazing as I remember him pushing me away last night, my lips stinging with rejection. *"You never did."*

I run the tap, splashing the gushing water on my burning face, tears stinging my eyes as all my hopes of us getting back together dissolve to nothing.

So that *is* what happened. *That's* why he was so keen to stop when the phone rang that night, *that's* why he went traveling without me. He'd gone off me. Gone off in search of someone new. *And he found her . . .*

I wrench my eyes open, searching the photos for more pictures of her, of other girls, other girlfriends—*How many have there been?* I scour the snaps—parties, people, places—then, suddenly, a familiar face grins out, and instantly the rest of last night comes rushing painfully back. *Kyle . . .* the party . . . kissing Andy . . . kissing Kyle . . . Kyle sneering . . . his mocking impression of Mum . . .

A jolt like electricity hits me without warning.

Mum.

Sarah's words scream back at me as the room begins to sway.

Trudie was not your mother.

I clutch the edge of the sink, my stomach lurching as the nightmare flashes back, starker, more painful, more terrifyingly real in the cold light of day.

Trudie was not . . . she was never my mother . . .

And she never told me. How . . . *how* could she keep something like that a secret, after everything we'd been through with the disease?

Especially when she found out about the disease . . .

The room spins, and I plunge my face down, down into the icy water, trying to drown the questions, the pain, the images flooding my head . . .

After Bex called that night, I took a taxi straight back to school—if Mum was angry about me staying at Andy's, he'd be the last person she'd want to see—but by the time I got there she'd gone.

Mum'd turned up at the prom looking for me, Bex said. Apparently she'd forgotten I'd told her I was staying at Bex's, then, when I wasn't at school, she'd gone mental. She'd stormed into the school hall, tottering around in her favorite heels and nightdress in front of everyone, searching for me, screaming at the top of her lungs. Bex tried to explain, tried calling me, but of course I hadn't answered my mobile . . .

Then Mum'd headed back to the car. The teachers tried to stop her, said she was in no state to drive, but Mum just shoved them out of the way.

33

Then she walked into a tree, fell over and broke her ankle. One of the teachers took her to hospital, and it was there that they noticed that she wasn't drunk. That there was something else wrong, really wrong, with her. And her life changed forever.

And so did mine.

Andy's bedroom door flies open.

"I have got better things to do on Christmas Day than wait around for you, you know?" he snaps.

"I bet," I say, dropping the photo at his feet.

He stares at it, surprised.

"Rosie, I . . . It's not what you think."

"Whatever." I look away.

"That was just a fling—*ages* ago—"

"About eighteen months ago, in fact."

"Rosie . . ." He falters. "She's not . . . We're not . . . It didn't mean anything."

"Whatever." I swallow, try to move past him.

"Rose—" He grabs my arm, his touch like ice.

"Let me go."

"Rosie, I—"

"*Andy*—"

"What did you *expect* me to do?"

I stop short, my breath stuck in my throat.

"What did you expect me to do, Rose? Just wait around for eighteen months on the off chance that you might finally call? That we might get back together?"

34

My throat is paralyzed.

"Tell me, Rosie, what was I supposed to do?"

"I don't know," I mumble helplessly. "I thought you loved me."

"I did," Andy says sadly. "But you shut me out." He snaps his fingers. "Just like that! I didn't know why, you wouldn't tell me, wouldn't even answer your phone the fifty times I called to find out why you weren't at the station like we'd arranged. I was standing there on the platform like an idiot, Rosie—I almost missed my train!"

"But you didn't," I say quietly. "You left."

"Yes, I left. I was hurt, I was angry, and I'd used all my savings on a Eurail ticket that was about to go to waste. You wouldn't tell me why you wouldn't come, didn't give me a reason to stay, you just sent me a text—a *text*—saying sorry, you couldn't come anymore. No explanation, nothing!"

I look away.

"It's a pretty shitty way to dump someone, Rose."

I stare at him. "I wasn't *dumping* you! I just . . . had a lot to deal with. I couldn't—"

"Couldn't talk to me about it? Couldn't tell me?"

"I couldn't!" I protest. "Not then."

"Why?" he explodes. "What could be so terrible that you couldn't tell me?"

I struggle to breathe, even now it's impossible to find words to describe the horrible uncertainty and confusion and terror of that awful, life-changing day when Mum was finally diagnosed.

He sighs. "As if I don't know."

"What?"

He looks away. "It was pretty obvious, Rose. The timing . . . what happened . . . or didn't . . ." He shuffles his feet, his cheeks coloring. "I'm sorry if I did something wrong, if I pushed you into nearly doing something you didn't want to . . ."

I stare at him, stunned.

He looks at me, his eyes pained. "But you could've just talked to me, you know? I was happy to wait."

"What? No!" I protest, my own cheeks burning. He thinks *I* dumped *him* because of that night? "No—no, it wasn't . . ." I take a deep breath, trying to get my words straight. "Andy, it wasn't you, anything to do with you. It was Mum—"

"Then why couldn't you tell me that? Why couldn't you call?"

"I was at the hospital, my phone was off, I couldn't."

"You could've if you'd tried, Rose. You could've called me, could've explained, could've let me know what was going on so I didn't keep *hoping* . . ."

I stare at him, speechless.

"Every city, every station—in Rome, in Athens, Barcelona—I prayed you'd changed your mind, that you'd be there waiting to explain, to join me for the rest of our trip, the adventure we'd planned for so long." He shrugs. "But you didn't come. You didn't come, and it became obvious you never would." He sighs. "I got tired of waiting for you."

"But you didn't wait very long, did you?" I gesture to the photo. "What? A few weeks? You couldn't have loved me that much."

He falters.

"*I* was waiting for *you*," I tell him. "I couldn't believe you'd gone without me. All summer I was waiting for you to call, to come and see me when you got back. I needed you." I swallow hard. "But you never did."

He looks away. "I thought . . . I thought you'd dumped me."

"And I thought *you'd* dumped *me*," I say sadly. "But I didn't jump into bed with the next guy who came along!"

"She wasn't—"

"And how dare you, how *dare* you try to tell me who I can and can't be with *now*?!"

"What?"

"You're such a hypocrite, Andy. Here you are with another girl *immediately* after we break up, and yet now, *a year and a half* later, you go mental when I'm with someone else!"

"That's not what happened!"

"*What?*" I ask incredulously. "You practically ripped Kyle off me!"

"Well, yes—but only because I was worried about you!"

"*Worried* about me? Is that why you snogged me too?"

"Actually, *you* snogged *me*," Andy reminds me.

"Yeah? Well . . . I was drunk!" I retort bitterly, my cheeks burning.

"Exactly!"

"What?"

"Rose . . . you were off your head. You didn't know what you were doing, and . . . after last time . . ." He swallows. "I'm sorry. It should never have happened. It was a mistake."

A mistake. My heart crumples as I look away, my gaze snagging on a picture right at the edge of the montage, almost hidden behind the others. It's me. Me and Andy. Our first date. We'd gone ice-skating, followed by fish and chips, of all things, sitting out under the stars with our newspaper wrappers. I stare at the photo. Our cheeks are flushed, our eyes bright with laughter. We look so happy. I close my eyes against the tears.

"Rosie," Andy sighs. "Look, I'm sorry, okay? I was just trying to look out for you last night—I didn't want you to do anything you'd regret."

I swallow hard.

"But you're right, if you want to go out with Kyle, with anyone . . ." He sighs. "That's your business."

I screw my eyes up tighter. *There's only you. There's only ever been you . . .*

"I know you've had a rough time lately, with your mum and everything . . . ," he says gently. "But I really wish you'd told me about her. I would've understood, Rose. I would've been there for you."

My throat swells with regret. *If only I'd called him that day—explained. He's right. What was he supposed to think? What did I expect him to do? This is all my fault—if I'd only told him the truth, things might've been so different . . .*

"But I understand why you didn't," he admits. "It's a bit embarrassing, isn't it?"

I look up sharply.

"I just mean it can't have been easy," he says quickly. "Giving up Sixth Form to look after your alcoholic mother."

My jaw drops. "What?"

"Rosie." He hesitates. "I know you tried to keep it quiet, but we all saw her, okay? Staggering down the street, slurring and spilling things everywhere . . ."

I stare at him, dumbfounded, an icy numbness gripping

38

my insides. An image of Kyle's stupid tottering walk floats through my mind.

He sighs. "I know she couldn't help it, it was an addiction, but look what she put you through. Missing your A levels, your friends—eighteen months of your life!"

"What?! No!" I interrupt, my cheeks hot. "Andy, Mum was not an alcoholic!"

"Rose, come on—"

"I can't *believe*— How *could* you!" I stare at him incredulously. "I mean, *Kyle's* one thing, but *you*, how could *you* think she . . . You knew Mum. You *knew* her!" I push past him and thunder down the stairs.

"Rosie!" He races after me. "Rosie, I'm sorry!"

I fling open the front door.

"Rosie, wait—" He catches my arm. "I'm sorry, I know she was your mum—you loved her—I didn't mean—"

"You don't know anything!" I yell, wrenching away from him, rage pounding in my ears. "She wasn't an alcoholic!"

He sighs, sadly, pityingly. "Rose . . ."

"She had *Huntington's disease*, okay? *That's* why I couldn't just hop on a train, *that's* why I dropped out of Sixth Form. She wasn't an *alcoholic*—it wasn't her fault—she had Huntington's!"

My heart racing, I run out the door, sprinting down the street, tears streaming down my face.

I can't go back—I can't ever go back to how things were. Andy doesn't want me—he feels *sorry* for me. He feels sorry for me because he thought my mum was an *alcoholic*! That night, that awful, horrible night her life changed forever, mine effectively ended.

And now she's gone. She's gone, and I'm left with nothing—no friends, no life, no future—

And she wasn't even my mother!

My heart racing, I sprint into the garden, my stomach churning as I lunge for the flower bed.

"Oh, sweetie." Melissa appears beside me, brushing my hair back from my forehead. "Was it the punch? Did I make it too strong? Should I call your dad?"

I shake my head vehemently, then immediately wish I hadn't, as my stomach empties itself yet again. She rubs my back.

"Oh, babe. You need a glass of water? Coffee?"

"Water." I nod weakly, clutching my belly.

"Coming right up!" She grins, ruffling my hair. "Don't worry, next time I'll leave out the vodka. Or maybe the rum." She kisses my forehead. "Maybe neither would be a good idea for a few days, though!"

She winks and disappears into the house.

I lean my head against the cold wall and close my eyes.

I didn't even have any freaking punch.

Chapter Four

The Christmas wreath tumbles to the floor as I shove the front door open and lean my head against the cold glass. I close my eyes, struggling to catch my breath, to summon the strength to step inside, to face the house that's no longer my home.

Nearly everything had to be moved, cleared away or locked up after the diagnosis: anything Mum could trip over or smash into as the jerky movements—*chorea*—progressed; anything she could hurt herself, or anyone else, with when the paranoia set in; all our trinkets and ornaments, our throw rugs and photo frames and memories, all boxed up and stored in the garage, empty since we'd sold the Mini.

The car was the biggest blow. By law, Mum had to tell the DVLA her diagnosis, and they made her retest. When she failed, that was it. They revoked her license.

"This is crazy!" Mum screamed at the test center. "Even *Jenson Button* failed his driving test the first time—I demand

a retake!" They refused. And without the car, in our little rural village, she lost her independence.

So I deferred Sixth Form. Despite Nana's protests about the importance of my education, I couldn't bear the thought of Mum being stuck at home on her own. I wanted to be there for her, look after her, do my best to cheer her up. It wasn't easy. I hated the way strangers stared at her wherever we went, nudging each other and whispering that she was crazy or drunk. But her mood swings were the worst.

She'd be high as a kite one minute, then fly into an uncontrollable rage over the smallest thing. She got so angry because *Neighbours* was canceled one bank holiday that she started hurling things at the TV, and smashed the screen. I tried to calm her down, tried to explain, but there was no reasoning with her—she needed her routine and didn't understand why she couldn't watch her beloved soap. In the end Sarah's husband, Steve, had to physically restrain her to stop her hurting herself. Then, when he finally let go, she called the police, showed them her bruises and had him arrested for assault.

The only thing that seemed to calm her down was her cigarettes, but like with her temper, she didn't seem to know when, or how, to stop. She'd just smoke one after another—up to fifty a day—inhaling compulsively until they burned down to her fingers. Then, if there weren't another dozen full packets ready in the cupboard (something she'd check obsessively), she'd freak out about that too.

Other times, she'd get utterly depressed, despairing at what was happening to her, frightened about the future, paranoid that I was going to leave. But I didn't. She was my mother, my whole world.

And I felt so guilty. She'd been struggling for years and I'd never twigged what was really going on, never realized. So I learned how to cope: to stick to a routine, to keep episodes of all her soaps recorded just in case, to buy cigarettes in bulk and leave ashtrays everywhere. To stop her burning her fingers I even bought her an old-fashioned cigarette holder that she absolutely adored—she said she felt like Audrey Hepburn.

Nana and Sarah helped as much as they could, worried about me dropping out of Sixth Form, losing touch with my friends, my future . . . Nana wanted me to take the predictive test straightaway, but I wasn't allowed—at sixteen I was too young. Plus there were other factors to consider.

Bex bombarded me with questions: What would I do if the test was positive? Would it be worth going to uni, or learning to drive? Should I really get married? Or have kids, if they could get it too? Wouldn't that be cruel, or irresponsible, or selfish? Endless painful, impossible questions that left me confused and sick and dizzy.

I kept quiet after that, told Bex to, too—tried to be normal, to keep up with my friends as they started Sixth Form without me, with odd days out, phone calls, Facebook. But all they ever seemed to do was gossip about their new mates, giggle about guys or moan about their course work, and it all seemed so petty suddenly. So meaningless. It was actually a relief when they finally stopped calling.

And besides, I had new friends—online friends from the

Huntington's Disease Youth Association. Teens who understood what I was going through, who'd lived with the disease for years, watching as it slowly sapped the independence and vitality from their loved ones day by day. Though we now realized Mum'd had symptoms for years before her diagnosis, we met people at her support group in much later stages of the disease—people whose families had deserted them because of their volatile behavior, not realizing they had HD; families torn apart by denial; parents whose children wouldn't visit them for fear of witnessing their own future; pensioners who'd envisaged their retirements spent indulging their hobbies and grandchildren, not visiting their formerly strong, healthy spouses or adored grown-up children withered and bedridden in care homes.

Mum was so frightened of becoming a burden like that. She couldn't bear to imagine that someday she might need someone to spoon-feed her and wipe her bum—that wasn't who she *was*. Though it pains me to say it, in a way, she was lucky.

And for a while she was reasonably okay. The doctors prescribed medication that toned down her anger, depression and chorea, and on really good days she developed a jubilant carpe diem attitude, throwing her worries to the wind as we went swimming in the sea, boating on the river, and picnicking on the Downs. For her birthday Nana, Sarah and I even took her to Paris for cake beneath the Eiffel Tower. She was even due to start a clinical trial for a new drug, which they hoped would slow the disease's progression.

But then, a few weeks later, she went upstairs for something in the middle of the night, lost her balance and tumbled all the way back down, smacking her head against the wall, causing a brain hemorrhage. That was the beginning of the end. Her symptoms seemed to advance much more quickly after that. She became completely bedridden. She struggled to swallow her food. Then she developed pneumonia.

It was awful. Nana and Sarah both did their best, coming over day and night, and care workers rallied round, but I was the only one there twenty-four-seven. The only one watching my mother slipping away. The only one witnessing what might happen to me.

What I *thought* might happen to me.

But she knew it never would.

The thought comes like a burning scythe through my chest as I stare at the grab-bars, the child-locks, her chair—things that have haunted my future—things that I'll *never* need—*and she knew!* All that time she let me believe I was at risk, *and all the time she knew!*

I grab a pair of scissors from a child-locked drawer and dive at the chair, screaming as I stab the sharp blades into it again and again, slashing and hacking at its wipe-clean surface, leaving great gashes bleeding foam. I hate this chair *so much.* I hate its carefully padded limbs, its folding back-support, its urine-proof coating. *So* practical. *So* functional. So ugly and terrifying and waiting for me—my destiny. Well, not anymore! I shove the chair onto its side, kicking and wrenching at it with all my might until finally an arm snaps off, sending me slamming painfully into the wall, but I don't care. Never again, never again will anyone sit in it, rely on it, succumb to it.

My eyes scan the room greedily, searching for more targets;

then suddenly the front door flies open and a man bursts in, wielding a cricket bat.

"All right, you—" Steve stops when he sees me. "Rosie?"

"*Rosie?!*" Sarah pushes past him. "Rosie! What on earth are you doing?" Her eyes take in the savaged chair, the scissors. "Are you okay?"

"I'm fine." I stare at her coolly, the scissors cold and hard in my hand, blood pounding in my temples.

"We heard all the noise and thought"—she glances at Steve—"I thought it was burglars!"

"Well, it's not," I say. "So you can go."

Sarah glances at Steve and pats his arm. "You go."

He frowns. "You sure?"

"You too," I tell her.

"Off you go." Sarah smiles at her husband as he leaves. "I'm staying."

"There's no need." I grit my teeth. "Just go."

She folds her arms and meets my gaze evenly.

I explode. "*What do you want?*"

"I don't want anything."

"Then get lost! Just get lost! This is my house, and I don't want you here, you and your lies—you make me sick! You're just . . . you're just . . ." My eyes fill with tears. "You're just like *her!*"

"Rosie—" She reaches for my arm.

"Get off me!" I wrench away. "How could you? How *could* you?!" I glare at her, rage pumping through me. "For *eighteen months* I watched my mum suffering, watched her slipping away, watched her *dying* . . .". My eyes flood. "Always fearing that I could have it too, that someday that could happen to

46

me. But it couldn't, could it? It was never going to happen to me—*because she wasn't my mother!*"

"Rosie—"

"And all the time she knew! Eighteen months, and she never thought to mention it, to let me off the hook? *Oh, by the way, Rosie, you can't have Huntington's*. That's all it would've taken—one simple sentence to erase a life sentence. *Eighteen months!* And if she hadn't got pneumonia it could have been longer, couldn't it? It could have been years and *years*—and would she *ever* have told me?"

"Rosie," Sarah begins, flustered now. "Rosie, she didn't know—"

"Oh, I know she didn't know! *I* didn't know. *You* didn't even know she had Huntington's, and you're a nurse, for God's sake! But once she was diagnosed she *should* have told me—how could she not? How could she sit there in that *hideous* chair *knowing* I'd *never* inherit the disease *and not tell me?* What did she think I'd do? *Leave* her? *How could she be so selfish?!*"

"Rosie, stop it! Rosie—she didn't *know!*"

"She did! She knew there was *no* chance of me *ever* getting the disease, and yet—"

"No, Rosie, she didn't!" Sarah grabs my wrists, her eyes intense. "She didn't know you weren't her daughter!"

I stare at her, the anger frozen in my limbs.

What?

She holds my gaze, her breath coming in gulps. "Rosie, sit down."

I open my mouth to speak but can't, and my legs crumble as I sink onto the sofa, my head spinning, trying to figure out what I've missed, what she means—hitting brick walls every time.

She didn't know . . . ?

Sarah sits down next to me, takes my hands.

"Rosie," she says carefully, searching for the right words. "I want you to listen to me, to let me explain—without interrupting." She swallows. "Okay?"

I nod, not sure I can speak anyway. My throat's like sandpaper.

"Okay," she sighs. "Okay." She takes a deep breath. "You know that Trudie always wanted a child so, *so* desperately. But she—I don't know if you know—she suffered a number of miscarriages . . ."

I nod again, my chest tight.

"She and David tried to adopt, but they were too old, too many stupid rules and red tape." She sighs. "Then finally she got pregnant again. David was so angry with her, we all were, so worried she was putting herself at risk. But she kept saying how she knew that this time it was going to be okay—she just *knew.* And for ages it seemed she was right. Everything was going so well, she'd got to her third trimester and they were over the moon.

"But then one horrible stormy night, just as I was finishing my shift at the hospital, your nana rushed Trudie in with stomach pains, weeks before she was due. David wasn't there, he was out somewhere in his cab, but they'd called his dispatcher—he was on his way. Trudie was frantic, terrified of losing her baby, anxious about the storm, desperately needing David beside her, so I stayed on, determined to do everything I could for her and the child.

"But there were . . . complications. The baby was born, but she wasn't breathing properly. She was rushed off to the Special Care Baby Unit and put on a ventilator while they organized an urgent transfer to the Neonatal Intensive Care Unit at Westhampton Hospital. I felt so helpless. All I could do was watch as she struggled to survive. She was so tiny, so frail.

"Then my friend Jamila who works in the SCBU started sympathizing, saying how life isn't fair—how some babies die while others aren't even wanted. I wasn't really listening, but she kept on about this other premature newborn, how her seventeen-year-old mother was going to give her up for adoption. She was doing my head in. I wanted to tell her to shut up, as if silence would save Trudie's baby—with every breath she seemed to be slipping away . . .

"Then Jamila asked me to cover for her. Her shift was meant to be over, but her replacement hadn't arrived yet. *Please,* Jamila begged—she was going on holiday, had to catch her flight—and as I was staying anyway, I told her to go. Anything for some peace and quiet."

Sarah swallows, takes a deep breath.

"The next thing I knew, an auxiliary nurse ran in, shouting that Jamila's teenager had done a runner. I hurried back to the labor ward and nearly ran straight into your nana, who'd come to find me. Trudie was desperate to see me, she said, so together we rushed back to the delivery rooms, and sure enough, the teenage girl's bed was empty. Security confirmed she'd left—they'd had no idea she was abandoning her baby. Then we heard Trudie. She was in hysterics, I'd never seen her so distraught. The police had arrived—there'd been a crash—David had been . . ." She glances at me, her face deathly pale. "He'd been so unlucky. There was nothing they could do . . ."

I swallow hard.

"It was awful. Your nana tried to comfort her, but Trudie was beside herself. Then, when she saw me, she just wanted her baby, was desperate to know if she was all right. She was so frightened, so upset, I *couldn't* tell her the truth. I said I'd go and check, and hurried back to the Unit. But her baby looked worse than ever and the ambulance *still* hadn't arrived. I was desperate. The baby was going to die, I just knew it. She wasn't even crying—she didn't have the strength. I couldn't face Trudie, couldn't go back and tell her—not after David . . .

"And then the other baby started to cry. The teenager's baby. Big, hearty sobs. I looked across at her—she was so much stronger, healthier, and about the same size . . ."

Sarah's breathing quickens.

"I didn't think about it," she says. "Not even for a second. There was no one else around, so I took my chance. I switched the identity bracelets and incubator tags. Just like that. Then the ambulance team arrived asking for baby Kenning. I told them there'd been a mistake about the child's name—it was Woods, not Kenning—and they believed me—it was obvious which child was sick, and they took her away." She swallows. "It was done. I couldn't have undone it if I'd wanted to. But I *didn't* want to—it was the right thing, I *knew* it was . . . for everyone." She looks at me and I drop my gaze, my head reeling.

The teenager . . . two babies . . . *switched?*

50

"Then Jamila's replacement arrived, and I rushed straight back to Trudie." Sarah smiles, her eyes watery. "You should've seen her face when I told her her baby was okay. She couldn't believe it, not till she finally saw her—saw *you*." She squeezes my knee, her lips trembling. "Oh, Rosie, it was love at first sight."

I stare at the cigarette burns polka-dotting the carpet as they spin and blur, thoughts flooding my head.

"So I'm . . . That teenager was . . ."

Sarah nods. "She was your biological mother, yes."

I swallow. "And she never knew? Mum never knew . . . ?"

She shakes her head. "Nobody knows. I've never told anyone."

"Not even Steve? Not Nana?"

"No." She sighs. "I knew if I did, if anyone so much as *suspected*, you could be taken away." She closes her eyes. "I'd never have forgiven myself."

"And Mum . . . she never suspected?"

"Never." Sarah looks at me. "As far as she was concerned, you were her little girl, her baby." Sarah squeezes my hand. "And you *were*, Rosie. She was your mum, she always will be. It doesn't matter about—"

"And the other girl?" I interrupt quietly, looking away. "What was her name?"

"Rosie, I can't really . . ." Sarah trails off, sighs. "Her name was Holly. Holly Woods."

"Holly." I test the name on my lips. A young name. A teenager's name. "And she—my mother—she just left me?"

"Oh, sweetie," Sarah says gently. "There could have been a thousand reasons why she ran away, why she'd decided to

51

put you up for adoption. Imagine if you had a child now, at your age, it's hardly the best—"

"I'd keep it."

"Yes, well . . . maybe she couldn't. Maybe she thought you'd have a better life that way." She squeezes my hand. "The point is that Trudie *did* want you, more than anything in the world. You saved her that night. You saved each other."

I stare at the doorframe, my height marked in Mum's loopy purple handwriting every birthday. I remember how I stood on tiptoe each year, impatient to reach the same height as her. How strange I felt when I realized I'd outgrown her.

Suddenly a pain hits my chest so hard that I crumple. "I miss her," I gasp. "I miss her so much."

"Oh, sweetie, I know!" Sarah wraps her arms around me, pulling me close. "I know. Me too."

"Why did she have to go? Why did she have to have stupid Huntington's? It's not fair!"

"I know, darling. I know." She kisses my hair fiercely, holding me tight. "But *you* don't. You're young and healthy and everything she wanted you to be. She was so proud of you, you know that? She loved you so much."

I nod, tears streaming down my cheeks.

"And she'll always be your mum, no matter what. Nothing can change that. Remember that. Remember *her.*" She fumbles in her purse, pulling out a photo strip. *"Look at her."*

I do. It's the photos we'd got from one of those passport booths. In each picture we're wearing wacky clothes and pulling different silly expressions. I look at Mum, dressed up in a boa, her cheeks painted bright red, fluttering her huge fake eyelashes, and smile despite myself. It was the day she sacked her physiotherapist.

"Poor Eileen, she barely got in the door, did she?" Sarah smiles.

"*Poor Eileen?* She didn't have a clue!"

She'd come in, introduced herself, then spoke to Mum ve-ry slo-wly and loudly. Mum had just stared at her, looked at me and Sarah and then said, "I'm sorry, are you quite well?"

"The look on her face!" Sarah laughs. "Priceless!"

We'd cracked up laughing but Eileen hadn't seen the funny side. That was the end of her. Mum said if she only had a limited time left she wasn't going to waste it with ignorant idiots, thank you very much.

"Then Trudie just said, 'Come on, if people are going to stare, we'll give 'em something to stare at!'" Sarah laughs.

And we did. We donned our wildest clothes and hired a pink stretch limo to chauffeur us down to Brighton, where we strolled along the pier, ate ice cream and fish and chips and candy-floss, then rode the rides till we felt sick, all decked out in our boas and crazy hats.

And you know what? Nobody stared, nobody gawped. We barely got a second glance all day.

"God, and then it started to rain, do you remember?"

I nod. "But I couldn't even *drag* her under the shelter—she was too strong—and too busy dancing!"

"And singing!" Sarah laughs, and I giggle as I remember Mum whirling and twirling around the lampposts singing loudly.

"I can't believe you convinced me to join in—what did we look like?"

"Who cares!" Sarah smiles. "She was happy."

She was. I hadn't seen her so happy in a long time. Singing her heart out in fancy dress in the middle of Brighton.

"And then—" Sarah can hardly speak for laughing. "Then when she got to the chorus of 'It's Raining Men,' she just stopped dead—"

"Yes! And just stood there, straight-faced, looking round the seafront—"

"And said—"

"'It bloody well isn't!'"

We crack up in hysterics.

I laugh till I can hardly breathe, the memory of that insane, wonderful sight dancing in my head, crazy and hilarious. Tears of laughter stream down my face, covering the tracks of their unhappy predecessors.

"It's raining now." I smile, looking out the window.

"Men?" Sarah asks, and I giggle, until suddenly a car pulls into the drive.

It's Nana. I pull away from Sarah, my smile gone. *Nana.*

"Sarah, it's—"

"Shhh now, you'll be fine. Everything will be okay, I promise," she insists.

"How will it?" I stare at her. "Sarah, I—I can't. She doesn't know. You said she doesn't know!"

Sarah stands up and takes my shoulders firmly. "She doesn't," she says, looking me in the eye. "But it's okay. Just be normal."

I stare at her. *Be normal?*

"She's still your nana, and she loves you," she tells me, stroking my cheek. "We both do."

The doorbell rings and I freeze.

"Look, whatever happens," Sarah says gently, "it's up to you. You can tell her if you want to, if it helps, if it makes it easier for you."

She looks at me sadly.

"Rosie, I'm so sorry. Sorry you had to find out this way, for everything you've been through." She sighs. "But it's your life now, and you have to make your own choices. But no matter what, no matter what you choose to do, just know I'm always here for you, any time, day or night, okay?"

I nod. "Okay."

She kisses my cheek, then goes to answer the door.

I take a deep breath. *Just be normal.* Be normal. *It's just Nana.* Just Nana . . .

Suddenly there she is, stepping into the room, beaming at me.

"Hi, Nana." I smile tentatively, feeling sick to my stomach.

"Hello, darling!" She gives me a hug, her small frame fragile in my arms. "Steve rang—are you all right? Andrew said he'd drop you off—"

"Oh, Nana, I'm so sorry—Christmas dinner . . ." I glance at my watch. "I should've called . . ."

"Don't be silly." She smiles. "It's all keeping warm, and besides, it's good for you to get out and see your friends. Especially now." She squeezes my hand. "When I think of the parties Trudie used to throw—goodness me, she wouldn't surface till *teatime* the next day!"

I smile weakly. Same old Nana, always making the best of things.

"Well, I'd better get back," Sarah says. "Steve's family will think I'm avoiding them! Bye, Laura." She hugs Nana, then blows me a kiss. "Bye, Rosie. Merry Christmas."

Merry Christmas.

I watch her walk away down the gravel drive.

"Shall we?" Nana smiles. "There's a great big turkey with our names on it at home, and I want to hear all about your wonderful party. Ooh, and *Holiday* is on later—I do love Cary Grant, and— Brrr!" She shivers violently as the wind blows in. "And I don't know about you, but I could do with a nice big mug of hot chocolate. Warms you from the inside out, Trudie would always say!"

I smile weakly as she takes my arm—just as normal—and I step out into the cold, dark night, lifting my face to the falling rain.

Rain patters heavily against the window as I lock the bathroom door and hold my breath.

Please, I pray, my fingers crossed tightly as I pull down my pants.

Please, this time . . .

Nothing. Shit.

I crumple to the floor, my fingers twisting frantically in my hair.

Relax, I tell myself. *It doesn't mean anything, it's not that late . . .*

Six weeks . . .

Raindrops slide like tears down the dark windowpane, blotting out the stars.

I screw my eyes shut, concentrate on breathing.

It could just . . . it could just be stress. It happens. You hear about it all the time—false alarms. It doesn't mean . . .

My breath catches, ragged in my throat.

Get a grip, girl. Everything's cool, everything's fine. It'll come . . .

I bite my lip, take a deep breath and force myself to stand up and splash cold water on my face.

Everything's fine.

I open my eyes and the girl in the mirror stares back at me.

She looks as unconvinced as I am.

Chapter Five

The little glow-in-the-dark stars swim above me as I stare at the ceiling of Nana's spare room, my head buzzing. Images of Sarah, Nana and Mum swirl wildly against the blank faces of my real mother—Holly—and Mum's dead baby, the events of that fateful night whirling like a tornado in my mind, questions battering like hailstones, puncturing and destroying all the truths I've ever known, leaving a void as black and as vast as the night sky, but with precious few stars to guide me.

My future.

A person cannot exist without a past. Someone famous said that. But what if your entire existence is a lie? It's like I've been wearing stilettos all my life, leaving footprints everywhere I go, and then one day someone says, "Hey! Those shoes don't belong to you!" and they take them away. And I look back, and all I have left are the old footprints, which don't even fit my feet anymore, so I can't go back, but I haven't got any new shoes to go forward in, so I'm stuck. Frozen in that place. Not even existing.

I sigh and reach into my purse, pulling out the list I've kept with me ever since I decided to take the test:

If Positive—Fight HD by:
Eating nutritiously—a strong body is a healthy body.
Exercising regularly—ditto.
Taking vitamins, fish oils, etc.—if there's ANY chance they could help, it's worth it.
Keeping my mind sharp—learn Italian, play chess, go on "Mastermind."
Taking part in clinical trials and research.

If Negative

The page beneath is blank—I couldn't bear to hope, to imagine the endless daunting possibilities . . .
And now?
I sigh. Now my past *and* future are blank.
I heave myself out of bed, grab my dressing gown, and pad into the lounge, curling up on the sofa and flicking blindly through the muted TV channels. The clock on the wall ticks endlessly, each second throbbing against my skull as the minutes crawl by. I glance up at it, and without warning, the family portraits beam down at me: black-and-white photos of Nana and Granddad when they were young; their wedding day; Mum as a baby, with Granddad—so smart and proud in his police uniform—just months before an armed burglar blasted him and his genetic secret into an early grave.
There are lots of Mum as a girl, then with Dad: laughing

as they cut their wedding cake; suntanned and windswept on a beach somewhere; Mum on a park swing grinning at the camera, her arms wrapped tightly round a small dark-haired toddler.

I stare at them incredulously—how did I never see it? We look nothing alike, it's blindingly obvious. Nana and Mum have the same chestnut hair, the same hazel eyes, but I've got black hair, and my eyes are green. It's not even as if Dad was dark—he was blond! How could I have been so blind? I'd never thought, never guessed, never *imagined.*

The faces smile blurrily back at me, but it's not real, it's not my family. Not anymore. The pieces are broken, and they can't be patched over with cuddles and cocoa and bloody Cary Grant. The lies glare through, like cracks in a stained-glass window, ruining everything.

"You're so like her, you know."

I look up quickly, blinking away the tears. Nana is standing in the doorway, her snowy hair crumpled from her pillow.

"The number of mornings I'd get up to find her curled like you are on the sofa with a mug of hot chocolate." She smiles. "Couldn't sleep?"

I shake my head, and she sits down next to me, following my gaze.

"She was so proud of you." She beams, her face crinkling like tissue paper. "She loved you so much, from the moment she first held you." She strokes my hair behind my ear the way Mum used to, and my chest hurts. "You were the best thing that ever happened to her, Rosie. A gift of hope, of happiness—just when she needed it most."

I swallow hard, her words echoing Sarah's: *You saved her that night—you saved each other* . . .

Nana squeezes my hand. "You brought so much joy to her life, through everything . . ." Her voice cracks, but still she smiles, the light from the silent TV catching every wrinkle on her face. "I honestly don't know what she'd have done without you. Our gift. Our miracle." She clutches my hand tightly. "My precious granddaughter."

Her face splinters as I blink fiercely, fighting the tears.

I'm not her granddaughter . . . Not any relation at all . . .

My eyes flick back to the family photos.

We're the only ones left, I realize suddenly. I'm all she's got left—and I'm not even hers . . .

"So." Nana smiles, her eyes watery. "What's next for the bright and beautiful Rosie Kenning?"

I look at her, my mind an utter blank.

Where do I go from here? How do I even start?

"What about Sixth Form?" Nana suggests. "You could pick up where you left off, and you'd be back with all your old friends—"

"They've got their A levels this year," I say miserably. "They'll be gone by June."

Everyone'll be gone. Off to uni, or jobs, or taking gap years. There's only me left behind. Me and Nana. A Nana I have to lie to—or break her heart.

"Well, how about traveling?" she suggests. "You've always wanted to travel, why not go now?"

I look at her, surprised.

She smiles. "What's stopping you?"

"I—I can't," I protest. "I couldn't leave you, not now . . ."

"Nonsense!" She laughs. "I'm quite capable of looking after myself, thank you very much. And you can afford it—you know Trudie put that money aside for you."

"What? No, Nana. I can't. That's for the future."

"The future starts today, Rosie," Nana says firmly. "If Trudie's taught us anything, it's that life's too short to put things off. We mustn't waste a single precious moment."

"Nana—"

"Rosie," she interrupts, her eyes serious. "You've put your life on hold for far too long. You're nearly eighteen." She squeezes my hand. "Have you thought any more about taking the test?"

"What?" I look up, surprised.

"The predictive test—for Huntington's. You can't let it overshadow your life, Rosie—"

The doorbell rings.

"I'll get it!" I say quickly, jumping to my feet and darting past her, my head throbbing as the walls of lies close in.

How can I tell her? How can I possibly tell her I don't *need* the test results anymore, because I know it'll be negative *because Trudie wasn't my mother*—I'm not her granddaughter after all—I'm just some *stranger*, an *imposter. A fraud* . . .

I can't tell anyone, I realize with a jolt. I'll have to lie, have to live with this secret—this terrible, *awful* secret—for the rest of my life . . .

I open the front door to find Andy shivering in the cold morning sunlight. I stare at him in surprise.

"Reckon I'm the last person you want to see right now, huh?" He looks at me nervously. "I'm really sorry—about yesterday."

I shrug. "Forget it."

"And about your mum—having Huntington's—about thinking . . ." He shakes his head. "I'm so sorry. No wonder you couldn't come traveling, couldn't call . . . I should've waited, should've stayed, should've *been there* for you." He looks at me, his eyes pained. "I'm so sorry, Rosie."

I shake my head. "It's okay."

"I looked up Huntington's online—I haven't slept. Have you been tested? Do you have it too?"

"Rosie?" Nana calls from the lounge. "Rosie, who is it?"

"It's just Andy, Nana! We'll be in in a minute!" I call back, pulling the front door closed behind me.

"Well?" he asks urgently. "Have you had the test?"

"Andy, I . . ." I hesitate as his blue eyes pierce mine. "Yes." I sigh, already weary of lying. All that sneaking around, going to the clinic for counseling, taking the test without anyone knowing, any pressure, anyone to talk me out of it . . . and all along I'd only had to ask Sarah.

He looks at me fearfully, his voice a whisper. "Have you got the result?"

I shake my head. "My appointment's tomorrow, but—"

"I'll come with you."

"What?"

"I'll come with you. I'll drive you there."

"No, Andy, thanks, but—"

"Please, Rosie," he says earnestly, his eyes clear, intense. "Let me go with you. Let me be there for you this time." He takes my hand in his. So soft, so warm. "Please, Rose," he begs. "I feel like such a shit."

I squeeze his hand. "You're not," I whisper. "You didn't know."

"But I do now." He gazes down at me. "I'm here now."

My chest aches as I look up at him.

It couldn't hurt, could it? To go to the clinic, to get my results—though I already know what they'll be. It'd put Nana's mind at rest, after all, and it would mean one less lie to tell . . . And it couldn't hurt to double-check, to be sure . . .

"Okay," I whisper.

Andy's face lights up, and he pulls me suddenly into a tight hug. I let myself relax in his strong arms, my face buried against his chest, inhaling that familiar warm musky Andy smell.

No, it couldn't hurt.

The clinic waiting room is daffodil-yellow and filled with bright posters and big, leafy potted plants, the coffee tables strewn with glossy magazines covered with beautiful smiley women—every trick and tactic possible to lift the spirits and thoughts of its occupants.

They needn't have bothered. I've probably leafed through every one of these magazines—and never read a single word. No distraction works when you're waiting to discover your fate. Not really.

When mum was first diagnosed I did what Andy did and looked Huntington's up online. I'd never heard of it before, so I was amazed at how many sites there were offering information and advice.

Essentially, I gathered, Huntington's is a genetic mutation

that causes a progressive degeneration of your brain cells—something along the lines of the physical effects of Parkinson's plus the mental deterioration of Alzheimer's—slowly stripping you of your ability to walk, talk and reason. Most people develop symptoms between the ages of thirty and forty-five, but there're also juvenile and late-onset forms. Mum had the latter.

I was surprised to read that there are currently about 6,700 reported cases in England and Wales, and around 30,000 in the United States, though most of the websites I looked at seemed to think that there are probably twice as many cases as the "official" numbers reported, because people often hide the condition due to stigma, insurance or family issues, or just decide not to be tested. Once the symptoms start it usually takes ten to twenty years to kill you—although the suicide rate is scarily high—and children of parents with HD have a fifty-percent chance of inheriting it. Oh, and there's no cure.

Basically, it's the worst thing I could possibly have imagined.

The more I read, the more surreal it felt—the discovery of the disease, its progression . . . None of this could really be happening to my mum, could it? But when I got to the symptoms, several seemed to jump out at me: involuntary movements (chorea), slurred speech, mood swings, outbursts of anger, difficulty multitasking, forgetfulness, clumsiness, slow reactions, weight loss, depression, paranoia . . . Suddenly the last few years seemed littered with signs, each screaming out at me that there was something wrong.

But they'd all seemed so trivial, so unimportant at

the time. Mum had always been flighty, forgetful, easily flustered—she couldn't cope if I changed my plans at the last minute or asked her to do several things at once, like test me on my revision while she cooked dinner or washed laundry. I remember I got so cross with her for dyeing my school shirt pink once, then she'd blamed me—said I'd been distracting her—and we'd had a huge row and I'd stomped up to my room, slamming my door behind me.

But that was normal, wasn't it? Teenagers are supposed to argue with their mothers, aren't they? Bex certainly did— she had screaming rows with her mum. Fortunately, my mum always calmed down really quickly—way before me. She'd just get very upset, have a huge outburst, and then it would be over. Friends again. I just thought she was going through the menopause.

But after her diagnosis I suddenly had to reassess every argument, every fight we'd ever had, trying to untangle Mum from the disease, the terrible things I'd said echoing guiltily in my ears.

Even the physical signs, like the chorea, I'd never noticed. I thought nothing of the familiar jingle of bracelets announcing her approach, used to nag at her for fidgeting while watching TV . . . and even as far back as my childhood, there were little things. Like, Mum was never any good at Snap. Her reactions just weren't quick enough, and I'd always beat her, hands down. It was one of my favorite games—because I always won.

And now . . . I look around the waiting room guiltily, wondering who's affected, what stage they're at. Half the people in this room will have the disease, statistically.

But not me.

I'd decided months ago that I needed to know, once and for all. I'd had a bad day with Mum, lost my temper, and dropped a bowl of pasta, smashing, to the floor. And then I panicked. I started analyzing everything I did, scouring myself for symptoms. It drove me crazy. So I rang the clinic and booked my first counseling session. You're usually supposed to be eighteen, but as I was only a few months off they let me in a bit early, so long as the counseling went well. They had to be convinced that I was psychologically ready, that I knew what I was letting myself in for, whatever the result. Because there is no going back. There's no cure. There's just knowing or not knowing. Having it or not. Fifty-fifty.

Unless, of course, you suddenly find out that you're not actually related to anyone with Huntington's after all. They didn't cover *that* in our sessions.

"Rosalind Kenning?" The nurse looks up from her clipboard.

Andy squeezes my hand, and we follow her in.

"Nice to see you, Rosie," Dan, my genetic counselor says. "And you've brought a friend. Good."

I introduce Andy, and he sits next to me, gripping my hand tightly. I've never seen him so nervous.

"Now, we've had your result back," Dan begins. "And it's *good news*, Rosie." His face breaks into a wide smile. "You do *not* have the gene that causes Huntington's!"

I exhale deeply. I hadn't even realized I was holding my breath.

"Are you sure?" Andy asks anxiously.

"Positive. By analyzing the number of CAG repeats on

her chromosome four—fifteen and seventeen—we can determine that Rosie has definitely *not* inherited the gene. If she had, one of her counts would be somewhere up around forty. Rosie is well below that. She's completely unaffected."

"Oh, God!" Andy grabs me in a tight hug. "Oh, thank God!"

I let him hug me, my body limp and numb in his arms.

Fifteen and seventeen . . . Mum's were forty-five and nineteen—I don't share either of them . . .

I knew. Of course I knew, but now . . . it's real.

I don't have Huntington's. I never will have Huntington's. Everything I dreaded and feared will never come true. It'll never happen to me like it happened to Mum.

Because she wasn't my mother.

Hot tears trickle down my cheeks.

"Hey." Andy pulls back gently and wipes my eyes. "Are you okay?"

I nod and look away, swallowing hard.

"Rosie, this is fantastic!" Andy grins.

I force a tight smile.

Yep. Fantastic.

"It's normal to experience a sense of shock," Dan says gently. "With the relief can come a sense of disbelief, and even guilt. It's perfectly normal, Rosie."

I smile at him, the tears still streaming down my cheeks.

She was right. Sarah was right. There's no going back. You either spend your life wondering, worrying, pretending . . . or you find out for sure.

And now I know.

For sure.

I stare at the little plastic wand, waiting for my fate to be decided—*revealed,* really. It's already decided, after all. Positive or negative. This is just proof. Scientific confirmation of what already is—or isn't.

Despite everything, I can't help praying, can't help hoping that somehow it's all been a coincidence—a bad case of food poisoning, a belated growth spurt, a late period . . .

I squeeze my eyes shut, *wishing, hoping, praying.*

I hold my breath as I force one eyelid open.

My heart stops and I snap my eye shut again quickly, as if I'll get a second chance . . .

I bite my lip and open my eyes.

But it's still the same. Of course it is. Wishing can't change it. This isn't a magic wand—it can't perform miracles.

Hot tears trickle down my cheeks and I bury my head in my hands.

I knew—of course I knew. But now I *know.* For sure. Completely and irrevocably and scientifically.

Positive.

I'm pregnant.

My life is over.

Chapter Six

Negative.

Not at risk.

Not my mother.

God, it's true. It's all true. Everything Sarah said. Though, as it turns out, she needn't have told me after all—they didn't compare our results, didn't find out.

I close my eyes, my head reeling.

Negative.

How can one word bring so much joy and so much despair?

"What's it to be? Red? White? Rosé?" Andy grins, putting on a French accent as he surveys the wine bottles in his kitchen. "Rosé for Rosie?"

I smile weakly. "No, thank you."

"No?" He frowns. "I know! Champagne! I think we've even got some flutes somewhere—this is a celebration, after all!"

He disappears through the doorway and I look away,

out of the window. Black clouds gather menacingly over the fields, blotting out the sun.

I thought I'd be pleased to get the all-clear, that it would set me free . . . but instead I just feel . . . lost . . . It seems like whenever I finally get an answer to one question, a million others pop up right behind it: I don't have the disease, I'm not Trudie's daughter—*so who am I?* And who's this girl, this Holly Woods, my real mother? Is she still around? Why did she run away? *Why did she abandon me?*

"Okay . . . champagne and flutes!" Andy returns, proudly flourishing a bottle and two glasses. "Now all we need is cake!"

"No, really, I don't want—"

"What have we got?" He opens a cupboard. "Swiss roll . . . flapjack . . ."

"Andy—"

"Battenberg! Do you like battenberg?"

"Andy, I'm fine! Really."

"Really?" He turns.

"Really."

"*Really?* Because you've barely said two words since we left the clinic, Rosie." He looks at me. "You don't want to go out, you don't want to celebrate . . ."

I look away.

He sighs. "I could understand it if the test were positive, but you're acting like you've got the weight of the world on your shoulders—and it's negative! You're healthy!" He sits down beside me. "Why aren't you happy about it?"

I shift uncomfortably.

"And don't say it's that guilt bollocks the counselor was on about." His tone softens and he covers my hand with his.

"Rose, you've suffered enough—your mum would be thrilled that you're in the clear."

I pull my hand away. "You don't understand."

"No," he sighs. "You're right, I don't."

"Andy—"

"I *don't* understand, because you never tell me anything!" He stands up, paces the room. "You just lock yourself away in your own little world and try to deal with everything by yourself. That's why we broke up—because you couldn't tell me, *wouldn't* tell me, what was wrong!"

I stare at him, my cheeks burning, my eyes hot. I look away.

"I could've handled it, Rosie—I could've helped—I could help now, if you'd let me."

I close my eyes.

He sighs. "I know it must be difficult—I know it's a lot to take in . . ."

"It's not," I mutter.

"Of course it is."

"It's not a lot to take in, all right?" I glare at him. "Because I—I already knew."

Andy frowns. "What do you mean?"

I look away.

"I don't understand, Rose," he says slowly. "I thought Huntington's was hereditary?"

"Exactly! Exactly, it's hereditary!"

He looks at me for a moment, then shakes his head. "You've lost me."

"It's hereditary!" I look at him, the pain prickling my

eyes. "But you can't inherit a disease from someone who's not related to you—who isn't even your *mother!*"

He stares at me.

"She wasn't my mother, Andy—she wasn't . . ." I trail off, close my eyes, my throat swelling painfully.

There's a long silence. Then he takes a deep breath and reaches over, his hand warm and soft on mine.

"Okay," he says gently. "I think it's time to spill, don't you?"

"Wow." Andy sighs after I've told him everything. "Wow."

"Yeah." It feels good to finally let it all out. I feel . . . lighter. But exhausted.

"And Trudie never knew?"

I shake my head.

"Wow, Rose. I mean, God, I don't know what to say . . ." He sighs. "How do you deal with something like— Have you told your nana?"

I shake my head. "I can't, Andy. I'm all she's got left—of Granddad, of Mum—how can I possibly tell her that it was all one big lie, all these years? That her real granddaughter died the day she was born? It would break her heart." I swallow, the pain in my chest swelling. "It's broken mine."

"Rosie, it's okay."

"No. No, it's not. You don't know what it's like, Andy. I'm stuck here, trapped in this life that's not even mine with a grandmother I have to lie to, *no* friends, *no* qualifications, *no life*—there's nothing left!" My voice cracks. "It's all right for you, you're buggering off around the world—you can escape!"

"Then come with me."

"Yeah, right."

"I'm serious—why not? You said it yourself, what's keeping you here?" He looks at me. "We always wanted to travel, didn't we? This is our second chance!"

I hesitate, and he squeezes my hand, his eyes softening. "Come with me, Rose. It wasn't the same without you—I missed you the whole time. This was *our* dream, after all. *We* planned it, *we* dreamed of it and then *missed* it because of a stupid misunderstanding—so let's go *now!*"

I look at him, the idea dancing enticingly in my mind—to just fly away with Andy, leave everything behind, pick up where we left off, but . . . it's too much, too sudden.

"No strings," he promises, reading my doubts. "I've missed you, Rosie. I've missed *you*—just being with you . . . hanging out, educating your taste in music." He grins, those dimples making me falter. "Come on, Rose. It's just what you need, it'll take your mind off everything."

"It will not!"

He looks up at the anger in my voice.

"You have no idea, do you? You think dashing off around the world will make me forget that my mother's dead? That she wasn't actually my mother?" I look at him. "How could I ever come back, Andy? To this mess of—of lies and deceit and, and . . ." I trail off and look out the window, but all I can see is my tearstained reflection and the dark clouds beyond. "It's such a mess, it's all such a mess, and I just . . . There's nothing left, Andy. None of it's real . . ." I close my eyes.

He sighs, rubs his brow.

"So, what now?"

I shrug. "I dunno."

We sit in silence for a moment.

"Actually, I do," I say eventually, taking a deep breath. "I'm going to find her."

"Who?"

I swallow hard. "My real mother."

"Hello? Mr. Woods? Hi!" I cross my fingers tightly. "Hi, I'm a friend of Holly's, and— Sorry? Holly Woods? She doesn't?" My heart sinks. "Sorry to bother you. Bye."

I sigh heavily, dropping the receiver into its cradle and my head into my hands. There were thirty-five Woodses in the phone book. That was the last one.

"Tell me you've had better luck with the birth records?"

Andy shakes his head at the computer screen. " 'Fraid not. According to this birth records site, no seventeen-year-old Holly Woods even existed in the year you were born."

"What?" I look up. "That's impossible! Maybe Sarah guessed her age wrong. Try the years either side."

"I have," Andy sighs. "I've tried five years either side. No Holly Woods."

"None *at all*?"

He shakes his head.

"I don't understand." I frown. "That's impossible. We know she was here—she was seventeen, she ran away, she had a baby . . ."

I drop the phone book and pick up my jacket. "Come on."

Andy stares at me. "Where are we going?"

"To the one place we know she *has* been."

The snow has all but melted as we drive into town, mounds that were once snowmen glinting in the fields and gardens as the afternoon sun struggles through the clouds.

"All set?" Andy asks as we pull into the car-park.

I take a deep breath and hug my clipboard. "All set."

He squeezes my shoulder, and we head into the small country hospital, the stench of disinfectant stinging my nose as we follow the signs down the lino-lined corridor to a ward painted in pastel colors.

Maternity.

Little goose bumps break out down my back. This is it. This is where it all happened. Thank God Sarah's got this week off, so there's no chance of bumping into her.

"Can I help you?" A cheerful-looking nurse approaches us.

I force a bright smile and clear my throat. "Hello, we're students at Maybridge Sixth Form College, and we're doing a project on the day we were born." My tone is professional, polite, as I recite the rehearsed lines we devised in the car.

"I see." She smiles. "How can I help you?"

"Well, I was born here," I say confidently. "And I was just wondering if you could tell me how many . . ." My eyes flick to her name-badge. *Jamila Price.* "How many . . ." Jamila . . . "How . . ."

She raises her eyebrows.

"How many other babies were born on the same days we were," Andy finishes for me. "And any information you can give us about them."

"I'm sorry." Jamila smiles apologetically. "We can't give out that information. Patient confidentiality, you know."

"Of course," Andy says. "Thanks anyway."

"What about you?" I ask desperately as she turns away. "Maybe I could just ask you some questions. Have you ever had to deal with mothers running away—abandoning their child?"

She stares at me. "I'm sorry—I'm afraid I can't help you."

"Come on, Rose," Andy says quickly. "Let's go."

"But—what about teenagers with unwanted babies? Adoption?"

"I'm sorry." She turns away.

"*Come on.*" Andy grabs my arm and pulls me back through the door.

"Crap." I kick the snow gloomily as we walk back to the car. "Utter crap. Fat lot of use that was."

"Well, I don't know what you expected, to be honest, Rose. They're hardly going to say, 'Oh yes, I remember that mother, here's her name, address and telephone number,' are they?"

"*She* might have." I round on him. "*She* might have, because *she's* the one who told Sarah about me!"

He stops walking.

"She was *there,* Andy—she *met* Holly. She might remember her, might be able to tell me—"

I turn back but he grabs my arm.

"She's not going to tell you anything, Rosie—there are laws, you know?"

"I know," I admit sulkily. "But—"

"And Sarah *broke* the law, Rose," Andy continues, his voice a whisper. "She'll get into a *lot* of trouble if anyone finds out—you have to be really careful about this."

"I *am* being careful." I hug the clipboard tightly. "But Andy, how else am I going to find my real mother?"

He sighs. "Maybe she doesn't want to be found."

I look at him.

"Think about it, Rosie. She was seventeen. Seventeen and pregnant and alone. She was going to give you up for adoption, she ran away, she probably even gave a fake name—there were no seventeen-year-old Holly Woodses, remember?"

I sigh heavily, digging my toe into the loose gravel. Andy's right, the trail's gone cold. It's nearly eighteen years cold. All I have is a name, and if that's fake . . . then I have nothing. My mother walked out of that hospital and just disappeared into thin air, leaving me behind—the only proof she ever existed.

She doesn't even have a birth record.

I dig my foot deeper into the stones, losing my toes in the dirt and grit.

No sign of her, even five years either side.

I rewind my conversation with Sarah miserably in my head. She was *seventeen*, she was *here—the girl's name was Holly Woods* . . .

Suddenly my heart begins to race.

The girl . . .

I march back to the car. "We need to check the records again."

"What? Rosie, wait—"

"The birth records," I tell him, sprinting now. "We got the wrong year!"

"Rosie, we checked," Andy argues. "Five years either side—there was no Holly Woods born at the right time to be your mother!"

"No." I grin, my cheeks warm in the icy air. "Not my *mother* . . ."

My fingers trip over themselves as I type into the database. I hold my breath, tapping my foot nervously as the computer scans the birth records.

A page of details pings up before me.

"Bingo," I whisper, clicking the mouse.

Holly Marie Woods, it reads.

Mother's Maiden Name: Sinclare.

Registration District: Maybridge.

Date of Birth . . .

The fifth of January, the year I was born.

I stare at the record, hardly able to believe it. There she is in black and white. *Holly Woods*—the *baby's* name, not the mother's. Sarah must've misunderstood when I asked her—or I did. But here she is. The other baby. *Holly Woods.*

"This is morbid," Andy mutters beside me. "This is so morbid, Rose. This girl died—Trudie's baby died . . ."

I look at the screen, goose bumps prickling my arms.

Mum's baby. If she'd lived, she'd have had my mum—she'd have my life. But she died. I blink hard, imagining her tiny body, a tiny coffin. Sarah swapped us, and she died—and Mum never even knew. She died . . . and I lived in her place.

I stare at the record, guilt wrapping heavily around my shoulders.

The day I was born. My town. I could be looking at my own birth record, it's so similar.

Suddenly, an icy shiver trickles down my spine.

This is my birth record.

I stare at the page again, my eyes wide, the facts screaming out at me, clear as day. This isn't some other girl, some stranger, even Trudie's daughter . . .

These are my details: my name, my mother.

I scroll down quickly, scanning, searching.

Mother's Maiden Name: Sinclare.

"That's weird," Andy says, reading over my shoulder. "Why would you give your child a different surname? Why Woods, not Sinclare?"

I shrug. "Maybe it was my father's name?"

"I thought she was alone?"

"She could still have named me after him."

"Or maybe she wanted to distance herself . . . ," Andy suggests carefully.

"From my real dad?" I frown.

"Yes . . ." Andy hesitates. "Or . . . from you."

I stare at him.

"Rosie . . ." He sighs. "All I'm saying is . . . she was going to put you up for adoption. Perhaps it was just easier to call you something else. Maybe she wanted to be harder to find."

"That's ridiculous," I say, my cheeks hot. "There could be a million reasons why she called me that—maybe she's a movie buff? . . . Maybe she just liked the name! The point is, *we don't know*, Andy. We can't ever know, unless we find her."

"How?" Andy asks. "We don't even know her first name—it's impossible!"

I stare miserably at the screen. All we've got is a surname. And a town . . .

Quickly, I click on a new search. I type Sinclare into the database, and, instantly, a short list appears in front of me. A smile spreads over my face as I scan the screen. There're only a few entries for thirty-five years ago . . . and only one in Maybridge!

"Bingo!"

Katharine Sinclare.

My mother!

My heart pounding crazily, I grab the phone book again and flick through it clumsily.

I gasp. There's only one Sinclare . . .

In Maybridge.

I stare at the page. I've found her. I've really found her . . .

Andy looks at me, his eyes serious.

"Now what?"

Now what?

I stare at myself in the mirror.

I pull off my baggy T-shirt and turn sideways, running my hand over my belly.

You can't even tell, not really. I look normal—a couple of pounds heavier, maybe, but no one would know to look at me. They'd never guess . . .

I bite my lip.

I can't have a baby—how can I? It would ruin everything! I've got a life, a dream. A dream that *doesn't* include becoming a single teenage mother . . .

I watch as a hot tear slides down my cheek.

I can't do this. Not on my own. I'm too young—there are a thousand reasons . . .

I just can't.

I take a deep breath.

It's time to make a decision, choose my future.

I pull my top back on, shivering suddenly.

And no one would ever know.

Chapter Seven

The first lampposts are flickering on as we pull up a few doors down from the pebble-dashed semidetached house. I stare up at it, spellbound, Christmas lights twinkling around the windows, a flashing reindeer guarding the gravel drive.

I can't believe how close she was all this time. I've driven past this house a million times—it's on my way to school, for heaven's sake!

"Rosie . . ." Andy hesitates. "I don't think this is such a good idea."

I turn. "What?"

"You can't just waltz up to some stranger's house and start making wild accusations."

"They're not wild accusations," I protest. "She's my mother!"

"She *might* be your mother," Andy argues. "You don't know, not for sure."

"She *is*," I insist. "Andy, it all fits—Holly Woods was her daughter, born the same day as me, when she was seventeen years old, and she lives in Maybridge—it's her!"

Andy sighs.

I look away. "I know you think I'm crazy, but—"

"I don't," he says quietly. "I don't think you're crazy. I just think you *want* this too much." He sighs. "You're setting yourself up for a fall."

"Well, maybe I am." I unsnap my seat belt. "But that's my decision."

Andy puts his hand on mine.

"You're right," he says. "It is your decision. But please, think about it—"

"I *have!*" I pull my hand away.

"Have you?" Andy challenges. "Have you really thought about *her*? About Katharine? About Sarah?"

"Sod Sarah!" I snap. "This is all Sarah's fault—she *did* it! She *lied* about it—to Mum, to everyone!"

"Yes, she lied," Andy admits. "But does she really deserve to go to jail for it?"

I look at him.

"Because that's what will happen, Rosie. Jail, because she tried to help three desperate people—a teenager too young to cope with being a mother, an abandoned baby, and a grieving widow, desperate for a child." He looks at me. "Sarah put her neck on the line for *your* sake, not hers. And now you want to unravel it all?"

I look away.

"And what about Katharine?" Andy persists. "She ran away, Rose—she abandoned you—*eighteen years ago*. She'll have a whole new life now—maybe even a family. How's she gonna feel if you waltz up and claim to be her daughter?"

I close my eyes, my thoughts whirling painfully.

"I just . . . I just want to *see* her . . ." I sigh. "Get to know her. Give her the choice—the chance to know me . . ."

"But it won't be her choice, Rosie," Andy says gently. "It'll be yours."

I look at him.

"She made her choice," he says. "She left."

I look away.

"Rosie . . ."

"So, what? I should just give up? Give up when I'm this close?"

He looks away.

"Andy!" I stare at him. "But . . . but then why did you help me search for her? Why help me get this far?"

He sighs. "I just . . . I didn't think you'd find her, Rosie— not this soon! This is all happening so quickly—just this morning you got your Huntington's results and now . . ." He shakes his head. "I thought it'd take ages, that you'd have time to think it through. That you just needed to get this out of your system to be able to get on with your life."

"Get on with my life?" I stare at him. "What life, Andy?"

He looks away.

"Great, Andy. That's great. You'll help me, fine—as long as I'm hitting brick walls, but as soon as I actually *find* something, find *her*, you suddenly back out? Thanks a lot!" I open the car door.

"Rosie . . ." Andy grabs my arm, but I wrench it away.

"Fine!" he snaps angrily. "Go—whatever! But you'd better know what you're doing, Rosie, because if you don't, you're about to ruin a lot of people's lives!"

I grit my teeth and slam the door behind me.

He doesn't understand, I tell myself as I march down the road. *It's all right for him, with his normal life and normal family and future all planned out. But I don't have that—I don't have anything anymore, and I need to know, I need to . . .*

I slow down as I approach the house. The front window is dark, the curtains drawn. A pizza-delivery leaflet sticks out of the letter-box.

I take a deep breath and lift the knocker. This is it. *This is her door . . .*

Suddenly I hesitate, Andy's words filling my head. Am I about to make the biggest mistake of my life . . . ?

I swallow hard, the knocker icy cold in my hand.

Maybe . . . maybe I *should* take some time, think about this more. This is a big step—it's *huge*—maybe I shouldn't rush into it . . .

The wind whispers round my ears as I look up at the dark house.

Andy's right, there's no hurry. She'll still be here. I can come back anytime, plan what I'll say, what I'll do—shit, what I'll *wear*—I glance down at my scruffy jeans and sweater.

Do I really want to meet my mother looking like *this*?

I take a last long look at the house, then sigh as I let the knocker go. It bangs gently as I turn to leave.

Immediately, a black barking shape hurls itself against the frosted glass. I jump back, my heart in my mouth as a light flicks on, exposing me in its yellow glare. The door opens and a woman peers out, gripping the dog's collar as he strains toward me, her hair wrapped in a towel turban.

"Sorry, love," she says. "Don't worry—he's all bark and no bite, this one. Can I help you?"

"I . . . I . . ." I stare at her. A dark tendril of wet hair escapes the turban and curls round her face. "Are you Katharine Sinclare?"

"Lord, no!" she laughs. "She hasn't lived here for years!"

My heart plummets. I haven't found her after all. And if she's not here . . . I'll never find her. The trail's gone cold.

"But perhaps I can help you?" The woman smiles. "I'm her mum—Pam."

I stare at her. *Her mum?* She's *Katharine's mother?* I blink. *My grandmother!*

"Um, yes, yes please—I . . ." This is it. No going back. "I'm Rosie Kenning," I say, my heart thumping. "I'm a student at Maybridge Sixth Form College, and I'm doing a school project—" The words are out in a rush before I can stop them. *What am I doing?* "But I . . . could come back—if it's not a good time?"

"What?" She touches her turban, then laughs. "No, don't be daft, come in, come in! Down, Toby! Come on in." She ushers me inside. "Grab a pew and I'll be back in just a mo." Pam flicks the lounge light on and disappears down the corridor. A hair dryer blasts into action.

I step slowly into the room, my eyes everywhere, drinking it in like a museum: the strings of colorful Christmas cards hanging from every wall, looping round framed school photographs and children's paintings; the heaving Christmas tree with its homemade decorations and lopsided angel;

the flowery chintz sofa and the rocking chair covered with a patchwork throw . . . And everywhere, crammed onto the mantelpiece, the television, the windowsills, are crowds of trinkets: postcards and souvenirs and photos, medals and trophies and certificates—all clues about my mother, her life, my family . . .

"So, what's your project about?" Pam calls as the hair dryer clicks off.

"Oh, it's, er . . . a sort of 'where are they now?' piece," I lie quickly, my eyes landing on a photo of two smiling schoolgirls.

"Oh yeah?"

I pick up the photo, and my heart skips a beat. Two little girls with gleaming black hair and bright smiles. One of them has to be Katharine.

"We're supposed to pick someone who was a teenager when we were born, and—"

"So you chose Kitty."

I turn as Pam enters behind me, running a brush through her thick dark hair.

"Well, I suppose that figures." She smiles at the photograph in my hand. "After all, she's the famous one."

"And here's Kitty in her first school play." Pam turns the pages of a photo album. "Bitten by the bug right then and there, she was. You know, she fought off five other girls to play Mary in the nativity that year—including the rector's daughter!—and then she went and lost her two front teeth, bless her!" She points to a photo of a little girl with a gappy grin and a tea towel on her head.

"And here she is in *Annie*, and *Joseph*, and as Sandy in *Grease*. Spent far too much time rehearsing and not enough revising for her GCSEs, if you ask me!" Pam chuckles. "Still, grades aren't everything—she was straight off to London for the summer with the National Youth Theatre, and then snapped up by an acting agent!"

"Wow!"

"We were so proud." Pam beams. "Didn't get to see much of her, of course, she was so busy auditioning and filming and living the high life in London. Not that she even stayed there very long—she left just after Christmas!"

"How come?" I ask carefully.

"She was spotted! Again! Can you believe it?" Pam laughs. "We got a call at the end of January—she was off to Los Angeles." Pam sighs. "Off to follow her dream."

Or to forget her past.

"She's been starring in a sitcom over there." Pam beams. "*For Richer, For Poorer.* Here." She untucks a large photo from the back of the album and I gasp. Kitty's black hair gleams beneath an Alice band, and her green eyes penetrate mine. Any doubts I had vanish in an instant.

She looks just like me.

"Lovely, isn't it?" Pam smiles. "And there's her stage name, Kitty Clare. Washing away her sin my husband, Keith, says—Get it? *Sinclare*?"

I grin, excitement thrilling like a fever through my veins. "Do you have any contact details for her? It would be great to do an interview or something."

89

"Of course," Pam says, handing me the photo. "The address of the studios is on the back, and you'll need a photo for your project. I've got plenty more."

"Thank you." I take the photo reverently. *My mother . . .*

Suddenly, Toby springs to his feet, barking madly as a key turns in the front door.

"Gracious, is that the time? Doesn't it fly?" Pam jumps up. "Sorry, love, that'll be my other daughter, Jenny, and her boys—we're off to the panto. It's all go in this family, I'm afraid!"

"That's fine. Thank you so much for your help." I smile, getting to my feet.

"Mum! Are you ready?" A woman bustles in, swiping her long black hair from her face. "Oh, sorry, I didn't realize you had a visitor. Hello." She smiles warmly.

"Hi." I beam back. *My aunt!*

Two little boys hurtle past her, lunging at each other with plastic swords. *And cousins!*

"Boys—careful!" She grins apologetically. "Sorry! They're a bit excited—we're off to see *Peter Pan*."

I beam as I edge past them. *A whole family!*

"Sorry to rush you off like this," Pam says, holding the front door for me. "Please do call round again if there's anything else you need—it's always lovely talking about my girls."

She smiles at me, and suddenly I give her a spontaneous hug, breathing in the fruity scent of her shampoo as she hugs me back.

"You take care, now." She beams. "And remember—anytime!"

"Goodbye!" I wave as she closes the door, hugging my jacket tighter, a warm feeling glowing inside me.

I've found her, I've actually found my mother! And Pam too, and Keith and Jenny and the boys—a whole other family! *My real family.* The wind whips against my cheeks, and my eyes water. My *mother.* Yes, she's in L.A.—practically the other side of the world—but I've found her! I've actually found her!

Andy looks up as I open the car door. "Well?"

I falter, remembering his harsh words, his cynicism.

"It wasn't her, was it?" He sighs, reaching over and brushing a tear from my eye.

I hesitate, can't meet his gaze.

"Oh, Rose." He pulls me into a tight embrace. "I'm so sorry, but you know, it's probably for the best."

Over his shoulder, my eyes are on the house. The front door opens and the family spills out onto the driveway, laughing and chattering happily.

"Do you want to talk about it?" Andy asks gently.

I shake my head. This is too fragile, too precious a moment to talk about right now. Especially with Andy. I can't tell him, can't let him ruin this—not now . . .

He starts the car, and I gaze into the rearview mirror as we drive away, watching the Sinclares laugh as they squash and squeeze into their car, Toby racing in excited circles around them, my head dancing with excitement, with possibilities. *My family . . . my grandmother . . . my mother . . .*

"You don't need her, you know?"

I turn, startled, as Andy's hand squeezes mine.

"Just coz she gave birth to you, it doesn't make her—"

"Let's talk about something else, okay?" I interrupt quickly, pulling my hand away.

He looks at me, concerned.

"Please." I swallow. "Tell me about your trip."

"Okay . . . ," he says uncertainly. "Well, I'm starting out in the States. I've got family in New York and Washington, so I'm going to crash at theirs on the cheap."

"Sounds good," I reply absently.

"Yeah, my cousin's a taxi driver—a bona fide New York cabbie—so he's promised to show me the sights. Then my aunt'll feed me up before I fly on to Chicago, San Francisco, then catch a Greyhound bus down to sunny L.A."

"L.A.?" I turn.

"Yeah, I thought I'd do the whole showbiz thing—Mann's Chinese Theater, Walk of Fame, Hollywood."

Hollywood . . . *Holly Woods*. I lean back against the head-rest and smile. *That's* why! What better name for the child of a starstruck seventeen-year-old?

"Then on to Southeast Asia—Vietnam, Cambodia, Thailand . . . ," Andy continues, but I zone out, still buzzing with thoughts of my family—so close by! And my mother—in Los Angeles . . .

Finally we pull into Nana's drive.

"Andy—"

"Rose—" We say each other's name together.

"You first," I insist.

"I just wanted to say . . . I *am* sorry we didn't find your mum. I know how much it meant to you, I just . . ." He rests his hand on mine. "I didn't want you to get hurt."

My cheeks burn and I look away. "I know," I say quietly.

He squeezes my hand. "Your turn."

"What? Oh, no, it was nothing." I shrug.

"What is it?" He smiles.

"I was just wondering . . ." I hesitate. "I mean, about your trip . . ."

He frowns. "I could always put it off for a bit, if you like? If you want me to stick around?"

I shake my head quickly. "No, no, it's not that, it's just . . ."

"What?" he asks gently.

"Would you mind . . . if I came along after all . . . maybe . . . ?"

"On the trip?"

I nod.

"Rosie, that would be *awesome!*"

"Yeah?"

"Ye-ah!" He grins. "Are you kidding? We'll have the best time!"

I smile at him. Then shiver as the wind whips past.

"Listen, go in, you're freezing. I'll call you tomorrow, okay? We'll meet up, sort everything. Rosie, this is going to be so great!" His eyes sparkle as he pulls away. "You won't regret it!"

I smile weakly.

"And Rosie?"

I turn.

"Trudie would be so proud." He beams.

His headlights dazzle my eyes as he turns the car around and disappears down the hill, leaving me dark and cold and guilty.

A cold, guilty sweat trickles down the back of my neck as I fidget restlessly, flicking through the litter of leaflets on the clinic coffee table, nervously waiting my turn.

Unwanted Pregnancy?

Your options:

a) Adoption.

Nope—I need this over with.

b) Abortion.

I take a deep breath, scan the page . . .

Up to Seven Weeks: Manual Vacuum Aspiration

Ugh. My stomach turns.

Medical Abortion (Abortion Pill)

I bite my lip. That seems easy enough. Take a pill—no more baby.

Simple.

"Hayley Wilson?"

I jump as the receptionist calls the next patient. But it's not me. Not yet. I watch as the girl stands up, head bowed as she passes through the double doors.

I wipe my palms on my jeans and pick up another leaflet, anything to keep my hands busy, distracted.

Your baby—week by week

Despite myself, my eyes slide down to the picture for seven weeks as words leap out at me—*fingers, toes, elbows, knees, nostrils, eyelids*—this clump of cells is no bigger than a pencil eraser, yet it already has *eyelids*? It's already moving on its own? Its tiny heart pulsing at 150 beats a minute—twice the speed of mine?

Before I know it, I've walked out. I walk out the door and keep walking, the air cold on my cheeks and fresh in my lungs. I take deep gulps of it, sucking it in till I feel dizzy with oxygen, with life, walking away, far away from the clinic . . .

Toward a future I never planned.

Chapter Eight

"Taxi's here!" Andy cries, slinging my rucksack over his shoulder and pretending to stagger under the weight. "Good God, woman, what have you got in here? Anyone would think you were going away for eight months or something!"

Sarah laughs as he reels down the driveway while Nana squeezes me so tight I think I'll burst.

"Eight months! Oh, sweetheart!"

I hold her close and my chest aches—she feels so small, so fragile. "I'll miss you, Nana."

"Oh, you'll be having far too much fun to miss anything round here!" Sarah grins.

"Now, you take care, all right?" Nana says, clutching my hands. "You're very precious."

"You too," I tell her tenderly.

"I want lots of postcards—and maybe a call once in a while?"

"I promise." I grin. "Now, no wild parties while I'm gone—I know what you're like!"

She laughs. "Just you try and stop me!"

"Good luck, sweetheart." Sarah hugs me and I stiffen involuntarily, then smile for Nana's sake.

I don't really know *how* to feel about Sarah anymore—whether to be angry with her, or resentful, or *grateful*, even . . . Everything's been such a blur these past few days, rushing around frantically packing and planning, there hasn't been much time to think about anything else. Not even Kitty. With Nana and Andy constantly around and the only computer in Nana's bedroom, I've only managed to Google her once—hungrily devouring a feast of new photographs—before Nana walked in and I quickly shut the site down, stung with guilt.

I climb into the taxi and look back at her waving madly from the doorway, and I feel sick. She's so happy for me—thrilled that I'm officially negative, delighted that I'm finally going traveling. What would she think if she knew the truth?

I watch as Sarah wraps her arm round Nana's thin shoulders and blows me a kiss.

How does she do it? How did Sarah keep her secret all these years, look us in the eye, all the while *knowing*? It's been killing me lying to Nana, walking on eggshells, double-checking everything I say and do . . .

I sigh as we turn a corner and she disappears, the trees and fields and houses crowding in, filling the distance between us.

At least now I won't have to lie for a while.

Not to Nana, anyway.

"Hey," Andy says softly. "Do you want to stop by the graveyard on the way? We've got time."

"No." I shake my head, looking away. "I've already been."

Another lie. It's been one thing holding it together in front of everyone else, but I just haven't been able to face visiting Mum's grave—not with my bags packed and a ticket clutched in my hand to go and find Kitty. A ticket paid for with Mum's inheritance.

"I'm so glad you changed your mind." Andy beams, his eyes bright. "We're gonna have such a great time, Rose. Me and you against the world."

I smile weakly, squeeze his hand, then turn to look out of the window as we head onto the motorway, my stomach tight.

What's one more lie? It's like they're contagious—every time I leave one behind, a new one rears its ugly head. But Andy wouldn't understand, he's made that clear. And I don't need his approval, not really. This is my life, my decision.

Besides, we'll have a wonderful time traveling together— just as we always planned—and then, when we get to Los Angeles . . .

My heartbeat quickens as the familiar scenery streams past and disappears behind us, leaving the tiny village, the familiar houses and fields, and my life as I've always known it far, far behind.

Who knows . . . ?

The ground is sprinkled with snow but the sky is a brilliant blue as finally we land in New York.

My eyes widen as we enter the crowded arrivals hall,

everyone pushing and shoving, waving signs and placards as they jostle for position. I inch closer to Andy.

Suddenly, a guy in a thick tartan jacket grabs Andy in a bear hug that lifts him off the ground. "Hey, shrimp! How're ya doin?" he cries. "And you must be the lovely Rosie." He grins, kissing my hand.

"Okay, enough of the charm," Andy laughs. "Rosie, Casey; Casey, Rosie. Now let's get going, I'm freezing my arse off!"

"Aw, and it's such a pretty ass, too," Casey teases, slapping Andy's bum and winking at me as he hitches my bag onto his shoulder. "Anyone for breakfast? I'm starved!"

"Breakfast" is unlike anything I've ever seen in my life— sausages, eggs and toast tussle for space next to long streaks of bacon, golden hash browns and a huge stack of fluffy pancakes drenched in sticky-sweet maple syrup. The image of my heaped plate stays with me all day—especially as the ferry bounces over the choppy waves toward Liberty Island.

"Ugh! I shouldn't have eaten so much!" I groan as my stomach lurches back and forth. "Either that, or I should've stayed on dry land!"

"Yeah, but she's worth it." Andy grins. "Just look at her!"

I gaze up at the massive green lady, her torch held high above the lights of Manhattan. The view of the city across the bay is just stunning, the skyscrapers shooting like rockets up into the blue, blue sky, the air crisp and clear, the waves sparkling far below. What a sight to greet all the immigrants about to start a new life in the Land of Opportunity.

"Quick, take a picture!" Casey cries, grabbing Andy and striking the *Titanic* pose.

I laugh and delve in my bag for my camera, my fingers tingling as they brush Kitty's photo. I wonder if she felt like this, arriving for the first time? So full of hope and expectation. Ready to start her new life. To follow her dream.

My heart soars with the seagulls high above as I take the shot, the wind in my hair, my seasickness suddenly gone.

The streets are rammed as we crawl back through the city in Casey's yellow cab. I've never seen anywhere so busy, so bustling, so *alive*! From every direction horns blare and drivers yell abuse as shoppers weave through the endless river of traffic to the bright lights and fancy window displays on the other side.

"Well, Toto." Andy winks. "Guess we're not in Kansas anymore!"

He's not kidding. Gazing out at this urban jungle, I feel a million miles away from sleepy little Bramberley.

"Everybody out!" Casey says suddenly, pulling up beside Central Park. "I'll take the bags—you can walk from here."

"What?" Andy cries.

"Trust me." Casey winks. "You'll love it."

He's right. The walk through snowy Central Park is beautiful, the lights of the city glittering like stars high above us. A guy on Rollerblades whizzes past, smooth as a train, weaving easily through the crowds of Japanese tourists, balloon sellers, joggers—a constant stream of people.

"Pretty cool, huh?" Andy grins.

I grin back at him, my senses bombarded with new sights and sounds and smells—it's like anything could happen!

No wonder Kitty came to America.

As if to prove me right, we step through an archway and

a fairy-tale castle suddenly appears in front of us—right in the middle of the park!

I gaze at it, enchanted, as a clock above me starts to play "Jingle Bells," little bronze animals dancing round while monkeys strike a bell five times, ringing out the hour. It's beautiful. Magical.

Andy grins, his eyes sparkling as he looks at me.

"What?" I ask suspiciously. "Have I got bird poo in my hair?"

"No!" he laughs. "No, I'm just—I'm really glad you came, Rosie."

I smile as I hook my arm through his, a warm feeling flooding through me despite the icy cold.

"So am I."

We finally arrive, exhausted and rosy-cheeked, at Casey's apartment, and I feel like I'm in an episode of *Friends*—except it's actually about half the size of Monica's apartment, and looks out on the brick wall of the neighboring building.

"Welcome!" Casey grins, slinging a tea towel over his shoulder. "Make yourselves at home—Lola, shift!"

"Two minutes!" the petite blond girl begs, her eyes glued to her laptop. "It's almost finished! Hi, guys—sorry—nice to mcct ya!"

"Guys, meet Lola—waitress extraordinaire and hopeless TV addict." Casey rolls his eyes. "Can't pry her away from her sitcoms—even to do the washing up!"

"It's your turn!" she protests good-naturedly.

Sitcoms. *Kitty.*

"You can watch online?" I scan the screen urgently. "What's this one?"

"They're all the same!" Casey groans. "Coupla guys, coupla girls, awful jokes and lots of canned laughter . . ."

Lola sticks out her tongue. "They're *live* audiences, *actually.*"

"Seen one, seen 'em all!" Casey grabs the computer, and Lola shrieks.

"You do it, you die—Brad's new boss is about to come in and find him dressed as a gigolo! But he doesn't realize she actually has a crush on him and thinks—"

"Well, fancy that," Casey says seriously. "Just how credible and believable and downright—ow!" he laughs as Lola hits him. "You can catch up later—it's New Year's Eve!"

"All right, already!" Lola grins, grabbing her jacket and turning to me. "What're you guys doing tonight?"

"Yeah, d'you wanna come to the bar?" Casey hits his head. "D'oh! You're not twenty-one, are ya?"

Andy hurls a cushion at him.

"You're coming to Times Square with us, though, right?" Lola asks.

"Actually, I'm pretty knackered." I yawn.

"But it's only seven-thirty!" Lola protests.

"Yeah," Andy says. "But that's half past midnight at home. We've already celebrated New Year!"

I smile. We toasted each other with mugs of hot chocolate in a little café before calling home.

"*Happy New Year, sweetheart!*" Nana had cried above

the noise of Sarah's house party. "Don't waste a single minute of it!"

I glance at Lola's laptop. I don't intend to.

"Then celebrate *twice!*" Lola insists. "Come on, you can't miss the ball drop!"

"Babe, they've been on a transatlantic flight, they're jet-lagged, and they *stink!*" Casey holds his nose theatrically, and I laugh.

"Well, just call us if you wanna meet up." Lola smiles. "Or we might see you there?"

"Yeah—you and two million others!" Casey laughs. "Have fun, guys—see ya later!" The door slams behind them, leaving us in sudden silence, a siren wailing somewhere in the distance.

"Well!" Andy grins. "It's been quite a day!"

I smile at him. "It certainly has."

"I'm going to take a shower." He grabs his rucksack. "Casey's right, I reek!"

I wait until I hear the water running, then I pick up the laptop. My fingers trembling, I type *For Richer, For Poorer* into the search engine, and immediately the theme tune blares loudly. I grab the headphones and plug them in quickly, holding my breath as I listen down the hall.

The sound of running water is joined by Andy's loud off-key singing. I sigh with relief and turn back to the screen.

The latest episode starts playing and I watch as two impossibly good-looking guys comically struggle to coax a kitten down from a fire escape. I wait impatiently, nervously, my eyes flicking over the rest of the webpage.

Episode Guide—Catch up quick!

Backstage Gossip!—Are Luke Reynolds and Kitty Clare secretly engaged?

Engaged? I stare at the photo. Kitty's *engaged?* Her face beams back at me, her arm linked with the tall, dark-haired man from the clip, those catlike green eyes sparkling brightly.

Photos; Interviews; Meet the Stars!

Eagerly, I click the icon.

Come join our studio audience! We're currently on hiatus, but shooting will recommence on March 16 . . .

No! I stare at the page. Not till March? That's months away! And we're going to be in L.A. in *three weeks . . .*

"Bathroom's free!"

I jump as Andy throws me a clean towel. His eyes flick to the screen.

Too late, I click the webpage closed.

"Oh, no," he says gravely. "Oh, Rosie."

"Andy, I—"

"I bring you all the way to New York and you wanna watch TV?" He shakes his head disapprovingly.

"What? Oh! No, no, I was just . . . looking, that's all."

"You won't mind me checking my email, then." He grins. "Shift!"

Numbly, I surrender the laptop and lock the bathroom door behind me. I pull Kitty's photo out of my bag and sink to the floor.

On hiatus till March. Till *March*, when we'll be God knows where—Cambodia or Thailand, or . . . And we're gonna be in L.A. in three weeks.

I sigh heavily, tracing Kitty's smiling face with my fingers. She'd felt so close . . .

But she could be anywhere.

New York City.

The thought thrills through me like electricity. I can't believe I've never been before. All these years, it's been just a plane, or train, or *bus* ride away . . . but now I'm finally going. I beam at my ticket—my passport to the Big Apple, the city that never sleeps, the town that's inspired more songs than any other, from Frank Sinatra to Jay-Z, home of Carrie Bradshaw, Will and Grace, Central Perk, Broadway . . .

The smile splits my face.

It's a dream come true. *All* my dreams are finally coming true.

My stomach flutters suddenly and, despite myself, I reach into my bag, pulling out the well-thumbed ultrasound image that lives there, carried with me always.

I trace my finger over the tiny black-and-white form, remembering how scared I'd been when I'd had the scan, how unsure . . .

And now . . .

"Sweetheart?" I hide the picture quickly and turn to look up at him, so tall and dark and impossibly handsome. The man of my dreams.

"There you are." He smiles, my insides melting like chocolate as he kisses me. "You ready for a brand-new year?"

"Absolutely." I beam, sliding the photo secretly into my bag and pushing it behind me as I slip my hand into his, following him outside as the minutes tick by quickly, leaving the past far behind. Somewhere high above us a rocket explodes in the sky and everything sparkles.

I smile, the bad memories fading with the fireworks, replaced by bigger, brighter, better ones every moment.

"I can't wait."

Chapter Nine

I pull the blanket up to my chin and shift position on the sofa for the umpteenth time as a premature firework explodes somewhere above us, the lights from passing cars chasing across the room like searchlights, dancing over the books and glinting blindingly on the picture frames. I pull the blanket over my head and close my eyes.

I can't sleep. Kitty's face keeps dancing in front of me, taunting, tormenting. She feels so close now, so *real*. All the time at home she'd seemed so far away, so distant—a dream. And now here I am in her country—and I've lost her! She could be anywhere, and I'm here, on some sofa in the middle of New York—doing what? I sigh heavily. I don't even know anymore.

"Can't sleep?" Andy rolls to face me from his sleeping bag on the floor.

I shake my head. I couldn't be more awake.

"Me neither. It must be jet lag, or anti–jet lag or something!" He smiles. "Come on, let's go out."

"*Now?*"

"Why not?" He grins, wriggling out of his sleeping bag. "It's the city that never sleeps, remember?"

The park is even more beautiful by night, glowing with thousands of tiny lamps, but it does nothing to lift my mood. *What am I doing here?* A million miles from home, from everything familiar, lying to Andy, using *Mum's* money. My heart twists. For what? I'll never find Kitty, not now. This country's so vast, so busy, so *full*—she could pass me on the street and I'd never even notice. Andy was right. It was stupid. It was a stupid idea to try to find her. I should never have come, never have left Nana, never lied to Andy . . .

And now I've got eight long empty months of traveling ahead of me when all I want to do is go home and curl up in my own bed.

"It's beautiful, isn't it?" Andy beams, misinterpreting my sigh as he gazes over at a gleaming ice rink surrounded by glowing stars, the skyscrapers soaring high above.

I watch, hypnotized, as the skaters whiz by, some laughing and giggling as they slip and slide perilously, others gliding lazily by without a care in the world. I envy them.

"Come on then, let's get your skates on," Andy says, grabbing my hand and heading over to the queue for skate hire.

"What?" I stare at him. "I can't! I haven't skated in ages, not since—"

"You don't forget." His eyes linger on mine, and my stomach flutters despite myself, remembering the last time we went ice-skating . . . our first date. I eye the shimmering surface uncertainly, my cheeks burning in the frosty air, as memories flood my head. Then he smiles that oh-so-familiar smile, his blue eyes sparkling as those dimples overcome all my doubts.

"Come on, Bambi." He grins, his arm strong and warm around me as we step toward the slippery ice. "I won't let you fall."

On the rink it's impossible to think about anything but staying upright—I cling to Andy as we slip and giggle round the ice till my bum's bruised from falling, and our sides kill from laughing so much.

Suddenly Andy checks his watch and grabs my hand.

"Quick! We've got to hurry!"

"Hurry where?" I laugh. "It's the city that never sleeps, remember!"

"You'll see—come on!"

We've barely returned our skates before Andy's dragging me through the streets, racing down block after block, until suddenly we round a corner, and I gasp.

I have *never* seen so many people. The ocean of bodies floods the streets, sprawling as far as I can see, crammed between the buildings, swaying together harmoniously as music blasts from loudspeakers, their blue *Happy New Year* top hats bobbing merrily as they dance, hug, cheer and squeal with excitement beneath the towering buildings ablaze with blinking billboards—twinkling and chasing and dazzling all different colors, shapes and pictures, beside the enormous glowing Broadway placards. The atmosphere is electric.

"Just in time." Andy grins, checking his watch and weaving us deeper into the throng.

Suddenly the music stops and the whole crowd begins to chant: "Fifty-nine! Fifty-eight! Fifty-seven! Fifty-six!"

"We couldn't miss the ball drop!" Andy laughs, pointing, as there, high above the brightest building, a glowing globe twinkles like a star, sparkling a million different colors and patterns as it slowly sinks toward an enormous ticking countdown.

"*Ten! Nine! Eight!*" My skin tingles and my heart beats fast as I clutch Andy's hand.

"*Seven! Six!*" He squeezes my hand and grins at me.

"*Five! Four! Three! Two! One!*"

The sky explodes in fireworks—bursting showers of blinding blue, red, green, gold—colorful confetti streaming down all around as the crowd goes crazy, the cheers deafening as everyone leaps up and down, hugging each other, and kissing to the strains of "Auld Lang Syne."

"*Happy New Year!*" A complete stranger grabs me in a bear hug and I laugh as a pink-haired woman lands a smacker on Andy's cheek. He grins at me as the confetti rains between us.

Suddenly "New York, New York" bursts on, and I shriek as Andy grabs me and starts dancing, singing at the top of his lungs. I giggle as he twirls me round, giddy with the buzzing atmosphere, the infectious excitement, the hope.

"Happy New Year." Andy grins, his breath warm on my face as he pulls me close, my skin tingling at his touch.

A brand-new year . . .

Suddenly all the strain and stress of the past year—with

Mum, with Sarah and Kitty—seem far, far away. The other side of the world. Another life. I can find Kitty anytime, after all. There's no hurry.

But here I am *now,* in incredible, vibrant, spine-tingling *New York City,* on the brink of a dazzling new year and a thrilling adventure. With Andy. Andy, who's gazing at me the same way he used to so long ago.

"Happy New Year." I beam into those familiar sparkling blue eyes.

And though we're surrounded by a million rowdy strangers, in the busiest city in the country, on the loudest, craziest night of the year, suddenly we're the only two people in the world.

The feeling lasts all week, as together we hurtle round the city, exploring everything it has to offer—we shop at Bloomingdale's and walk across the Brooklyn Bridge; have breakfast outside Tiffany's and dinner on Fifth Avenue; see *Wicked* on Broadway and the Knicks at Madison Square Garden; visit art museums and history museums and science museums, sending postcards from everywhere we go—until finally, on our last night in New York, there's only one place we haven't been.

My stomach flips as we travel up and up and up— until eventually the doors open and I race outside into the fresh night air, Andy a split second behind me. Then—just as I'm about to reach the edge—he grabs my waist and spins me round.

"I win!" he cries, one arm tight around me as he seizes the rail triumphantly.

"*Cheat!*" I protest, breathless and giggling. Then my jaw drops. There it is, the whole of New York glittering below us, beautiful and boundless. I breathe it in, feeling dizzy and light-headed and on top of the world. It's the perfect end to the perfect week, like all those movies that have ended here—*Sleepless in Seattle* and Nana's favorite Cary Grant film, *An Affair to Remember*.

"I feel like Meg Ryan," I whisper, staring down at it all, sparkling in the dark.

"Not Naomi Watts?" Andy asks, his eyes twinkling. "In *King Kong*?" He lifts me up as I shriek, my giggles piercing the night air.

"You great gorilla," I tease, but he stops my mouth with the gentlest, softest kiss.

Somewhere a clock chimes.

"Happy birthday," Andy whispers, his eyes dancing as he pulls out a black velvet box.

I stare at him, surprised. "It's not till tomorrow, wally."

"Ah." He grins. "But at home it *is* tomorrow."

I count the bells. Seven p.m. I smile. Midnight at home. He's right.

Carefully I open the box, to reveal an exquisite garnet birthstone necklace I'd admired in a little boutique in the Village. I gasp. "Andy!"

"Happy birthday, Rosie." He beams, pulling me closer and looping it deftly round my neck, his eyes shining. "I love you." He strokes my face, looking deep into my eyes. "I never stopped loving you."

112

I stare at him, my heart full, my insides glowing.

I can't believe my life has changed so quickly—so dramatically. Just a couple of weeks ago everything seemed so bleak, so empty . . . yet here I am now, my future glittering with excitement, with promise, with Andy—my Andy—the only guy I've ever loved—on top of the world. Literally.

"I love you too," I whisper. "I've always loved you."

He kisses me again, his lips soft, his body warm against mine, my head spinning somewhere high in the stars above as finally we pick up where we left off on that night so long ago, in the city that never sleeps . . .

The Empire State Building winks back at me in the sunlight as I gaze out of our fiftieth-story hotel room window, the city buzzing and bustling far below, as perfect as I've always dreamed.

There's so much magic here, so much history—the Empire State Building, the Brooklyn Bridge, the aching hole where the Twin Towers once stood. It's incredible—this city with all its scars and heartache doesn't dwell, doesn't wallow, doesn't sleep, even. It's too busy thriving, rushing and bustling into the soaring hopes and excitement of the future, and I feel swept up in its spell—like a little girl again.

But I'm not.

I tilt my hand and the light twinkles on the ring as it winks back at me.

"Marry me," he'd said, dropping to one knee right in the middle of Central Park, his eyes sparkling in the sunshine. "I love you. Marry me?"

I can barely believe it, even now. I grin down at the ring, glittering like a promise on my finger. A promise of love, of a future so bright that all the worries of my past fade away . . .

I close my eyes.

I wish you could see this, baby, I wish you were here now—I wish . . .

I take a deep breath and close my eyes tight, making a secret, silent wish as I blow out the candles.

I look down at the cake, the scent of wax drifting on the clearing smoke, hoping against hope that my wish will come true.

Happy birthday, Holly.

Chapter Ten

I open my eyes, and for a moment have no idea where I am, or why I feel so incredibly, inexplicably happy. I try to remember what I was dreaming about as my eyes sweep around the unfamiliar bedroom, over the wide-screen TV and plush red carpet, to a huge window. Outside, the skyscrapers glitter in the morning sun, and the Empire State Building winks back at me.

Suddenly, I remember.

My face explodes in a smile, and quickly I roll over.

"Good morning." Andy grins, his eyes sparkling in the sunlight, his blond hair crumpled sexily against his pillow. "How are you this morning?"

I beam at him. "I'm wonderful."

"I agree," he whispers, his eyes dancing as he brushes my hair from my face. "Completely and utterly."

My heart flutters as his hand glides slowly down to my waist, and with one smooth movement he pulls me closer, my entire body tingling as his smooth skin meets mine.

"Happy birthday." He kisses me gently, his mouth hot against mine, leaving me breathless. "So the hotel was a good idea?"

"The best." I nuzzle closer. "Though I can't say I got a very good night's sleep."

"No, me either," Andy agrees, his fingers trailing up my back and tangling in my hair. "Strange, that."

"Mmm. Maybe it was the pillows?"

He kisses my neck. "Or the mattress?"

"Or the linen?" I smooth my hands over his back.

"Hmm. Perhaps we should complain?"

"Oh, I'm not complaining." I smile, hooking my leg over his.

"No?"

"Besides, maybe we haven't given them a proper chance . . ."

"Excellent point." He grins. "You think we need to do more research?"

I shrug. "It would only be fair . . ."

I squeal as he rolls me underneath him, onto the smoothest bed linen, the softest mattress and the fluffiest pillows I've ever felt.

Nope, it wasn't a dream . . .

"Washington, here we come!" Andy grins, squeezing my hand as we head into the station, Casey a few steps ahead of us. "No more yellow cabs, no more Central Park, no more Empire State Building . . ."

"*Aw . . .*" I pout.

"*But,*" he says quickly, squeezing me tight, "in Washington they have the Lincoln Memorial, the Pentagon and the White House!"

"Wow!" I grin.

"*And* they have the Smithsonian—the largest museum complex in the world!"

"*Much* better!" I smile up at him. Actually, I couldn't give a monkey's where we go as long as we're together. Just the two of us, back how we used to be. Better. I beam, thinking about the hotel. Me and Andy against the world, finally *traveling* the world—just as we always planned. I grin. I can't think of a better way to spend my birthday.

Nana couldn't believe I'd texted her from the top of the Empire State Building—"You should have gone on Valentine's Day!" she chided when I called her this morning. "You might have met Cary Grant!"

I squeeze Andy's hand. Who needs Cary Grant?

Andy winks. "So long, New York. No more silly statues and pitiful little buildings . . ."

"No more tiny breakfasts and early nights . . . ," I join in, grinning.

Andy laughs. "No more posters for tacky Broadway plays, no more smelly cabs—hey!" Andy yelps as Casey throws him over his shoulder and runs off round the station, Andy's legs flailing in the air.

I laugh at the two of them goofing around, and my eyes flick over the poster—*A Midsummer Night's Dream*—an awful version, by the looks of it. The guy playing Oberon looks like a drug addict, and the woman—

117

I freeze. It can't be.

Kitty's green eyes meet mine as I stare at her, unable to believe it . . . It's her. *Here. In New York* . . . My heart pounds as I scan the poster—the play's been on all week and finishes tonight. *She's been here all week* . . .

And now we're leaving . . .

"'Starring *For Richer, For Poorer*'s Kitty Clare,'" Casey reads, shuddering. "Thank God Lola didn't hear about this—she's her favorite!" He grins, grabbing me in a hug. "Good to meet ya, Rosie."

"Oh—yes—yes, you too."

We wave goodbye and I follow Andy numbly toward the ticket barriers.

How is this possible? How could this *happen?* I feel dizzy, sick.

"Andy . . ."

"Hmm?" he mumbles, checking the screens. "Platform three."

"Andy." I stop dead. "I—can't do this. I can't leave New York."

He grins. "It's been fantastic, hasn't it?" He kisses my nose. "But wait till you see everywhere else!"

"No." I pull on his hand, stopping him. "No, you don't understand. . . ."

He frowns. "What?"

"Andy." I look at him sadly. "I can't come with you. Not now."

"What?" He looks at me, his blue eyes filled with confusion. "But—why?"

I sigh. How can I tell him?

"Rosie, what is it?"

"I . . ." I take a deep breath, trying to find the words.

"Is it us?" he asks seriously, looking deep into my eyes. "It's last night, isn't it? We shouldn't've—I shouldn't've—it was too much, too soon. I'm so sorry, I—"

"No, no—it's not that at all!" I kiss him quickly. "You're amazing—last night was *amazing*." I squeeze his hands. "So was this morning."

"Then what is it?" Andy's eyes flick to the clock. "Can't we talk about this on the train? We haven't got long, Rose."

"I know, but—"

"The seven-oh-five Vermonter to Washington, D.C., is boarding at platform three" a man announces over the intercom.

I look at Andy. "You'd better go." I sigh, turning away.

"Rosie!" He grabs my handbag strap and it snaps, the contents spilling everywhere.

"Oh God, I'm sorry." He starts gathering up my things.

"You'd better go," I say again, scooping my bag up off the floor. "You'll miss your train."

"I'm not going without you."

"I can't, Andy—"

"Rose, no—you're not doing this to me again." He holds my gaze determinedly. "What *is* it? What's wrong? *Tell me*."

"It's . . ." My eyes fall on the photo of Kitty, which has fallen out of my bag. I sigh, then hand it to him.

"I don't understand," he says. "Who's Kitty Clare? An actress?"

I nod, swallowing painfully. "She's Katharine Sinclare."

"Katharine who?" Andy stares at me, then at the photo. "I don't under—" His expression changes.

"It's her, Andy, she's here—"

"Don't." Andy interrupts, shakes his head. He stares at the photo, his features tense. "This . . . *this* is why you came?" He looks at me hard. "Of course it is!" He turns away angrily. "God, how stupid am I?!"

I grab his hand. "You're not stupid!"

"Yes I am!" He pulls his hand away roughly. "I thought you—I thought we . . ." His jaw tightens. "Never mind what I thought. I was wrong. Obviously." He turns away.

"Andy, wait!"

"I've got a train to catch."

"Andy!"

"Goodbye, Rosie. I hope you find what you're looking for."

"Andy, please—"

He marches through the ticket barrier.

"Andy!"

I watch him slowly disappear into the crowd, my insides ripping in two—desperate to run after him, to be with him, to explain . . . but somehow frozen to the spot.

I have to do this, I tell myself, blinking fiercely as I finally force myself to turn away, my chest tight. *It's what I came here for—the reason I came with him in the first place.*

So why does it hurt so much?

It takes me ages to find the theater. It's not on the main Broadway strip at all, but tucked down a little side street, opposite a McDonald's. I cross my fingers and rush up to the box office, breathing a sigh of relief as I finally slide into my seat beside a group of teenagers. They chatter and giggle, passing around photos of Kitty, while a young couple in front share a program, their heads bent close together as they whisper and kiss.

My stomach tightens painfully and I look away, blinking quickly as the lights dim and the curtain begins to rise.

The first few scenes are a blur. I sit impatiently through courtly disputes and lovers' squabbles, waiting for her to appear. And then, suddenly, there she is—a whirl of wispy chiffon, surrounded by glittering fairies—and everything else fades away.

It's her. It's really her. There, live onstage in front of me, just meters away. Kitty Clare—Katharine Sinclare—my *mother*—gliding around the stage, her dark hair gleaming in the spotlight, her melodious voice ringing round the auditorium. I watch, mesmerized, drinking in every precious moment, hooked on her every move, every word, every emotion—her tears, smiles, frowns—etching her into my mind.

Finally, the curtain drops, and still I can't breathe. I push my way out of the theater, down the stairs, through the foyer and out into the rain, my rucksack bulky on my shoulders as I weave clumsily through the dark busy street, heading for the stage door. There's a crowd gathered already, and I stand on tiptoe, craning my neck, trying to get a better view.

Suddenly, a thousand flashes go off as the stage door opens—and there she is!

A burly bodyguard holds an umbrella over her sleek black bob as, beaming, she waves at the crowd.

The girls go crazy, squealing and jumping and pushing, thrusting photos toward her, begging for autographs.

"Hello, everybody!" Kitty calls in a crisp English accent. "Thank you all so much for coming! I'll miss you, New York!" She blows a kiss.

"We'll miss you, Kitty!" a girl screams behind me. "Kitty, we love you!"

Kitty smiles and waves at her, catching my eye for just an instant. My heart stops. "Kitt—"

"*Kitty!*" the crowd screams as she starts down the steps, everyone pushing and shoving, trying to get closer to her.

"Kitty!" I cry, watching her weave past, lost in the crowd. "*Kitty!*"

She smiles and walks straight past me to a waiting limousine. "Thank you, thank you all!" she calls with a little wave. "And goodnight!"

"Kitty!" The crowd swarms toward the limousine.

"*Kitty!*" I shout. "*No! Kitty, wait!*"

The car door slams shut.

I push through the throng and grab the bodyguard's sleeve. "Please!" I beg. "I need to talk to her! I'm—"

"Her biggest fan, yeah, I know," he says, shrugging me off and climbing into the front seat.

"No! I'm . . . Hey!" Someone pulls me backward as the crowd surges forward.

"I'm—I'm her daughter . . . ," I mutter miserably as the car glides away, disappearing into the stream of traffic flowing into the night. I watch it helplessly, the rain falling in big wet heavy drops, until finally I'm the only one left.

I slump onto the curb.

I can't believe I actually found her—she was close enough to *touch*—but now she's gone. A stabbing pain hits my chest, and I hug my knees hard.

I lost her.

A taxi pulls up and beeps at me, but I shake my head.

Where would I go? I can't go back to Casey's, I can't go to Washington with Andy.

Andy . . .

I close my eyes and the tears spill over, stinging my throat. Just hours ago I was on top of the world, so happy. But I threw it all away—on a fantasy, a dream. I stare miserably at the photograph of Kitty, spattered and smudged by the falling rain. I found her—her fame made her easy to find—but it's made her impossible to reach too. I'll never get near her. Not now. She's gone.

The taxi beeps again and I shake my head harder, rubbing my eyes. It beeps again and I stand up, annoyed.

The taxi door opens and a guy steps out.

I glance at him briefly, then look back in disbelief as he walks toward me, hands deep in his pockets.

"Hey," Andy says. "Fancy seeing you here."

"She's staying at the Ritz!" Lola turns in her seat. "I read it in *TV Extra!* This is so exciting!" she gushes. "Rosie, why didn't you tell us your mom was Kitty Clare?"

I look at Andy, my head still reeling. He looks away.

Lola glances at Andy, then me, then turns and closes the partition.

We drive in silence for a while, the city lights sliding over the space between us.

"Andy, I—"

"Was any of it real?" He interrupts quietly, staring at his lap. "Was last night—has *anything* this week actually been real? Or was it all just . . . part of some plan, keeping me sweet, biding your time till you found her?"

"No!" I tell him urgently. "No, Andy, it was *all* real—all of it—it's been the best week of my life!"

He doesn't look up.

I hesitate. "I mean, yes, coming to America seemed like the perfect way to find Kitty, but everything that's happened since . . ." I look at him earnestly, desperate to hold him, kiss him—*show* him. "Andy, it's been more than I ever hoped for!"

He finally looks up, his eyes uncertain.

"She wasn't even meant to be in New York—I thought she was in L.A., that I'd have ages to find the right time to tell you, to explain. But then I saw the poster and . . ." I trail off. "She's my *mum*, Andy, and she was so close. If I hadn't *tried*, if . . ." I sigh. "I'm so sorry."

He nods silently.

"I thought you'd got on the train," I say gently.

"I did," he admits. "I was sitting there in the carriage by myself, consumed with déjà vu—I couldn't believe you'd bailed on me *again*, hidden things from me, *lied* to me."

I close my eyes.

124

He sighs. "And then I remembered why you did it last time. That you had a pretty good reason."

I look at him. "Andy."

"And while I'm not crazy about being used, or lied to, I am crazy about you, Rosie Kenning." He squeezes my hand and my eyes fill. "And I want to be there for you—you can trust me, you know."

I nod. "I know."

He sighs. "Why didn't you tell me?"

"I don't know." I shrug miserably. "You were just so down on the whole idea. I thought you'd be mad at me, spoil it all, and I just wanted to find her, to *see* her." I sigh and stare at my lap, my throat swelling. "But it didn't work, did it? It's over."

Andy looks at me for a moment, then shakes his head. "Nope, not good enough, I'm afraid."

I look at him. "What?"

"Rosie, if you've come all this way to find her—if it really means that much to you—you're not going to bloody well give up now."

"But—it's impossible, I'll never get anywhere near her. You weren't there—she's got all this security—"

"Well." Andy winks. "That's where the master plan comes in."

"Sweetheart." He checks his watch for the millionth time. "Are you nearly ready? We're gonna miss it completely if we don't leave soon!"

"My darling fiancé." I smile, the word tingling deliciously on my tongue. "We've got heaps of time. You go get us a cab, I just want to change."

I pull my dress over my head and his arms are instantly around my waist.

"Don't ever change." He beams, his eyes deep in mine. "You're so beautiful, have I ever told you that?"

I laugh. "Once or twice."

"You look"—he kisses my neck, my shoulder—"like a movie star."

A thrill tingles down my spine.

"Babe . . . ," I mumble. "Cab?"

"But you said we've got heaps of time!" he complains, kissing my arm, my ring finger.

"We have." I smile. "We've got the rest of our lives."

"The rest of our lives." He beams at me. "Just you and me."

Chapter Eleven

"This is never going to work," I moan, struggling to carry the wobbling silver platter along the hotel corridor without the lid falling off.

"Well, it won't if you give up," Andy urges. "Now come on, you must've inherited some of Kitty's acting talent! Next room."

I groan and stop outside the next door.

"Room service!" I sing for the umpteenth time.

A middle-aged man opens the door, his belly hanging over his boxers.

I plaster on a smile. "Room service?"

"I ain't ordered no room service," he grunts. "Whatya—"

"Sorry, wrong room!" Andy interrupts, steering me on down the corridor as I tug the tiny black skirt farther over my bum.

"I feel ridiculous!" I hiss. "Besides, this is a waitress's uniform, not room service!"

"Well, it's all Lola had." Andy grins. "And it is very cute."

I glare at him.

"Andy, we don't even know which room she's in," I protest. "She hasn't even *ordered* room service—and what if someone else actually has? All we've got are chocolates!"

"Who doesn't like chocolates?" Andy smiles. "Come on, next room."

Lola's master plan—as seen on one of her favorite sitcoms—involved her causing a distraction in the hotel lobby by pretending (?) to be a crazed fan while Andy and I snuck in and got changed in the toilets. Now, starting at the top of the hotel, we're knocking on every single door holding Lola's covered silver platter, pretending to be room service, until we find Kitty. We've gone through two whole floors already, but there's still no sign of her.

The next door opens almost immediately. An enormous man in a suit glowers down at me, his bulk filling the doorway.

"Yes?" he grunts.

"Er, room service?" I say timidly.

"Typical!" Another man strides forward and the Incredible Bulk steps aside. "Grab the cases, will you, Stan? Trust Kitty, ordering room service at the last minute. We're never gonna leave! I think she's fallen in love with your town." He winks at me, the warmth of his smile making my cheeks burn. "Please, go on in. And tell her I've gone to see what the hell's happened to our cab, will you?"

"I, er, I will!" I call after him, watching him stroll away down the corridor, the Bulk following behind, laden with heavy suitcases.

"Oh. My. God!" I hiss, turning to Andy. "That was Luke Reynolds!"

"Who?" He frowns.

"Kitty's costar—they're engaged!"

"Well, we've got the right room, then, haven't we? Come on!" He pushes me inside.

"Oh my *God!*" I stop dead in the doorway. My jaw drops as I gaze round at the marble fireplace, the roaring log fire, the silver candlesticks, the beautiful bouquets, and the luxurious deep-pile Indian rug sprawling across the expansive floor. It's absolutely incredible—and a far cry from her parents' cramped semi in Bramberley.

"You forget something, babe?" Kitty pads out of the bathroom.

I stare at her, my breath catching in my throat. Here she is, in front of me, in the flesh. Her black hair swings smoothly as she stops and looks at me, her green eyes penetrating mine.

"Can I help you?" she asks, her accent a muddle of American twang and round English vowels.

"I, um, er . . ." I glance at the platter in my hands. "Room service!"

She frowns. "I didn't order any . . ." She lifts the lid, surprised. "Chocolates? I don't eat chocolates."

"Oh, I'm sorry. I—"

"He *knows* I don't eat chocolates." She beams suddenly. "I love that man. He spoils me rotten." She winks as she pops one in her mouth. "Where'd he go, anyway?"

"Uh, he—"

"He went to see about the taxi, ma'am," Andy interrupts,

bowing and closing the door behind him as he steps back into the corridor.

"Have I found the perfect guy, or what?" She grins. "Now, let me get you a nice fat tip." She picks up her purse and a tiny frown flickers over her features. "Do I know you?"

"I—" I nod helplessly, my throat paralyzed, butterflies dancing circles in my stomach. Could it be? Could she really recognize me . . . ?

"Ah, I know!" She points a finger at me. "You were at this afternoon's show, weren't you? Huge backpack, no umbrella?" She smiles.

I nod quickly.

"So?" she says eagerly. "Did you like it? I never trust the critics."

"Oh, I thought it was wonderful," I gush.

She beams at me. "Cigarette?" she offers, opening a packet.

"No, thanks."

She settles back in her armchair. She looks so young, so beautiful.

"You're not really room service, are you?" she says suddenly. "Unless the Ritz suddenly changed their uniform since this morning."

I feel my cheeks grow hot.

"And the chocolates—are they from you too?"

"I—" I struggle to breathe. "I'm really, really sorry—"

"Relax!" she laughs. "I've done some crazy things to meet stars in my time, believe me. And thank you—they're delicious." She grins. "So, what can I do for you?" she asks, placing a cigarette between her lips and feeling for a lighter.

"Autograph? Photo? I'm afraid I haven't got long—my taxi to the airport will be here soon. I'm off to sunny Las Vegas."

She smiles at me expectantly.

The butterflies go crazy. It's now or never.

"My name's Rosie." I swallow. "Rosie Kenning."

"Nice to meet you, Rosie."

"And I'm—" I take a deep breath, my cheeks burning. "I'm your daughter."

She looks up quickly.

I hold her gaze fearfully, a rabbit pinned in headlights, not daring to breathe. I can't believe I just did that—just blurted it out like that!

She stares at me for a long moment, my heart hammering wildly. This is it. The moment of truth.

And then she smiles, cocking her head to one side. "I didn't know I had a daughter." She exhales coolly.

"I know," I say, my breath shallow. "I'm sorry, I—"

"Oh, don't worry, I'm always the last to know," she says, waving her cigarette. "Usually I'm just handed a script and it's 'Action!' Nice to have a heads-up for a change."

I frown, confused.

"Actually, Janine's been on about getting me a kid on the show for a while now—change my image, keep things fresh." She shakes her head. "She keeps saying I need a hook, you know, to capture the public's imagination, attract media interest, constantly raise my profile . . ."

"No," I interject. "I'm—"

"Do you know, I was up to play Maria in the remake of *The Sound of Music* but they said I wasn't a *star name*— never mind that I've been on prime-time telly for the last

131

eight years—and that no one would buy me as a motherly nun after *For Richer, For Poorer*! Offered me the Baroness instead—*the Baroness*! Well, we'll show them, huh? We'll show them motherly."

She smiles at me, looks me over.

"They've done a pretty good job too, I must say. Black hair, green eyes—you're even British!" She leans forward. "Or is that just a really good accent?"

"No, I—I am."

"Well, I'm very impressed." She beams, leaning back in her chair and looking me up and down. "You're a bit old, though, aren't you?"

"Sorry?"

"Well, I mean I'm sure they could make you look a bit younger with makeup, but—what are you, seventeen? Eighteen?"

"I'm eighteen."

"Well, exactly! I'm not old enough to—"

"You're thirty-five."

She chokes on her cigarette smoke. "And you're a cheeky minx!"

"I'm eighteen," I say again. "Eighteen today, actually. It's my birthday."

"Well, happy birthday, but that's really no excuse for—"

"And eighteen years ago today, when you were seventeen"—I take a deep breath, seizing my opportunity— "you gave birth to me."

She stares at me, then coughs. "What?"

I hold her gaze expectantly. "In England."

132

She looks at me for a long moment and then gives a little laugh and stands up, hugging herself.

"Well, you're good, I'll give you that—a backstory and everything! The studio must've pulled out all the stops for this one, though I can't think why they never told me, I mean—"

"It's nothing to do with the studio!" I interrupt loudly. "I'm not an actress! I'm real. I'm your real daughter!"

She turns deathly pale and just stares at me. "Stan . . . ?"

"Please, listen—"

"I don't know what you want, but—"

"You gave birth to me in St. Anne's hospital, Maybridge."

"I really don't think—"

"You ran away after I was born, you—"

"Look," she says suddenly, turning to me. "Hon. I'm sure you're very nice, and I hope you find your mum, I really do, but you've got the wrong lady."

"It was a stormy night and—"

"*Rosie*," she interrupts. "Look, I don't know who you've been talking to, but—"

"Your mother."

"What?" She stares at me.

"I've spoken to your mother, Pam Sinclare." I hold her gaze. "My grandmother."

She looks at me, speechless.

"That's how I found you. She told me how you'd always wanted to be an actress, how you came to America when you were seventeen. But she doesn't know the real reason you left, does she?"

"I—"

"She doesn't know that you'd just had a baby, that you were scared, that you ran away."

"Now, listen—"

"But after you ran away, Kitty, there was a mistake—"

"Damn right, there's been a mistake!" she shouts, striding to the door and flinging it open. "Stan's always telling me—*Stan?*"

"Kitty," I beg. "Kitty, please."

"Rosie . . ." Andy steps inside.

"And who the hell are you?" Kitty demands.

"Kitty, I'm your *daughter!*"

"I don't have a daughter!" She rounds on me, eyes blazing. "Now please leave—both of you!"

"No. Kitty—"

"Stan!" she calls again. "*Stan!*"

"*Rosie,*" Andy hisses. "Are you *sure* about this?"

"Yes!" I shrug him off. "Kit—"

Andy catches my arm again and holds it tightly. "*Really* sure?"

I look at him.

He lowers his voice. "What if you're wrong? What if it's not her?"

"What?" I stare at him. It *has* to be her.

Doesn't it?

I look at Kitty, who's punching a number on the hotel phone. She *looks* like me—same hair, same eyes . . . She's the right age. She had a daughter called Holly Woods . . . My breath catches.

Didn't she . . . ?

Sinclare . . . There were several on record—just because Kitty lived locally, it doesn't necessarily mean . . .

134

I swallow.

My mother was a runaway—she could've come from *anywhere* to have her baby in secret . . .

A shiver runs down my spine. Pam never mentioned a baby, a pregnancy—I assumed because Kitty'd kept it a secret, but what if . . .

I stare at Kitty as she clutches the receiver. "Security?"

What if there was no baby?

My heart hammers painfully.

What if she'd just gone off, as Pam said, to follow her dream?

I was so sure. So *sure* . . . But what if it was all a huge mistake? *What if she's the wrong Sinclare?*

"Rosie," Andy says gently, wrapping his arm round my shoulder. "Maybe we should go."

I stare at Kitty, doubt gripping me with icy fingers.

It's not her . . . All this, and it's not even her!

"Come on, Rose." Andy steers me toward the door, the room spinning wildly.

I was so sure . . . I've come all this way, left Nana, lied to Andy—all for nothing. I got it wrong, so wrong . . . *She's not my mother . . . I'm not her daughter, not—*

"Wait—" I stop suddenly in the doorway, my last chance. "Holly Woods." I turn to Kitty desperately. "Kitty, I'm Holly Woods."

She stares at me for a second, her green eyes wide. Then, trembling, she replaces the telephone.

"Who sent you?" she whispers, her breath ragged, her face ashen. "Did Jack send you?"

"Nobody sent me!" I insist, my pulse racing.

"What does he want? Money?"

"No, Kitty, you don't understand."

"No, *you* don't understand!" she cries, eyes wild as she stares straight at me. *"I do not have a daughter!"*

The words sting like boiling water. I stare at her. Her face is white and she's shaking.

"What's going on?"

Luke appears in the doorway.

Kitty stares at him. For an instant something like terror flashes over her features. Then it's gone.

"Oh, thank God!" she gushes, rushing to his side. "Oh, darling, they just burst in—they're stalkers—they wouldn't leave!"

Stalkers?

Luke pulls out his mobile and dials. "Police?"

"We're leaving," Andy insists, taking my arm.

"But—" I stare at Kitty helplessly. "Wait—"

"Oh, darling, I was so scared—she was saying such crazy things!"

My jaw drops.

"It's all right, sweetheart, they're leaving." Luke puts down his phone and pulls Kitty close, glaring at me.

"Come on." Andy drags me away down the corridor, my head reeling.

Crazy things? She *recognized* me—she *knew* I was telling the truth!

I droop against the mirrored wall of the lift, the glass cold and hard against my forehead as we travel down, down, and Andy walks me numbly outside, the lights from the hotel splintering on the wet pavement as an icy wind whips my cheeks.

"God, Rosie, you're shaking! Where're your clothes? Are they still inside?"

I shrug, my body shivering uncontrollably. But I don't feel cold. I don't feel anything.

"Wait here, I'll go and get them."

I stare blindly out at the street, at people bustling by, a blur of color and movement.

I can't believe it. I found her. I *met* my real mother . . . *and she kicked me out.* I slump against the wall, the conversation reeling round my head—her shock, her anger, her denial—her *recognition.* The look in her eyes when I mentioned the name Holly Woods—that whimsical name she gave me before she ran away . . .

Suddenly it hits me, as hard and as painful as a punch to the stomach.

She ran away. *From me. That's* why she gave me a different name. She didn't want me—she never had—she was going to give me up for adoption . . . Andy was right, she made her choice. There was no mistake, no regret. Her voice rings painfully in my ears—*I don't have a daughter!* She'd never wanted a baby, and now, as far as she's concerned, she never had one.

A yellow shape looms up in front of me. A taxi. Casey. I struggle forward, gripping the wall for support as the driver approaches the hotel. But it's not Casey. He walks straight past me, opening one of the hotel's heavy glass doors as a couple hurries out, the woman's high heels clacking noisily over the pavement. She turns, brushing her black bob out of her eyes as she slides into the car, and I shrink into the shadows as it pulls away, disappearing into the sea of traffic.

There she goes. My mother. Out of my life forever—just as she always wanted . . .

"Here you go!" Andy rushes back out. "Come on, it's pissing it down." He wraps my coat around me, hugging me close as the rain beats down harder, dodging pedestrians and puddles until finally we find Casey's cab.

"Is she okay?" Lola whispers as I slump into the warm backseat.

"I think she's in shock," Andy says quietly, shutting the door. "It didn't go so well."

"Oh, no," Lola sighs. "I'm so sorry. Here, Rosie, honey, take some of this."

She passes a bottle through the partition and Andy wraps my fingers around it.

I tip it upward, the smooth liquid warm as it slides down my throat.

"Good girl." Lola smiles, and Andy kisses my forehead.

"Okay." Casey starts the engine. "Where to?"

"Rosie?" Andy asks gently, his voice a million miles away.

"Anywhere," I mumble. "Anywhere but here."

I lean my head against the cold window, my eyes heavy as I watch the raindrops streak across, changing color as they smudge their haphazard way down, down, blurring the world outside as we pull off, leaving the hotel, my mother, and all my hopes far, far behind. Forever.

Goodbye, Kitty Clare.

I sigh.

Goodbye, Holly Woods.

I watch the raindrops streak quickly across the window as the city lights stream past, trying to ignore the sick feeling in my stomach.

My fingers play with the ring, new and strange on my finger, weighing heavily on my conscience. I think of the photo nestled in my bag, of my new life, my new fiancé, my secret . . .

"Babe?" I turn to him, but he's already asleep, his head lolling heavily against the seat.

I stroke his cheek. He looks so happy, so peaceful.

I glance again at the ring, gleaming on my finger, then kiss it tenderly.

Goodbye, Holly Woods. I sigh.

Hello, future.

Chapter Twelve

I wake suddenly, startled and disorientated. Warm sunlight streams onto my face, and I'm curled under a blanket on the backseat of the empty taxi.

My neck aches as I stretch and struggle upright to look out of the window—at the ocean. *The ocean?* Where am I?!

Rap-rap-rap!

I turn to see Andy outside the opposite window, his arms filled with bags, a flower between his teeth. I reach over and open the door.

"Not quite a rose, I'm afraid, but the best I could find at short notice." He grins, putting the bags down and presenting the flower to me. "Happy birthday."

"What?" I smile, confused, stroking the delicate, velvety petals, my stomach growling as the rich aroma of coffee fills the cab.

"Happy birthday!" Andy repeats, reaching into a bag and handing me a steaming Styrofoam cup and a muffin. "I decided that yesterday wasn't so great, as birthdays go . . ."

"No kidding," I sigh.

"So," he says. "Today we're going to start again. Do it properly."

"Hence the waking up in a cab in the middle of nowhere?" I smile, gazing out at the pale blue sea and soaring seagulls.

"Come on." He grins, taking out his own coffee. "All the best birthdays begin by waking up in a cab in the middle of nowhere." He winks. "Welcome to Plymouth!"

"*Plymouth?*" I stare out the window. "How long have I been asleep?"

Andy laughs. "Plymouth, Massachusetts, New England. Though I am surprised you slept all night, especially in a car. You must've been shattered."

"Yeah." I take a sip of my coffee. "*Shattered.*"

"I'm so sorry, Rose," Andy says gently. "I never dreamed Kitty'd react like that."

I sigh. "What doesn't kill you, right?" I smile weakly.

"Right." He sighs. "She's the one who's missing out, okay?"

I look up at him, my throat swelling. "Thanks." I take another deep breath. "I just want to forget about it, really."

"Of course," he says. "And that's what today's all about. A fresh start. Casey and Lola have buggered off sightseeing for the morning, so it's just us, I'm afraid—you, me, the beach and the sea." He grins.

I beam. "Perfect."

"Almost," he says, pulling a candle from his pocket and sticking it into my muffin.

I smile as he lights it, the warmth of the flame spreading through me, chasing away the shadows of yesterday, of the past eighteen years.

"Make a wish." He grins, his eyes twinkling in the candle-light.

I take a deep breath, close my eyes and blow.

New England is the perfect antidote to New York. Peaceful and sleepy, with its quaint little picket fences lining the gardens of the pretty white clapboard houses, it feels like it's tucked away from the world and all its worries and problems. Mum would've loved it.

We spend the morning wandering lazily round Plymouth. I buy some postcards and call Nana; then we meet Casey and Lola and drive right along to the farthest tip of the Cape, to Provincetown. The tiny town is practically shut up for the winter—letters that once spelled OPEN now rearranged to NOPE in the shop windows, while others cheerfully proclaim SEE YOU IN APRIL!; streets and restaurants that are probably crammed with tourists in the summer, now reclaimed by the laid-back locals: the fishermen with their enormous Christmas tree built from lobster pots, the families digging for clams along the empty shore. It's perfect.

After a delicious seafood lunch, Andy and I finally wave goodbye to Casey and Lola and book into a gorgeous little B&B. We unpack, shower, and then wander slowly down to the boardwalk pier, the Pilgrim Monument spearing the clear blue sky behind us, the huge black-and-white faces of fishermen's wives staring out from the wharf walls as little brightly colored boats bob up and down beside us, the waves splashing wildly below. For the first time in ages I feel like I can really breathe.

"Surprise!" Andy announces as we reach a shiny white boat with *Wesley's* painted on the side.

"Sorry?"

"This is your birthday surprise—I organized it this morning!"

I raise my eyebrows. "A boat?"

"A boat *trip*," Andy corrects, helping me aboard. "But not just any boat trip—now, take a seat and keep your eyes peeled."

"For what?"

"It's a surprise, just—watch the waves."

We ride for what seems like hours, salty spray peppering my lips as the wind tugs wildly at my hair, the glittering waves glinting blindingly as I stare out at the distant horizon—blue sea merging into blue sky. The sun beams down on my face, sea air filling my lungs as the steady rise and fall of the boat lulls me with its lazy rhythm, my thoughts drifting with the seagulls reeling high overhead—wings outstretched, surrendered to the wind like great white kites.

Mum bought me a kite for my sixth birthday. It was beautiful. Snowy white with a long tail of ribbons. She held the string, and I ran and ran as fast as I could, but it kept dropping to a clumsy heap on the ground. When I got tired Mum took over, holding it high above her head and running and running until, all at once, a sudden wonderful gust of wind took the kite soaring high, high into the sky, so I had to squint to see it.

"Hold on, Rosie!" Mum had called. "Hold tight!"

And I did, gripping the string with all my might as the kite danced high up above, gleaming bright white against the blue sky, its ribbons sparkling in the sunlight as it flew, soaring and dipping like a bird, forever pulling at the string in my hand—higher, higher—tugging to get free.

Then I let go. The string snapped from my grip and was gone. Mum raced after it, but it was too fast, soaring up, up and away, higher than the trees. She scooped me up in a hug and told me it was all right, she'd buy me another one. But I didn't want another one. That was my kite, and it was free. I'd let it go. It'd wanted so much to be free that I just couldn't hold on, couldn't hold it down. I smiled as I watched it whirl away—above the trees, above the birds, above the clouds, sparkling into the heavens, dancing free.

It was the most beautiful thing I have ever seen.

"Hey!" Andy nudges me, and I open my eyes. "You're meant to be watching!"

"Watching for *what*?" I laugh. "Give me a clue! The pier, the beach? We're almost back!"

"No—we can't be!" Andy says, panicking. "We haven't seen them!" He rushes round to the other side of the boat.

"Seen who?" I ask, following him.

"The whales! We're meant to see whales!" He leans over the rail and strains his eyes.

I look too. Nothing but sparkling water. "Whales?"

"It's supposed to be a *whale-watching trip*!" Andy moans. "If we don't see any whales, it's just—it's just a boat!" He slumps against the rail as the boat slows to a stop, glowering at the empty waves. "Some surprise, huh?"

I laugh at his mournful expression.

"It was wonderful." I squeeze his hand as we clamber down the gangplank back to dry land. "Thank you." I kiss him. "For everything. For today, for this . . . for everything yesterday . . ."

"You're welcome," Andy says gently, his hand warm in mine as we wander back along the jetty. "I'm just sorry how it turned out."

"Yeah," I sigh. "Well, maybe it's for the best."

He looks at me. "Really?"

I shrug. "Now at least I know who she is—where she is—and I told her who I am." I swallow. "That's all I wanted."

Andy frowns.

"I mean, of course it would have been great if she'd wanted to get to know me, to have some kind of relationship," I admit, slipping my shoes off as we step onto the beach. "But it's clear that's not what she wants—what she ever wanted. And I have to respect that. That's her choice." I sigh again, the sand freezing beneath my bare toes. "Besides." I smile. "I've already had the best mother in the world, so Kitty would never have compared anyway, despite all her glitz and glamor. So"—I take a deep breath—"it's for the best. Now at least I know."

"Really?" Andy squeezes my hand. "You're still glad you found her? Despite everything?"

"Yes." I nod. "I just—I couldn't spend my whole life wondering what if, you know? It's like the Huntington's—I could have dealt with having it, but no one could tell me if I had it or not. I had to watch Mum suffering, wondering if the same thing was going to happen to me, but not *knowing*." I sigh. "But now . . ." I fill my lungs with the fresh, cool, salty air. "Now I *can* move on. I'm eighteen years old, after all—it's about time!" I smile. "Time to be my own person, live my own life—make my own mistakes."

I look up at him. "I'm sorry I lied to you, Andy."

He shakes his head. "It's okay."

"No, it's not. I should have told you," I argue. "Secrets just . . . they always seem to make things worse, don't they?"

Andy nods.

"So. No more secrets, no more lies," I promise. "I'm old enough to handle the truth—about anything."

Andy nods. "No more secrets."

I squeeze his hand as I glance behind us, back at the jetty, the beach, and the long trail of clear footprints leading to where we're standing now. My *footprints*, I realize with a smile. My *path*.

"So," Andy says finally. "What now?"

I take a deep breath. *What now . . . ?*

That's the million-dollar question. A big fat dizzying future lies in front of me, with a million paths to choose, decisions to make, dreams to follow . . .

But not tonight. I smile. Not tonight.

"Food!" I grin. "I'm starving!"

"Excellent!" Andy grins, linking his arm with mine. "I know just the place . . ."

"Fish and chips!" I laugh as we stop before a huge wooden sign: WOODY'S PLAICE. "We're having fish and chips?"

"Just the place . . . get it?" Andy grins. "Just the *plaice* . . ."

I groan and cuff him round the head. "You need a new joke book, mister."

"What do you mean?" he protests. "It's my own material!"

"I wouldn't admit that!"

A bell jangles as Andy pushes the door open, and it's like stepping into a ship's cabin. We're surrounded by nautical curios: weird and wonderful fishing equipment, gleaming compasses, nets and telescopes hang from the rafters; coral curls with driftwood on the walls; and a beautiful carved mermaid masthead guards the old-fashioned till. It should look tacky, but it doesn't—it's like an Aladdin's cave of treasures, illuminated by flickering lamplight and filled with the warm vinegary smell of crispy batter.

We order fish and chips and gaze out across the bay.

"It's beautiful," I sigh, popping the last chip into my mouth and watching the sun sink slowly beneath the sparkling pink waves. "Everything today was beautiful. Thank you, Andy."

"You're welcome." He smiles, his eyes glowing in the candlelight. "Happy birthday—again."

"Whoa, it's somebody's birthday?" A dark-haired man stops as he passes our table. "Why didn't you say so? I would've put a candle in your cod!" He grins. "Congratulations!"

"Thank you." I smile.

"English, too! Always a pleasure to meet people from back home. I'm Jack—I own this place, for my sins. Did you enjoy your meal?"

"It was perfect," I tell him. "Just like home."

"Praise indeed!" He bows low. "I thought New England could do with some proper Old English cuisine—especially since they've stolen all our place names!"

I laugh.

"So, what do you fancy for pud? I can recommend the chocolate cake, or we've got an amazing homemade apple crumble."

"Oh, I couldn't eat another bite." I laugh. "I'm stuffed!"

"Come on, Rosie, you've got to have some cake," Andy protests. "It's your eighteenth!"

"Wow! Then *double* congratulations! Oh, and here you are in the States, where you can't drink—legally, I mean." Jack winks. "Bummer! Well, many happy returns, Rosie." He starts to collect our plates, then stops. "But actually . . . Listen, I've got an idea," he says, his eyes twinkling. "I'll be back in a jiffy with your dessert."

He rushes off with our plates and I giggle as he disappears into the kitchen.

"Can you believe him?" I smile at Andy. "We didn't even order any dessert!"

"Yeah . . . ," Andy says distractedly.

"What's wrong? Aw, did you want the homemade apple crumble?" I grin, ruffling his hair.

"What? No, no it's not that." He stares at the table.

I look at him. "Andy?"

"Rosie . . ." He runs his hand through his hair. "It's just . . ." He hesitates, leans forward. "Listen, you know what you were saying earlier, about the truth and secrets, and how you said you were glad you'd found Kitty even though it didn't work out—because you finally knew the truth?"

"Yes . . . ," I say carefully.

"And we agreed . . . no more secrets, right?"

I nod nervously.

"Well." Andy takes a big breath. "Don't get mad, but when I went back into the hotel toilets to get your coat, Kitty came in . . ."

"What?" My stomach tightens.

"She didn't see me—she was on her mobile." Andy pauses and looks at me. "She was calling the operator and demanding to be connected to a Jack Woods."

I look at him. *Jack Woods? As in Holly Woods?*

Andy holds my gaze. "A Jack Woods in Provincetown."

I stare at him, my skin prickling, Kitty's words ringing loudly in my ears: *Did Jack send you?*

"Well—I called the operator too," Andy continues quickly, taking my hands in his. "Rosie, this is the only address for a Jack Woods in Provincetown. This restaurant."

I stare at the menu. "Woody's . . ."

Andy nods.

And he's English.

Suddenly the lights go out, plunging us into darkness. I grip Andy's hand, startled.

"What the . . . ?"

"Happy birthday to you!" the waitresses sing, parading out from the kitchen. *"Happy birthday to you! Happy birthday, dear Ro-sie . . ."*

Jack appears behind them, beaming as he carries a large cake covered in burning candles.

"Happy Birthday to you!"

Jack places the cake on our table, but I can't take my eyes off him.

"Make a wish," he urges, his eyes sparkling.

I look at him for a moment longer, then take a deep breath

149

and blow with all my might, wishing hard. When I open my eyes all the candles are out and everyone is cheering.

"Happy birthday, love." Jack smiles. "Many happy returns."

"Thank you!" I beam, looking at the cake—it even has HAPPY BIRTHDAY written over it and a large number 18. I swallow. "Do you have special cakes ready for all your customers' birthdays?"

"No!" Jack laughs. "No, you were just lucky this time. It was my daughter's birthday yesterday, but she—well, she's not here to eat it, so happy birthday!" He grins as he turns back to the kitchen.

I stare at the cake.

"Are you okay?" Andy whispers.

"It's him, isn't it?" I swallow. "It's really him?"

"Seems so."

"I never even thought—I mean—my *father*?" I look back toward the kitchen. "Do you think he knows? About the baby—me?"

"Rosie, he just said it was his daughter's birthday yesterday."

"I know!" A warm tingle shivers down my spine. "And he still celebrates it—he makes a cake . . ." I stare at it, the knife trembling in my hand. "Andy, this is *my cake*!"

We both stare at it with its beautiful icing and its candles—all eighteen of them. *After all this time, he still makes a cake for me . . . for the child he never knew.*

My heart constricts.

For the baby who he thinks died.

"I have to tell him," I decide suddenly. "I have to tell him who I am. It's fate, I know it is. Finding him here, now, my birthday, the cake . . ." I turn to the kitchen, my heart

150

aching for this poor man and his tragic annual ritual. "Andy, he thinks I'm dead."

"Rosie—" Andy starts.

"Everything okay?" A waitress appears beside me. "Can I get you anything else?"

"No, no—I was just wondering, is Mr. Woods busy?" I ask hesitantly, my heart pounding. "Only I'd love to thank him for the cake and—"

"I'm afraid he's just left," the waitress says. "Sorry."

I stare at her. "He's gone?" *I can't have missed my chance* . . .

"We can come back tomorrow," Andy says. "Talk to him then."

"Do you know where he went?" I ask the waitress desperately. *I can't wait—I can't.*

"Yeah, his wife just called," she says, wiping down the table next to us. "He had to hurry home."

Andy glances at me.

"Do you know where that is?" he asks. "Do you have an address?"

"Yeah." A puzzled smile flickers over her face, and she points at the ceiling. "Right there. Jack lives in the apartment over the restaurant."

"Okay." I stare at the lighted windows above the restaurant, my heart pounding. "This is it. No going back."

"No going back," Andy agrees.

"Oh, God!" I say, sinking back down onto the bench for the umpteenth time. "But what if he's not interested? What if—"

151

"Rose, there are a million what-ifs," Andy says gently. "But only one way to find out. Look at it this way, it can't be worse than Kitty, can it?"

I sigh heavily. "No," I agree reluctantly. "But—maybe I should come back tomorrow. It might not be a good time, it's late . . ."

"It's seven p.m."

"Yes, but—"

"Rosie, it's up to you." Andy smiles. "We can leave now if you want. We can come back tomorrow, or never come back at all. It's entirely your choice."

I sigh, staring at the house. "I need to do this, I'm ready, I'm just . . . scared."

"I know." Andy squeezes my hand. "There's no rush."

I nod absently, eyes glued to the door.

"But what if he *is* like Kitty?" I whisper. "What if he doesn't want me either?"

"Rosie." Andy strokes my hair from my cheek, looks into my eyes, smiles. "He made you a cake."

I smile too, a warm feeling spreading deep inside me. "He did, didn't he? He made me a cake."

I take a deep breath, stand up, cross the road and climb the steps before I have a chance to change my mind. Andy squeezes my shoulders as I knock on the door, my hands clammy as I cross my fingers tightly.

A blond curly-haired woman opens it, and I freeze.

Oh, God. *Not* part of the plan!

"H-hi," I stammer. "My name's—my name's Rosie, I—"

"Nice to meet you, come in, come in, quickly—didn't

152

Jack tell you to use the back door?" She ushers us inside and shuts the door. "I'm Megan." She smiles. "Thanks so much for coming at such short notice—as you know, they weren't meant to be back today, but then they called from the station, so we're a bit all over the place! There're snacks over there, drinks in the kitchen, okay?"

"I . . . ," I begin, but she's already hurried off.

"Looks like a party," Andy comments.

The house is full of people milling around drinking beer and munching crisps, laughing and chatting. I look around for Jack, but there's no sign of him. My eyes wander over the soft cream furniture, the stripped pine bookshelves, everything in shades of the sea. A beautiful seascape hangs in pride of place above the crackling fire, and twisted pieces of driftwood lie scattered decoratively around the room, their limbs curling and reaching like living creatures. I gaze around, fascinated by one thing after another, until I notice a photo collage hanging on the wall. I move closer.

Suddenly something small and blue collides with my knee.

"Hello!" I smile, looking down at a little boy in Spider-Man pajamas, his dark fringe flopping over his eyes as he stares up at me.

"Sorry!" Megan rushes over and scoops him up. "Ben! What are you doing out of bed?"

"I wanted to say surprise!" Ben whines, rubbing his eye with his fist.

"Well, we'll see what Daddy says, okay?" Megan smiles, mouthing "sorry" at me as she carries him away.

"Isn't he cute?" I beam at Andy.

"Yeah . . . ," he says, nodding toward the kitchen. "And look who 'Daddy' is."

I turn and look as Jack walks out, swinging Ben high onto his shoulders.

"Oh, my God!" I look at Andy, my pulse racing. "You don't think . . . ?" I look at the little boy giggling as Jack bounces him along. *I have a brother?*

"Shh." Andy nudges me as Jack approaches. I take a deep breath, struggling to compose myself as excitement bubbles through me.

"Well, hello again!" He smiles.

"Hi! Sorry—I tried to find you at the restaurant but the waitress said you'd left and that you lived here and we just knocked on the door and . . . thank you so much again for the cake!" I gush clumsily, my cheeks on fire.

"Oh, you're welcome!" Jack grins. "Sorry I had to rush off—had to rustle up a sudden surprise party! But now you're here you can have that birthday drink you missed out on." Jack winks, reaching for a couple of beers. "You've gotta have a drink on your eightee— Wait—" He freezes. "What's that?"

There's the sound of a car in the driveway.

"Quick! Everyone hide!" Jack cries, flicking the light off, grabbing Ben and diving behind the sofa. Everyone ducks and hides, and Andy and I glance at each other, bemused, before crouching awkwardly behind an armchair.

"What are we doing?" Andy hisses in my ear.

"I have no idea!" I shrug helplessly.

A key turns in the lock, and Jack shushes everyone again. The front door opens and the light flicks on.

"SURPRISE!"

Everyone jumps to their feet, and Jack rushes to the door, Ben hot on his heels.

"Surprise!" Andy grins at me as we straighten up, none the wiser. I crane my neck but there're too many people. Everyone's crowding round the doorway, cheering and whooping.

"Happy birthday!" people call out, to a chorus of party poppers and camera flashes.

I freeze, flooded with an eerie sense of déjà vu.

"Happy birthday, sweetheart!" Jack cries. "You didn't think we'd let your eighteenth go by without a party, did you? Even if it is a day late!"

My stomach lurches.

"Thanks, Dad," a girl's voice laughs. "Josh, did you know about this? Melissa?"

Feeling very hot, I stand on tiptoe, craning this way and that, but still I can't see.

"Wow, this is awesome!" she laughs again. "Do I get a cake and everything?"

The sick feeling grows in my stomach.

"Now, that's a funny story, sweetheart. I, er, I gave it away—you said you were staying in New York, and—"

"You *what?*" she laughs.

I back away quickly, edging past Andy toward the kitchen.

"Rosie . . ." He catches my arm.

I shake my head as I push past, my chest tight.

I need to get out of here. It's a mistake. It's all a mistake. I've got it wrong—I've got it wrong *again*. He's not my dad—he's got a daughter—a real, live eighteen-year-old daughter.

Tears prickle at my eyes as I push desperately, needing to get through, to escape . . .

"Sweetheart! Over here! Here she is!" Jack's voice booms directly behind me and I freeze. He taps me on the shoulder and I turn round numbly.

"Hi!" The girl grins at me, brushing a strand of chestnut-colored hair behind her ear as my heart stops dead.

"So you're the one who ate my cake?" Her hazel eyes sparkle as she holds out a hand. "Nice to meet ya! I'm Holly."

"I—" The breath catches in my throat. *She looks just like* . . . Suddenly it clicks.

Holly.

Holly *Woods.*

Jack's daughter . . .

Jack's daughter . . .

No!

I stare at her, the blood freezing in my veins.

It can't be . . . *It's impossible* . . . The chestnut hair . . . the hazel eyes . . . my age . . . my birthday . . . *Holly Woods* . . .

I stare at her helplessly as the room spins dizzily around us . . . It's her . . . I close my eyes, but her face is burned deep into my mind, inescapable. *She's here* . . . *She survived* . . . *Somehow she survived* . . . *Somehow* . . .

She's me.

PART TWO

Someone Else's Life

We know what we are, but know not what we may be.
—William Shakespeare,
Hamlet

Holly

The sunlight hits my eyelids and a grin tugs at my mouth, even before I remember why. I reach tentatively under my pillow and a tingle shivers down my spine.

It wasn't a dream.

Glancing at the door, I pull out the ring and carefully, so, so slowly, slide it onto my finger, the same rush of giddiness, the same dizzying excitement thrilling through my veins as when he first gave it to me.

It may not be a diamond—I press the plastic gem and smile as it lights up—but if anything, that makes it even *more* perfect. How many other guys would be thoughtful enough to let their fiancée choose her own ring?

"You're the one who's gonna be wearing it for the rest of your life, after all." He'd beamed, his eyes sparkling as brightly as the glowing neon gem. I grin as the light changes color, and kiss it impulsively.

The rest of my life . . .

"Holly?" Dad knocks, making me jump. "You awake?"

"Mm-hmm—yep, come in!" I call, plunging my hand beneath the duvet as the door opens.

"Morning, Holly-berry!" He grins, his black hair still messed up from sleep. "I brought you some brekkie!" He reveals a tray laden with greasy bacon and eggs. My stomach swims.

"Da-ad!" I laugh, trying to wriggle the ring off my finger. "You know I just grab some cereal—"

"Well, that may have been adequate for a little girl." He smiles. "But not for a grown woman of eighteen!" He brings the tray over.

I yank desperately, but the ring won't budge.

"Besides," he continues. "I didn't get to make your birthday breakfast . . ."

"Not this again." I grin, finally tugging my finger free and sitting up quickly to take the tray. "I told you, it was a once-in-a-lifetime trip—Josh won it—and when else would I get to go to New York?"

"And it just happened to be on your eighteenth birthday?"

"And it just happened to be on my eighteenth birthday, yes." I smile, gingerly taking a bite of toast. "Come on, Dad, I'm here now—and you've given away my cake!"

He pulls a face. "Sorry. I'd forgotten I'd ordered it, and then, you know, you were *away* . . ."

I roll my eyes.

"And it was just sitting there, all sad and lonely, and you weren't due back till late *tonight* . . ."

I bite my lip. My bad again.

"And as it was a *specially made fresh-cream* cake, I didn't think it would keep for two whole days . . ."

"All right, already! I'm *sorry!*" I laugh. "I'm a terrible daughter and she deserved it more than me." I stick out my tongue. "She up yet?"

"Rosie? No, she's out for the count. Megan's gonna take her some breakfast in a bit, see how she is."

"That was weird, huh?" I say, taking another bite. "How she just fainted like that?"

"Yup. One look at your ugly mug and—bam!"

"Watch it." I grin. "Or I'll go back to New York."

"We weren't expecting you back till today anyway," Dad says, his tone softening. "I thought it was meant to be a long weekend?"

I raise my eyebrows. "You complaining?"

"Not at all. Just making sure my little girl's okay."

I roll my eyes again. "I'm fine."

"Sure?"

"Sure. Grown woman, remember?"

Dad grins. "You had a good time?"

I beam, thinking of the ring nestled under my pillow. "I had the time of my life."

"Good." He smiles, kissing my forehead. "You deserve it."

I wait till he closes the door. Then I exhale.

It feels weird keeping this from Dad. I'm bursting to tell him— that's the whole reason we've rushed home early, after all—but then . . . I grin, remembering Dad's face as he jumped out from behind the sofa. Trust him to spoil my surprise with one of his own!

I glance at the door, then carefully pull the ring back out, stroking the little gem with my fingertips. He'd know by now, if it weren't for the party—and if Josh weren't so old-fashioned. I can't believe he wants to ask Dad's permission before we tell anyone—as if he's gonna say no! Typical Josh. It's all very well to do things by the book, but it's *killing* me keeping this secret—Dad and I usually tell each other everything!

Well, almost everything. My hand falls to my stomach. I wonder if Mom were still alive if I'd have told her yet . . . Probably not, not before Josh. I smile. He's not the only one who can keep secrets. I still can't believe he took me to *New York* for my birthday—the first time I've ever been on a plane!—just because he knows how much I want to travel! That he *proposed*! I tilt the ring so it sends rainbows dancing around the room.

Now I can't wait to tell him *my* secret, can't wait to see his face! But first things first—not till we're officially engaged. If Josh wants to be traditional, I'll keep things traditional—I can at least do *something* the right way round!

I take a last long look at the plastic ring, then slide open my bottom drawer, home of all my secret dreams—the journals I've kept since I was twelve; cut-out photos of singers, movie stars and cute guys Melissa and I fantasized about marrying; brochures of exotic places we dreamed of traveling, tucked inside the empty passport I've had since I was sixteen—just in case our dreams ever came true.

And dreams can come true. I smile, tucking the ring carefully between the brochures and the photo of Josh, who's been top of my list—circled with a heart—since the very first day I met him . . .

I slide the drawer shut, then lie back on my pillow, grinning at the ceiling, enjoying the delicious feeling of my buried treasure, my precious secret, just waiting to be revealed . . .

Rosie

It's dark, terribly dark—I can't see a thing. I grope around helplessly, clawing and clutching, stumbling and scratching, through endless stones and brambles and what feels like ice. Then, suddenly, my feet sink into something soft, and it's sand I'm walking on, its gentle caress cool and soothing between my toes.

A light flickers in the distance. I walk blindly toward it, a warm breeze whispering in my hair.

The wooden door opens easily, and a man looks round and smiles, his black hair curling round his ears as a little boy—his miniature—scrambles to his feet.

"You found us." The man beams as they enfold me in a tight hug. I hold them close, sandwiched between the man's strong embrace and the child's warm cuddle. A perfect fit, the missing piece. "Rosie, you finally found us." I close my eyes. "You're finally home . . ."

"Rosie?"

"Mmm . . ." I turn my head, enjoying the warmth surrounding me, the softness against my cheek.

"Rosie?" a woman says. "Are you awake?"

"Wakey-wakey!" Suddenly the whole world shudders and quakes and my eyes fly open.

The little dark-haired boy bounces over me, giggling happily as sunlight fills the room.

I blink hard and stare at him. Then I smile.

"Ben!" a blond curly-haired woman chides. "Ben, get down!"

She sets down a tray and grabs him round the belly as he squirms.

"Sorry about that!" She smiles apologetically. "How're you feeling?"

"Um, fine thanks." I stare at her blankly.

"I'm Megan," she says. "From the party?"

Party. Pieces of last night float back to me like a puzzle. Fish and chips, the cake, the party . . .

"Right, sorry." I gaze round the unfamiliar bedroom. "Thanks for letting us stay over." I smile as Ben grins through her legs at me, his dark fringe flopping over his eyes.

"Oh, honey, you're welcome—there was no *way* I was letting you guys go back to that B and B after your fall. I had to make sure you were really okay."

"Oh, I'm fine, thank you." I struggle into a sitting position, and instantly my head pounds. "Ow!"

"Easy, honey." Megan lays a cool hand on my forehead. "I'll give you some lotion for that bruise when you come downstairs, but first: breakfast!" She plops a heaving tray of bacon and eggs onto my lap.

"Wow!" I gasp.

"Don't blame me!" Megan grins. "Jack always insists on a greasefest when he does breakfast. You don't have to eat it all."

"Thanks." I smile, my heart racing as I remember more.

Jack. *My dad.* My real dad. And he's made me breakfast, a real English breakfast—eggs and proper bacon, none of that streaky American stuff—and not a pancake in sight!

"The bathroom's just across the hall, when you're done. There's a towel and a spare toothbrush, and feel free to use anything else you find."

"Thanks, Megan," I tell her. "I'm sorry to be such an inconvenience."

"Don't be silly," she laughs, tucking a stray ringlet behind her ear. "Make yourself at home."

My heart soars. *Home.* With my dad—I grin, winking at Ben as he pinches a piece of my toast—and my little brother!

164

"Shout if you need anything. We're just downstairs." Megan smiles, scooping up Ben. "And Holly's around too—if she ever gets out of bed!"

The toast sticks in my throat as the door clicks closed.

Holly.

My appetite gone, I slide the tray onto the bedside table, knocking something clattering to the floor.

"Shit!" I lean down and gingerly pick up the broken picture frame. I turn it over and my heart stops. There they are. The happy family. Jack and Megan and Ben—and Holly, sticking out like a sore thumb with her chestnut hair against Jack and Ben's black, Megan's blond.

Holly Woods.

Trudie's daughter.

She looks just like her. The same hair, the same eyes, the same bright smile . . . I drop the picture like a hot coal, sweat cold on the back of my neck.

I have to get out of here. I can't see her, can't—

There's a knock at the door. I stare, paralyzed, as it swings open.

"Morning." Andy smiles. "How're you feeling?"

"Fine," I say, jumping out of bed and scowling at the unfamiliar jogging bottoms and T-shirt I'm wearing. I scour the room. "Where are my clothes?"

"Well, since you drenched us both in Coke with your dizzy spell last night, Megan's doing a wash for us downstairs," Andy tells me, wearing a similar pair of makeshift pajamas. "She insisted—said she couldn't let us leave with dirty clothes. She's even doing my socks." He grins. "She's brave!"

"Great," I say, pacing the room. "Fantastic. Brilliant!"

"Are you okay?" Andy frowns.

"No." I shake my head. "I've got to go. We've got to go. Now."

"What?"

"We shouldn't be here!" I cry. "We should never have come—we have to go—"

"Rosie." Andy catches my arms. "What's going on? What's wrong?"

"Didn't you *see*?" I stare at him, trembling. "Didn't you *see* her?"

"Who?"

"Jack's daughter!" I stare at him incredulously.

"What? Yeah, briefly, but I was more concerned about you when you conked out."

"It's *her*, Andy," I say meaningfully. "*She's Trudie's daughter.*"

Andy stares at me.

"Rosie . . . Trudie's daughter died."

"Well, obviously not!" I stare at him wildly. "Obviously not, Andy—that's just one more mistake to add to the list!"

"But wait, I mean—are you *sure*?"

"Andy, she's *Holly Woods*."

"What?" His eyes widen. "She's called Holl—"

"Holly." I nod grimly. "Holly Woods. And she's the same *age* as me, she's got the same *birthday*, she's living with *my* father and she's the bleeding spitting image of Trudie—look!" I thrust the photograph at him.

"Knock, knock!"

I freeze as the bedroom door creaks open. Holly peers round with a friendly smile.

"Hi there! How're you doing? Did you sleep okay?"

166

I nod helplessly, the blood draining from my head.

"I'm not surprised after that fall!" she says sympathetically. "Anyway, I know Megan's washing your clothes, so here's a pair of my jeans and a T-shirt and a hoodie. We're about the same size, huh?" She holds them up.

I nod again, staring at her hair as it gleams in the sunshine—the exact same shade . . .

"Is there anything else you need?" She smiles, her hazel eyes shining.

I shake my head numbly. She even has the same kink at the top of her ear . . .

"Okay." She beams, looking from me to Andy. "See ya later!"

She closes the door behind her and I sink onto the bed.

"Oh, my God." Andy sits down next to me. "Oh. My. God."

I stare at the door. "Do you—do you think she heard us?" I whisper, my voice cracking.

"No." He shakes his head. "No, I don't think so."

"I just can't believe it, Andy. She survived. She's alive. She's *here*. How did this happen?"

He looks at me. "I don't know. I really don't know, Rosie. There must have been . . . a mistake. The baby must've recovered."

"But *how*?" My voice comes out high and shrill as hot tears spring into my eyes. "And how did Sarah *not know*?"

Andy squeezes my hand. "I don't know." He shakes his head. "I suppose she was too concerned about Trudie and . . . and you."

"Me?" I stare at him. "*Me? She's me*, Andy! *She's* Rosie

167

Kenning—*she's* Trudie's daughter." I stare at him miserably. "Don't you see, there was *no need* for Sarah to switch us—no need for any of this—*because Trudie's baby didn't die!*"

Andy pulls me to him tightly, my heart thumping against his.

"She—*she* should have stayed with Trudie, she should've . . . and *I* should've . . ."

"Shhh . . ." He strokes my hair.

"This is my family, Andy," I whisper against his chest. "My dad, my *brother* . . ."

"Then you have to tell them."

I sigh heavily. "I can't. Andy, they're a family. A *happy* family."

"They're *your* family."

"No." I shake my head, the word scratching my throat and stinging my eyes. "No, they can't ever be. Not now. It's impossible. They're hers." I bite my nail. "Sarah switched us, so they're Holly's. They're her family, they love each other. They deserve to be together."

"But Rose—"

"I can't—I can't break them up, Andy, I can't tell them—can't be that selfish." I sigh again, rubbing my eyes with my sleeve. "I've lasted this long without them, haven't I?" I swallow hard. "I'll survive."

"Rosie . . ."

"No, Andy." I stand up. "We have to go."

"Rose, just listen to me for a sec. If you're right, if she *is* Trudie's daughter—"

"She *is!*"

"Then Rosie, you *have* to tell them."

"Andy! You're not listening to me—"

"You have to tell them," he interrupts, "because Holly could have inherited Huntington's."

Holly

The wind tugs wildly at my hair, the salty breeze filling my lungs as I head along the harbor. I love this time of year. The chill in the air, the winter sunshine glistening on the waves, the old year gone and done with and the promise of a whole fresh new one to come. A new year, a new start, a new *name* . . .

I grin, suddenly warm despite the frosty air.

"Mrs. Holly Samuels." The name tingles on my tongue, and I giggle like an idiot. I can't wait. The first time I ever laid eyes on Josh I knew he was The One. I smile, remembering how serious and sexy he looked, studying in the school library—till Melissa flicked a spitball right at him! I can still see his face as he turned around— outraged—and flicked one straight back! And then he grinned, that wide infectious grin, and that was it. I was a goner.

I wonder what he sees in me . . .

It's hardly my brain—not compared to Mr. Ivy League Samuels. Not that I'm dumb, but it beats me how anyone can study that hard; can use all that power and strength in those huge sexy arms just to carry schoolbooks; can *enjoy* being stuck in a dusty library for hours on end when the sun's shining so bright you just *have* to be outside, when the pool sparkles so invitingly, or the sky's so blue you *have* to go sail around the point to see if the sea matches—when there's a *whole world* out there just waiting to be explored!

Safe to say, it's not our common interests that attracted him either . . .

So . . . my glittering personality? My hilarious sense of humor? Ha-ha.

Looks? I glance briefly at my reflection in a window.

Hardly.

So . . . what? What *do* we have in common?

My pace slows, and I shiver suddenly, slipping back into the shadowy doubts that have plagued me ever since Josh started Harvard, remembering how frightened I was every time he called, always expecting him to tell me it wasn't working out, that he'd realized we're total opposites, that he'd met someone else . . .

But instead he took me to New York for my birthday—and proposed!

All my doubts fade with the sparkling memory of my ring, my gleaming proof of his feelings.

Who cares *why*? Opposites attract, after all. We love each other—that's all that matters. *We're engaged!*

The grin splits my face as I race the last few blocks to his house, unable to wait any longer, to suppress the buzzing, fizzing thrill of this incredible secret longing to burst right out of me, desperate to shout it from the rooftops.

We're getting married!

Rosie

The clothes are almost a perfect fit. I look at myself in the full-length mirror in Holly's faded jeans and green Gap hoodie, and shiver suddenly. It's like I'm looking into another life—the life I would've had: the clothes I might've worn, the house I'd be living in, the family I'd have—the person I'd be. I look myself in the eye. Holly Woods. I try the name on my lips, whispering at first, then out loud.

"Holly Woods."

The shapes are alien to my mouth. It's not me—it doesn't sound right. I try again, lengthening the vowels and attempting an American accent.

"Holly . . ." No. "*Holly*," I correct. "*Holly Woods.*"

I shudder, the girl in the mirror unrecognizable.

"What are you doing?"

Andy stands in the doorway.

"This is a mistake," I tell him. "I can't do this. This is her life, not mine."

"I know." Andy frowns. "But you have to tell her." He looks at me. "Don't you?"

I slump down onto the bed. "Yes—no!" I run my hands through my hair, pulling it tight. "I don't know!"

"Rose," Andy says gently, sitting down next to me. "Remember how you felt when you didn't know if you had Huntington's?"

I nod miserably.

171

"And you said the not knowing was the worst bit, right? Well, Holly hasn't got a clue!"

"I know! But *that's* the difference!" I look at him. "*That's* the difference, Andy. I *knew* there was a chance of inheriting the disease—well, I *thought* I knew—and I saw what it did to Mum. I had to live with it hanging over me every day. But Holly doesn't even know there's a *possibility*. She could live for years and years without any signs—she might not *have* Huntington's, Andy! So what good would knowing do?" I shake my head. "It'd ruin her life."

"So ignorance is bliss, huh?" Andy says quietly. "You want her to live Trudie's life? Not knowing till it's too late?"

I look away.

"What if she has children, Rose? What if she passes the disease on to her kids because she doesn't even know she has it?"

"I don't know! I don't *know*, Andy." I stare at the floor. "What's worse? Living your whole life normally until one day you discover you've got Huntington's—or suddenly being told you're not who you think you are, your family's not your family—oh, and there's a fifty percent chance you could inherit a fatal disease?"

He looks away.

"It's impossible!" I shrug helplessly. "How can I make this life-changing decision about a girl I don't even know?"

"You can't," Andy sighs, taking my hand. "Because it's not your decision to make."

I look up.

He squeezes my hand. "It's hers."

I stare at him hopelessly for a moment, then sigh heavily and collapse back onto the bed.

"It'll ruin her life," I say simply, closing my eyes. "Either way, I'll ruin her life."

Holly

When there's no answer to Josh's doorbell, I head around to the backyard, to find Melissa midlunge.

Immediately, every inch of me itches to tell her my news, to squeal and scream and leap around celebrating with my best friend.

Not till after Dad, I remind myself for the hundredth time, biting my tongue.

"Holls!" Melissa grins, looking up. "Perfect timing. Wanna come for a run? It's, like, a total record—I've managed to keep my New Year's jogging resolution for a whole week!"

"Congrats!" I say, struggling to keep the grin from my face. "But not right now, thanks. Your brother around?"

"Nope." She jogs on the spot. "Still in bed."

"Still?"

"Uh-huh. You two must've had a pretty *eventful* weekend, huh?" She winks. "He's exhausted, and you look like the cat that got the cream."

I beam. "You have no idea."

"Please—spare me!" She grins, rolling her eyes as she jogs off down the driveway. "See you later, then—some of us have to exercise *alone.*"

I laugh as she blows me a kiss and disappears around the corner, then I push open the back door. Slipping off my sneakers, I creep carefully upstairs, tiptoe to Josh's bedroom door and listen. Silence. Gently, I ease the handle down . . .

Josh is lying in bed, grinning at me.

"You're awake!" I accuse, disappointed. "I wanted to surprise you!"

"You have." He reaches for me, as I pull off my baggy sweater. "You're more and more beautiful every day . . . Is that a new shirt? Wow!"

"Eyes on the *face*." I grin, climbing onto the bed beside him.

"Always, baby, always," he insists, stroking my hair. "I meant it brings out the color of your *eyes*." He grins, pulling me close as I settle into his chest, my fingers twirling and tangling in the soft black curls. He catches my hand and slides his fingers through mine. We look like a candy bar: chocolaty brown striped with creamy vanilla.

"Where's the ring?" he whispers.

I smile. "Somewhere safe."

"You've managed to keep it a secret?" he asks. "Even with your big mouth?"

"Hey!" I slap his chest and cuddle closer. "For now," I sigh. "But you're gonna ask Dad today, right? You go back to Harvard tonight."

"Yes," Josh promises, his heart beating faster against my cheek. "I'll ask him today. After lunch."

"*Before* lunch," I beg, sitting up. "Please, Josh, I can't stand it. I can't wait any longer!"

"Okay, okay. Before lunch," Josh relents, pulling me back down and hooking his leg over mine. "Just as soon as I get up the courage."

"Hey!" I giggle. "That's not courage you're getting up!"

He leans his head into my neck, his huge warm body pressing against me, pushing me down into the mattress . . .

"No!" I laugh, pushing him away. "Joshua Samuels, I don't believe you're taking me seriously!"

"Holly Woods." He grins. "I'll take you whichever way you like."

He slides his hand under my top as he nibbles the kink on my
right ear, sending shivers tickling deliciously down my spine as I collapse against the pillows . . .

"No!" With an immense force of will I push him away, struggling
upright. "Come on!"

"Not even the pixie ear?" he asks innocently.

"*Especially* not the pixie ear!" I laugh, pulling my sweater
back on.

He looks at me mournfully. "You're really serious?"

"Deadly." I grin, kissing his nose and fixing my hair. "Not till after
lunch! When we're *officially* engaged." I lean forward. "Then we can
do whatever"—I kiss his cheek—"we"—his nose—"want." I cup his
face and kiss him deeply, pressing myself against him for a long moment. Finally I break away, leaving us both breathless.

He stares at me for a second, then suddenly lifts me, shrieking,
over his shoulder.

"Well then, what are we waiting for?" he cries. "Come on!"

Rosie

"Ready?" Andy asks.

I nod, my heart racing. "As I'll ever be."

He squeezes my hand, I take a deep breath, and we push
into the kitchen.

"Oh, good!" Megan looks up from her ironing board.

"Holly lent you something to wear—sorry—didn't mean to leave you without anything! But I thought I'd better get to your clothes before they stained, I hope you don't mind?"

"Thank you." I smile. "And I'm sorry—"

"Don't be silly, it was a party! Ben's always spilling things—try cleaning up after a toddler!" She grins. "Besides, I think you got the brunt of it, judging from your clothes! All clean now." She nods at a pile of fresh laundry. "Holl's are a good fit, though, huh?"

"Yeah." I shift uncomfortably and glance at Andy. "Is, er, is Holly around?" I clench my fists, digging my nails into my palms nervously.

"Nope, sorry, she's gone out." Megan shakes her head, her blond curls bouncing as she irons a T-shirt. "She'll be back for lunch—you'll stay, right? Then I'll drop you back at your B and B."

"Thanks." I smile, relieved. *She's not here. There's still time.*

"Hello—you're up!" Jack grins, stepping into the kitchen.

"Hi." I beam, staring at him. I can't help it. His black hair, his sparkling green eyes. My dad.

"How's the head?" he asks.

"Oh, fine—fine, thank you," I stammer. "Sorry, I don't know what came over me."

"Don't be silly." Jack winks. "You've gotta black out on your eighteenth, one way or another—it's tradition!"

I smile. "And thanks for breakfast, too."

"Not at all—proper English, eh? None of this pancake malarkey."

Megan rolls her eyes.

"It was wonderful." I beam. "Just like home."

"Hear that?" Jack turns to Megan. "Maybe we should do breakfast at the restaurant too—show 'em how it's done?"

"We have enough grease as it is, thanks." Megan laughs. "Besides, you can't handle the customers you've got—there're seven messages on the machine this morning."

"Already?"

"Uh-huh." She looks at him. "You did check it yesterday?"

Jack looks at her blankly. "I . . . er . . . um . . ."

"Jack!" Megan exclaims. "*What* is the point of us having an answering machine if you never check it?"

"I *do*," Jack protests, looping his arms around her waist. "I *do*—when I remember . . ."

"And when was the last time you remembered?" Megan asks skeptically.

"Um . . . yesterday?"

"We'll see, shall we?" She pushes the button on the machine.

"*First message: received Friday, January fifth,*" the machine intones.

Megan cuffs Jack round the head. "*Friday!*"

"What can I say?" Jack shrugs. "We had a weekend without the kids—I got distracted . . ." He nuzzles her neck.

"Jack!" she giggles, pushing him away. "We have company!"

"It's okay," I say quickly. "We were just going to—uh—go and change, anyway!" I grab our clothes and head out of the room, Andy following quickly.

"*Hello?*" the woman on the answering machine snaps impatiently. "*Jack? Are you there? Jack?*"

I freeze in the corridor, the familiar voice stopping me in my tracks.

"*Jack!*" she shouts irritably. "*Jack, answer the goddamn phone!*" It's Kitty.

Holly

"You ready?" I ask, gazing up at Josh as he straightens his jacket. He looks so nervous, standing there in his uncomfortable suit, sweating despite the January chill.

"You're gorgeous," I tell him, standing on tiptoe to kiss him. "You're smart, and you're a Harvard scholar!" I straighten his tie. "What man wouldn't want you for a son-in-law?"

Josh glances down at me, an anxious smile flickering across his tense features. "Your dad?"

"Don't worry!" I laugh lightly. "He loves you. Almost as much as I do." I flash him a grin and push through the back door. To my surprise, both Dad and Megan are sitting at the kitchen table.

No time like the present!

"Daddy . . ." I smile, taking a deep breath and squeezing Josh's hand. "Dad, Josh and I have something to ask—"

"Josh, go home, please."

My smile freezes. *"Dad!"*

"Holly," Megan says softly. I look at her, then back at Dad. His face is tight, tense.

"Please, Josh." Dad doesn't look up. "We have some family business to attend to."

"But Dad—" I glance at Josh. "Daddy, Josh—"

Josh squeezes my hand. "Maybe I should go," he whispers.

"No!" I hiss, gripping his hand tightly. "No, Josh . . ."

"It's not a good time," he says meaningfully, gently disentangling his fingers and kissing my forehead. "I'll see you later."

"Josh—"

I watch as he closes the door behind him, then turn on my father, my blood boiling.

"*Well?*" I demand. "*Well?* What's so important that you had to be so rude?"

"Why don't you tell me?" He doesn't look up.

I stare at him. "What?"

"Why don't you tell me," he continues, "what you were doing in New York?"

"What do you mean?" I ask, my cheeks flushing. "It was just a holiday."

"Just a holiday," Dad repeats, nodding slowly. "So, what happened?"

"What?"

"Why'd you come back early?" he says tersely. "Why'd you cut your 'holiday' short?"

"I—"

"The flight back was paid for, right? Josh won the tickets?"

I stare at him.

"So why didn't you stay the whole weekend?"

He looks up and I falter.

"Okay," I sigh. "It wasn't a prize . . . Josh bought the tickets."

He closes his eyes, nods grimly.

"I'm sorry I didn't tell you, Daddy, but it was the only way we thought you'd let me go—you'd never have let me miss my eightee—"

179

"So why'd you get the bus back early?" he interrupts, staring at the table. "If Josh paid so much for flights, why miss them?"

I sigh. "We didn't have flights back," I confess miserably. "We were always going to get the bus. We only flew down there because Josh got a cheap deal—because I'd never been on a plane before—it was my present."

"Your present." Dad nods, his jaw tight.

I move toward him. "I'm sorry, Daddy."

"Then why don't you tell me the truth?" He looks up sharply, stopping me short.

"What?"

"Why don't you tell me the *real* reason you went to New York, Holls?"

"I—"

"And what exactly happened to make you come home early."

He looks straight at me. He knows. I don't know how, but I can see it in his eyes.

"If you already know, I don't see why you need me to tell you," I mutter.

Megan shifts uncomfortably.

"*Because,* Holly, I'm your father and I have a right to—"

"I'm eighteen years old, Dad, I don't need your permission," I say bitterly. "Or your approval."

"My approval? My *approval*?" He stares at me. "Holly, you obviously thought I wouldn't approve, or you'd have told me yourself!"

I look away, tears stinging my eyes. I never thought he felt that way. Never. I thought he liked Josh—I thought Josh was just being formal by asking his permission. I never dreamed Daddy might say no . . .

A chill trickles through me.

What'll he say about the baby?

"Holly, you must see what a mistake this was."

My insides twist. *A mistake?*

Dad sighs. "I don't think you should have any more contact."

I stare at him. *"What?"*

"It's for the best."

"You can't—you can't mean it! *Megan!*" I beg her for help, but she looks away. "I won't," I say defiantly. "You can't make me. This is *my* life and I'll decide who's in it!"

"No."

"Dad!"

"I'm sorry, Holly," he says, rubbing his brow. "I really am, but I can't just stand by and watch while—"

"Then you don't have to," I interrupt quietly.

"What?"

I bite my lip. "If that's really the way you feel . . ." He looks away. ". . . then I'll move out."

Dad's head snaps up.

"We'll live together," I tell him, tears trickling down my cheeks. "I'll leave."

"Holly!" He stares at me, dumbfounded.

"I don't want to," I say, my voice cracking. "But if you make me choose . . ."

He stares at me, then suddenly stands up. I back away, but to my surprise, he moves over to the counter and clicks a button on the answering machine.

"Jack? Are you there? Jack?"

Dad turns to me. I frown, confused, then glance at Megan, who looks away.

"Jack? Jack, answer the goddamn phone! How dare you send your daughter to me, Jack? We had an agreement. She has nothing to do with me. Do you have any idea what this could do to my career? To my relationship? My life? I knew this was a mistake. I should never have trusted you. I should never have had anything to do with you!"

The message clicks abruptly and there is silence.

Rosie

Oh, God! I can't bear this. Can't bear to hear that awful message again—to stand here behind the half-open kitchen door, watching what it's doing to Jack—to Holly—but I can't move either, can't go back in, can't speak . . . Andy's hand finds mine.

"I'm sorry you had to hear that, sweetheart," Jack sighs. "But it's for your own good."

Holly stares at him. "What's going on? Who was that?"

He sighs again. "Holly . . ."

"What!"

"Holly, I'm not angry, I just want to know the truth."

"What truth, Dad? What are you talking about?"

He shakes his head. "We could've worked it out, we could've handled this together, if you'd just come to me, trusted me. We've always trusted each other, haven't we?" He looks at her, his eyes sad, tired. "It was for the best. Everything I did, I thought it was all for the best." He squeezes her hand. "How did you find out, Holls?"

182

She stares at him. "About *what?*"

He presses his eyes shut, screws them so tight it looks painful. "About Katharine."

Oh, God . . .

She looks at him blankly.

"I *know*, Holly," he sighs. "I know you went to New York to find Katharine." He opens his eyes, his features strained. "To find your mother."

Holly's mouth drops open as she stares at him, her face deathly pale.

The frustration in Jack's eyes slowly melts into fear. "*Didn't* you?"

"Daddy . . ." She hesitates, her eyes wide. "My mother is dead . . ."

Oh, God!

"But—but you went to New York—" Jack insists. "You went to find her . . . you *found* her! . . ."

Holly shakes her head slowly, her lips trembling. "My mother is dead," she repeats faintly. "You told me, Daddy. Mommy died. She died when I was born . . ." She stares at him, swallows. "Didn't she?"

He just stares at her, horror-struck.

"Daddy?" Holly whispers. "Is my mom alive?"

I close my eyes, praying the ground will just swallow me up.

"But then how . . . why . . . I don't understand . . ." He falters. "If you didn't find her—if you didn't go looking for her . . ."

"It was me," a tiny voice mumbles. I'm startled to recognize it as my own. The door swings open and my cheeks burn as

183

everyone turns. I can't breathe, can't believe I just said that, but I couldn't watch any longer.

Jack stares at me. "I'm sorry—what?"

"I—I went to New York—I . . ." I trail off, the words stuck in my throat as my eyes lock on to Holly's, so scared, so confused. Oh, *God* . . . My heart races and I start to panic. *I can't—I can't do this!*

"Honey." Megan smiles kindly. "Look, I think you're a bit confused—could you just give us a minute?"

"Of course," I breathe, flooded with relief. "Of course, I'm sorry, I—"

"Actually," Andy says gently, blocking my exit, "you all need to hear this." He meets my gaze evenly. "It's really important."

I stare at him desperately.

"Go on, Rose," he whispers, squeezing my hand encouragingly. "You can do this."

I swallow hard and force myself to turn back round.

"I—" I begin, but the words die on my lips as I meet Jack's gaze. He looks so sad, so lost. And I'm about to make everything a million times worse . . .

Andy squeezes my hand again. I squeeze back—hard—then take a deep breath, my knees trembling.

"It was me," I tell them. "I went to New York and found Katharine Sinclare . . ." I hesitate, search Jack's big green eyes. "It's me she's talking about in her message."

He frowns, rubs his brow. "I—I don't understand."

"I'm her daughter," I say quickly, the words tumbling out clumsily. His eyes widen, and I look away, burning beneath his gaze. "I'm—I'm *your* daughter."

Holly

The silence is deafening. I'm not sure I'm even breathing. I stare at her, this strange girl standing in my kitchen, wearing my clothes, hardly daring to move.

What? I glance at Dad, who's just staring at her, frozen to the spot. His *daughter?* My *sister? I have a sister?*

Dad runs a hand through his hair, and suddenly I see her there, in his black hair, his green eyes. His *daughter.* My mind frantically tries to connect the dots . . . We share a birthday—an *eighteenth* birthday—oh, my God, *we're twins!* Which means . . . we share a mother—a mother who's alive—she's *alive!* My heart thumps against my chest. After all these years, *my mom's alive*—she's in *New York!*

"Wow!" I gasp, breaking the silence, excitement bubbling inside me like champagne. I cross the room to get a better look at her, take her hands in mine—my sister—my twin! "Wow, wow, wow! This is . . . this is amazing!"

I beam at her but she just gazes at me uncertainly, then glances at Dad. Why didn't he tell me? So many secrets—my mom, my *twin sister!* It's like *The Parent Trap!*

"I don't understand," Dad mutters quietly, clearing his throat. "How . . . how . . . Katharine is your mother . . . ?"

She nods. "I was born at St. Anne's Hospital, Maybridge, the night of January the fifth, eighteen years ago," she begins, speaking quickly but clearly—as though she's rehearsed this. "I was premature—"

"Daddy—we're twins!" I interrupt, laughing at his apparent confusion.

Rosie stares at me then, faltering midflow. She lets go of my hands and sinks into a chair, her face draining of color.

"I was born prematurely," she continues, clearing her throat and staring at the table. "To Katharine Sinclare—"

"*We* were," I correct her, smiling. She closes her eyes.

"And rushed to the Special Care Baby Unit."

A cold chill shivers through me—oh, God, is she sick? Did they think she'd died—is that how we were separated? I watch her intently, twirling my finger in my hair.

"Then"—she takes a deep breath—"there was—there was a *mix-up* at the Unit," she continues, glancing at me.

I hardly dare breathe.

"I was brought back to a different mother. Not Katharine." She glances at Dad. "This other woman, Trudie, she brought me up—I thought all my life she was my mum." She stares at the table. "But she wasn't. Katharine was," she states, hesitates. "And you are my father."

Wow. Oh, my God. I watch as she struggles to control her emotions, my heart aching for her. I want to hug her, to let her know it's okay, that we'll accept and love her—my lost sister. But something in her eyes stops me.

Dad stares at her for a long moment. "But . . . twins . . . ? Katharine didn't have . . . ."

She trembles as she shakes her head. "No, no, she didn't . . . ." She glances at me, looks away. Her boyfriend squeezes her shoulders.

I freeze, utterly lost now. I look from her to Dad, trying to make sense, to rewind the conversation in my head.

"There was a . . . another baby," she says, her breath coming in starts. "The woman I was given to also gave birth to a daughter—a

186

beautiful baby girl." She smiles at me now, her eyes shining with tears. "And she . . . Katharine . . ." I stare at her as she swallows hard, looks away. "Like I said," she whispers. "There was a mix-up."

My heart stops. I swear, it just stops stone-cold dead. I stare at this girl, at my dad, this wild story whirling dizzily around my head.

"What are you saying?" I ask quietly.

She looks at me, her face pained. "Holly, I—I only just found out, I—"

"What are you *saying*?" I repeat, my voice harsh, brittle.

"Holly," she whispers, taking my hand. "You and I—we were swapped at birth."

The words rip through me like a knife as my hand grows limp in hers.

"I—I don't understand . . ." I look at Dad, who's just staring at her. "I—I don't . . ." I run out of words.

She sighs. "I know—I'm sorry, I know this is a huge, *huge* shock, but—"

"What would make you think such a thing?" Dad interrupts, his face ashen.

She looks at him then, her eyes sad.

"I'm sorry, I know this is hard to believe—I didn't believe it at first either—I couldn't . . ." She hesitates and glances at me. "But then I had a—a test done, and it showed I wasn't a genetic match with my mother. When I was born, Katharine was at the same hospital at the same time, and when I met her . . ." She pauses, smiles weakly. "Well, it was obvious."

My chest tightens as I look at Dad, praying he'll disagree—but recognition blossoms in his eyes. She looks like Mom—the mom I've never met—the mom he told me died. The mom who's . . . who's not my mom.

187

Rosie swallows. "But I didn't know for certain—for definite—until I met you, Holly."

I look up sharply.

"You're so—you're just . . ." She smiles. "You're beautiful—"

I eye her warily.

"And you're the spitting image of my mum, of Trudie." She slides a photograph across the table.

I turn away, refusing to look, though every part of me itches to see—to know—to prove her wrong.

I watch, frozen, as Dad slowly picks up the photograph. He gasps, then stares at me, his jaw hanging open.

It can't be true, it can't—

I snatch the photo from his hands, a shiver racing down my spine as I stare at it, unbelieving, horrified.

It's me—it's me, only older . . . The chestnut hair, the hazel eyes, the freckles—even the kinky ear . . .

"This is horseshit!" I reel backward, laughing loudly at the absurdity of it all, but then I look at this girl, so sad and sympathetic, and at Megan, so confused, and then I see my dad—my daddy—who's staring at me like he's never seen me before, and my laughter dies.

"Daddy, tell her!" I beg, my voice laced with panic now. "Tell her it's not true—it's ridiculous!"

"It's impossible," Dad says, his frown deepening. "It can't be . . . and yet . . ."

"Get out!" I scream at her, wrenching open the back door. "Just *get out!*"

"Holly . . . ," Megan says gently.

"*Get out of my house!*" I yell, my whole body shaking. "Dad, tell her!"

"Please, let me explain—" she begs. "There's more."

188

"How dare you? How *dare* you! After we've given you some-where to stay, given you food, a *birthday cake*—my *fricking birthday cake!*" Tears burn my eyes. "And my *clothes!* You're even wearing my fricking *clothes!*"

I lunge at her and she tumbles to the floor as I tear at her sweat-shirt—*my* sweatshirt—trying to yank it roughly over her head.

"Hey!" Her boyfriend tries to pull me off.

"Get off me!" I yell, kicking him so hard he falls. "This has *noth-ing* to do with you! This is my house! My *life!*"

"Holly!" Megan reaches for me.

"She can't have it!" I scream, clinging to the sweatshirt, pulling, struggling, desperate to get it back. *"She can't have my life!"*

"Holly!" Dad bellows, lifting me roughly by my arm. "What the *hell* are you doing?"

Everyone's staring at me like I'm some sort of freak show. I look at Dad helplessly, my heart breaking into a thousand jagged splinters.

"Tell her it's not true," I gasp. "Tell her she's a liar—tell her to go away and leave us alone!" I beg. "Daddy, please!"

He looks at me, his face aged with lines I've never noticed before.

"No, Holly-berry," he sighs, the familiar nickname breaking my heart. "I—I can't . . ."

I stare at him for a long moment, the splinters turning to ice.

"Then she's welcome to you."

I turn my back on them all, slamming the kitchen door hard behind me.

Rosie

Shit. I look at Andy. He helps me up, rubbing his leg where Holly kicked him.

Well, that went well.

Jack is frozen, staring at the door Holly just slammed, the shudders still rippling through the room.

"Look," Megan says quietly. "This has all been quite a shock, I think we just need some time . . ."

I nod. "I understand. I'm so sorry . . . it's just—"

"Unbelievable . . . ," Jack murmurs, gazing out the window, frozen in time, in shock. "You're Katharine's daughter?" He turns, his eyes unreadable. "You're really Kathy's daughter?"

I look at him for a moment, uncertain suddenly, in spite of everything. Then I nod tentatively, my voice a whisper. "I'm *your* daughter."

His eyes soften visibly for a moment; then he looks away.

I stare at the floor, aware of every heartbeat pounding in my chest, my head.

"I'm sorry," he sighs, sinking into a chair. "It's just so . . ."

"Unbelievable," I agree quietly.

"Sweetie." Megan turns to me. "Have you . . . I mean, would you . . . consider . . ." She hesitates. "A test—or something . . . to confirm . . . ?"

"Of course." I nod quickly, my cheeks burning fiercely.

"I'm sorry, I don't mean to imply . . ." She stumbles. "Just to be certain, to be sure—just because you and Holly were born the same night . . ."

"It's fine." I swallow. It's not like I can tell them about Sarah, about the identity tags she switched . . . I think that would push them over the edge—more than I already have.

Somewhere overhead a plane hums through the sky. I wish I were on it.

I glance around the kitchen, my eyes flicking over anything, everything—anything to avoid looking at Jack or Megan—and my gaze snags on a framed photo by the sink. The same photo as in the bedroom—the happy family: Jack, Megan, Holly and Ben.

Suddenly the enormity of what I've done crashes down on me. I've ripped this whole family apart—not just Holly's life, but Jack's and Megan's and even little Ben's. And there's absolutely no way to go back now, to undo it.

"I'm so sorry," I blurt out. "This was never—I didn't mean—I didn't even *know* about Holly until last night. I thought the other baby died, and I . . . I just wanted to find my real parents . . ."

Jack nods slowly but doesn't look up.

"Shhh, sweetie. It's okay." Megan pats my hand gently. "Do your par—do the people looking after you know you're here now?"

I shake my head. "She thinks I'm traveling—I didn't want her to worry . . ." I look at Jack, my throat tight. "But—but I had to tell you." I look at the photo, my heart aching. "I had to tell you . . ."

Jack nods, still staring at the table.

"Because there's more."

He looks up, his face worn and weary. "More?"

Andy squeezes my shoulder.

"Perhaps whatever it is could wait, sweetie?" Megan says. "It's a lot to deal with as it is."

I shake my head, determined to get it all out and over with. Any delay will just cause more grief, more pain.

"No. No, I'm sorry," I sigh. "I would never have come crashing into your life if it weren't for this—if it weren't important."

Jack holds my gaze, his eyes tired, fearful. "I'm listening."

I take a deep breath.

"Have you ever heard of Huntington's disease?"

Holly

"Tell me you love me."

Josh looks up, surprised, as his bedroom door slams against the wall.

"Tell me you love me!" I demand, standing over him, tears scorching my eyes, blurring my vision. "Tell me you love me, no matter what."

"Of course I love you, baby." Josh scrambles to his feet and pulls me close. "Hey, what's going on? What's the matter?"

He folds me into his arms, and I can't speak, the tears pouring too fast now, my breath hot gasps against his shirt.

"Hey, baby girl, it's okay, it's all right." He pulls me closer, tighter. "Shhh now. What happened? Is it your dad?"

My dad. The sobs surge harder, swelling painfully in my throat. *He's not—he's not my dad!*

"Hey, sweetheart, it's okay, it's all right." Josh brushes away my tears, his eyes serious, sad. "He doesn't approve, does he?"

"What?" I frown, confused. "No! No, it's not that." I swallow hard, stroke his cheek. "It's not you."

"Well . . . what, then?" Josh frowns. "Baby, whatever it is we can fix it, okay?" he soothes, his eyes deep in mine. "I love you." He kisses me gently. "I'll always love you."

"Really?" I search his eyes.

"Of course." He smiles, brushing my hair from my face.

"Even when I'm old and wrinkly?"

He grins. "Even when your boobs hit the floor and you leave a trail of drool behind your walker."

"Eww!" I smile. "Promise?" I sniff.

He cups my face in his hands. "Holly Marie Woods, I will love you till my dying day."

I stare at him, my insides twisting harder than ever.

Holly Marie Woods . . .

My eyes fill and I screw them shut, the tears streaming down my cheeks as my world collapses around me.

"Holly?" Josh panics. "What is it? Holly?"

That's not even my name.

Rosie

"Wow," Jack says when I've finished. He rubs his brow as Megan strokes his back soothingly. "Wow."

"I'm so sorry," I mumble, lost for words now everything's spilled out in the open. Andy looks at me with a small reassuring smile.

"So Holly . . ." Jack trails off. "There's a chance she might *develop* this . . . this disease . . . ?"

"There's a fifty percent chance, yes." I look away.

"But she's so healthy . . . so beautiful . . ." He gazes at the picture by the sink. "My Holly-berry . . ."

I nod, my heart aching with guilt.

"Okay." He swallows. "So what do we do if she has? Chemo? Therapy? Drugs?" He looks at me.

I shake my head miserably. "There's research going on all the time, new developments, but at the moment . . ." I hesitate. "I'm sorry, there is no cure."

"What?" Jack stares at me. "There must be—there has to be!" He slams his fist against the table, jumps from his chair. "I'll sue!" he rages. "I'll sue that bloody hospital—this is their fault!" He grabs the phone and my heart leaps in panic.

"I don't think that'll help anyone, Jack," Megan soothes, resting her hand gently on his. "Besides, let's do the DNA test first—make sure we've got our facts straight."

Jack drops the phone and collapses at the table, head in his hands, clawing at his hair. "I can't just . . . she can't . . .

she's my daughter, my little girl . . ." He trails off, wiping his tears roughly. Megan slips her arm around him, kisses his shoulder.

I wish I'd never come here, wish I'd never found out, wish I'd never been born. This man is breaking into pieces before me and it's all my fault. My chest tightens and all I want to do is run.

"But you know," Andy says gently, warm by my side. "You know, there's a fifty percent chance that Holly's completely unaffected—that she's perfectly healthy. Right, Rose?"

"Right." I nod gratefully at him. "And even if she *has* inherited the gene, she'll probably be perfectly fine for years—decades, even. It can start really late, Mum was in her . . ." I hesitate, remembering how Mum's early symptoms were overlooked. "She wasn't diagnosed till her fifties."

Jack looks up, searching my eyes carefully. "Your mother . . ." He clears his throat. "You watched her die of this disease?"

An icy clamp closes over my heart as I think of Mum staggering around the prom, ranting at the neighbors, lying in her hospital bed . . . herself and yet so very, very far from herself.

I close my eyes, swallow, and nod. "Yes."

Slowly, he places his large hand over mine. "Then *I'm* the one who's sorry."

I look at him then, this man whose life has just been shattered, his eyes filled with sadness and compassion—for me. *He's* sorry for *me*. My throat swells as he squeezes my hand.

"I'm so sorry . . . ," I say again, the only words left in my vocabulary, as the tears flood up from nowhere.

Then, suddenly, I'm folded in his arms, breathing in the musky smell of his shirt, his hold tight, protective.

"It's not your fault," he soothes, stroking my hair. "Okay? It's not anybody's fault."

I close my eyes, trying to convince myself he's right, that I haven't just single-handedly destroyed his life—*all* their lives. That this *was* the right thing to do, not just for me, but for Jack, for Holly . . . My gaze snags on the window and I freeze, stung with guilt, as Holly stares back at me, her eyes wide, pale as a ghost against the glass.

Holly

"Holly!" Dad calls after me as I race away down the steps, my heart on fire, pounding as hard as my footsteps. "Holly, wait!" he calls again. "Holly, please!"

I shake my head fiercely, trying to erase the image of Rosie in his arms—his daughter—his *real* daughter.

"Holly." He catches my arm. "Holly, please, come back inside."

I pull away.

"Holly." He blocks my path. "Holly, please."

"Tell her to go," I say, biting my lip against the tears. "Tell her to go, and I'll come back."

He looks at me for a long moment, his eyes pained.

My throat swells and I pull away.

"Holly—where are you going?"

"I'm moving in with Josh," I call over my shoulder. "He's going back to college, and I'm going with him!"

"Holly, wait—you're not moving in with your boyfriend—"

"He's my *fiancé*!" I round on him. "If you'd bothered to listen to me for a second, you'd know that. Josh proposed in New York—*that's* why we came home early. We're getting married."

He stares at me. "You're *what*? Holly—you can't—you're *eighteen*!"

"I can do whatever the hell I like—and you can't stop me!" I yell at him, tears swimming in my eyes. "After all, you're not my father!"

He freezes, trapped in the cage of light from the window, pain blasted across his features.

I turn away, my cheeks blazing and run, just run, as fast as I can. I fling open Josh's car door and throw myself inside.

"Let's go."

"Holly . . ." Josh pulls me close. "Baby, you should've let me go with you. Was she still there?"

"Oh, yeah!" I laugh, blinking fiercely, trying to stop the stupid tears streaking down my face. "Oh, she was still there, all right." The image of the two of them burns my eyes.

Josh strokes my knee. "Babe, I'm sure your dad—"

"Can we just go?" I interrupt. "Please?"

He looks at me, then starts the car. "Sure." He pulls into the road. "Where would you like to go?"

I turn, surprised. "With you. Back to Harvard."

"You want to stay with me? In my dorm room?" he laughs. "Trust me, that dorm ain't no place for a lady."

"Please," I beg. "I don't seem to have *any* place right now."

Josh sighs. "Baby, there is nothing I'd like more than to take you with me—but at college? Holly, you'd be on your own all day while I'm at class . . . Besides, running away isn't the answer—you have to stay here, work things out with your dad."

197

"He's not my—"

"Yes, he is." Josh pulls over, looks me straight in the eye. "He'll always be your dad. He brought you up—and all on his own before Megan came along. Now, that can't have been easy—you're a little spitfire when you get going—"

"I am n—!" I protest, but Josh places his finger on my lips.

"But he's done a pretty fine job, if you ask me." He moves his hand to my cheek. "Now, Holly, Minnie Mouse or Donald Duck—whoever you are: you're still you." He leans closer. "And I love you."

He kisses me and I feel myself beginning to melt.

"And so does your dad."

I bite my lip.

"So, Donald, where would you like me to escort you to? If you're not quite ready to go home, I'm sure Melissa would love to have an impromptu slumber party and a chance to show off what is now, I believe, the state's largest collection of Johnny Depp DVDs . . ."

"Who needs Johnny Depp?" I whisper, leaning in as he wraps his arm around me, strong and warm and safe.

"Well, that's true," he agrees, kissing the top of my head. "But she also got a nauseating amount of chocolate for Christmas, and it would be an act of pure human kindness to help her eat it. I've done my best, of course, but there's only so much a mere man can do. Time to call in an expert."

I grin and slap him playfully.

"And then of course there's the pièce de résistance—Dumbledore, the farting cat who's guaranteed to drool on your face . . ."

"Sold!" I laugh, nuzzling closer.

"Everything's gonna be okay, okay?" he whispers, smoothing my hair.

"Okay," I sigh, ignoring the insistent buzz of my cell phone in my pocket.

Rosie

"I should have gone after her." Jack slams the phone down and paces the kitchen. "I should've—"

"No," Megan soothes. "No, she just needs some space, that's all. It's a lot to deal with."

"But she's my daughter—and she's out there on her own—"

"She's with Josh," Megan corrects him. "He'll look after her. He's a good kid, Jack."

"A good *husband?*" Jack challenges. "A good husband for my *teenage daughter?*"

"She's eighteen, Jack—"

"I know that!" Jack snaps. "Don't tell me about my own daughter!"

Megan looks away.

He sighs and leans against the counter. "I'm sorry," he mumbles. "It's just—she's *only* eighteen. She's my baby—my little girl."

"I know," Megan smooths his hair gently. "And *she* knows too. She knows you're her dad and she loves you." She kisses him.

I glance at Andy, who nods and clears his throat.

"Um, we should—we should really be getting back to the B and B," I say, moving toward the door.

"Do you need a ride, honey?" Megan offers. "I need to go pick up Ben from my mom's anyway."

"Thanks." I smile. "That would be—"

"No." Jack looks up. "No, you can't go—not you too." His gaze locks on mine. "You should stay here."

I hesitate. I don't want to leave, not now I've found him—but part of me wants to run as far and as fast as I can.

"Jack—" Megan begins.

"I'm not sure that's a good idea," I say, my cheeks burning. "You and Holly need some time alone, you need to talk . . ."

"It's just to a B and B, Jack—she'll still be in town," Megan reasons.

"No," Jack says, his voice firm. "I've gone eighteen years without knowing my daughter." He swallows hard. "Don't you think that's long enough?"

Megan looks at him, then at me, then closes her mouth and looks away.

My heart thumps loudly in the stillness.

"Rosie," he says gently, his green eyes so wide, so nervous, so vulnerable. "Will you stay?"

Holly

"That is *so cool!*" Melissa exclaims, squealing and hugging her pillow, startling Dumbledore who immediately leaps off the bed and scurries downstairs.

I scowl at her. "Weren't you *listening*? Exactly which part of my life falling to pieces is cool?"

She rolls her eyes. "Don't be so melodramatic—this is unreal! *Holly,* don't you get it? You have a *mom*!"

Despite myself, my heart flutters. *My mom.*

"Holly!" Melissa squeals, grabbing my hands and squeezing them. "You probably have a whole other family in England—land of Shakespeare and castles and kings and—"

"I don't want another family—I want *my* family!" I snap, pulling my hands away and hugging my knees. "I want my dad back."

"Holls." Melissa places her hand on my knee. "He's always gonna be your dad—like, *duh,* you couldn't even get rid of him at the prom, remember? How he wouldn't go home? How he offered to chaperone? To DJ?"

A smile tugs at my lips.

"He's not going *anywhere,* believe me—look how many times he's called you just tonight." I glance guiltily at my muted cell phone. "But you're telling me you don't wanna meet your *mom*? Your actual *mother*? All these years you thought she was dead, fantasized about what she was like, how things might've been, and now . . ." She squeezes my knees, her eyes sparkling with excitement. "She's *alive*! Holly, your mom's alive!"

"She's *always* been alive—don't you get it? Melissa, Dad lied—he *lied* to me, all this time. He told me she'd died."

"Well, *yeah*!" Melissa rolls her eyes. "Well, he would, wouldn't he? That bitch on the phone is obviously a waste of space—who wouldn't rather have a mom who's dead than one who tells her daughter to get lost when she turns up at her door? What a cow."

I twist my finger tightly in my hair. I hadn't thought of it like that.

"Holls, he was just trying to spare your feelings. Imagine if you'd gone looking for her like that Rosie girl did and she slammed the door in your face? How crushed would you be?"

I bite my lip, imagining it—the hope, the excitement, the earth-shattering rejection. It would be devastating. It must've been devastating. I frown, reluctant to feel sorry for Rosie.

"Well, he still shouldn't have lied."

"Well, duh," Melissa says softly. "But then, he's a guy, what do you expect? Emotional issues aren't exactly their strength."

"You're not kidding." I smile despite myself. "You should've seen how he flipped when I said I was going to stay with Josh at Harvard. *'You're eighteen—you're too young to get married!'*"

Melissa's jaw drops and she stares at me. "Shut *up*! You're *engaged*?"

Before I can react, Melissa screams and leaps on top of me, strangling me in a bear hug.

"Oh, my God! Oh, my Goooooooddddd!" She releases me momentarily. *"When? How?* Wait!" She looks at me urgently. *"Promise* me I'll be your maid of honor! Please, Holly! I've never been a maid of honor, and—"

"All right, already—you can be my maid of honor!" I laugh, and she lunges on top of me again, her squeals, if possible, louder than ever.

"Oh, my God! Oh, my *God*! This is awesome! This is the best day of my life! My best friend is gonna be my sister-in-law, and I'm finally going to be a maid of honor!" She squeezes me hard. "And *you*! What the heck is your problem? You're finally gonna meet your mom—your *real, cool English* mom—and you're *getting married*! Your mom can come to the wedding! Hey—you can probably get married in a castle, lucky thing!"

"Whoa, there!" I laugh. "One step at a time!"

"I've gotta call Josh—I can't *believe* he didn't tell me!" Melissa grabs her cell, punches in the number, puts it on speaker, then squeals loudly as he answers.

"I can't believe you're getting married!" she shrieks, flying at me in another hug as Josh laughs, all my worries fizzling away as excitement bubbles up inside me.

We're getting married!

Melissa squeezes me tight, her grin splitting her face as this time I squeal too. She's right, I am lucky. I have my friends, my family—Dad, and Megan and Ben; I have Josh and the promise of our new life together, *our own family.* I smile, hugging my secret. And somewhere, far across the Atlantic, I have a mom. My heart cartwheels at the thought. My *real* mom. Not some woman who gave birth to me and then couldn't be bothered to stick around. It was an accident—we were separated by accident. She never meant to leave me at all.

And now I can't wait to meet her.

Rosie

"What you doing?"

I look up to see Ben watching me in the bathroom mirror as I rub the two cotton buds against the inside of my cheek. I turn and smile.

"I'm doing a test," I tell him. "For DNA."

"Oh." He screws up his nose. "Like ABC?"

I laugh. "Not really." Though actually, it's almost as easy. I can't believe all it takes is two cotton buds rubbed inside each of our cheeks, sealed in two labeled paper envelopes, posted off to the lab with a check and a downloaded form—and hey presto: 99.9 percent accurate DNA results in less than a fortnight. It's scarily simple.

Ben watches intently as I seal my cotton buds into the envelope with my name on, and I smile.

"You want a go?" I pull a fresh bud out of the box, and he eyes me uncertainly for a moment before opening his mouth, displaying rows of tiny pearly white teeth.

Ever so gently, I rub the cotton tip against his cheek and he giggles. "That tickles!"

"You're not ticklish, are you?" I gasp, tickling under his armpit. He collapses to the floor, squirming gleefully, his laughter filling the room.

"What's going on in here, then?" Jack grins, appearing round the doorframe with Megan.

"Daddy!" Ben cries, leaping into his arms.

"Hello, trouble." Jack grins, rubbing his nose against Ben's. "How's my monkey?"

"I'm not a monkey!" Ben protests. "I'm Ben!"

"Of course you are." Jack smiles, kissing his forehead. "And do you know who this is?" He points at me.

Ben shakes his head furiously, his hair flying in his eyes.

"This is Rosie," Jack tells him, brushing his fringe back and looking at me. "She's your big sister."

Ben stares at me, eyes wide, and my breath catches.

"*Might* be your sister," Megan amends quickly. "Let's wait till it's official, huh?" She looks at Jack sternly. "That's the whole point."

"Of course, of course." Jack nods. "You done with yours?" He nods at the envelope by the sink.

"Yep," I say, handing it over. "All done and dusted."

"Great," Jack says. "I'll go drop them in the mail."

"Now?" Megan says.

"The sooner the better, I think." Jack smiles at me wearily. "Then we'll all know where we stand." He passes Ben to Megan and jogs downstairs.

Megan looks at me awkwardly.

"I'm sorry if I seem . . ." She falters. "I don't mean to be skeptical, just with children it's better if things are definite, before . . ."

"I understand," I tell her, hugging my arms. "Have you heard from Holly?"

"No," Megan sighs. "She's still not answering her cell phone, but her friend's mom called—she's staying with them. So at least we know she's safe."

"Good. That's a relief."

"Yes." Megan nods. "It is. Anyway, I'd better get this one to bed." She ruffles Ben's hair. "It's been a long day."

I nod. "I think I'll get an early night too."

"Okay, well, you know where everything is." Megan smiles. "Good night."

"Night."

"Night, Rosie."

I look up, my heart jumping at my name on Ben's lips as he waves to me over Megan's shoulder. I smile and wave back until they disappear through the doorway.

I sigh, flooded with conflicting emotions, then push open

the door to the spare room and collapse into Andy's waiting arms.

"Are you okay?" he whispers, stroking my hair.

I nod, my cheek pressed tight against his chest, my eyes glued once more to the family photo in its broken frame—the warmth I feel gazing at my dad, at my gorgeous little brother, fading as I look at Holly, the terrible casualty of this reunion. I close my eyes, feeling sick to my stomach.

"You did really well down there, you know?" Andy says. "That took a lot of balls."

I smile despite myself.

"I know it wasn't easy—especially after Kitty . . ." He squeezes me tight. "But you did it. You found your dad and you told him. I'm proud of you." He kisses my head, his words tickling my ear. "You did what you came to do."

I open my eyes.

"That's just it," I whisper, feeling sicker than ever. "Now what?"

Holly

Something bats at my nose and my eyes fly open. A white paw prods my cheek and a long trail of drool dangles precariously over my face.

"*Dumbledore!* Dumbledore—get off!" I hiss, sitting bolt upright and swiping the cat away. He jumps off the bed, nose in the air, his little bell jangling petulantly as he trots off to find his next victim.

Ugh! I wipe my cheek. *Gross! Why does he always pick on me?*

I glance at the bedside clock. *Four-thirty a.m.?* I groan and flop back on my pillow, wide awake now.

I stare at the window, the faint moonlight glowing through the thin curtains, the dark branches dancing back and forth with the breeze.

Four-thirty-two a.m.

I look across at Melissa splayed on her bed, snoring loudly, oblivious. Typical. I roll over, burying my head in my pillow, restless and wakeful. This is so unlike me! Normally I sleep like a log, straight through my alarm and into next Tuesday, given half a chance. Not like Dad, who's always up at the crack of dawn.

Dad.

My heart twists suddenly, remembering him standing there, so hurt, so dejected. It wasn't fair. He didn't know—he didn't *know* he wasn't my dad all these years . . . This has all been an incredible shock—for both of us. And how do I react when I find out? My words ring painfully in my ears.

You're not my father!

I fumble for my cell phone. Fifteen missed calls. My heart sinks as the first message begins:

"Holly—Holly, sweetheart, please come home. I love you so much, just please come home—"

I click it off, scramble into my jeans and run downstairs, the cold air hitting me like a slap in the face—my wake-up call—as suddenly I'm running down the street, the wind in my hair, the lampposts smiling down at me.

I'm coming, Dad, I'm coming.

I'm coming home.

Rosie

I open my eyes and stare miserably at the ceiling. It's no good. I've been lying here, wide awake, for ages, the events of the past twenty-four hours swirling and spinning round my head, refusing to let me sleep. What they said—what I said—what I didn't say—what I *should* have said . . . whether I should've said *anything* . . .

I sigh and gently slide out of bed, careful not to wake Andy snoring softly beside me. I shiver as my feet hit the floor, and pad out onto the landing.

I flick the bathroom light on and stare at myself in the mirror.

So this is what they see. This is the girl who waltzed in and turned their world upside down. Who took everything they knew and threw it out the window. Who's imposed herself on their lives—their family. I sigh heavily, covering my face with my hands.

It's up to them now. It's all up to them. I've done my bit. The snow globe is well and truly shaken up. Who knows how it will settle this time . . . if it ever will.

I close my eyes and dip my head to the tap, drinking the cold water as it flows over my lips, cool and soothing and numbing.

"Holly?"

I jump at the voice, bashing my lip on the tap and spilling water down my front.

"Sorry!" Jack says, backing out of the bathroom. "Sorry, Rosie—I didn't mean to scare you, I thought you were— Sorry."

"What time is it?" I yawn, taking in his jeans and woolly sweater. It's still pitch black and freezing.

"Four-thirty-three," he says. "Couldn't sleep?"

I shake my head. "My mind won't keep still."

He nods. "Yes, there's—well, there's a lot to think about."

I nod. "You?"

He shakes his head. "I've been looking up Huntington's online, trying to get my head around it all." He rubs his eyes. "But there's only so much you can take in."

Don't I know it. "If you want to talk, or have any questions . . ."

"Thank you." He nods. "But right now I just need some air—I'm heading down to the fish market. No rest for the wicked." He smiles. "Good night."

"Good *morning.*" I smile, heading into my bedroom.

"Actually, Rosie . . ." He follows me. "Rosie, would you—"

Andy grunts in his sleep and rolls over.

"Oh!" Jack starts, backing away into the hallway. "Oh, God, I'm sorry—"

"It's okay." I pull the door closed, following him. "Jack?"

"Sorry, I—I didn't know—I was just going to say—to ask, really—since we're both up . . ." He clears his throat. "I'm heading down to the market now—as I said—and I just wondered . . ." He frowns suddenly. "Sorry. Forget it, go back to bed."

"I'd love to come." I smile.

"You would?"

I nod. "Just give me five minutes to throw some clothes on and I'll see you downstairs."

He stares at me, surprised. "Right. Great!" He turns to leave but doesn't move.

"So, you and Andy . . . ," he begins. "The two of you, you're . . . close?" He glances at me.

I smile. "Yeah, we're . . . close."

He nods, takes a deep breath. "Right. Lots to learn." He smiles shyly. "I'll see you downstairs?"

"Five minutes," I confirm.

"Right."

I smile as he disappears down the stairs. He's right, there is a lot to learn. Father and daughter and we don't know the first thing about each other. Well, there's no time like the present, even if it is the middle of the night—and freezing!

Holly

A stitch stabs at my side as I finally round the corner onto our street. I race up the steps at the back of the house, scrabble under the mat for the spare key and rush into the kitchen.

"Dad?" I fumble for the light switch and knock something off the counter. "Dad?" I race upstairs. "Dad?"

"Holly?" Megan opens her bedroom door. "Jeez, you scared the life out of me. Are you okay?"

"Where's Dad?" I ask urgently, looking past her at the empty bed.

"He's gone to the fish market, sweetie," Megan says. "It's Monday."

The fish market. My heart sinks. I should've remembered.

"Are you all right?" she asks anxiously.

"Yes," I say, my breath in starts. "Yes, I'm fine, I just—I just really wanted to see him—to tell him . . ."

"Oh, sweetheart, he knows." Megan pulls me into a tight hug. "He'll be so glad to see you." She kisses my hair. *"I'm* so glad to see you."

"Holly?" Ben's door opens and he rubs his eyes sleepily.

"Hey, Benji-bear!" I smile, hugging him close, breathing in his sweet little-boy smell. "How's my favorite cuddle monster?"

"Good!" he cries, giving me a sloppy kiss and clamping his pudgy arms around my neck.

"We're just glad you're home," Megan says, stroking my hair tenderly, and I crumble, melting in their warmth. *Home.*

"Yeah." I smile, drying my tears against Ben's soft pajamas as he snuggles up to me, so warm, so familiar. "Me too."

"Do any of you know where Rosie is?"

I look up, surprised. Rosie's boyfriend is standing in the doorway of the spare room. In pajamas.

"I just woke up," he says. "She's gone."

Megan glances at him, then looks at me. She hesitates.

My stomach hardens. "He's with *Rosie?*"

Rosie

It's still pitch black when we reach the fish market, but the place is already bustling. Fishermen unload their glistening wares while customers jostle and crowd round the counters, scouring the writing mass for the biggest and best fish from the morning's catch. I huddle deeper into the padded jacket Jack's lent me, burrowing my face away from the biting cold—and the stench!

"Fragrant, huh?" Jack returns proudly with his fish gleaming like treasure in his box. He lifts it up and inhales deeply. "Poo-ee! I love the smell of fresh fish in the morning!" He grins at me, his cheeks pink from the cold, his eyes sparkling. "Brr! We're lucky it's not snowing."

I stare at him. "Are you serious? You come down here in the snow? In the middle of the night?"

Jack laughs. "It's not night—it's morning! See?" He nods toward the churning mass of black sea slapping at the shingle, and the horizon beyond. The sun is just creeping up over the edge, and the beginnings of color are returning to the world. "Isn't it beautiful?"

I shiver in his jacket and he laughs.

"Come on," he says, "let's dump these and grab a hot drink to warm up. There's a greasy spoon over there that does a mean hot chocolate."

"With marshmallows?" I mumble through the coat, my nose an icicle.

"Is there any other kind?" He grins, leading the way.

Holly

"She's still here?" I look at Megan accusingly as she pours tea into three mugs. "She stayed the night? *Here?*"

"I'm gonna—I'm just gonna go get . . ." Rosie's boyfriend gestures to the door. "I'm just gonna go." He disappears back upstairs.

"It was late, sweetie." Megan hands me a mug and leads me into the living room. "She had nowhere else to go."

"How about back to England?" I mutter, taking a sip of tea. It burns my tongue.

Megan sinks onto the sofa and sighs. "I can't imagine what you're feeling right now. It's an awful shock, but . . . Rosie might be his daughter, sweetie."

"*I'm* his daughter!" I protest, my eyes stinging. "Aren't I enough?" I stare at her, daring her to answer. "Maybe I should just go away and leave them to it."

"Don't be ridiculous. Holly, you mean the world to your dad. You should have seen him last night—he was beside himself with worry."

"Yeah, so worried he replaced me, huh?"

"Holly!"

"Well, it's true, isn't it? He's got a new daughter now." I hug my knees. "His real one."

"That's not true! Holly, don't even think it. Your dad loves you so much—"

"Yeah, but he's not my dad, is he?"

"He'll always be your dad!"

"It's not the same, though—it's not biological. He's *her* dad now."

"Holly, we don't even know that—not for sure! They did a test last night—let's wait for the results before—"

"What's the point?" I sigh. "He *knows* she's his—he looks at her and he sees *her mother*—Katharine—doesn't he? Look at me! I'm a redhead—I stand out like a sore thumb! No wonder she didn't want me—she *knew* I was a mistake, an impostor . . ."

"Holly, that's ridiculous."

"Is it?" I bite my lip hard, twisting my finger tightly in my hair—my horrible ugly, traitorous red hair.

"Look at me," Megan says suddenly. "Look at me, Holly. I'm not your biological mother—I never was and I never will be." She squeezes my hand. "But do you think that I love you any less? That any of this matters to me? To Ben?"

I look at him, carefully building his tower of wooden blocks—painstakingly adding one and then another, only for them all to come crashing down. Like my life. My heart aches. *Dad's not the only one I could lose . . .*

"That's not the same," I sigh. "Ben doesn't know the difference."

"Exactly. Exactly, Holly—that's the point!"

"It's not! It's different!" I insist. "It's different when it's your child, a part of you . . ." I trail off, a stabbing pain in my chest.

"Okay," Megan says carefully, leaning closer and looking me in the eye. "Okay, then. Do you honestly think I love you any less than I love Ben?"

I look at her, then look at Ben, hugging my knees hard. "You must—he's *yours,* you gave birth to him—"

Megan shakes her head. "Oh, sweetie, it's just not that simple. Giving birth doesn't make you a mom," she says. "Look at this

214

Katharine woman. She abandoned her baby—she's nobody's mother. But your dad—your dad would move heaven and earth for you, and not because he thought you shared his genes, but because he loves you *so much.* It's that love that counts—that bond. You're a team. You'll get through this."

I stare into my tea, biting my lip.

"And what about Rosie?" I whisper. "How does she fit into all this?"

Megan sighs. "That's just something we're gonna have to figure out."

Rosie

We slide into a booth by the window and I clamp my hands around my steaming hot chocolate, the feeling slowly returning to my fingers, the fishy aroma lingering persistently around us.

"Isn't it spectacular?" Jack sighs, gazing out the window. "My favorite time of day."

I must admit the scarlet sunrise is beautiful—a lot more so now I'm sitting indoors feeling warm marshmallows melting in my mouth.

"If only it rose later," I muse.

Jack grins. "Sorry about that. I'm used to getting up early. My dad ran a chippie, so after my A levels I worked there for a bit while I tried to figure out what to do with my life. He always sent me down to the market at the crack of dawn to get the best fish, but I didn't mind. I kind of loved it. I fell in love with the sunrise. The peace. The promise of a brand-new day." He stares out at the golden light spreading over the horizon. "That's how I met Katharine, actually."

I stare at him. "At a fish market?"

"No!" he laughs, a deep warm sound. "No, Kathy wouldn't be caught dead at a fish market. No, she'd gone down to see the sea, she said. She was standing there, right on the beach, shivering in her miniskirt and fluffy white jacket." He pauses. "I'll always remember that jacket . . ."

I watch him closely.

"Sorry." He clears his throat. "I'm rambling. It's been so long since I've spoken of her . . ." He shakes his head. "Anyway, how'd you like your hot chocolate?"

"Please," I whisper. "Tell me."

Jack looks at me for a moment, his eyes uncertain. Then he takes a deep breath.

"She was the most beautiful girl I'd ever seen." He sighs, looking out the window, into the past. "Her hair was tangled from the wind, her mascara streaked across her cheeks, and she'd lost her shoes somehow—she was standing there barefoot on the pebbles, with goose bumps all down her legs—she was freezing—but she wouldn't leave. I offered to call her a taxi, but she refused, said she wanted to see the sun come up, that she wouldn't leave until she had."

"She'd been there all night?"

"That's what she said. At least, she'd been out all night. I doubt she'd got all dressed up to go to the beach." Jack blows on his hot chocolate, clasps the mug tightly. "Actually, she seemed sort of upset, so I decided to wait with her, make sure she was all right."

"What happened?"

"She told me to sod off!" Jack laughs. "You can't blame her, really—middle of the night, some stranger chatting her up—but I wasn't going anywhere, and neither was she. We were stubborn as mules, the pair of us. And eventually we got talking." He smiles, staring at the table.

"I kept asking her name, but she wouldn't tell me, wouldn't tell me anything about herself. She said the night was too beautiful to talk about ordinary daytime things— anything serious or personal or real. So we just talked . . . about nothing, really. Star signs and dreams . . ." He trails off, sips his hot chocolate. "Then, before we knew it, the sun had come up. She had to go and I was late with the fish. I gave her my number, hoped she'd call, but to be honest, I didn't think I'd ever see her again. But the next morning, when I went down to the market—there she was."

I smile, the cup warm in my hands.

"Well, after that it became kind of a ritual. Every night I'd go to the beach, earlier and earlier, and she was always there, staring at the sea. I took warm clothes, coffee, sleeping bags and blankets, even, anything to keep her warm—she seemed so cold all the time, her skin like ice inside her fluffy jacket. And we'd just lie there on the beach, staring at the stars, talking about nothing, or not talking at all, till the sun came up." He grins at me suddenly. "I got last pick of the fish for two whole weeks, but you know what? No one noticed," he laughs. "They didn't even care."

I look at him. "Two weeks?"

"Two wonderful weeks . . ." He sighs, swirling his cup.

217

"And then one night I turned up and she wasn't there. I waited for her all night and well into the next morning. But she didn't come. She never came again. She just disappeared."

"Did you try to find her?"

"How could I? I didn't know her name, where she lived, her phone number—I didn't know anything about her. Only her star sign. Scorpio." He sighs. "It was like she'd never existed, like I'd dreamed her up—the girl of my dreams . . .

"And then, the following winter, in the middle of the night, I get this phone call. It's Kathy, she's having our baby, she's scared. Can I come? I didn't think twice—I just dropped everything and jumped in the car. I drove for hours in the dark, hitting this dreadful storm on the way—I didn't think I'd make it. Finally, just as I was approaching the hospital, I saw Kathy running up the road. She looked exactly the same, the same fragile beauty, the same frightened, haunted look in her eyes, except this time there was something else—an urgency about her.

"I pulled over and she just stared at me for a moment, frozen. Then she burst into tears. I opened the car door and she climbed inside, crumpled over in the seat, and sobbed her heart out. I asked her about the baby—what had happened, why she'd left the hospital—but she wouldn't answer, just begged me to drive—to take her away somewhere, anywhere. So I did. I drove us to a little park and I pulled over. But still Kathy couldn't stop crying. She kept saying over and over how she'd thought I wasn't coming, that I'd left her. I tried to comfort her, told her I'd never leave her—that I'd do anything for her. She stared at me then. Just stared at me, for the longest time.

"Then she smiled, her beautiful face streaked and blotched with tears as she took my hand. 'You're a father,' she whispered, the words filling the air around us, tingling in my ears. 'You're a daddy.'"

His eyes fill and I swallow hard.

"We drove back to the hospital and Kathy took me inside, but the baby had been moved—taken to a bigger hospital for special care."

I stare at him, the breath caught in my throat. *She came back . . .*

"So we followed," Jack says, his expression softening. "I couldn't believe it when I saw her—this tiny precious little person, so small, so fragile inside her incubator, fighting for her life.

"'She's yours,' Kathy told me, showing me the identity bracelet—the name she'd chosen. *Holly Woods.* 'She's all yours.' I just stared at her, at this tiny miracle with my name, and the earth moved beneath me. It was the most incredible moment of my life. Suddenly I was a father." He looks at me and smiles. My insides glow.

"Kathy seemed so relieved. She started collecting her things, giving me instructions. I was confused, I didn't understand. Then it dawned on me. She was leaving—and she wanted to leave the baby with me.

"I tried to convince her that everything would be all right, that I'd look after her and the baby, but she refused—she couldn't be a mother, she said, she was only seventeen. I hadn't known she was that young . . . She grew hysterical, saying no one knew, no one *could* know—that it was *our* secret. That she was relying on me.

"Nothing I said made any difference. The baby was mine, Kathy said, or else she'd give her up for adoption—end of story. She was so upset, I agreed. Of course I'd take the baby, look after her, love her. I was convinced Kathy would change her mind, you see. I thought if I just stuck around long enough she'd have a change of heart—that we'd be a family . . .

"And for a while it seemed to work. Holly had to stay in the special unit at the hospital, so I booked us into a nearby hotel in town, and the next day Kathy seemed much calmer, we even registered the birth together, that's how I finally discovered her name. Katharine." He smiles. "I always think of her as Kathy—like Cathy from *Wuthering Heights*—so wild and untameable, so fragile . . .

"I visited Holly in the Unit every day, and sometimes Kathy would come with me. She seemed to be getting much better—I was convinced that once the shock wore off, that once Holly was fully recovered and we could bring her home . . ."

Jack sighs suddenly. "But the day I brought Holly back from the hospital, Kathy was gone."

I stare at him, frozen.

"She left a note—she was sorry, she'd gone to California, I shouldn't try to find her, please look after Holly." He rubs his brow. "I . . . didn't know what to do. I took Holly home to my parents, and they went ballistic, told me I was an idiot—how did I know she was even mine?—that I shouldn't let some slapper ruin my life. Then, when I told them I was keeping the baby, they threw me out."

I gasp.

Jack shrugs. "They didn't understand. Holly was my *daughter*—I loved her more than anything in the world, except—" He swallows. "So I left. My grandparents lived in San Francisco, so Holly and I got on a plane, stayed with them, and I got a job in a fish restaurant while I tried to find Katharine. I was sure she'd have come to her senses by now, knew she'd regret abandoning her baby for the rest of her life . . ." He sighs. "But it was hopeless. She'd vanished. Again. By the time Holly was old enough to ask questions I decided to tell her that her mother had died. It seemed easier somehow. Kinder . . .

"Then I met Megan." He smiles. "The girl with the sunshine in her hair. And the rest is history. Her folks lived on the East Coast, so we moved here, and when her granddad died we took over his restaurant, got married." He smiles. "She was so beautiful, and warm and funny, and so good with Holly—it was like everything had worked out.

"Then, about eight years ago, I got the shock of my life when I saw Katharine on TV. Calling herself Kitty now. *Kitty Clare*—no wonder I hadn't been able to find her. It was so surreal—I couldn't believe it, after all that time . . ." He shakes his head incredulously. "I wrote to her through her agent, telling her where we were, sent photos of Holly, but she didn't reply. Perhaps she never received the letter, I told myself, so I kept trying—letters, photos, a couple of times a year—via her agent, her studios, determined to give her every opportunity possible to know her daughter. But when I never heard from her again I knew I'd been right to lie to Holly. It's better to have a dead mother than one who abandoned you, right?"

He looks at me, stricken. "Rosie, I'm so sorry—I mean—"

"It's okay," I say quietly. "I know what you mean."

He sighs. "I'm not sure Holly'll see it that way, though."

"You were just trying to spare her feelings," I reason.

"Well, yes," Jack admits. "But how did you feel when you learned the truth about your mother—that she wasn't dead after all, that she was alive on the other side of the world?"

"I was angry," I admit. "I was hurt that I hadn't known the truth. But then that was all mixed up with the fear of Huntington's—of inheriting the disease. It wasn't the same. Holly's never known her mum, so she's probably more upset about you—she's frightened of losing her dad."

"She'll never lose me."

"I know." I smile. "And deep down I'm sure she does too. I'd already lost my mum when I found out she wasn't my mother. In the end, though, it doesn't affect how I feel about her. She's still my mum, she always will be. But watching her die from Huntington's . . . dreading it happening to me . . . I always thought I'd rather know the truth—about everything. Then you can find a way to deal with it."

"And now?"

"Now . . . I don't know." I sigh. "I mean, your life was a lot simpler before I came along, huh? And as for Holly . . ."

Jack sighs. "It's been a bit of a bombshell for everyone."

"Yes." I nod. "But for Holly it's going to be worse. My bombshell was finding out my dead mother wasn't my mother, that my real one was still out there, and that I was never going to inherit Huntington's—Holly's is that you're not her dad and she's at risk from a disease she's probably never even heard of. Would you want to know? Really?"

Jack considers for a moment. "There's definitely no cure?"

"No," I sigh. "Not yet."

He pauses. "And yet you wanted to know—you took the test."

I nod.

"Why?"

"I suppose I needed to know one way or the other—so I could make informed choices . . ." I trail off. "My mother . . ." My voice catches. "Trudie . . . said she might not have had children if she'd known."

Jack looks at me for a long moment, his expression unreadable, then stares into his cocoa. "Well," he says softly, stroking his thumb round the rim of the cup. "That really would have been a tragedy."

I look away, my cheeks hot, the lump in my throat the size of a watermelon.

Jack sighs. "I'll tell Holly about Huntington's. Take her out for the day, just the two of us. It should come from me."

I look up.

"She needs to know." He nods. "You're right, she needs to make an informed choice. I can't make this decision for her, and I won't lie to her anymore." He smiles sadly out the window. "My little girl's growing up." He looks at me. "Both of them are."

Holly

"It's gonna be okay," Megan says for the millionth time, pouring Ben a glass of milk while I cook pancakes, the butter swirling in the pan making my stomach turn.

"Remember, she's the outsider here." Megan squeezes my shoulders. "You and your dad—you're a rock, you're solid. Okay?"

A rock. I swallow. The only rock I'm sure of is the one lodged in my gut, growing every minute they're alone together.

Suddenly, footsteps pound up the steps outside and I freeze.

"Holly!" Dad cries, rushing through the back door and grabbing me in a hug that lifts me off my feet. "Holly-berry, thank God!"

I can't breathe, he's squeezing me so tight.

"I'm sorry I left, Dad—"

"Oh, sweetheart, I'm just so glad you're home!"

I close my eyes, the rock inside me beginning to crumble as his familiar salty smell washes over me.

Home.

"I'll just go and shower," Rosie says, squeezing past. I flinch at her touch, her voice.

"Don't you want some brekkie first?" Dad asks. "Holly makes the best pancakes." He grins at me.

"Yummy pancakes!" Ben agrees, his mouth full, and I smile tightly.

Say no, say no, I pray into the soft folds of Dad's jacket, clinging on tighter, holding my breath. *Let it just be us.*

"Thanks, but I'm not really that hun—" Her stomach growls loudly and Dad laughs, sending vibrations trembling through me.

"I think your stomach disagrees." He grins. "Come on, pull up a chair. It's been a long morning."

My heart sinks as he slips out of my grasp, leaving me cold suddenly, standing by the stove.

He pulls out a chair for Rosie and smiles at me. "You coming, Holls?"

I hesitate, unwilling to join them, reluctant to leave them alone.

"Wow!" Rosie says suddenly, taking a bite. "These are amazing!" She grins at me.

I look at her. Megan's right. Remember how Rosie must be feeling—her mother slammed the door in her face, and she's in a new place, a new country, meeting a new father . . .

My father! I slump into a chair and stab a pancake.

"Does your dad never cook you pancakes, Rosie?" I ask innocently. "Dad used to make them for breakfast for me every day when I was little." I slice a piece off and pop it in my mouth. "Did yours?"

Megan shoots me a look, but I don't care. I chew without tasting, waiting.

"Actually, no," Rosie says quietly. "No, my dad died the night I was born."

"Oh." I swallow, the pancake heavy as guilt in my stomach. "Oh, I'm sorry."

She smiles. "It's okay. I never knew him, and me and Mum did just fine on our own—though she wasn't much of a cook! She only made pancakes on Shrove Tuesday."

"Shrove what?" I ask.

225

"Shrove Tuesday, honey," Dad replies. "It's the day before Lent—pancake day."

"Oh." I frown. Some stupid British custom.

"Mum tried and tried to make pancakes, but they always stuck to the pan—or the ceiling!" Rosie laughs. "So in the end we had ice cream instead. Ice Cream Tuesday, we called it, courtesy of Saint Ben and Saint Jerry."

Dad laughs out loud, his mouth full.

"Now, that's my kind of saint's day," Megan chuckles, Ben giggling as she wipes syrup from his chin.

I hack off another piece of pancake.

"She did make mean eggy-bread, though," Rosie continues.

I frown. "What's eggy-bread?"

She looks surprised. "Oh, it's—it's like um . . ."

"It's a bit like French toast, only savory." Dad smiles. "It's delicious."

"Oh," I say, my pancake suddenly seeming very ordinary. Again with the Britishness!

"Maybe I could cook it for you sometime?" Rosie offers.

Sometime? Sometime? How long is she planning on staying?

I take another bite, tasting nothing.

"So, how was the fish market, honey?" Megan asks, sipping her tea.

"Oh, fine, fine," Dad says. "I showed Rosie all the different kinds of fish, but I don't think she appreciated them—her nose got the better of her!"

"The stench!" she laughs. "I don't know how you can bear it!"

"You get used to it." Megan smiles.

"Actually, I kinda like it," I mumble.

"I was thinking." Dad takes another pancake. "Maybe we should

226

take the boat out this morning—see if we can catch anything our-
selves?"

I glance at Megan. "What about the restaurant?"

"Oh, I'm sure Pete can cope for one day—he's always on about
wanting more responsibility." Dad smiles.

I spear another pancake. Great. Dad *never* takes days off work.
But now he makes an exception for a day alone with Rosie—how
cozy. It's so unfair. How come she gets to go traveling, to spend the
day sailing with Dad—to do whatever the hell she wants—while I
have to go to school—when we're exactly the same age?

"And I think the school will cope without you for a day—just this
once." Dad winks at me. "What d'you reckon, Holly-berry? You up
for it?"

I look up, surprised, then hesitate, imagining sitting in a boat
with Rosie and Dad all day. I think I'd actually prefer to be at school.

"I'm not sure . . . ," I begin, reaching for the maple syrup. "I've
got a swim meet this afternoon, and—"

"Come on, Holly, you love sailing. I can't go out on my own—I'd
be a right Billy-no-mates."

I look up. *On his own?* "But I thought—" I glance at Rosie.

"Megan and Ben have got a playdate, and Rosie here has got
plans with her—her young man. Isn't that right?"

Rosie nods, smiling as she chews.

"So, what do you say?" Dad grins at me. "Just the two of us?
Unless you're ashamed to be seen out with your old dad?"

I smile at him, the mug of tea toasty in my hands. "Okay."

"That's my girl." Dad winks.

I glance at Rosie, who looks quickly at her plate.

Okay, I think, so maybe I should give her a chance. I take a sip
of my tea.

"So, tell me about your mom, Rosie," I venture, the tea warm and sweet as it slides down my throat. "Besides that she's not the world's greatest cook."

She smiles. "World's most dangerous cook, more like. I've lost count of the number of explosions that came from our kitchen. Once we even had to call the fire brigade!" She laughs. "She was trying to cook potatoes in her new pressure cooker—and it just exploded! We were scraping mashed potato off the ceiling for weeks!" She grins. "But she made it into a game—she pretended it was snow, and we made little potato snowmen and drew faces on the windows—pretty gross, really, but I was only little and I loved it." She smiles wistfully.

"She made everything fun like that. Like we never had ordinary toast—it was always cut into animal shapes or smiley faces. When it was really burned she'd cut it into bats and pretend it was *supposed* to be black!"

I smile despite myself. "What else? Tell me about her."

Rosie smiles, chewing thoughtfully. "Well, besides the fact you're the absolute spitting image of her . . ."

I feel my cheeks grow warm.

"She used to be a children's book illustrator—she loved to paint, draw, sculpt—she adored creating stuff out of nothing."

I think of my driftwood sculptures. So that's where I get it from.

Rosie grins. "For my fifth birthday I desperately wanted a doll's house—this fancy one I'd seen in the toy shop, but it was really expensive. So Mum made me one. A gingerbread house. God, it was wonderful. It had fairy lights all round the roof, and the driveway was made of popping candy. It was magical. I loved it so much I couldn't bear to eat it."

I smile, imagining it twinkling on the table.

"She used to dance when she was younger, too—she once dreamed of becoming a ballerina, my nana told me."

Nana? My heart flips. *I have a nana too?*

"She'd run, swim, dance, anything to release her energy—it was boundless!"

My hearts beats loudly. So she was a swimmer too.

"And her sense of humor!" Rosie laughs. "God, the stitches I've suffered from her jokes and pranks—she was hysterical. And her fashion sense . . . Inimitable." She grins. "Nobody could ever tell my mother what to wear."

"She sounds wonderful," I muse dreamily.

"She was," Rosie sighs. "She really was."

My heart stops.

Did I hear her right?

I stare at her, my voice a whisper. *"Was?"*

Rosie looks up at me, surprise turning to confusion, then fear. She glances quickly at Dad.

"You mean she . . ." I falter, the words forming hollowly on my lips. "She's *dead*?"

Rosie looks away.

"My mom is *dead*?" I feel sick, all my resurrected dreams of my mother melting away like last year's snow, trampled to dirt. *I don't have a mother. I still don't have a mother. I never will . . .*

"Holly . . ." Dad squeezes my arm. "Sweetheart, I'm so sorry. I—"

"How?" I ask suddenly, turning to Rosie. "When?"

She hesitates, and looks at Dad.

"Holly," he soothes. "Holly, I really don't think—"

"When?" I persist, my voice mottled with tears. "She was *my* mother. I have the right to know." I look at Rosie. "Well?"

229

"Last month," she says quietly. "She died just before Christmas."

I stare at her. So recently. She was alive last month. There's a DVD in my room, a Christmas present, still in its cellophane, unwatched. She was alive when it was bought—when it was wrapped, maybe. I stare down at the table, at nothing.

"How?" I whisper.

Silence.

"How?" I demand. Rosie's looking at Dad, fear etched across her face.

"I can't—"

I slam my fist on the table, making her jump. "Tell me!"

"I *can't!*"

"Why not?" I yell at her. "What difference does it make? She's still dead!"

"Holly—" Dad squeezes my hand as Ben begins to whimper.

Rosie looks away. "You don't understand—"

"Oh, I understand, I understand just fine." I spit the words at her. "Your family died, so you thought you'd come on over the Atlantic and take *mine*? You thought you'd just waltz over here and pick up a mom in New York and a dad in New England and everything would be hunky-dory?" I lean closer. "Except it didn't work like that, did it? Your mom didn't want you. She never did. She slammed the door in your face—"

Rosie flinches.

"Holly!" Dad barks.

"So you thought you'd come here?" I continue. "Third-time lucky? To my home, my *family* and take *my dad*?"

Megan cuddles Ben close as they leave the room.

"It's not like that!" Rosie's voice is surprisingly strong, her eyes shining. "It's not like that—I didn't even know you existed—I thought you'd died!"

"Well, wouldn't that have been convenient?" I say, sneering.

"I thought you were dead," she repeats, "and when I found out you weren't, I . . . I wanted to just walk away. I never wanted to hurt you—"

"Then why did you?" I yell at her. "There are plenty of planes leaving every day—you could have left any time! Why didn't you?"

"I couldn't."

"Why? Because you'd found your dad, and that was all that mattered to you? Screw everyone else—who cares how many lives you ruin?"

"No!"

"Holly—" Dad takes my arm.

"Yes!" I scream at her, shrugging him away. "Yes—you're a self-ish bitch!"

"No." Rosie's voice is quiet now, determined. Her eyes meet mine. "You had to know."

"Really?" My voice drips with sarcasm. "I just *had* to know that my dad's not really my dad, that my whole life is one big lie, except—oh, yeah—my mom's still dead!" I glare at her. "I just couldn't live without that knowledge a second longer, could I?"

"You had to know—"

"Rosie—" Dad warns.

"She has to know!" Her eyes are desperate, fraught.

"Know what?" I stare at him, icy dread trickling slowly down my spine. "Dad? Know what?"

"Trudie died—" Rosie begins.

"Yeah, thanks, I got that."

231

"Of Huntington's disease." She looks at me, then drops her eyes to the floor, screws them shut.

Dad sighs heavily.

"What?" I frown, staring at her, at Dad. Have I missed something? "Like I said, what difference does it make?" I look from one to the other insistently. "What the hell is Hunting's disease, anyway?"

"Huntington's disease," Rosie corrects me quietly, her voice strained, her gaze glued to the floor. "It's a terminal illness—a deterioration of the mind, the body . . ."

I stare at her, mystified. *So?*

She looks at me, her eyes sad, regretful. "Holly, I'm so sorry . . ."

I don't breathe. I just watch her eyes well up with pain and regret, my heart poised on a knife edge.

"It's hereditary."

Rosie

My words slice through the room, sharp and swift and brutal, leaving everyone deathly silent. Holly stares at me numbly, but I can't meet her eyes.

"Holly—" Jack whispers. He takes her hand but she doesn't move.

I stare at the floor, my cheeks burning. Now I know how Pandora felt.

"Sweetheart, it's okay, it's gonna be okay," Jack soothes, stroking her hand.

"How?" She looks at him with the same blank expression. "It's hereditary . . . I'm gonna die?"

"No," Jack tells her, his eyes intense, his voice breaking. "No, you're not—it's not even definite you've inherited it—it's just a chance."

She stares at him. "What chance?"

Jack hesitates, swallows. "Fifty percent. Right, Rosie?" He looks at me.

I nod absently. I feel Holly's eyes on me but I can't look.

"That's all, just fifty percent—you're just as likely not to have it. Okay, Holly-berry?" he says, his voice infused with determined hope, with fear. "Okay?"

I squeeze my eyes shut tight, remembering those same words being said to me, feeling Holly's pain as the realization sinks in. I was wrong—it's not always best to know the truth. Ignorance is bliss, isn't that what they say? And I've just shattered her ignorance, her bliss, her life, with this one foul sledgehammer of truth.

Holly's right. I am selfish. If only I could have left well alone, walked away . . .

I scrape my chair back, shattering the silence.

"I'm sorry." I stand up, my face hot as I stumble toward the door. "I'm so sorry. I'll get out of your way, I'll—"

"Rosie . . ." Jack's voice is gentle but still stings.

"I'm so sorry." I flee quickly through the door, running as I hit the steps, the raindrops spitting at my face.

She *had* to know, I tell myself, blinking hard, trying to block out the image of her face—blanched with shock, staring wide-eyed as I ripped her world apart. *She had to know . . .*

Didn't she?

Holly

I watch Rosie leave, hammering down the steps like thunder. Dad looks at me anxiously, his grip tight on my hand, waiting for me to react. But I can't.

Everything feels unreal, somehow—like I'm watching myself from a distance, like I've left my body. Like I'm already dead.

Even the sharp buzz of my cell phone doesn't make me jump. I stare at the illuminated screen.

Josh.

God, Josh. My fiancé. The fiancé I was scared to burden by telling him I was pregnant. Now I've got a terminal illness too.

I stare at the phone as it shudders violently on the table. Megan glances at Dad, then silently reaches over and turns it off.

"Holly . . . ," Dad starts. "Holly-berry, talk to me . . ."

I shake my head, a tiny movement, all I can manage.

"It'll be okay, you'll see . . ."

I shake my head harder, cold sweat trickling down my neck.

"It will, I promise—you probably don't even have the disease—and even if you do— Holly!" I lunge for the sink, my knees buckling as I heave my guts out over the dirty dishes.

"Shhh," Dad soothes, his arms around me as he brushes my hair back from my face. "It's all right, it'll be okay . . ."

"How . . . ," I whimper, wiping my wrist across my mouth, my skin cold and clammy, my voice hoarse. "How did this happen . . . ?"

He sighs heavily. "I don't know, sweetheart." He looks at me helplessly, his eyes the saddest I've ever seen them. "I have no idea."

Rosie

The raindrops blur into my tears as I stare out blankly across the beach, at the wispy sea grass billowing in the wind, the boats bobbing up and down on the churning gray sea. I wish I could just get in one and sail far, far away . . .

"Rose? Rosie!" I turn at the sound of Andy's voice.

"What're you doing out here? It's raining!" He hurries down the road toward me, a rucksack over each shoulder. "Here, put this on." He drops the bags onto the sand and throws me a waterproof jacket. "Thought we might need our stuff from the B and B." He grins. "As we're staying."

I close my eyes.

"So where'd you get to, early bird?" he asks. "I woke up at the crack of dawn and you'd disappeared!"

"I'm sorry." I sigh, the words too familiar on my lips.

"Where were you?" he says. "I tried your phone . . ."

"I'm sorry, I forgot it," I say, rubbing my face. "I was with Jack, we went to the fish market."

"Right." He nods. "Well, next time leave a note or something, will you? I was worried."

"*I'm sorry!*" I turn on him. "I'm sorry, I'm sorry, I'm sorry—*okay?*" Tears sting my eyes and I look away, my breath shuddering in my chest.

"Rosie . . ." He wraps his arm gently round my shoulders. "Rosie, what's the matter? What's happened?"

I look at him, a wave of hopelessness crashing over

me. "Holly knows," I tell him miserably. "I told her about Mum—about Huntington's. Jack asked me not to—he wanted to tell her himself—but oh, no, me and my stupid big mouth!"

"Hey," Andy soothes. "Rosie, she was going to find out sometime. It doesn't really matter how . . ."

"No," I shake my head wretchedly. "You weren't there, Andy, you didn't see her face . . ." I close my eyes. "She's just so . . . broken. And it's all my fault!"

"No." Andy says firmly. "No, Rosie, none of this is your fault."

"Yes, it *is*!" I insist. "I've *ruined* their lives, Andy! I could have walked away—I *should* have walked away. This was a huge mistake. I have to go!" I grab my bag and sling it over my shoulder, standing up.

"Okay." Andy stands. "Okay, we'll go—we'll go on down to my aunt in Washington, we just need to call a cab, say goodbye, then—"

"No." I shake my head. "I can't—I can't go back in that house."

"Rosie, you owe Jack that much. You can't just disappear without telling him," he says softly. "He's your dad."

I dig my shoes into the sand, thinking of the fish market, the café, the warmth of Jack's arms as he hugged me close. My *dad* . . .

"Just . . . say goodbye, and we'll go, we're out of here—we don't ever have to come back, okay?" Andy searches my eyes. "If that's really what you want."

I take a deep breath, my throat swelling as I gaze up at

the clapboard house, the restaurant with its wooden sign creaking in the salty breeze . . .

I swallow hard. "It is."

Holly

I watch the raindrops sliding like tears down the window as Megan pours me yet another cup of tea.

"So . . ." I stare into the swirling depths of my mug. "How long do I have?"

"Oh, sweetheart," Dad sighs. "It's not like that—you might not even *have*—"

"How long?" I look at him.

He glances at Megan, then sighs again. "I did a bit of research last night, and most of the Websites I found said it usually doesn't even start until middle age. Trudie didn't even know she had it when Ro—" He stops himself, strokes my hand. "When you were born."

I nod, considering. "Then how long till I die? Once it starts?"

"I don't know," he admits. "It varies I think—it depends . . ." He frowns. "You should talk to Rosie."

I look at him quickly.

He squeezes my hand. "She knows better than anyone," he says gently. "She was her mother's caregiver."

I stare at him. A caregiver? I'm going to need a *caregiver*?

"But sweetheart, we don't even know you've got it," he says swiftly, reading my fear. "There's a test you can take, if you want to, to find out if you definitely have the gene—"

"If I *want* to? Why wouldn't I?"

"Well, some people don't, they'd rather not know—afraid a positive result will affect their lives too much—"

"Well, duh—they're gonna die!" I laugh, a short sharp bitter sound.

"No," Dad says gently. "Their life before the disease. Their jobs, their careers, their marriages . . ."

"Why?" I frown. "Why would it affect that?"

"Well . . ." Dad hesitates. "From what I can gather online, some people are scared their employers might discriminate against them, or they're afraid they'll become a burden on their partners—"

"Josh would stand by me," I tell him firmly. "He loves me."

"I'm sure he would." Dad smiles, stroking my hand. "But does he want children?"

"Why?" I freeze. "What do you mean?"

"Sweetheart." He swallows. "Some people . . . they decide—they're afraid to have children . . ." He looks at me, his voice careful, his eyes sad. "I mean, it is hereditary . . ."

My hand goes limp in his, his words forming an icy fist around my heart.

This could get my baby too . . .

"Rosie said that Trudie—" He stops himself. "Sweetie—"

"What?" I interrupt. "What did Rosie say?"

"Nothing, it doesn't matter."

"Tell me," I command, my voice wobbly. The authority of the terminally ill.

He shifts uncomfortably. "Rosie said that Trudie, if she'd known . . ." He sighs. "She might not have had children."

I close my eyes.

She wouldn't have had children . . . I would never have been born . . .

"But she was so glad she did," Dad insists, squeezing my hand. "That's an argument *against* having the test, if you look at it that way. Maybe it's better to live your life, regardless of what may or may not happen in the future. Anyone could fall under a bus!"

His words wash over me, my head spinning in painful circles.

She wouldn't have had children—I shouldn't have children—I shouldn't have this child . . .

"He's right, Holly," Megan says. "Maybe it's better not to know."

"I have to know!" I yell, my words louder, harsher than intended. "I have to—this is my life—my *future* . . ." *My baby* . . . My throat stings. "I might have this . . . *disease,* and I don't even know what it is—I've never even heard of it!"

"You're right," Megan says gently, glancing at Dad. "We don't know anything about it, not really. But Rosie does."

"I'm not talking to her, that selfish bitch!"

"I know it's hard, but she knows what you're going through," Dad soothes. "She can help you."

"I don't need her help!" I explode. "I don't need anything from her—this is her fault!" I screw my eyes closed, the pain unbearable. "If she hadn't—if we hadn't—"

"If you hadn't been swapped at birth you'd have watched your mother die from Huntington's, just like she did," Dad says evenly. "You'd have wondered every day if you were going to inherit it, just like she did. And now you'd be in exactly the same position you're in now. But you'd be all alone," he says. "Like she was."

I look away, a lump in my throat.

"None of this is her fault, Holly. Who can blame her for wanting to find her real parents? But when she met you she was willing to walk away and leave us all. She only stayed because she knows how awful it is to live not knowing. She's been there, Holly. She's been through it all, and she thought you had the right to know, to decide for yourself, to choose."

To choose.

Images of the Planned Parenthood clinic flash back to me. *To choose . . .*

Trudie said she wouldn't have had children . . .

"I'm scared," I whisper, tears streaking my cheeks. "Daddy, I'm so scared."

"I know." Dad kisses my head fiercely, his stubble rough and scratchy as he holds me tight. "I know. Me too." His tears slide into my hair, warm and wet. "We'll get through this," he promises, his voice cracking and breaking my heart. "We will. You'll see. Together we can beat anything."

I cling to him like a child, desperately holding on, trying to believe him.

"You okay, Holly?"

I blink as Ben appears in the doorway, his eyes wide with concern.

I nod quickly, biting my lip, unable to speak. He pads over and climbs onto my lap, his short arms looping my neck tightly as Dad hugs us both, holding us together. I pull Ben close, my heart aching as I breathe him in, this precious child—perhaps the only child I'll ever hold this way—the nearest I'll ever get to a child of my own . . . I kiss his hair, pulling him as close as possible, tears flooding my eyes.

I never knew my mother; now I'll probably never be one.

"Why didn't you tell me, Daddy?"

"What?" he whispers.

"About Mom—Kitty, I mean." I swallow painfully. "Why didn't you tell me the truth?"

"Oh, sweetheart, I'm so sorry." He kisses my hair. "I thought I could protect you—I thought . . . She left us, Holly-berry. She didn't deserve you. She didn't know what she was missing . . ."

"She was still my mom," I whisper, Ben warm and heavy in my arms. "I mean—"

"You're right." Dad strokes my hair from my face, looks at me. "I'm sorry, I was wrong. You had a right to know. I'll never keep anything from you again, sweetheart. I promise." He links his pinkie with mine like we used to when I was little. "No more secrets, okay?" He wipes a tear from my cheek. "From now on, we'll tell each other everything. Okay?"

I look at him, his eyes so sad, and I nod, fresh tears spilling down my cheeks. I squeeze my eyes shut, take a deep breath. "Daddy—"

A knock at the back door stops my breath. Rosie slowly creaks it open, a large bag over her shoulder, Andy behind her.

"Sorry—I—didn't mean to interrupt," she stammers, her eyes glued nervously to mine. "I just—we just came to say . . ." She swallows. "We've called a taxi—we're leaving." The words tumble out quickly as she looks from Dad to me, her eyes filling. "I'm so sorry—I never meant to—" Her voice cracks as she blinks quickly. "I'm so sorry." She moves to leave.

"Wait," I say, my voice hoarse.

She stops, her hand on the doorknob.

"You don't—you don't have to go."

She hesitates, her eyes flicking anxiously from me to Dad. She shakes her head. "I really should—"

"Maybe it's for the best, Holly-berry," Dad says, stroking my hair. "Just for now, give us some time."

"No," I say, my voice stronger now. "No, it's okay." I can't believe what I'm doing, what I'm saying. I can't stand her, can't stand the thought of her in my house, my home, but . . . but I need to know more.

"You should stay." I swallow. "If you don't mind . . . I have some questions."

She looks at me, a sad recognition in her eyes.

"Of course," she says gently, sliding her bag to the floor. "Of course."

"Maybe we should give you guys some space," Megan suggests, lifting Ben gently from my arms and glancing meaningfully at Andy. "Some time alone together, to talk . . ."

"Good idea." Dad smiles gratefully.

Andy looks at Rosie, who nods absently, her gaze glued to mine, searching my eyes.

"Yeah." He nods, plunging his hands in his pockets and following Megan outside. "Yeah, good idea."

The door closes behind them.

And then there were three.

"So," Rosie sighs, sinking slowly into a chair. "Where should I begin?"

Rosie

We talk for hours, the shadows lengthening slowly across the kitchen as Holly twirls her finger endlessly in her hair, listening silently.

I tell her about Mum: about life before and after her

onset; about the test, the different stages of counseling I went through, what it was like waiting for the result. I try to emphasize the positive—that it's nowhere near certain she's got the gene, that even if she does, she could still have a long and healthy life—that there's no reason why she can't still do everything she's ever wanted . . .

But in her eyes I see it all: my own fear, my own hopelessness. In the end they're just words. In the end it's her life.

"Okay," Holly says finally. "Okay, enough for now."

I nod. "It's a lot to take in."

She nods, her thoughts a million miles away.

"How about I make us some nice hot soup?" Jack suggests brightly. "I don't know about you girls, but I'm starving!" He turns to Holly. "What d'you think, Holls? I'll even rustle up some crunchy croutons for you." He ruffles her hair.

"What?" She looks up at him blankly. "Oh, not for me, thanks."

"Are you sure?" Jack frowns. "Or are you just holding out for my famous fresh-baked rolls to dunk in it?"

She smiles weakly. "No."

"Okay then, anything you like. Pasta? Chili? Burgers? I know!" He grins. "Fish and chips!"

Holly smiles faintly.

"Thanks, but I'm really not hungry." She scrapes her chair back from the table. "I think I might go out on my bike for a while—I could do with some air."

"Are you sure?" Jack asks anxiously. "Shall I come with you?"

"I can leave," I add quickly. "You don't have to go—"

"I'm fine, really," Holly insists gently, her movements

243

slow, steady. "You guys enjoy your soup." She walks out the back door, closing it slowly behind her.

Jack sighs, his head sinking into his hands. He seems to have aged so much in just a day. "My little girl . . ."

"I really am sorry," I say helplessly.

"It's not your fault," Jack tells me, looking up. "And thank you for talking to her." He smiles weakly, his eyes tired. "It can't have been easy going through all that again, but I think it really helped."

I shake my head. "It's the least I can do, after . . . Anything I can do to help, anything . . ."

"I'm not sure there's much any of us really *can* do." Jack sighs. "Apart from just being here for her, as long as it takes."

I nod. That, at least, I can do.

"And you can help me eat some soup!" Jack pushes himself up from the table. "What flavor do you like? Tomato? Mushroom? Minestrone?"

"Anything as long as it's hot." I smile.

"Great. The same for Andy?"

Shit. Andy.

Holly

I ride on autopilot, just concentrating on breathing, on pedaling, the wind streaming through my hair, Rosie's words washing in and out of my mind like the tide.

Chorea.

Mood swings.

Disabled.

Nursing home.

Hereditary.

Fatal.

I cycle harder, trying to outpace them, to blot them out as I race through the dark dappled shadows of the forest. But they're still there. They always will be.

I break out of the trees and there they are, the endless undulating desert of dunes, beautiful and terrifying, windswept and barren, and as empty and bleak as my future.

Maybe this is my punishment for not being ambitious, for not being academic, for wasting my life on sports and sculptures and having no real aspirations or goals. You leave your future empty, and something's bound to come along to fill it up . . .

But I *did* have dreams. I blink against the wind, the tears. I had hopes. Maybe not academically, vocationally . . . but I'm *engaged*— that must mean *something*?

I sail down one dune and struggle up another, lost in the sea of sand. *But what now? What'll happen to me? To Josh? To our life together?*

To our baby.

I skid to a stop, throw down my bike and collapse onto the cool silky sand, hugging my knees as I watch the dying sun drown in the endless ocean.

It'll be okay, I tell myself, forcing myself to take deep breaths. *It'll be all right. Josh loves me—he promised—till death do us part . . .*

However long that'll be.

I blink quickly, reaching into my pocket for my cell phone; I turn it on.

Seven missed calls. All Josh. I press Redial, then hold my breath.

245

It rings for a few seconds, then goes to voice mail.

"Josh, please call." I hesitate, unsure what to say next, the words I need to say playing dangerously on my lips. I close my eyes, take a deep breath, but I can't—can't tell him. Not over the phone.

"I love you," I sigh, the words snatched away on the wind as I hang up quickly, swallowing hard, trying to stifle the questions, the fear rising in my chest.

Do you love me?

Did you mean it when you said you'd always love me, no matter what?

Even if I might have Huntington's disease?

I close my eyes.

And I'm pregnant.

Rosie

I check Andy's text again as I hurry up the hill toward the glowing neon-pink café, its rainbow flag fluttering proudly beside the Stars and Stripes. Provincetown keeps surprising me with its mix of old-world charm—clapboard houses, traditional churches and tributes to the Pilgrims—nestled harmoniously next to brightly graffitied shops, weird sculptures, vibrant art galleries and a liberal gay scene.

I double-check my phone, making sure there're no new messages. He's sent four since I saw him—the first from another café, then an art gallery, then the library and the last from right here. I push open the glass door, sending a little bell jangling merrily as I scour the white wicker tables, bean-bags and hammocks lit by a festival of colorful paper lanterns.

"I canceled the taxi."

I turn to see Andy sitting alone at a table beneath a fluffy pink lamp, his rucksack slumped beside him.

"There you are!" I smile, walking over. "I wasn't sure I'd got the right place—this doesn't really seem like your scene."

He shrugs. "It's dry, it's open. Nearly everywhere else shut at five."

"I'm sorry," I say, sliding into a chair. "I lost track of time. Holly wanted to talk—about everything. It helped, I think."

"That's good." He smiles tiredly.

"Yeah, yeah it is." I nod. "Anything I can do to make this better, right?"

"Right." He nods, stroking my hand. "So I take it you don't want to leave, then?"

"No." I shake my head. "No, they need me here."

He nods. "They're your family."

"*They are.*" I beam, warmth flooding through me. "And I think I might actually be able to do some good now—help Holly through this—salvage something from this whole mess."

"That's great, Rose." Andy squeezes my hand. "Really great."

"It is." I smile, weary with relief. "Anyway, we'd better get back, coz Jack's making us soup—I hope you're hungry!"

I stand up but Andy doesn't move.

"Andy?"

"Yeah." He hesitates. "Yeah . . . I think I might still go back to the B and B."

"Why?" I stare at him. "I told you, we can stay."

"You can stay," he tells me. "*You* can stay, Rose, and you should. This is what you came for—this is your family, your place." He sighs. "But I'm just getting in the way."

"You're not," I insist, sitting back down and grabbing his hand. "Andy, I couldn't have done this without you."

"But now you have," he says softly. "You're here. You've told them. You're helping Holly." He smiles. "But this is a difficult situation, Rose—it's really fragile, and my being here . . . it's not helping."

"It's helping me!" I protest. "I need you, Andy. I love you. You're the only one who knows me, *really* knows me. Don't leave me on my own."

"I've been on my own all day."

"I know," I say. "I know, and I'm sorry."

"It's okay—I understand." He sighs. "And it would be different if I thought you actually needed me, Rose, or even if I could help somehow. But I'm not family, I can't help, and you have to admit it's easier to talk to Holly when I'm not there."

I open my mouth to protest, then look away miserably.

"She doesn't need an audience, Rosie—it's hard enough already. It's easier if I make myself scarce while you all work through this . . . and that would be fine if we were still in New York—in any city, really—but this town . . . most of it's closed for the winter, I've been everywhere else and the only places open late are bars I can't even go in because I'm not twenty-one!"

"I'm sorry." I squeeze his hand desperately.

"Don't be!" Andy sighs. "You need to do this, you need

to give all your time and energy to Holly—without worrying about me. This is difficult enough for everyone without me complicating things." He strokes my hair away from my face. "How about I just give you guys some space, some time alone together as a family to work things out? I'll go on down to Washington, stay with my family—"

"No!" I protest vehemently.

"Rosie, it's just a few hours away, there's a direct train to Boston—I can be back in no time if you need me." He smooths my frown lines. "You're not really interested in all those stuffy monuments anyway, are you? And you'll escape my Aunt Patty's inquisition—she can be pretty brutal when it comes to her boys—ask Lola." He grins, his eyes softening as he gazes into mine, and my heart falters. "Then I'll come back, or you can come and join me, and we'll go on traveling together when . . ." He trails off. ". . . whenever."

I stare at him miserably. When will that be? In a week? A month? He's right, it's not fair to keep him here twiddling his thumbs indefinitely, and he wouldn't be far away, but . . . My heart twists. But I'd miss him so much.

"No," I decide. "No, just give me a few more days—I'll make this work, I promise. Tomorrow—tomorrow we'll spend the whole day together—just us," I say desperately. "I'll make up for leaving you alone today."

He sighs.

"We'll—we'll go whale watching, okay?" I clutch his hands. "Second-time lucky? You can't leave without seeing any whales!"

"Rosie . . ."

"I want to be with you."

He sighs heavily. "And what about Jack? And Holly?"

I hesitate.

"You see?" he says sadly. "It's impossible."

"It's not." I shake my head stubbornly. "It's not impossible—I love you . . ." I thread my arms around him, knotting him to me as he runs his thumb gently over my bottom lip, his gaze troubled.

"So, what do you say?" I search his eyes hopefully. "To-morrow? Just the two of us?"

"Scout's honor?" He raises an eyebrow. "Just you and me?"

"Dib dib dob," I say solemnly. "Just you and me . . . and a whole load of whales."

"Well," he sighs, pulling me closer and kissing me. "I suppose one more night can't hurt."

Holly

I stare at my cell phone as the first morning rays peep through my window.

It's 9:31 a.m.

I feel like I've been lying here for days, watching the minutes drag slowly, silently by. Just lying. Just breathing. Too weary to move, too tired for tears.

I pick up my phone and check it's not on mute.

It's not.

Full signal. Full battery. No missed calls. No texts—except from Melissa, who's left a dozen impatient messages demanding to know why I wasn't at school, why I'm not answering my phone, begging me to call her to fill her in on all the exciting news about my awe-some new family and my amazing new mom . . .

Yeah, I think. My *amazing* new *dead* mom, who's probably given me a fatal disease . . .

Awesome.

I try Josh again, but when he still doesn't answer, I don't leave a message. I've already left five voice mails—and ten texts.

Where are you, Josh?

Maybe he's lost his phone? Maybe it's been stolen? Maybe it's charging—plugged into his dorm-room wall while he's been out . . . all night long . . .

Come on, Holls, I tell myself. *Josh loves you—you're engaged! What more reassurance do you need?*

I stare at my ring, its plastic gem glowing reassuringly.

But that was before.

I glance at the computer screen, then close my eyes, which are red and sore from reading and surfing and searching and crying all night as I watch my future showcased on YouTube.

9:32 a.m.

I sigh and reach for my glass of water. Empty. Figures.

I weigh my options dully. Die of thirst or get up and face the world. Pretty even.

I take a deep breath, then heave myself out of bed, the blood rushing to my head as my feet hit the floor, the room spinning merci-lessly. Another deep breath and I open the door.

Nothing happens.

No tornado transports me to Oz, no snowy forest appears be-yond the doorway, no scenes of destruction and desolation. Just the landing and the stairs and the sound of Megan clattering in the kitchen.

251

The world hasn't changed at all, hasn't stopped turning, hasn't stood still.

So why do I feel like I'm falling so fast right through its center?

I make it safely down the stairs and wander slowly into the living room to find Ben watching cartoons.

"Hey, Benji," I say, kissing his head as I sink down beside him.

"Hey," he replies, flopping onto my lap and grinning up at me.

My heart lifts. "Who's winning, Tom or Jerry?" I ask, brushing his bangs from his sparkling eyes.

"Jerry," Ben giggles, pointing. "Duh!"

Duh. I smile, my fingers curling absently in his soft hair. Ben's watching cartoons, Jerry's eluding Tom. Nothing has changed. I close my eyes and let the loud cartoon music fade away.

Nothing has changed.

A loud knocking sound wakes me before I realize I'm asleep.

I glance at Ben, still glued to the TV screen. Maybe I imagined it.

Another knock and I hear Megan rush to open the front door.

"Oh, hello." A woman's crisp English accent floats through the doorway, "I wonder if you could help me, I'm looking for Jack? Jack Woods?"

I frown at the strange voice—she sounds oddly familiar, yet somehow I can't place her. Who do I know from England? Besides Hurricane Rosie.

I peer over the back of the sofa through the half-open living room door, but can only see Megan.

"Oh! Right. Please come in," she says, brushing her frazzled hair out of her eyes, leaving a streak of soap suds across her forehead. She wipes her hands on a dishcloth. "Can I get you a cup of tea? Coffee?"

"Lovely."

Megan steps aside, blocking my view as the woman enters, her heels clicking down the corridor to the kitchen.

Burning with curiosity, I slide Ben gently onto the sofa and stand up.

Then I see it.

There, on the street outside my house, is a limo. A bona fide stretch limo. I stare at it gleaming by the sidewalk, then pinch myself. This has to be a dream.

Dazed, I creep down the corridor and peek into the kitchen.

I wasn't dreaming.

The woman is gorgeous. Like, movie-star gorgeous—about thirty, but just so glamorous, her bobbed black hair gleaming in the morning sunshine, her makeup flawless, her tailored cream dress clinging immaculately to her curves. She's stunning. And strangely familiar . . .

"Black coffee, no sugar." She beams at Megan. "Thank you so much."

"Same, thanks," another woman says.

I blink—I hadn't even noticed her. She's a little older, with pointy features, a tight blond bun and an oversized Gucci bag. She reminds me of Meryl Streep in *The Devil Wears Prada*—only with Gucci.

"Jack should be here any minute." Megan smiles nervously, the best cups and saucers clattering in her hands. "I'm Megan, by the way."

The movie star steps toward her smoothly, hand outstretched.

"Lovely to meet you, Megan. I'm Kitty."

"Nice to meet you," Megan says, wiping her hand quickly on her skirt and shaking Kitty's hand. "Sorry, you look so familiar, have we met bef—" Suddenly her eyes pop. "Oh, my God!" she gasps. "You're Kitty Clare!"

Kitty Clare! Oh, my God! My heart beats quickly. I'm *such* an idiot—of *course* that's who she is—she's on our TV *every single week—For Richer, For Poorer,* Dad's favorite sitcom! Oh, my God, Melissa will totally flip when I tell her! Kitty Clare is in my house! In my kitchen! *And I'm in my hippo pj's!*

"I love your work!" Megan gushes excitedly, her curls frizzier than ever. "That episode where you and Mitch got stuck in the elevator—hilarious!"

Kitty smiles graciously.

"And then when the firefighter finally arrived and you said—"

"Megan?" Dad calls, bursting in through the back door. "Megan, have you seen my—" He stops midstride. "Katharine!"

I frown, confused, as he stares at Kitty Clare.

Katharine?

"Actually . . . it's Kitty now." She smiles, a hint of nervousness in her eyes as she stands up to face Dad, turning her back to me. "Hello, Jack. It's been a long time."

I watch as they stare at each other, my head whirling. *What's going on? How does Dad know Kitty Clare? And why'd he call her—*

My heart stops.

"Katharine?"

Dad spins around, horrified. "Sweetheart!"

I back away from the doorway as Kitty begins to turn, just as Rosie strolls down the stairs.

"Morning!" She smiles at me, walking obliviously into the kitchen.

"Rosie—" Dad starts urgently.

"Rosie!" Kitty cries, swooping toward her. "Oh, Rosie, darling, thank God!"

I freeze, paralyzed, as she engulfs Rosie in a tight embrace.

It's her. Katharine—Kitty. Kitty Clare. The mother who never wanted me.

I stare at her as she drowns Rosie with affection, a sick feeling growing in my stomach.

The mother who never wanted *me.*

Rosie

I stare at her, this woman who's squeezing me as if her life depends on it. It's Kitty—it's really Kitty, and yet . . . I need to pinch myself.

"Oh, Rosie," she whispers, stroking my hair. "I'm not too late, thank goodness!"

Behind her, footsteps pound quickly up the stairs.

Oh, God, Holly. Helplessly, I watch her go, Kitty's arms tight around me.

"Sweetheart, wait!" Jack moves to chase after her, then glances back at me. "I—I'll be right back." He sprints upstairs as Megan stares at Kitty, her face a strange shade of gray.

"I, um . . ." She falters. "I have to—Ben needs—" Head bowed, she hurries from the room.

Kitty watches them go, then turns to me, my heart beating wildly as I try to take it all in.

"Rosie, sweetie."

"I—I don't understand . . ." I stare at her, still not quite able to believe she's here. "What are you doing here?"

"Rosie—I . . . I just wanted to see you—*had* to see you,

I . . ." She glances quickly at her companion. "Why don't we sit down?"

She pulls out a chair, but I don't sit.

"Rosie, please . . . let me explain, apologize . . . You're my *daughter*, my—" She clutches my hand, tears springing in her eyes. "My little girl . . ."

My chest tightens as my own eyes prickle painfully.

"But . . . but when I came to see you, you said—"

"Oh, please, don't!" she protests, her expression pained. "*Please* don't remind me of what I said then—how I *behaved*." She sinks miserably into a chair. "I behaved abominably, Rosie. And I'm so, *so* sorry." She sighs, shaking her head. "I just—I have to be so careful. People come up to me all the time with outlandish stories, preposterous claims, blackmail . . ."

"I wasn't trying to blackmail you!"

"I know!" she gushes, squeezing my hands. "Oh, Rosie, I know, I just—I never expected . . . never dreamed . . . after so many years . . ." She blinks quickly. "I hadn't seen my daughter in *eighteen years*. I never thought I'd see you again . . ." She trails off, her eyes lingering on mine, filling with tears.

I sit down, numbly. "Aren't you meant to be in Las Vegas?"

"Yes." She nods. "Yes, I am. I'm meant to be shooting a movie there. I *was* there, but after you left—"

"After you kicked me out," I correct her.

Her perfect features crumple in pain as she nods, tears streaking her face.

"Rosie, I can't eat, I haven't slept . . . I just keep going over and *over* it in my head. My *daughter* found me—after *eighteen years*, you found me!—and instead of welcoming you with open arms, I . . ." She shakes her head wretchedly. "I will *never* forgive myself, Rosie. And I won't blame you if you tell me to leave—if you never want to see me again . . ." She looks at me desperately. "But I *had* to come, had to *find* you . . . had to *try*—I wouldn't have been able to live with myself if I didn't at least *try*—you're my *daughter* . . ."

My heart twists, her words echoing my own in New York.

"*That's* why I'm here. That's why I came all this way, why I'm in trouble with my director on the first day of shooting my first big movie—because there's nowhere on this *earth* I need to be more than right here, right now—with you. My beautiful daughter." She gazes into my eyes and my throat swells.

"And I understand if you can't forgive me, if you tell me to go—I do . . ." Her lips tremble. "But more than anything in the world I would really, *really* love the chance—a second chance—to spend some time with you. To get to know you . . ." She takes a deep breath, bites her lip. "If you'll let me?"

I stare at her, her green eyes mirroring mine, memories of New York fading to nothing as I recognize the undisguised hope glistening there.

"I'd like that," I say quietly.

"Oh!" she gasps, tears spilling over as she grabs me in a tight hug. "Oh, Rosie! Thank you!"

I hug her back, this stranger with my hair, my eyes.

My mother . . . , I think, my heart swelling as her perfume washes over me, exotic and intoxicating. *She came back . . . Again . . .*

"You won't regret it—I promise!" she gushes. "I'm going to take you for the most fabulous lunch, I know the best little seafood restaurant—you do *like* seafood?" She looks up quickly.

"Yes." I smile.

"Wonderful! Something in common already!" Kitty beams. "Oh, you'll love it—it's right on the edge of Boston Harbor, the view's incredible."

"Boston?" I look at her, surprised.

"Yes! It's just gorgeous, and the crab cakes are to *die* for—I hope you didn't have too much breakfast!"

I look at her. "You mean *now? Today?*"

"Yes!" She grins. "The table's booked for one o'clock!"

"Oh . . ." I think of Andy suddenly, of our day together. "Today's a bit . . . a bit difficult . . ."

"Oh." Her face falls. "Oh, right." She bites her lip. "My fault—I should've called, shouldn't've just . . ." She runs a hand through her perfect hair, then smiles sadly. "Never mind, next time—there'll be a next time, right?" She looks up anxiously.

"Of course!" I smile. "How about tomorrow? Next week?"

"Oh, darling, I can't." She looks crestfallen. "The movie's only given me two days off—I have to fly back tomorrow."

"Oh." My heart sinks. "Oh, I see. So when—"

"I've got a week off in March, before filming resumes," she suggests brightly. "Maybe you could come down then?"

I stare at her. *March?* That's two months away.

"Oh, darling, it's my fault. I just thought, just *hoped,* that you'd be free for a couple of hours. Total presumption on my part." She sighs.

"No," I hear myself saying. "No, it's okay. I can come with you."

"Really?" Her face brightens like the sun coming out. "Oh, sweetie, you're sure?" She grabs me in a hug. "We're gonna have such a good time—get some lunch, go shopping— just . . . spend some time together." She smiles, strokes my cheek. "I want to get to know you, Rosie."

I look at her, her eyes so full of hope, of expectation.

I smile. "Me too."

Holly

I slam the bathroom door and lunge for the toilet, heaving my guts out through painful, shuddering sobs.

She's *here*? After all these years—all my life—she's *here*? *Now*? And she's a freaking superstar? She's *Kitty Clare*?!

I collapse on the floor, trembling and cold, my throat sore and sour.

After all these years without so much as a birthday card—a letter!—now Rosie's her daughter, she suddenly wants to be a mother? And where's my mother? She's dead! Rosie already had her and now she's got Kitty too—*and* my dad!—And who've I got? *Who's left?*

As if on cue, my cell phone bleeps in my pocket and I grab for it desperately, so thankful, so relieved, that finally just when I need him most, Josh—

OMG! *Is that a STRETCH LIMO@ur house? WTF?! AWESOME!! SO JEALOUS!! Mxx*

259

I scream, hurling the phone, smashing it against the wall, and bury my head in my hands as the tears gush uncontrollably, burning my eyes, my throat, my cheeks. She's got everything. Rosie's taken everything. There's nothing left . . .

"Holly?" Dad knocks gently on the door and I try to swallow my sobs. "Sweetheart, are you okay? Can I come in?"

No! I scream inside. *No! You're a liar! You told me my mother didn't want me—you told me she was dead!*

"I'm in the shower!" I call, my voice horribly wobbly as I reach for the faucet and turn it on max, the water thundering in the stall.

"Holly!" He knocks again. "Holly, please!"

I close my eyes.

Leave me alone! This is all your fault! If you'd only told me about her maybe I would've gone looking for her, maybe I would've found her—and then she'd be here looking for me, *not Rosie!*

"Holly, talk to me!" Dad begs. "I'm gonna stand right out here until— Shit!"

Above the roaring water I hear Megan calling him from downstairs.

I close my eyes.

He knocks again. "Holly? Sweetheart, I'll be just downstairs when you come out, when you want to talk, okay?" He sighs. "I love you."

I hear him lean against the door, resting his weight on it for a moment before he walks away.

Figures.

I rest my head back on the wall, relieved that he's gone, angry at myself for feeling so hurt, so disappointed that he left. He left me. Just like everyone else. My "buddy," my "pal." My dad.

The steam fills my head, making everything fuggy and damp as I tear off my clothes and crawl into the stall, gasping as the hot water strikes my body. I close my eyes, hugging my knees to my chest, enjoying the heat, the noise, the pain that drown out the outside world, washing it away.

Who needs Kitty with her perfect hair and expensive clothes? She couldn't even be bothered to stick around after I was born. Who needs Trudie either? All she ever gave me was Huntington's disease. Who needs a dead father or a dad who lies—who's not even my real dad! And who needs a fiancé who can't even be bothered to answer his freaking phone? A fiancé who's always got his head buried in his books, who's always studying, always aspiring to something bigger, something better . . .

. . . *Than me,* I realize. We're living in different worlds, taking such different paths.

Especially now . . .

I bite my lip, my tears mingling with the water streaming over my body.

And who needs children anyway . . . More trouble than they're worth . . .

I choke on my sobs, drowning as I reach blindly for the shampoo.

I grip something sharp and drop it immediately, sucking at my stinging thumb. My blood tastes warm in my mouth. Warm and sweet and strangely comforting. I open my eyes and spot my razor lying a foot away.

Tentatively, I reach for it, the gleaming blades winking at me in the shimmering light. Gently, I run my thumb across them, watching, mesmerized, as bright fresh blood seeps from the cuts and is immediately washed clean by the gushing water, leaving two neat stinging lines. I suck my thumb again, running my tongue along the wounds, tasting their sweetness and feeling their pain. Losing my own.

I press the razor into my forearm, feeling the stinging, pulsing throb of my veins, watching my blood trickle down my arm, bright and gleaming and scarlet as it swirls away down the drain with my hurt and my pain, my arm painting itself more red with each cut—scarlet-red . . . rose-red . . . *Rosie* . . .

This is all her fault. All of it. If she hadn't come here everything would've been fine. But oh, no—the blood gushes faster now—oh, no, she had to come and stir things up, had to take *everything* . . . *everyone! Both* my fathers, *both* my mothers, my *brother*—and even any *future* family I might have had! She's taken everything, and what's she left me with? Nothing!

I hold my arm out to the water, the stinging pain a relief as it washes the redness away, cleansing and purging my wounds. I touch them gingerly, running my fingers across them like I'm reading Braille.

Yes, it's all Rosie's fault. Little Miss DNA. She's taken everything.

Well, maybe it's time I took something back.

Rosie

"Don't forget your scarf." Kitty grins. "It's freezing in Boston!"

I head for the stairs and nearly collide with Jack rushing down.

"Hey," he says, spotting the open front door. "What's going on?"

"Nothing's *going on*, Jack," Kitty says, glancing at Megan, who disappears into the living room with Ben. "I just asked Rosie if she'd like to spend the day with me, that's all."

"That's *all?*" Jack laughs bitterly. "Kitty, you abandoned your daughter eighteen years ago, and now you suddenly turn up here out of the blue, and—what? You think she's just going to drop everything and forgive you?"

Kitty blushes. "It's not like that."

"You're just going to pick up where you left off?"

"No, but—"

"No, damn right you're not! You really think after *eighteen* years—after what happened in New York—after—"

"She said yes," Kitty says softly.

He turns to me, stunned. "Rosie?"

I shift uncomfortably.

"Rosie—how can you? After all she's done, how can you just . . ."

"She's my mother, Jack," I say helplessly. "That's why I came here, to find my mother."

"Yes, and look how she treated you when you did find her!" Jack protests. "She kicked you out, Rosie, she abandoned you as a baby, she hasn't wanted to know you for eighteen years!"

"But now I do," Kitty says desperately. "Now I do—more than anything in the world."

Jack snorts.

"I know what I did was wrong," she sighs. "I was seventeen—I was scared senseless." She bites her lip. "I know that's no excuse, but I'm trying to make up for it now. I know nothing ever will, but . . ." She looks at me, smiles gently. "If Rosie can find it in her heart to give me a second chance . . ."

"It wasn't just Rosie you left," Jack says quietly.

She stares at him. "Jack . . ."

His jaw tenses as he stares at the coat-rack.

I gaze intently at my feet, my cheeks burning in the long silence.

"I'm sorry," Kitty says finally. "Jack, I really am sorry."

"Yes, well." Jack clears his throat, runs his hand through his hair, looking anywhere but at Kitty. "Whatever our issues may be, you're right, Rosie should come first. As you said, it's her decision." He looks at me again, a sad, tender look. "She's an adult now."

I feel awful as they both look at me, like I'm caught in the middle of a custody battle.

"Rosie?" Kitty says gently.

I look from her to Jack and back again, utterly torn. Jack's been so good to me—I don't want to betray him or hurt his feelings . . . but Kitty's come all this way—and it's my only chance to see her for months . . .

"Look, it's okay," Kitty sighs. "Jack's right, it wasn't fair of me to just turn up like this. We'll schedule something else, some other time, let things cool down . . ."

"No, wait—" I cry as she turns away. "I want to come with you."

She's the whole reason I came all this way, after all—I can't bear for her to walk out that door, not knowing when I'll ever see her again.

"If that's okay," I add anxiously, turning to Jack. "I'll be back later?"

"Of course." He smiles, his eyes tired. "Of course, if that's what you want."

"Thank you, Jack," Kitty says gently. "For everything."

He looks at her for a long moment, his expression unreadable, then swallows hard.

"Just . . . look after her," he says, before turning to walk away down the corridor.

"Goodbye, Jack," Kitty whispers as he disappears.

She sighs quietly. Then she blinks quickly, takes a deep breath and turns to me.

"You ready?" She beams. "Lunch reservations await!"

I rush upstairs for my scarf, then remember Andy. Shit.

I try the bathrooms but they're both locked, the sound of running water gushing behind the closed doors.

"Andy!" I call. "Andy, I'm really sorry, I've got to go—"

"I can't hear you!" he shouts back. "I'm in the shower!"

"Andy, open the door! Andy, it's important! I've got to—"

"Ten minutes!" he shouts back.

Ten minutes? I don't have ten minutes!

Kitty's car horn beeps outside. I swear under my breath, then run into my room and grab my notebook from my bag.

Andy, I scribble quickly.

Kitty's arrived—one day only. Have gone to Boston with her. Back tonight. Please forgive me . . . boat trip tomorrow?

I love you,

Rosie xxxx

I prop the note against my pillow and rush downstairs.

The door of the limo is waiting open for me—I can't believe the size of it! I slide onto the smooth leather seat feeling light-headed, like I'm in a dream. I'm going out for the day *in a stretch limo! To Boston!*

I'm going out for the day *with my mother!*

Holly

The front door slams downstairs and I hold my breath, listening carefully.

Silence.

I creep out of the bathroom and pad silently to the top of the stairs.

Still nothing.

Slowly, oh-so-carefully, I tiptoe to Rosie's door and gently push it open.

It's empty.

Feeling like a fugitive in my own house, I step cautiously inside and close the door behind me.

My eyes flick quickly around the room, skimming over the furniture I've seen a million times, to Rosie's toiletries on the desk, her bag on the bed, a note on her pillow . . .

I bite my lip, my heart deafening in my ears as I cross to the bed. This is wrong, so wrong, but I can't stop myself.

I scowl at the page, her loopy handwriting, her signature.

Rosie xxxx

Outside, a car door slams, making me jump. I cross to the window to see the stretch limo pull smoothly away from the curb and disappear down the street, Kitty and Rosie tucked smugly inside.

My vision blurs and the paper crumples in my fist, opening my stinging wounds. I stuff it in my pocket and grab Rosie's bag, new fire raging through my veins as I tear it open, yanking at its contents and strewing them over the bed. Clothes tumble out, books and hair clips . . . there must be something—she must have *something* I can use against her . . . I pick up a notebook, leafing swiftly through its pages for anything, anything at all—and a photograph slips out. Eagerly, I grab it—

Kitty smiles back at me like a knife through my heart.

I stare at her, her eyes bright and gleaming, and suddenly I scream, tearing at the photograph, ripping it into long jagged strips, clawing at her perfect face, that smug smile!

You didn't want me! I tear the photo again, my blood blazing. *You never wanted me—so why now? Why her?!*

I tear again and again, furiously, fiercely, slashing and shredding every last trace of her, the pieces scattering over the bed like ashes.

I grab at Rosie's clothes, eager for more destruction, more relief—then something small and pink tumbles out of a pocket. I pick it up. An address book.

"What are you doing?"

I spin around quickly, sliding the book into my back pocket.

Andy is standing in the doorway, tucking his shirt into his jeans.

"What are you doing in here?" he says warily. "Where's Rosie?"

"Out," I tell him defiantly. "She went out. More *bonding time,*" I add bitterly.

He frowns. "That's impossible, she—we were . . ." His eyes drop to the bed, all her things scattered wildly over it. "What the hell do you think you're doing, Holly—that's Rosie's stuff!"

"So what?" I yell, my remorse melting away as my anger boils. "So what? This is *my* house." I gesture around wildly. "This is *my* stuff! She's taken everything from me—why shouldn't I have something of hers?" I grab Rosie's things—clothes, shoes, books—and hurl them around the room.

"Stop it!" Andy snatches at them. "Holly, stop!" He catches my arm, and I wince. He looks down, then stares at me, shocked. I pull quickly away, yanking my sleeves down over my weeping cuts and folding my arms.

Andy just stands there, staring at me. His eyes fall on the shredded picture and he brushes the pieces apart, recognition in his eyes.

"What?" I challenge, his pity scorching my cheeks. "*What?* She was mine—she was my mom. Why *shouldn't* I?"

I feel his gaze on me like a spotlight burning as I snatch handfuls of the scraps and dump them into the trash can. When I turn back I am surprised that they're all gone. I look at Andy, his cupped hands full of paper.

I wipe at my eyes and sniff. "Well?" I demand.

To my surprise he moves slowly toward the trash can and drops the paper in. Then he takes something from his own bag.

A cigarette lighter.

I look at him, startled. He smiles and raises his eyebrows.

"Ever thought about cremation?"

Rosie

With a flick of her wrist, Kitty lights her cigarette, the flame dancing for a second before vanishing as she drops the lighter back into her clutch bag. She closes her eyes, sighing blissfully as she exhales, and I watch the thin plume of smoke curl like a ribbon toward the ceiling of the car, thinking of Trudie and her cigarette holder.

"God, I'm sorry!" Kitty cries stubbing it out quickly.

"I've been trying to quit, but there are moments when I'm stressed—or nervous . . ."

"It's fine, really," I protest.

"No," she says, flicking the cigarette out the window. "It's a disgusting habit, I've been meaning to quit for years."

"Really, it's not like I've never . . . I tried it once," I say clumsily, my cheeks growing hot.

"Did you?" she asks, her green eyes wide. "Tell me."

I shrug. "There's nothing to tell, really."

"Please," she says, her fingers soft and cool on my knee, her eyes insistent. "There's so much I don't know, so much I've missed."

I stare at my lap, my cheeks on fire. "It was just at school." I shrug. "Some of the girls were passing it round and . . . you know . . ."

"You didn't like it?" she asks.

I screw up my nose. "It tasted of . . . ashtrays and bad breath."

She laughs, a tinkling sound, and beams at me. "Very smart. I can see you didn't get your brains from me. I'd rather have got lung cancer than be thought uncool."

She smiles, but inside I'm back in high school gazing at the popular kids, feeling geeky and awkward. Kitty's assistant, Janine, catches my eye and looks quickly away, hugging the large bag on her lap.

"What about guys?" Kitty's eyes gleam. "Look at you—you're gorgeous. I bet you've had guys falling for you left, right and center, right?"

"Not really," I say, feeling even more uncomfortable and square. "There's just Andy."

"Right—the guy you were with at the hotel? He's cute." She grins. "Andy . . ."

I nod silently, staring at my feet. Andy, who I've left—again. Who I've broken my promise to.

Janine clears her throat.

"What else?" Kitty asks brightly. "Did you have any pets, growing up? I bet you're a cat person, aren't you? I *always* wanted a cat as a child, but Mum fell for this great big soppy dog—" She looks at me quickly. "Oh, no, you're gonna tell me you love dogs now, aren't you?"

I shrug. "I dunno, we never had any pets."

"Oh, right . . ." She falters. "What about hobbies?"

"Not really."

"Sports?"

I shake my head.

She bites her lip, the sparkle fading from her eyes. "Right . . ."

The car drifts into silence, and I stare out the window, gazing at the tree-lined avenues and clapboard houses as they rush past. Then I see Kitty's reflection in the glass, and my heart aches. I have so much to say, so many questions—but how to ask them of this confident, glamorous woman? She's supposed to be my mother, but besides our genes we're nothing alike. We may be sitting two feet away from each other, but we're worlds apart.

Outside, people point and stare at the limo as we pass, and I remember the trip to Brighton with Trudie and Sarah, how much fun we had in our pink limousine, our wacky clothes, how hard we laughed . . .

I pick at a hole in my jeans and look around the

luxurious car, afraid to touch anything, wishing I'd had a chance to shower, to change into something more suitable—wishing I had anything suitable to change into.

Wishing I had my mum.

Trudie.

Holly

The fire burns swiftly in the metal can, the bright flames licking the small pile of paper into powdery ash.

"Feel better?" Andy asks.

I shrug. But a small part of my pain has subsided, floating away through the window with the disappearing smoke.

He nods, slides down from the window ledge and crosses to the door. "Well," he says, picking up his bag. "Have a nice life."

"You're leaving?" I ask, surprised.

He pauses in the doorway. "It's for the best."

"Where will you go?"

He shrugs. "Back to the B and B for now, then . . . I dunno." He sighs. "We were supposed to be in Washington by now."

"Washington?" I look at him, considering. I take a breath and hop down from the sill. "Let's go."

"What?" He looks at me, startled.

"Washington," I say. "Let's go. Now."

He watches me for a moment, a smile playing on his lips, trying to decide if I'm serious.

I am. Deadly.

"No." He shakes his head eventually. "You can't just leave—"

"I can."

"Well, I can't."

"Why?"

"I can't just leave *Ro—*"

"Why? *Why not?* What's so special about her?" I demand, the familiar heat returning to my cheeks. "Weren't you supposed to be spending the day together?"

"We are. We will—"

"*Andy,* she's gone for the *whole day.* I saw her! She's gone to Boston."

He stares at me. *"What?"*

I nod.

"To *Boston?* What the hell? No, she wouldn't—she *promised—*"

I shrug.

Andy's eyes are wide, incredulous. He shakes his head. "She just *left?*"

I nod.

"Bloody hell! *Bloody* Rosie!—After she *promised* . . . We were going to see the whales . . ."

I look at him surprised. "Whales?"

"Yeah," he sighs. "If there actually are any round here—we saw bugger all last time."

I stare at him. Whale watching? In *January?*

"You didn't see *any?*" I ask, trying to keep a straight face.

He shakes his head. "Nope. *Wesley's Whale-Spotter,* my arse."

"Oh, no—you didn't go with them?" I laugh. "They're notorious—total rip-off!"

"Tell me about it," Andy groans.

"You wanna just hop on the ferry to Boston," I tell him, the lies spilling out before I can stop them. "You'll go straight across the Cape, see *hundreds* of whales."

Andy stares at me. *"Hundreds? Really?"*

"Uh-huh," I say, avoiding his eyes. "Come on, let's go."

"What, now?" He looks at me.

"Why not?" I look at him for a long moment, my heart thumping. *Rosie's not the only one who can go swanning off to Boston— not the only one who can take things that don't belong to her . . .*

"Unless of course you'd rather sit around here twiddling your thumbs waiting until she bothers to come back?" I suggest. *"Again."*

He looks at me, then drops his bag on the floor.

"Let's go."

Rosie

"Look up," Kitty instructs, and I do as I'm told, the bright lights making my eyes water. She strokes the mascara wand over my lashes, and I try not to blink. We're in the changing rooms at Chanel—*Chanel!*—and I'm completely paranoid I'm going to damage something expensive and get kicked out any moment, but Kitty seems right at home. She's picked out a dozen designer outfits for me to try on and has insisted on doing my makeup—she must have a ton of it stashed in that massive Gucci bag.

"There!" She smiles. "All done."

I stand up and turn to face the full-length mirror.

"Oh, Rosie," she gasps, her hand cool on my bare shoulder. "You're beautiful."

"Stunning." Janine beams. "And I know just the shoes you need . . ." She winks at Kitty and disappears behind the black velvet curtain.

I stare at the girl standing before me, struggling to recognize myself. My lips are a weird purpley-blue color to match my dress, which feels too tight round my ribs; my nose has all but disappeared beneath concealer and powder, while my eyes have become huge green saucers, surrounded by thick black eyeliner and glittering eye shadow. I seriously wouldn't recognize myself. I look like a . . . I look like someone out of . . . Then it hits me.

I look like Kitty.

My cheeks flush as I compare our reflections in the mirror.

That's what this makeover has been about—the manicure and pedicure we had done together, the makeup, the new clothes . . . all transforming me into the daughter she wants me to be. Glamorous, sophisticated, groomed.

Kitty Clare's daughter.

"I love that color on you." She smiles, stroking my dress. It ripples like water beneath her touch, and goose bumps prickle on my skin. "Isn't it gorgeous?"

I stare at myself. This isn't me. None of this is—it's weird, it's . . . I swallow, pulling at the material, trying to cover myself up, struggling to breathe.

"Rosie?" Kitty's cool hand lands on my shoulder. Her eyes search mine. "Are you okay?"

I nod furiously, look away.

"Don't you like the dress? I think it's beautiful."

"It is!" I insist. "It's great. The dress, the makeup—it's . . . fabulous!" I gush, risking another glance at my reflection and swallowing hard. "What a makeover, huh?"

Kitty looks at me for a moment, then pulls over a stool.

"Look, I've got a confession to make." She sighs, sitting down and looking me in the eye. She takes a deep breath. "I'm a bit out of my depth here . . ."

I stare at her—*she's* out of her depth?

"Give me a movie director or big-shot producer and I'm laughing." She smiles. "I've been there, done that. I know how to paint on a grin and turn on the charm. But you . . . you're my *daughter*." She takes my hands shyly. "My daughter," she whispers. "You're a part of me—but more. You're your own person—your own beautiful person, and"—her eyes swim with tears—"and I don't know you at all."

Her eyes search mine, sorrowful, anxious, and something inside me flips over.

Kitty Clare, super-sophisticated movie star, is as nervous as I am.

"And I'm sorry," she continues. "I'm so sorry for all the years I've missed—for not knowing what to *say* or how to act around you—for only having one day now and making a total mess of it . . ." She snatches a ragged breath. "And I know it's too late—too late for me to be a mother to you . . ." she trails off, her eyes shining. "But Rosie, I'd really like us to be friends."

She clasps my hands tightly.

"Are you okay?" she asks gently, her eyes deep in mine. "Has your life been okay?"

I nod, my throat dry.

"And you and—and Jack," she continues. "You get on okay?"

"Yeah." I smile. "He's great."

"I'm so glad." She beams. "I knew he'd be a good father."

I look at her then, realize.

"Kitty . . . Jack didn't—he didn't bring me up," I say. "We only just met a few days ago—I found him after I met you."

"What?" She stares at me, stunned. "I don't understand . . ."

"It's—it's what I was trying to tell you in New York. There was a mix-up at the hospital . . ." I look at her. "I was swapped at birth."

Kitty's jaw drops.

"I only came to the States a week ago to try to find you—my real mother."

She stares at me, white as a sheet, emotion flickering over her features. "I can't believe it . . . I . . ." She struggles for words. "That's why your accent . . . your hair . . . your *name* . . ." She looks at me, eyes wide. "I just thought that Jack had changed your . . ." She shakes her head incredulously. "*Swapped?*"

I nod.

"So who . . . Jack has another daughter?" She frowns. "I mean—"

"Yes, Holly. My mum's—*Trudie's*—real daughter. He brought her up instead of me, while I grew up with a different family, in England."

"Oh, Rosie—darling!" She holds me close, her heart racing. "I . . . I had no idea! And your . . . the people who brought you up . . . they didn't *know?*" She pulls back.

I shake my head, look away.

"I never knew my dad," I say, my voice dry and throaty. "He died just before I was born."

"Oh, Rosie!"

"But my mum—Trudie—" I smile, warmth flooding through me. "She was wonderful."

Kitty smiles faintly. "Good," she says softly. "I'm really glad. She must be so proud."

"I hope so." I smile tightly, swallowing hard. "She—she died, just before Christmas."

"Oh, God!" Kitty's hand flies to her mouth. "What happened, was she ill?"

"Yes." I nod. "She had Huntington's disease."

I can see it doesn't mean much to her, but now isn't the time to explain.

Kitty sighs, her eyes deep green pools. "What you must have gone through . . . And all that time . . ." She shakes her head. "You know, not a day has gone by that I haven't thought about you, wondered how you were, if you were happy . . ."

I pick at a thread on the dress.

"You probably find that hard to believe." She sighs. "I wouldn't blame you. God knows what people have told you—what Jack's told you—and I know it's no excuse . . . but I was just a child myself when I had you—younger than you are now. And I was so scared. I hadn't the first idea what

277

to do. I tried to hide my pregnancy, didn't tell anyone, not even my mum—I was terrified." She bites her lip.

"She was already worried about my future, thought I was stuffing up my GCSEs—she'd been on me like a ton of bricks all year. She'd even sent me to Granny's for the whole of the Easter holidays, thought banishing me to a desolate seaside town would convince me to knuckle down and revise. But instead I met Jack." I look up as she smiles.

"With him I wasn't a screw-up, a let-down. With him I could forget all my problems, be anyone I liked . . ." Her eyes dance wistfully. "And he was so sweet. He made me laugh, made me feel special."

She sighs. "Then it was back home to reality. I knew I'd failed my GCSEs as soon as I took them—and now with a baby on the way . . ." Her face crumples like a child's and suddenly I see the seventeen-year-old in her, the terror, the fragility. "My life was over. My parents were going to kill me—I'd made such a mess. I was so scared . . . I couldn't tell them . . ." She chews a manicured nail anxiously.

"Then, like a miracle, I got accepted into the National Youth Theatre—and my parents were suddenly so proud!" She shakes her head incredulously. "You should've seen Mum—it was all she could talk about."

I smile, remembering the way Pam had glowed as she spoke about Kitty and her glamorous career.

"So then I *really* couldn't tell her!" Kitty's voice cracks. "So I moved to London, where it was easier to just not think about the baby, to throw myself into rehearsals, performances, the show—then I got an agent and had more auditions, rehearsals, filming, performing . . . until finally, at twenty weeks, I couldn't hide it anymore . . ." She closes her eyes, her lip trembling.

"My agent was furious, said she'd had a complaint from a casting director, that I'd been utterly unprofessional by not telling her, that she couldn't represent me anymore. Then I was totally screwed!" Kitty laughs bitterly, tears shimmering in her eyes. "I had no agent, no job, no money coming in, too late for an abortion—not that I would have—I couldn't . . . I couldn't go home, couldn't tell my parents . . . Luckily they were still paying my rent, so I made excuses not to see them, got a job in a call center, worked all hours trying to save up money for the baby—for you." Her watery gaze meets mine and my throat swells.

"Then around Christmas, I realized . . . I just couldn't cope anymore. My flatmates had left for the holidays—one had even landed a TV job in L.A. I was all by myself for Christmas and New Year and it was utterly horrible . . . And I knew it would be even harder once I had a baby to look after. So I made a decision—a New Year's resolution. It was time to go home, finally face the music, tell my parents—whatever the consequences. I couldn't do this alone."

She swallows hard, her eyes frightened.

"But then—I don't know if it was the stress, or the train journey, or what—but my waters broke on the way home!" she cries. "I panicked—it was too soon, I wasn't due yet! An ambulance took me to hospital, but I was scared silly. I didn't know what to do, I needed my Mum . . .

"But then I realized—if I could just keep quiet for a few more hours . . . my parents needed never know . . . I could put you up for adoption—that would be the best thing all round. I wasn't fit to be a mother, and you'd have a much better life, go to someone who really wanted a baby, couldn't have one of their own."

I look away, thinking of Trudie, of Sarah.

"I was terrified. I was having a baby and I was alone. I couldn't call Mum, not now I'd made my decision, I couldn't call my friends—anyone who knew my family . . . So finally I called Jack. Funny, kind, caring Jack, whose number I'd kept, who lived miles away, who I'd only known for two weeks and who I totally expected to tell me to get stuffed. Who told me he was on his way before I'd even put the phone down . . ." She smiles weakly.

"But for hours he didn't come. I gave birth, had to give my baby a name for her bracelet, then she was rushed away to a special unit while the nurses cleaned me up. Then I started to panic all over again. I thought Jack had changed his mind, gotten cold feet and left me all on my own after all. I couldn't cope—couldn't be a mother—couldn't deal with it all, so I—I ran away . . ." She looks away, shame painting her cheeks scarlet.

"And then, suddenly, there he was, driving up the road. Jack, my knight in shining armor. I couldn't believe it. He promised he'd look after us both, that we'd be a family. But I . . . I just couldn't. I tried, I really did—we registered the birth together, visited you in hospital—but I was so scared of ruining your life the way I'd wrecked my own. You were already ill—premature—and I felt it was my fault, my punishment. I didn't deserve you . . ." She swallows. "So when Jack went to bring you home, I left. I told my parents I'd got a job in L.A., got on a plane and arranged to sleep on my friend's floor."

She shakes her head wretchedly. "I had to go—had to get away. You have to believe me, Rosie, I was no good for you—I was a mess—I'm *still* a mess . . ." She sighs miserably. "But don't ever think that I didn't love you, that I don't think about you—feel horrible for what I did. I've had to live with it every day of my life, eating me up inside, never able to tell anyone."

"What about Luke?" I whisper. "You're engaged."

"Oh, we're not engaged, Rosie, not really—Luke's gay! It's all a sham, a career move—my whole life's one big charade! It may look glamorous—the bright lights, the makeup, but it's all an act, Rosie. Nothing's real. *You're* the only thing that's ever been real. You and . . . and Jack . . ." She trails off. "I couldn't believe it when I got his letter all those years later. That he'd followed me to the States . . ." She gazes wistfully out the window.

"But it was too late," she continues, her eyes clouding over. "It was too late. He was married, and I couldn't risk wrecking that for him by crashing back into your lives—however much I wanted to. Too many years had passed and I was still so ashamed of leaving you, so frightened you'd reject me . . . I couldn't even open the letters that followed—it was too painful, seeing the photos, hearing about all the things I'd missed. You guys were obviously doing so well without me—you looked so healthy, so happy . . ." She squeezes her eyes shut.

"I had no idea . . ." Kitty groans. "*No idea*—that that

wasn't you at all—that you were on the other side of the world!" She looks at me, pain-stricken. "You're my *daughter* and I had no idea that they'd given me a completely different baby!" Black tears trickle down her cheeks. "What kind of a person does that make me? What kind of a *mother*?" She shakes her head miserably as she crumples on her stool. "Oh, Rosie, can you ever forgive me?"

I look at her, dressed to the nines, her lips painted an unnatural scarlet, her cheeks streaked with mascara, and tears flood my eyes as I think about what it must've been like to be so alone, so scared, so young.

I take a deep breath, then nod.

Immediately, she engulfs me in a tight hug, her ribs shaking with sobs.

Over her shoulder, I see Janine smiling at our reflections through a gap in the curtains.

"Reunited at last!" she sighs, dabbing at her eyes. "Mother and daughter."

I smile through my tears, a warm feeling growing inside me.

Mother and daughter. At last.

Holly

"I still don't see any whales," Andy says doubtfully, leaning over the rail of the boat and studying the murky depths.

"Patience," I chide, hiding a smile. "We're barely out of the harbor yet."

The salty air billows through my hair and shivers on my skin as the dark waves surge beneath us.

"Choppy today." I frown.

"Not seasick, I hope?" Andy grins.

"Don't you worry about me." I smile. "I've been out here a thousand times—it's your own breakfast you wanna keep a hold on."

"Whatever." Andy laughs. "That's what Rosie said before we went on *Nemesis* at Alton Towers. Wasn't too cocky afterwards when her ice cream sundae made a sudden reappearance! Though neither was I—she puked all over me!"

"Eww, gross!" I grimace.

"Must be love," Andy sighs, staring out to sea.

I look at him for a long moment, his eyes pained, his cheeks blasted pink by the wind, and I bite my lip. I shouldn't have brought him out here like this, under false pretenses. He's got nothing to do with this mess—I just wanted to hurt Rosie like she's hurt me. Make her suffer like I'm suffering.

"Like you and—Josh, is it?" He turns suddenly, catching me off guard.

My heart plummets and I stare at my feet. *Josh.*

"You're serious, right? You're engaged?"

"Yup," I say, my throat swelling. "Though how long that'll last . . ."

He frowns. "Why?"

"Oh." I shrug, embarrassed I've spoken the thought out loud. "No reason."

I stare determinedly at the sea, scouring the horizon for imaginary whales, ignoring the sick feeling in my stomach, the thumping of my heart.

"Only . . . ," Andy begins, then breaks off. "Nothing. Sorry. It's none of my business."

"What?" I ask, turning to him.

"Well . . ." He takes a breath. "It's just I hope it's not because of the Huntington's that you're unsure." His eyes search mine and I look away, my cheeks burning.

"Have you told him yet?" he asks gently.

"You're right," I say briskly, warm despite the biting wind. "It's none of your business."

He nods, turns back to sea. "Just like Rosie," he mutters.

"What?" I turn on him furiously. "What do you mean? I'm nothing like her!"

He smiles. "You're more alike than you think."

I stare at him.

"She never told me about the disease, Holly. She kept it all secret. We even broke up because she was too afraid to tell me." He looks at me. "You're telling me you're not feeling the same? You're not scared to tell Josh?"

I bite my lip.

"You know," he says gently, "if she had told me—even if she knew she'd got it—it wouldn't have mattered. It wouldn't have scared me away."

I stare at him, incredulous. "It wouldn't have mattered?"

He shakes his head. "Of course not."

"That she was going to die?"

"Everybody dies."

I stare at him. "It wouldn't have mattered that in ten, maybe twenty years' time you'd be feeding her from a *spoon*? That you'd have to be her *caregiver*? It wouldn't have mattered that you could never have *children* without worrying that they'd have it too?"

284

He sighs, a troubled frown clouding his brow.

"No." I shake my head, my stomach lurching with the surging waves. "No, you're wrong. It matters."

"Holly," he says gently. "You don't even know you've got Huntington's. You don't have to worry yet—"

"I do!" I argue, the boat rocking wildly. "You don't understand!" The icy wind whips at my face, stinging my eyes. "Nobody does, nobody knows . . ."

"Nobody knows *what*?" Andy asks, struggling against the roar of the wind, the crash of the waves against the boat.

"That I'm—" A sudden lurch of the boat sends me reeling into the barrier, heaving my guts into the swirling sea below.

"Not seasick, huh?" Andy grins, crouching down next to me and rubbing my back as I collapse, shivering, onto the deck.

"No," I sigh, swallowing painfully. "Not seasick."

He frowns at me, confused.

I take a deep breath and close my eyes, my head aching.

"I'm not seasick," I tell him, the words finally forming on my lips. "I'm pregnant."

Rosie

I gaze out the car window, craning my neck to try to see the tops of the brownstone buildings, but they're too high— stretching for the sky, snagging the clouds.

People walking by stare as we pass and I have to remind myself that they can't see me. I glance at Kitty. How do you ever get used to this?

"C'mon, come *on*," Kitty mutters under her breath as we stop at yet another red light, headed for lunch. She smiles apologetically at me. "Sorry—city driving is such a pain." She sighs and leans back in her seat. "It's really almost better to— Actually . . . Jerry, stop the car—pull over here."

I look up, surprised.

"What?" Janine stares at her. "But Nautica's still over a mile away."

"I've changed my mind. Jerry, just here will do fine, thank you."

"Where are we going?" Janine asks, hastily collecting her things as we pull to a stop.

"*We're* going for a walk." Kitty flashes her a smile as she blocks her way. "You stay here with Jerry, and I'll call you when we're done." She grabs her clutch and winks at me as I scramble out. "I think Rosie and I can manage on our own from here."

"What? But—" Janine protests, looking slighted as Kitty slams the door. "Wait—don't forget your tote!"

She thrusts her huge Gucci bag through the window at Kitty, who looks at her for a moment, then rolls her eyes.

"Don't need it." She grins. "Bye!" She waves as the limo crawls away, Janine anxiously staring after us.

"C'mon." Kitty smiles at me, tossing her scarf over her shoulder and hooking her arm through mine. "Quick, let's make a run for it!"

Holly

"Oh, my God," Andy says quietly.

"I know," I sigh.

"You're sure?"

I nod, biting my lip. "About eight weeks or so . . ."

"Wow . . . congratulations?" he says tentatively.

I glare at him.

"Perhaps not." He swallows. "What does Josh think?"

"He doesn't know," I admit miserably.

"What? What about your dad?"

I shake my head. "Nobody knows."

"Holly!" he stares at me. *"Eight weeks?"*

I nod. "Or so."

"But Holly—your arm—you could hurt the—"

"I know," I say, my cheeks burning. "It was stupid. I wasn't think-ing. It was a one-time thing."

"Are you sure?"

"I was just upset," I mumble, pulling my jacket tighter. "It won't happen again."

"Okay," Andy says gently. "Wow . . ." He takes a deep breath and sits down beside me.

I close my eyes, the motion of the boat gentler now, rocking softly, but I still feel sick, everything inside me sore and trembling.

Andy slips his arm around my shoulders awkwardly.

"It'll be okay," he says gently.

I stare at him. "How?"

"I mean—"

"I'm eighteen. I'm pregnant. Oh, yeah, and I might have Huntington's disease," I fire at him. "Please, Andy, tell me how it's all gonna be okay?"

"I only meant . . ." He hesitates, then looks at me, his eyes deep and blue. "Do you want it?" he asks, his voice a whisper. "The baby?"

I close my eyes, tears prickling as I remember the clinic.

"I'm just trying to understand why you haven't told Josh," he says gently. "I mean, before Rosie and I even arrived, before Huntington's was ever an issue."

I stare at the floor, my head throbbing, trying to untangle my thoughts, my feelings.

"Was it that you were afraid he wouldn't want it?"

I trace the grain of the wood with my fingers, stroking the knots.

"Or were you afraid that he would?"

My head snaps up. "How dare you!" I turn on him, angry and guilt-stricken. "You don't know me, Andy—you know nothing about me, so how *dare* you judge me?"

"I'm not!" he protests.

"Yes, I was afraid, okay? I was afraid of being pregnant, afraid of what that means, afraid that Josh would leave me—or worse, that he'd stand by me just because I was pregnant. Ever since he left for college I've been . . . I've been sort of expecting us to break up."

"Why?" Andy frowns.

"That's what happens, isn't it? It's what's happened to some of my friends, anyway. And Josh and I—we're from different worlds. He's so clever. He's going to be a great scientist," I tell him proudly, the words clogging my throat. "Someone really important. I couldn't

288

tie him down like that—couldn't let him throw away his dreams!" I shake my head. "I *can't* let him do that."

"So . . . what were you going to do?"

"I dunno." I bite my lip. "I just wanted to wait, to see . . ." I stare at my feet. "If we were gonna break up anyway, there seemed no point in telling him."

Andy sighs.

"And then we went to New York and he proposed and everything was perfect." I smile miserably. "I almost told him then—I should have—but I thought no, no I'll just hold out another day, wait till we get home, announce our engagement . . . it'll be so perfect—" Tears gush through my words. "But now it'll never be perfect because I can't tell him—I can't tell him about Huntington's because we're already engaged—he's already trapped. He'd never walk away from me now. And I can't tell him about our baby, because I might—because it might . . ."

Andy holds me tighter.

"And I don't know why I'm telling you all this." I sniff. "I hardly even know you!"

"It's okay," he soothes. "I do think you should tell your dad, though."

"I *can't*," I protest. "He's too busy running around after fricking *Rosie*! And even if I did, he'd think that was *why* we wanted to get married in the first place!"

"But if you talked to him," Andy says gently. "If you explained . . ."

"I can't." I shake my head firmly. "I can't tell anyone." I look at him suddenly. "And neither can you, Andy, swear it."

"Holly . . ."

"Swear it," I demand. "Not even Rosie. *Especially* not Rosie."

"Okay." He holds his hands up. "I swear. I won't tell anybody. Scout's honor."

I look at him carefully, his clear eyes, his concern.

"Thank you," I say quietly.

"You're welcome," he says. "But I do think you should talk to someone . . . a professional."

I look at him. "A shrink?"

"No." He smiles. "A genetic counselor, someone who knows about all this stuff. They'll be able to help you decide whether or not to take the test—"

"But I *want* to take the test!" I cry. "I have to!"

"That's fine," Andy soothes. "But it's the counselors who do the testing. Okay?"

I nod. "Okay."

"So in the next few days, you need to look up where the nearest clinic is and—"

"Why not today?" I ask suddenly. "We'll be in Boston in half an hour—they're bound to have one there."

He smiles. "You don't waste any time, do you?"

"Andy," I say gravely. "I haven't got any time to waste."

Rosie

The streets are swarming with busy pedestrians, but despite the hustle and bustle, Boston's quite different from New York. There's a more . . . civilized feel. I don't know if it's the colonial architecture, with its tall columns and grand façades, or the people themselves, but Boston has quite a

European feel, a sense of age and gravitas compared to the hectic dazzle of New York.

Kitty leads me down a cobbled street that could be straight out of a Dickens novel, past several street performers, to the edge of a vast park.

"I'm starving!" she says suddenly, turning to me. "Have you ever had clam chowder?"

"Clam what?" I ask, bewildered.

"Chowder," she laughs. "It's like a delicious creamy soup. You'll love it. Come on."

Heels clacking quickly across the pavement, she heads toward a very swanky-looking restaurant, and my heart sinks. There's a queue of smartly dressed people outside—all suits and dresses. I stare miserably at my scruffy jeans and trainers, wishing I still had on the purple dress. I'm going to stick out like a sore thumb. If they even let me in.

"Two chowders, please."

I look up, surprised. Kitty's not in the queue at all, but instead is standing in front of a stripy street stall. Steam billows as the vendor lifts the lid on a big metal pot and Kitty grins, handing me what looks like a loaf of crusty bread.

"I thought we were having soup?" I ask, confused.

"It *is* soup!" Kitty laughs, lifting the top of my loaf straight off to reveal a creamy liquid inside. "It's a sourdough bowl—delicious! Once you've finished your chowder, you eat the bowl—it's fantastic." She beams. "Don't tell Janine, though—I'm not meant to have carbs." She grins, popping a piece of bread into her mouth. "Come on," she says, hooking her arm through mine and leading me into the park. "Let's find somewhere to sit."

Holly

I stare up at the towering gray building, its windows gleaming in the afternoon sun. This is it.

It was surprisingly easy to find—right there on Google on Andy's phone, and now right here on the street. People walk straight past without a second glance, but I can't take my eyes off it. This is the place where my future gets decided.

Our future.

"You okay?" Andy asks. "You know, you don't have to do this today. You can always come back another time, when you've had a chance to think about it properly."

"No," I say, my voice surprisingly calm. "No, I need to do this now."

I only intended to make an appointment. I borrowed Andy's phone—mine being smashed up at home—and I punched in the number, half expecting no one to answer, or that I'd hang up if they did. Somehow, though, I asked for an appointment, and we were all set with a date next week—until I said I was pregnant. The woman on the other end went very quiet, asked me how far along I was, then put me on hold while a tinny panpipe played "Dancing Queen" in my ear for so long that I thought she'd forgotten me. Then she came back and said a counselor would see me now, today, if I could come in?

So here I am.

"Holly?" Andy asks, breaking my trance. "You ready?"

I take a deep breath, my knees quivering beneath me.

Ready as I'll ever be.

The waiting room is busy and stinks of disinfectant. I sit down next to a woman who looks like she's desperate for the bathroom—she keeps fidgeting, leaning forward, then back, and looking all around her—making me even more nervous. I turn away, reaching for a magazine, when this other man starts pacing the room, waving his arms around like he's doing some sort of new age slow-motion dance. I look around, beginning to notice twitches, nervous tics, fidgeting, among the other people in the room. This must be the waiting room for the psychiatric ward too. A man catches me watching him and I look quickly away, pretending to be engrossed in my fly fishing magazine.

Suddenly Andy gasps beside me and I look up as a drunk woman stumbles in, talking loudly and slurring her words. The receptionist helps her to a chair and I look back at Andy, about to make a comment about needing a stiff drink myself, but his face is ashen.

"What is it?" I ask, following his gaze back to the woman.

He swallows hard and shakes his head. "It's just—nothing."

"What?" I insist.

"She just . . ." Andy stares at his lap. "She just reminded me a bit of . . . someone."

"Okay . . ." I grin. "Someone's been hanging around too many bars . . ."

He looks at me, his eyes full of . . . what? Pity? He looks away quickly and suddenly I get it. *Trudie.* He knew Trudie. That woman reminds him of her . . .

I look around the waiting area and my pulse quickens.

Chorea, speech and movement impediments . . . Suddenly the words are embodied, alive, their meaning so much more horrific in the flesh. She's not drunk and they're not crazy. These are real people.

This is Huntington's disease.

293

Rosie

We stroll through the park, past the barren trees and lamp-posts, until we come to a duck pond.

"Perfect!" Kitty announces, sitting down on a damp-looking bench.

I eye her cream coat uncertainly. "Are you sure?"

"Best seat in the house, don't you think?" She grins. I stare at her, this woman in her designer dress—her carefully styled hair tangling in the breeze, Jimmy Choos caked in mud—perched, knees up on a park bench, drinking soup out of a bread bowl, and I smile. She's like a totally different person. She tosses some crumbs to a quacking family of ducks, which fall over themselves as they scrabble after the bread, and she laughs, beaming up at me as I sit down.

"God, I don't know what it is with you, Rosie, but I just suddenly feel . . ." She leans her head back, searching for the right word. "*Young,* I suppose!" she laughs, hugging her knees. "That's weird, isn't it? You'd think meeting my grown-up daughter would make me feel ancient—and it does, in some ways," she admits. "But being with you makes me remember being your age, seeing all this for the first time . . ." She sweeps her arm out to encompass the park, the surrounding buildings, the statues. "It's glorious." She sighs blissfully.

"It is beautiful," I say, taking a sip of chowder and looking around, the creamy soup warm and salty in my mouth.

"There's something so . . . peaceful about Boston, like it's been here forever."

"There is, isn't there?" She smiles thoughtfully. "This city has such a sense of history. The *Mayflower* landed just up the road at Plymouth. Boston itself is where the first shots of the American Revolution rang out, as well as being home of the first newspaper, the first university . . ." She looks at me and laughs.

"Don't look so surprised, Rosie." She grins. "I'm not actually a *complete* airhead. I used to love history when I was at school, it was like story time—all these amazing tales and characters, and all of them true . . . more or less, anyway." She giggles. "I'll never forget my old history teacher: 'Remember, children, the victors write the history books!'" Kitty laughs. "She was bonkers. For some reason she was crazy about the suffragettes, women's lib and all that. She had us make this mad *sculpture* out of coat hangers and clay and papier-mâché or something! Oh, it was horrible. Hideous! But she loved it, insisted it be installed in the playground as a reminder to us all. Of what, I'm not exactly sure. I think it was supposed to be Emmeline Pankhurst or something, but it looked more like a giant yeti in a tutu—"

"Betty the Yeti!" I cry, and she looks at me, stunned.

"Yes," she says slowly. "How did you . . . ?"

"That was my school." I grin. "Maybridge Grange."

"No!" she gasps. "You're . . ." She stares at me, gobsmacked. "You're not a Grangers girl?"

I nod and she shrieks with laughter.

"*No way!*" she squeals, clutching my hands. "My God! How is the old place? Tell me Belchers isn't still there, *please!*"

I nod, laughing, thinking of tiny wizened Miss Bellchamber, dwarfed by her stacks of ancient history books. "They kept trying to replace her, but she refuses to retire!"

"God!" Kitty laughs, her eyes watering. "She's an institution! She must've been sixty-odd when *I* was there! Tell me she doesn't still run the choir too?"

"Oh, yes, berets and all."

"The berets!" Kitty squeals. "Oh, God, they don't still make you wear those horrible orange monstrosities, do they? Ugh! Hideous!"

"Not according to Miss Bellchamber." I clear my throat to imitate the old lady's squeaky voice. "'We should be proud of our berets—the reason the Prince of Wales spoke to Grangers girls when he visited Maybridge was because they looked far smarter than any other school.'"

"*Bollocks!*" Kitty shrieks, spilling her soup. "I was *there*! The poor prince couldn't stop pissing himself giggling at us!"

"I *knew* it!" I laugh. "I wondered why he looked like he was crying in the photos!"

Kitty nods, her eyes streaming. "It took him five whole minutes to regain his composure, poor thing. He was meant to be meeting the mayor, but he couldn't keep a straight face! In the end his aide asked us to take them off completely in case we set him off again!"

I crease up in hysterics as Kitty giggles uncontrollably, the rich chowder warming my insides.

"My God, Maybridge Grange." Kitty wipes her eyes, beaming at me. "Jeez, Rosie, I'm so sorry—I wouldn't inflict that place on my worst enemy, let alone my daughter." She smiles. "It's a wonder you learned anything. Don't tell me you went on to Maybridge Sixth Form College as well?"

"No," I say, straightening my napkin on my lap. "No, I was meant to, but Mum—" I glance at her quickly. "Trudie, I mean—she needed me."

Kitty's smile fades. "Because she had Huntington's disease?" I nod.

"So you missed your A levels to look after her?"

I nod. "I wanted to."

"But it can't have been easy," she says gently.

I shrug, picking at the edge of my sourdough roll, watching the pieces crumble to the ground.

Kitty looks at me for a moment, then stares at her soup.

"It's awful to watch someone you love slip away," she says softly. "My granddad died of cancer when I was a little girl." She smiles weakly. "I remember running up to his bedside, not understanding why he looked so different, why he'd stopped picking me up and playing with me. It was like he wasn't my granddad anymore."

I nod. "That was the worst part. The way she changed . . ."

She nods sympathetically. "The disease affected her mobility?"

"Not just that—it was her behavior too. Her moods, her temper."

She frowns. "She was violent?"

"Not really—she didn't mean to be, she just got angry, frustrated. It was the disease, not her."

"Oh, sweetheart." Kitty squeezes my hand. "I can't imagine what you've been through . . . what you've given up—"

"I didn't mind," I insist. "She was my mum."

She looks at me. "And all that time you thought it might happen to you too? That you might inherit her disease?"

I nod, studying my chowder intently, my eyes swimming.

Kitty puts her bowl on the bench and pulls me close. "Oh, Rosie," she whispers, kissing my hair. "Imagine how different life would have been . . . *should* have been."

My heart twists in knots as I grieve for my lost mother—for all the years I've missed with the one I've found.

"I'm so sorry," Kitty sighs, stroking my hair as she holds me tight. "I am so, so sorry."

Holly

I close my eyes. This is surreal. A nightmare . . . I pinch myself, hoping I'll wake up.

"Holly?" I look up to see a smiling woman in a green dress. "Would you like to follow me?"

She leads us down a long hallway and into a small office that smells of oranges, then closes the door.

"Hi." She shakes my hand. "I'm Charlotte Atkins. I'm a genetic counselor. That sounds technical, but it just means I'm here to talk everything through with you." She turns to Andy. "And you've brought a friend. Excellent."

"Andy," he says, shaking her hand awkwardly.

"So," she says, sitting down and glancing at her notes. "You're thinking about testing for Huntington's disease?"

I nod.

She looks at me, her voice gentle. "And I understand you're pregnant?"

I nod again. "About eight weeks."

"Yes." She nods, her eyes troubled as she scribbles on her page. "Well, we'll come back to that. So, have you always known you were at risk?"

"No." I shake my head. "No, I just found out. My mom died—she had Huntington's."

"That must've been hard." Charlotte frowns. "Were you her caregiver?"

"No, actually I—I never met her, she . . ." I hesitate, glancing at Andy. "I was brought up by someone else."

"You were adopted?"

I look at her, then nod. Now is not the time—it's complicated enough.

Charlotte explains all about Huntington's. Most of it I've already heard from Rosie, but it's good to hear it from an expert—and from someone I don't despise.

She confirms that if I have inherited Huntington's from Trudie, my symptoms will probably develop at around the same age as hers did—not until my forties or fifties—and that my baby has a twenty-five percent risk of inheriting, which would rise to fifty percent if I test positive.

"Now, Holly." Charlotte leans forward. "Is your pregnancy the main reason you're thinking of testing?"

I nod miserably. "I mean, if I'm positive I need to consider . . ." I trail off.

"And Andy, is this what you want too?" Charlotte asks.

"Um . . . I . . . ," he stammers.

"No—Andy's just a friend," I say, embarrassed.

"Right." Charlotte smiles. "I see. Actually, that's better. You don't need any pressure, Holly," she tells me. "I'm not here to tell you what to do, and nobody else should either. This isn't anyone's decision but yours, okay?"

I nod, twirling my finger tightly in my hair.

"But if your pregnancy is your main concern, we can perform a prenatal test—to test the baby's DNA directly."

"You can test it before it's born?" I ask incredulously.

"Yes." Charlotte nods. "Through CVS at ten to twelve weeks or amniocentesis a little later."

"That's what I want," I tell her. "I want to know if my baby will have the disease."

"Okay," she says. "But we do advise that you test yourself first."

"Why?" I ask. "I don't need to know about myself right now—I need to know about the baby."

"I understand," Charlotte says calmly. "What you need to appreciate is that with these procedures there is a risk—up to one percent—of a miscarriage."

I close my eyes.

"Obviously, if you're negative there's no reason to risk the pregnancy. And I know you might not think so now, but even if you yourself are positive, you might decide you don't want the prenatal test after all."

I sigh.

"Most importantly, you need to understand that if the prenatal test comes back positive, then you won't have a choice not to know your own fate. You'll both definitely develop Huntington's disease."

I bite my lip. "I understand."

"Holly," Charlotte says quietly. "The only real reason to do this—to take a prenatal HD test—is if you're considering terminating your pregnancy if the result is positive."

She looks at me and I drop my gaze, her words hanging heavily in the air between us.

"Is that something you're prepared to do?"

Rosie

The limo smoothly and silently rounds the corner and Woody's Plaice rises into view, its wooden sign creaking in the evening breeze, the lanterns twinkling brightly in the windows.

"I wish I didn't have to go," Kitty sighs, pulling me close. "Today's been so wonderful. Thank you so much."

I hug her back, my throat tightening painfully as I inhale her rich perfume, breathing her in. *Don't go,* I beg inwardly. *Don't go, I've only just found you.*

"Promise me you'll come visit," she urges. "Just give me a call and I'll arrange everything. Promise?"

I nod, my eyes prickling.

"And no matter what happens—what's happened— know that I love you." She hugs me fiercely. "And I'm so, so sorry . . ." Her ribs shudder and she tightens her grip, holding me for a long moment before kissing me on the cheek. "Now go. Before my mascara starts to run." She grins. "Again."

I look at her uncertainly, unwilling.

"Go," she whispers, pulling a tissue out of her bag and

rolling her eyes. "Don't mind me, I'm an actress. My emotions are always at the surface. I'm fine." She smiles brightly. "Go, go."

I step out of the car and turn back to her as she winds the window down.

"I'll see you soon," I tell her.

"You'd better." She grins tightly, her eyes bright. "Goodbye, Rosie," she whispers, gripping my hand.

"Goodbye," I whisper, my eyes filling as her hand finally slips from mine as the car pulls away.

I watch it sail away around the corner, my heart both heavy and light.

Goodbye, Mum.

It feels like a dream. It seems impossible that just this morning I didn't know her at all, thought she didn't want to know me, and now . . . I smile. She's my mother. I mean, Trudie will always be my mum—Kitty will never replace her—but now I have a chance to get to know my real mother. My birth mother. A completely new, wonderfully different woman. I race up the steps to the house, brimming with excitement, and fly through the door, nearly colliding with Megan.

"Sorry!" I grin. "Have you seen Andy?"

"Andy? No—have you seen—"

"Holly?" Jack calls, rushing into the kitchen. "Rosie!" He stops in his tracks. "How did— Where's Kitty?"

"She had to go, but oh, Jack, we had the *best* day!"

"Really?" He smiles, relieved. "I was so worried."

"She's terrific!" I laugh. "She's amazing, she's just—"

"She's your mother." Jack smiles.

"Yes." I look at him, the word thrilling through every fiber of my being, bright and shiny and incredible. "She is. She really is!"

"That's so great, Rosie, after all this time . . ." Jack smiles, but something clouds his eyes.

"And she said she was sorry," I tell him quickly. "Sorry for leaving us. For leaving you—that she's regretted it every day of her life."

His expression changes as he looks down at me, surprise followed by something else, something softer.

"She said that?" he whispers.

I nod. "She said she was scared. Scared she'd ruin our lives, and then scared to come back—frightened that we'd reject her."

He frowns. "I'd never have rejected her," he whispers softly, searching my eyes. "She's . . . she's your mother."

"I know." I smile up at him. "She also said that she never worried about me, not for a minute, because she knew I'd be safe with you," I tell him. "That you'd be a wonderful father."

He looks at me, his eyes unreadable.

"She was right." I beam, a lump swelling in my throat.

Emotion streaks across his face.

"Thank you," he whispers, his voice hoarse. "Rosie, thank you."

Holly

The pier looms up ahead of us before I even realize we're back. I stare at it, disorientated, unsure quite how I got here, how to continue.

"You okay?" Andy asks and I turn, startled. I'd forgotten he was there.

I nod quickly. "Yes, yes, sorry, I was . . . somewhere else."

"Understandable." He nods, climbing off the boat. "You've been in a sort of trance the whole way back. You missed all the whales."

I look up, surprised.

"Oh, yeah," he says. "There were dozens—*massive* ones."

A smile tugs at my lips. "Liar."

"You'll never know, will you?" He winks, heading up the hill.

"Thank you, Andy," I tell him, following. "For everything. That was . . . it was . . ."

"Horrific," Andy finishes for me.

I grin. "Horrific," I agree, fumbling for my keys. "Thanks for lending me your cell phone, too."

"Hang on to it for now," he tells me. "In case the clinic rings about your appointment."

"You're sure? What if someone calls for you?"

"No one's got that number—no one except Rosie, anyway. I got the SIM especially to make calls in the States—keep it for now."

"Thanks." I smile, the expression freezing on my face as a black stretch limo rounds the corner and heads toward us.

"Holly?" Andy looks at me. "Holly, what is it?" He glances at the car.

I stare at it, frozen. "It's her."

He frowns. "Who?"

I swallow hard. "Kitty."

"Kitty?" Andy stares. "What the *hell*? What's *she* doing here?"

My heart pounds deafeningly, my skin prickling as the car gets closer, closer—then it's gone.

I close my eyes.

She's gone.

"Holly?" Andy says quietly. "Are you okay?"

I nod slowly, forcing myself to take deep breaths.

She's gone now.

Andy wraps his arm around me gently. "Are you sure?"

I nod again, swallow. "I just want to go home."

Andy nods, squeezing my shoulders tightly as we slowly round the corner onto my street. We make it up the driveway, up the steps, and then I stop, suddenly exhausted. The thought of taking another step, of opening that door, of facing Dad and Megan and dealing with everything, is overwhelming.

"I don't think I can do this," I breathe.

"It's gonna be okay," Andy soothes. "Remember, it's your decision."

I bite my lip. *My decision.* The hardest of my life.

"Come here," he says, pulling me into a hug. I lean into his warmth, closing my eyes and trying to pretend it's all been a dream—a nightmare—that soon I'll be able to wake up.

"Oh, Rosie." Dad's voice floats through the open kitchen window and I freeze. "I never stopped hoping, never stopped trying . . .

so many letters . . ." He trails off and I hold my breath, turning to look through the glass to see Dad holding Rosie tightly.

"Holly?" Andy glances at me nervously.

I can't breathe. My eyes are glued to the pair of them. My dad. With his daughter. His real daughter. His *healthy* daughter.

"If she'd just given us a chance, if she'd just tried . . . we could have been a family . . ."

My chest tightens as he strokes her hair.

"Oh Rosie, it could've been—it *should've* been so different . . ."

My heart stops.

Did he just say that? Did he really just say that?

"Holly?" Andy says distantly. "Are you okay?"

What about me—and Megan—and Ben? We're his family. Or at least, they are . . .

But not me, I realize, my legs trembling beneath me. *It's never been me.*

I stare at Rosie, folded so tightly in his arms, the world revolving around her, as always. Where I should be. Where I used to be.

She's taken everything.

"Holly?" Andy's face swims in front of mine as he searches my eyes, his hand soft on my cheek, his gaze clear and blue.

Suddenly I lean forward and kiss him, hard, pushing against him as if my life depends on it.

He breaks away and stares at me. I stare back, my lips stinging, my pulse racing, hardly believing what I've just done.

"Andy?" Rosie's voice is small, hesitant.

The look on her face is priceless—shock and surprise painting her cheeks a beautiful shade of gray.

Maybe now she'll know how it feels.

"Rosie . . . ," Andy starts. "Rosie, I—"

"Holly?"

I freeze at the familiar voice.

Slowly, I look down the steps, to where Josh is staring at me, his eyes wide, an inappropriately cheerful bunch of daisies hanging limply from his hand.

Rosie

"What's going on?" I say quietly, my blood running cold as I look through the open window at Andy, then Holly, then back again. He looks away. "Andy . . . ?"

He glances at Holly, then glares at me.

"Oh, sod the pair of you!" he mutters angrily, pushing past her and storming straight past me through the kitchen and thundering upstairs.

"Andy!" I cry, racing after him. *"Andy!"*

I find him in the bedroom stuffing clothes into his rucksack.

"What are you doing?"

"Leaving, remember? I wanted to go before, but you begged me to stay—said you needed me. And like a stupid sod, I believed you." He wrestles with his bag, his fingers fumbling in his hurry, his anger.

"Andy, what's wrong?" I ask quietly. "What happened?"

"You happened, Rosie. *You* happened." He shoves his clothes down, pushing and pounding as he struggles with the zip. "I warned you—I *warned* you that you didn't know what you were doing, what pain you could cause, what a *bloody mess* you'd make—but oh, no, *Rosie* knows best." He yanks the zip up finally, tightens the cord, then sighs, pushing his hair back from his face, his eyes closed. "Such a bloody mess . . ."

I step closer, wanting to hold him, to soothe away his anger, but something pins me to the spot.

"Is this about Holly?" I ask, my voice small, the words stinging my tongue as they rise unbidden. "Did you . . . did something happen?"

"Oh, here we go!" Andy laughs, lifting his bag off the bed.

"I'm only asking," I defend myself, hugging my arms. "Did you spend the day with her?"

"Why?" He rounds on me suddenly. "Why, where were you, Rosie?"

I stare at him. "I—"

"You were meant to be with me, we were supposed to go whale watching, remember?" He glares at me. "But when I get out of the shower: surprise, surprise, no Rosie. Again."

"I'm sorry!" I cry. "But Kitty just turned up—I had to go—I left you a note!"

"Really? A note?" Andy laughs. "Where? Where, Rose? I don't see any note, do you?" He sweeps his arm around the room. "And even if you did, you *promised* we'd spend today together, Rosie. You promised." His eyes bore into me. "But no. You left me. *Again.* And it wasn't even for Holly! You left me for Kitty—*Kitty!* After the way she treated you in New York, the message she left on the answering machine—she just snaps her fingers and off you go? Are you crazy?"

"She's my mum!"

"No, you had a mum, Rosie. A terrific mum. She loved

you, she cared for you, and yes, she's gone, but I'm telling you now, if you think Kitty's going to be some magical replacement, you're in for a big disappointment."

"That's not what I'm doing!"

"Well, I don't know *what* you're doing anymore—what you want, where you're going. You're coming traveling, then you're not. You're finding your mother, then you're not. You're spending the day with me, then you're not—I can't keep up!"

I stare at him, speechless.

"I'm sick of it, Rosie!" His bag thumps to the floor. "I've been working shitty jobs since July to save up for this trip—it's my gap year! I'm supposed to be seeing the sights, digging wells in dusty villages or getting off my face at full-moon parties—not chasing around after messed-up girls with their incessant issues who piss me about, then screw me over at every turn!"

My cheeks burn. "That's not fair."

"Well, you know what? Life's not fair. It wasn't fair that Trudie died, it wasn't fair that she turned out not be your mother. But you can't just take another person's parents because yours have gone, then flaunt them in their face with fishing trips and hugs and bloody *limos*—*that's* not fair, Rosie!"

"They're my parents!" I protest. "She's my *mother*, Andy! He's my *father*!"

"He's *Holly's* father!" Andy rounds on me. "He's been her father for eighteen years, and now you've ruined her life!"

"Me?" I stare at him, dumbfounded, anger rising against the guilt and shame. "I didn't even know about Jack—it was *you* who found him, *you* who brought me here, Andy. I was going to walk away, leave everyone well alone, but you *made* me tell her. *You* said I had no choice!"

309

"Well—"

"No, Andy, you're in this as deep as I am, but it's so much easier to just blame me, isn't it? To do a runner when things get complicated—like you always do? When the truth is, we wouldn't be standing here if it weren't for you!"

"Well, maybe you're better off without me, then," he counters. "You're right, I'm wrong, whatever." He shrugs. "I'm well out of it." He swings his bag onto his shoulder and pulls on his Yankees baseball cap.

My heart hurts, beating frantically. I bought him that cap in New York—we'd laughed so hard.

"Andy, wait!" I grab his arm. "Please!"

"Why?" His eyes bore into mine.

"I—"

"You don't need me, Rosie—you've got your family now. The whole reason you came, remember?" His eyes blaze at me.

"Andy—"

"Goodbye, Rose." He yanks open the door. "I hope it was worth it."

Helplessly, I watch him go, pinned to the spot by his words—the truth—as the door slams shut behind him.

Holly

"Holly?" Josh looks up at me. "Holly, what's going on?"

I can't look at him, can't face him. My cheeks are burning and I feel nauseous.

"Holly? Could you come down here, please?"

I close my eyes, then walk slowly down the steps, my grip tight on the handrail, my eyes on the ground.

"So?" he says when I reach the bottom. "You wanna tell me what's going on?"

"Nothing," I mumble, my eyes glued to the path. "Nothing's going on."

"Right," he says, nodding thoughtfully. "I get a dozen missed calls, plus texts and voice mails begging me to call you—there's something urgent you have to tell me—yet when I try calling you today you don't answer your phone, then when I come all the way down here I find you kissing some other guy!"

I close my eyes.

"So tell me, Holly, what was it that was so urgent? What was it you just *had* to tell me?"

He looks at me and I look away, take a deep breath, willing the words to come, the impossible, awful, life-altering truth.

He laughs bitterly. "I suppose that's a stupid question."

I frown. "What do you mean?"

"*This* is what you were so desperate to tell me?" he says. "That you're dumping me for someone else?"

I stare at him incredulously, the blood pumping wildly through my veins, the enormity of my news overwhelming as I look at him, so agitated, so outraged. Then suddenly I laugh—a brittle, edgy sound.

"Yes, Josh," I tell him. "Yes, that's exactly it. I've found someone else—I'm in love with Andy."

"What?" He stares at me dumbfounded. "Who the hell is Andy?"

"I'm sorry." I close my eyes, forcing the words out painfully. "It's over."

"Holly . . ."

I march away from him.

311

"Holly, wait—"

I bite my lip, don't turn.

"Holly!" He grabs my arm. "What's going on? What's happened?"

"It's over!" I tell him, pulling roughly away. "Are you stupid or something? Do you need me to spell it out?" I stare at him, my blood racing, out of control. "It's over, Josh. I've *moved on.* Deal with it, okay? You're free—go screw as many college girls as you want."

"What?" Josh stares at me. "Holly—"

"Why didn't you answer your phone, Josh?" I ask miserably. "Where were you?"

"What?"

"You knew how upset I was, how much I needed you, yet you wouldn't let me come with you, wouldn't answer your phone . . ." Hot tears streak down my face. "I needed you, Josh. I needed you and you weren't there."

"Holly, baby, I'm sorry—I'm here now, I—"

"It's too late." I turn away sadly. "You're too late."

"Holly . . ." He sighs. ". . . I didn't get your calls, I couldn't answer. I didn't have my phone—I left it . . . in a friend's room and when I got it back I called—I came straight over!"

I bite my lip.

"Jeez, Holly, it was just one day!"

One day? Is that all? One day and my whole world has fallen apart.

He looks at me for a moment, then sighs heavily. "Look, Holly, I don't know what's happened, what's changed, but—"

"Everything," I mumble. "Everything's changed. I'm—" I sigh. "You don't understand."

"Then help me understand." He cups my face, his hands trembling. "Holly . . . Look at me. You're what?"

I look at him and see our future in his face. The sacrifice he would make—the future I'd destroy.

"I'm . . ." I take a deep breath, trembling on the brink, the precipice. "I'm . . . not in love with you." I turn away, closing my eyes against the hurt in his eyes, the lies in mine. An awful silence trails behind me, and I shiver at the enormity of it, the great abyss I've created, filled with shock and hurt, as I walk away from him, from our life together.

"I—I don't believe you," Josh says, panic lacing his words like arsenic. "Holls, I don't believe you. Holly . . . this is *me*!" He grabs my arm. "This is *us*!"

His eyes are full, deep wells of sorrow. "Holly . . . is this about that kiss? About kissing another guy?"

I close my eyes.

"It's okay—it didn't mean anything—I understand . . ."

I shake my head miserably. "You don't understand."

"Holly, I do . . . ," he says, his voice trembling. "I do understand."

He looks pained suddenly, distraught.

"The guys, they . . . they told me I was crazy to get engaged so young—insisted on taking me out last night, drinking, clubbing . . . They wanted to show me what I'd be giving up, what I'd be missing out on, and I . . ." He sighs, his face crumpling. "That's why I didn't get your calls . . . My phone was—"

"In a friend's room," I quote, the blood leaving my body.

"Holly, it's not what you're thinking—nothing happened—I couldn't! I love you!"

I look away.

"Baby, I'm so sorry." He shakes his head. "I feel sick. I came straight here when I got my phone. I haven't eaten, haven't slept—"

"I bet." I bite my lip so hard it bleeds.

"Holly . . ." He shakes his head wretchedly, his eyes swimming. "Baby, nothing happened, I swear! I left before anything happened—I realized it was a mistake. Like you and him, right?"

I turn away, tears flooding my eyes.

"It's this engagement, it's freaked us out, made us crazy, that's all!" he insists desperately. "I knew you were scared, that you were worried about our future when I left for college. That's why I took you to New York, to prove to you that nothing had changed, that I'm yours—I'm yours as long as you'll have me."

I close my eyes.

"And New York . . . it was so incredible, so perfect—and then I saw that ring vendor and suddenly realized there was one way I could truly convince you, one way I could prove my commitment to you once and for all . . ." He sighs.

"But we're too young, Holls, we're teenagers, for God's sake! It was too much, I get that now. I understand . . . *That's* why we both freaked out—that's all it was—a knee-jerk reaction, a melt-down, right?" He searches my eyes, his gaze pleading, desperate. "Let's just take a step back, okay? No ring, no pressure. Just you and me. We're great together—so great—let's just go back to the way we were."

The way we were . . .

"Holly, please," he begs. "Just you and me. I love you."

Just you and me.

I shake my head. "It's too late."

"No," he insists, squeezing my hands hard. "It's not too late,

Holly, please. You're still you and I'm still me and I love you so much . . ." Tears streak his face. "Please forgive me, Holly. Please." His voice cracks, breaking my heart. "I love you, Holly Woods."

Tears blur my vision as I look up at him, biting my lips to stop them from trembling. Here it is—my excuse for leaving him, for setting him free, handed to me on a plate. But somehow it doesn't make it any easier.

"I forgive you," I say, closing my eyes, the tears spilling down my cheeks. "But it's too late." I swallow hard, pulling gently away. "It's over."

I turn and run blindly up the steps, past Andy coming down, into the house and up to my room before I can change my mind—before I turn back and crumble into Josh's arms and ruin his life forever.

This is for the best, I tell myself. *It's better this way. It's the right thing. For both of us.*

I throw myself on my bed and curl up around my stomach.

For all of us.

So why does it feel like the end of the world?

Rosie

I watch helplessly through the bedroom window as Andy walks away down the back steps, out of my life.

Suddenly Holly rushes up past him and he looks back after her for a second, as if undecided, before continuing on down. He walks up to Josh, starts to say something, then Josh turns and punches Andy hard round the face. I gasp. Josh's eyes blaze with tears as he turns and stalks away, hurling the daisies scattering to the ground.

Andy just stands there for a moment, staring after Josh, holding his jaw, and every part of me wants to run to him, comfort him—but then he looks up at me, scowls, and disappears round the corner.

I close my eyes, a wave of loneliness washing over me as I clasp the beautiful birthstone necklace he gave me, hanging heavily next to my heart.

He's gone. This time he's really gone.

And it's all my fault.

My throat dry and sore, I slump down to the kitchen for a glass of water.

Andy's wrong, I *do* have a right to be here. Jack *wants* me here—and Kitty. They're my *parents*, they want me—I *have* to stay.

I'm about to run the tap when I hear Megan's voice, raised in anger.

"Is this what it's all been about, Jack? All these years? Finding Kitty?" she yells.

I freeze, my eyes drawn to the closed living room door.

"Is this why you came to the States? Jeez, Jack, is that why you *married* me, so you'd be able to *stay?*"

"Don't be ridiculous," Jack's voice is low, defensive.

I put the empty glass down carefully.

"*Is* it ridiculous?" Megan asks, her voice shrill, so unlike the happy-go-lucky Megan I've gotten to know these past few days.

"Then how come you never mentioned her, huh, Jack?" she demands. "How come you gave me the same spiel you gave Holly about her mom being dead—when all along you've been sending her letters? All through our marriage!"

Despite myself I wander into the hallway, drawn like a moth to the flame of destruction.

"It's not like that! I was only sending her photos of her daughter—of Holly!"

Megan laughs bitterly. "*Her daughter*, is she? No matter that she'd never laid eyes on her mother till this morning— that she thought she was dead? No matter that I'm your *wife*—for all intents and purposes Holly's mom too—but you didn't think to mention that her *real* mother was still kicking around somewhere, not so far away—on our television every week, for Christ's sake—*being sent regular updates?* That she might just turn up at our house one day and stand there in our kitchen letting me *gush* about her *stupid show?*" She snatches a ragged breath. "Do you have any idea how *humiliated* I feel, Jack? How *betrayed?*"

"Megan . . ." Jack sighs. "Yes, I sent her letters, okay— she's Holly's mother, I wanted to give her a chance to know her. But she didn't want that. She didn't want anything to do with me, or Holly. I didn't think I'd ever see her again!"

"And now you have."

"Yes, now I have."

There's a long pause, then Megan's voice, clear and controlled. "Are you still in love with her, Jack?"

I hold my breath, the silence so long I'm convinced I've missed his answer. Then finally it comes, quiet, almost a sigh.

"Don't be stupid. I love you, Megan."

Megan sighs. "You know what?" she says, her voice bright

with tears. "I think I need some air. Can you pick up Ben? You know, your second child, born of your second choice?"

"Megan—"

I retreat quickly to the stairs as the door flies open and she storms through the hallway and out the kitchen door, Jack in pursuit, but she's too fast for him. I hear her quickly pattering down the steps outside as Jack watches her through the kitchen window, his head bowed over the sink. Suddenly he punches it hard, the dirty cutlery clattering in the bowl, my empty glass shattering on the floor.

I pad slowly, softly, back up the stairs to my room, careful of every footstep on the soft carpet. But still the trail of destruction continues.

How? I think. How did this happen? Just half an hour ago I raced into this house, on top of the world, buzzing with excitement, desperate to tell Andy about Kitty, thrilled that everything was somehow, amazingly, falling into place . . .

But actually everything was falling apart. I twirl my necklace miserably. Andy's right. I caused this. I caused this whole mess. And now he's gone. I just let him go. Again.

Well, not this time. I pull out my mobile and punch in his number, a thousand apologies poised on my lips. But he doesn't pick up. I sigh. I don't blame him.

"Andy, I'm so sorry," I tell his voice mail. "You were right. I've screwed everything up. Sarah changed everything when she swapped me with Holly and, whether she was right or wrong, I should've had the sense to just live with it. To get on with my own life and make the most of it. With you. I love you, Andy. I miss you." I sigh, clutching my birthstone tightly. "Please call me."

I click off and stare at the phone, willing it to ring. It doesn't.

I curl up on the bed, my head throbbing in my arms, loneliness descending around me like a cold fog.

What have I done?

Holly

I dive into the pool, the cool rush of water swallowing me whole as I swim for all I'm worth, slicing through the water, barely time to snatch a breath as I propel myself forward, one length and then another, kicking faster, pulling the water past me in swift power-ful strokes. I push myself harder and harder, until suddenly I break the surface, gasping for air, adrenaline still surging madly in my veins.

It's no good, I realize, throwing my head back and rubbing the chlorine from my eyes. I used to be able to escape anything by swimming, to lose myself in the water. But not now. Not this time.

I take a deep breath and sink below the surface, the world dis-solving instantly, all sounds of the pool, of people, of life outside, fading as my hair swirls around me like a mermaid's. Down here, everything's in slow motion, the sounds muted, the blue water and the lights rippling above, so peaceful . . .

Is this what it's like for you, baby? I think. *Floating in there, so peaceful and quiet? So safe?*

It seems impossible that only a week ago I went to the clinic — it's been the longest week of my life. How is it that I've never noticed how slow a second is, how the hours stretch endlessly through the morning, the long afternoon, into the eternal black night. Day after endless day. But finally it's almost here. Tomorrow is my appointment. Just one more sleep. One more endless night. Then decision time.

Think about it, Charlotte said. I've done nothing but.

What if . . . What if it's negative? That's easy. Hurray, we're safe. My life can go back to normal—ish—and I can start trying to deal with my pregnancy like any other teenager.

What if . . . What if it's positive? A shiver runs down my spine. Then I know what to expect. I've read enough now, watched enough heartbreaking videos online. I know exactly what's going to happen to me. What might happen to my baby.

My eyes sting from the chlorine and my lungs begin to burn as I watch the air bubbles float silently to the surface.

Would I treat my child any differently, knowing? Knowing his or her future? Knowing mine? Will people treat me differently, judge me, make assumptions if I'm positive? If I tell them . . .

Charlotte said that I should consider applying for benefits like long-term-care insurance now, before I get tested, because if I'm positive it'll be more difficult—impossible, even. It could affect my employment, my life insurance, my *baby's* insurance . . . unless I can find five hundred dollars to pay for the test anonymously.

Though the answer to that one's offered itself on a plate, I think bitterly, remembering Kitty's letter—the first *ever*—that arrived this morning. After *eighteen years, now* she suddenly writes to me, apologizing for missing my entire childhood, offering me money—ten thousand dollars—as back payment for all the birthdays and Christmases she's missed.

Yeah, like *that* makes up for a lifetime of abandonment.

My blood boils in my temples.

320

I don't need her, don't need anything from her. Ever. She can stick her freaking money. She can't *buy* my forgiveness—not after what she did. I'll find another way. Somehow.

I close my eyes and float like a starfish to the surface, my lungs exploding with the burst of oxygen, tears brimming my eyes as I surrender to the water, to fate.

I always thought I'd like to see the future, what life had in store for me. What I didn't realize was that some things are set in stone. I'm not like Ebenezer Scrooge, who can see the misery in his future and change it. This is DNA. It's unchangeable. There's no cure. If you've got the mutated gene you'll definitely develop Huntington's. If you don't, then you're free. Fifty-fifty. All or nothing. The toss of a coin.

If only it were that easy.

Charlotte's given me an information packet—testimonials from other people who were at risk. Huntington's is not the end of the world, she says; lots of people lead fulfilled, happy lives, even knowing they're positive. Scientists and athletes and academics—brilliant people who might not have achieved what they did if people had treated them differently. If their horizons had been fenced in. Thirty to forty years is a long time, they say. You can either live while you can, or treat it like a prolonged death sentence, overshadowed by the future.

I know it's meant to be comforting—inspiring, even—but I'm pregnant, there's another life at stake here. I know Charlotte says I can abort at up to twenty weeks, but I honestly don't think I could bear it. My baby already seems so much a part of me that I need to decide before then. Before I'm showing. Before everyone has to know. When I might still be able to try to pretend that none of this ever happened.

Tell people, Charlotte had said. But how can I? Melissa keeps calling and coming around, but I can't face her, can't talk to her. How can I tell her why Josh and I broke up without telling her about Huntington's? How can I tell her about Huntington's without telling her about the baby—her *brother's* baby—Melissa's niece or nephew—while Josh doesn't even know I'm pregnant?

While I'm still considering abortion.

I can't. I can't tell anyone. Even Dad. As much as I've tried, as much as I want to tell him . . . there's just too much. I can't spill one drop without the rest coming pouring out in an endless flood, and I'm afraid I'll drown in it. I'm afraid we all will. I squeeze my eyes shut, giddy in this endless circle, fumbling around desperately for the way out. There is no way out, I realize, no Get Out of Jail Free card, only a choice to stay in the dark or to know where I'm headed.

Where *we're* headed. It's not just me anymore. There's my baby. Josh's baby.

Josh. God, Josh. He sat outside my room all night, begging me to talk to him, then left me a letter saying that he understands I need some space, some time to deal with everything, but that he's there, ready, waiting for me whenever I need him. That he loves me . . .

My eyes sting.

I made the right decision, ending it with Josh, I know I did. I'm saving him, just like I'd be saving this baby. From a life of misery—of endless heartache.

It was the right decision—the hardest decision of my life.

So far.

With a rush I turn and heave myself onto the side of the pool, shivering in the sudden cold, the harsh lights, the echoing noise of the real world.

I grab my towel and hug it around me, reaching into my purse for my notebook, and pull out the photo inside. To my surprise, two pictures slide to the floor—the scan image and Rosie's photo of Trudie, her chestnut hair gleaming in the sun, so like mine.

My heart twists. How did Trudie do it? How did she cope, knowing that her child, her little girl, was watching her deteriorate, watching her die, *knowing* she might develop HD herself one day? I brush my finger gently across the photo, across the kink in her ear, noticing for the first time her finger curled in her hair. I untwirl mine self-consciously, a funny shiver tingling down my spine. *She did that too.*

There are so many things I don't know—so many questions I'd ask her. Would she have done things differently if she'd known? Would she have taken the test? *Would she have had an abortion?*

My eyes flick to the scan picture, my heart twisting painfully as my fingers trace the tiny form.

The only reason to take a prenatal HD test is if you're considering terminating your pregnancy . . .

Memories of the clinic rush back at me. *Manual Vacuum Aspiration . . .* I shiver.

What if I couldn't? What if I couldn't face it, if I changed my mind? We'll always know what's in the crystal ball, I'll have stolen the child's choice and he or she will get a live-action preview when I start having symptoms.

But if I go ahead with an abortion . . . My chest hurts. I'll be saving my baby a future of misery, a preordained destiny of suffering . . . A woman in the news even killed her sons because of what HD was doing to them, thought they'd be better off dead . . .

But I'd be robbing my child of thirty to forty years of healthy life . . .

Which is the right choice? And who am I to decide what's best—a life destined for suffering . . . or no life at all?

Maybe I should just go ahead with an abortion anyway; then

I wouldn't have to decide about testing for myself for another ten, twenty years—no pressure, no rush. My decision. Maybe that's what I should've done to start with, saved all this misery and heartache and stress. I never wanted to be pregnant, after all—I should sue the stupid condom company—and now suddenly here I am, forced to make all these life-and-death decisions.

And Kitty left her baby, after all—maybe teens just aren't meant to be parents.

I stroke my stomach. But if it's negative, if I don't have Huntington's . . .

I close my eyes, my head spinning in endless circles as I pull on my clothes and head home.

Still holding my breath.

Still waiting to surface.

Rosie

I can't believe only a week ago I was in Boston with Kitty. It feels like a dream, her appearing out of the blue like that, and then that wonderful afternoon in the park. And now she's disappeared again, as quickly as she arrived. I know she's just busy, but I keep calling and emailing her anyway, keep thinking of new things to tell her—we have so much to catch up on.

It's just as well she hasn't called back, really, I think, glancing at Jack as he dresses a lobster—though things between him and Megan seem to be a little better, thank goodness. Jack's been bringing her huge bouquets of flowers every day and the house smells wonderful, though Megan complains that they keep dropping petals everywhere. She loves them, though. Whenever Jack's not around, she lingers over them, inhaling their perfume and constantly rearranging them in their vases. Which is why they keep dropping petals everywhere.

At least someone's love life's working out. I sigh. I keep calling Andy's mobile in the vain hope he'll answer, but he never does. I went round to the B&B, but he's left. Gone without a trace. I don't even know if he's traveled down to Washington like he suggested—if he's even still in the country! He's probably a million miles away by now, seeing the world just like he planned. Like we planned.

I tuck my necklace under my hoodie and sigh, determined to learn from my mistakes. I'm not going to run away from my problems anymore. I've caused this mess and now I'm going to stick around to try to sort it out.

Somehow.

All week I've been trying to make myself useful wherever possible, babysitting gorgeous Ben whenever I can and helping Jack at the restaurant every day, as half his staff have gone down with a bug.

This, officially, is also what's wrong with Holly, who's been off school for a week and has barely left her room. She won't answer to anyone, not even her friend Melissa, not even Josh. He sat outside her door for a whole night, but still she wouldn't see him. And when she does come out, she doesn't talk, just goes off swimming or for long bike rides by herself. I've been trying to think of ways to reach out to her, help her, but after Kitty, I'm worried I'll just make

325

things worse. I can't force this, I have to be patient, wait till she wants to talk, till she's ready. And when she is, I'll be here, waiting. However long it takes.

"Oops—missed a spot." Jack points at a pool of tomato sauce that has somehow leapt from the pan I'm stirring onto the floor.

"Thanks," I say, kneeling to wipe it up, and he grins as he arranges a tray of crab cakes a sous chef has just prepared.

"If a job's not worth doing right—"

"It's not worth doing at all," I mutter good-naturedly, swabbing the tiles.

"Right you are— Holly!" he says suddenly, staring at the doorway.

I freeze, hidden from sight on the floor.

"Hello, stranger!" he cries, rushing over to hug her. "I was beginning to forget what you look like. Want some lunch? You look a little pale. Lucky kippers are today's special!"

"No—no thanks," she says. "I've already eaten."

I peer round the counter. She does look pale, like a ghost, ashen and drawn, heavy bags dark under her eyes.

"Dad . . ." She takes a deep breath, her finger twirling in her hair. "Dad, do you think you could lend me some money? Just a loan . . ."

"Sure," Jack says. "How much?"

She hesitates. "Five hundred dollars?"

Jack whistles. "That's a lot of money, sweetie. What's it for?"

"It's important," Holly bites her lip. "It's . . ."

As she hesitates, a deliveryman pushes through the door into the kitchen, laden with vegetables. "Mr. Woods?"

"Guilty," Jack says, taking the clipboard. "What's it for, Holls?"

"It's just—I've decided . . ." Holly falters, her eyes flicking to the deliveryman. "There's just something I really need."

"For five hundred dollars?" Jack asks, looking up from the clipboard.

She nods.

"Sweetie, if I'm giving you that much money I wanna know what it's for," Jack says, signing the delivery note and handing it back.

She hugs her arms as she watches the deliveryman leave.

"It's just . . ." She hesitates. "It's . . . I want to take the test."

The breath catches in my throat.

Jack stares at her, swallows. "The Huntington's test?"

She nods, her eyes wide.

"Sweetie . . ." He sighs. "Don't you think we should talk about this? Take some time? There's no hurry . . ."

She shakes her head. "I need to know."

"Jack!" A waitress bursts into the kitchen. "The Prescott party's just arrived—they want to talk to you about catering for a wedding."

"I'll be there in a minute," Jack tells her, turning back to Holly.

"Holly-berry, this is a huge decision, okay? We need to sit down and talk about it properly, discuss everything. I really don't think this is something you want to rush into—"

"But Daddy, I *have* to—"

"You don't *have* to do anything, sweetheart, okay?" He strokes her hair behind her ear. "But if you still want to go ahead after we've talked about it all properly . . . of course I'll pay, okay?"

"Jack!" The waitress appears again, looking frazzled.

"Okay, Holly-berry?" Jack repeats.

"Okay." She nods, staring at the floor. He kisses her forehead before following the waitress into the restaurant.

Holly closes her eyes and sighs heavily.

I take a deep breath and stand up. "Holly?" Her eyes fly open.

"Rosie!" she gasps. "I didn't see you there."

"Sorry, I didn't mean to startle you—I was just . . . mopping." I show her. "Your dad's a slave driver." I smile. *Your,* I think. Careful to say *your.*

"Right," she says, hugging her arms around herself. "Tell me about it." She smiles weakly, leaving through the back door.

"Holly, wait." I follow her outside. "Listen, you shouldn't have to pay—for the test, I mean. Either of you."

She turns.

"This is my fault, my responsibility, and . . . I owe you."

"You don't owe me anything, Rosie," she says coolly. "Least of all money."

God, that came out wrong—like I'm trying to buy her off or something.

"No, I didn't mean . . ." I swallow, choosing my words carefully. "What I mean is . . . there's Trudie's inheritance money."

She looks at me, surprised.

"It's yours, Holly. It belongs to you, not me. You should have it."

She bites her lip, hesitating.

"I can't get it for you all at once, obviously, but look, here's fifty dollars," I say, fishing in my purse. "I can get more from the bank later." I hold the money out to her and she hesitates.

"Thank you," Holly says finally, taking it. "I'll pay you back."

I shake my head. "It's yours."

She smiles. "Thank you."

She folds the notes up carefully and tucks them into her jeans pocket.

"Well," I say, anxious not to ruin the moment by saying or doing anything stupid. "I'd better get on." I head for the door.

"Wait," she says suddenly. "Rosie . . . are you doing anything tomorrow?"

Holly

Rosie's eyes immediately light up, and I hesitate.

Is this crazy? Have I gone nuts? *What am I doing?* Of all the people in the whole world . . .

But then, of all the people in the whole world, who better? Andy's gone, and she's been through this already. She's my other half, the flip side of this coin. She thought she was at risk and now she's not. I thought I was fine and now I'm not. She had her mother's disease to worry about, I have my baby's. She's the girl in the looking glass with my life—only backward.

"I'm free," she tells me eagerly. "Tomorrow. All day."

329

I smile weakly. "And . . . do you have Trudie's medical records?"

She looks at me, surprised. "I . . . no, but I could probably get them . . ."

"Thanks," I say awkwardly. "It's just . . . it would be good to see them. Find out if there are any more genetic surprises, you know."

Rosie's face fills with pain. "I think it's just the Huntington's," she says quietly.

I nod.

"What made you want to get tested?" I blurt suddenly.

She looks at me, surprised.

"I . . ." She takes a deep breath, considering. "I couldn't live with the not knowing," she says simply. "I watched my mum—Trudie, I mean," she corrects herself quickly. "I watched her suffer and then die and I had to know if it was going to happen to me too."

I nod again.

"But a lot of people choose not to get tested," she says quickly. "Jack's right, you need to take some time, think about it all properly—"

"It's *all* I think about," I counter. "All I *can* think about."

"I know." Rosie nods miserably. "Holly, I'm so sorry, I should never have told you. All I've done is ruin your life—"

"No," I say, though it kills me to admit it. "No, Rosie. You did the right thing. I needed to know." *I need to know.*

She stares at the floor. I look at her. My reflection.

"Rosie, it's not your fault," I tell her, a gift.

She looks up at me, her eyes filled with tears, then suddenly flies at me in a hug, holding on to me as if her life depends on it— this girl who's stolen my life and trampled on my dreams. I should hate her, but how can I? She was me; now I'm her. This mistake that switched us, that placed us in each other's worlds, each

330

other's lives, has linked us forever. She's the only one who *can* understand.

And she didn't steal my life, not really. She couldn't have taken it if it wasn't rightfully hers. She brought the truth, and all the harsh realities that carries with it. But no, she hasn't stolen my life.

The truth is, I've been living hers.

Rosie

I hold on to Holly tightly, this girl, this amazing girl, whose life I've managed to single-handedly obliterate, who's actually accepted my olive branch. It's just a beginning, but I can be there for her, I can understand . . . It won't ever make up for the pain I've caused, but I can at least do some good.

"Holly, if there's anything—*anything*—I can do for you—if you want to talk, if you need anything at all—"

"Actually," she says hesitantly. "Tomorrow I'm . . . I've decided that—"

"There you are!" Jack calls, opening the kitchen door. "Someone's arrived to cheer you up."

We both look up in surprise. Then I follow his gaze to where Andy stands awkwardly.

Andy. My heart soars. This moment, this very moment I'm making peace with Holly, now Andy's come back too. Someone up there's smiling on me today.

"Hi!" I beam. "You're back."

"Hi," he says awkwardly, his hands deep in his pockets. He glances at Holly.

331

"I'll—I'll leave you to it," she says, moving toward the door.

"Actually," Andy says, stopping her, "it's Holly I've come to see."

Holly

"I wanted to check if we're still on—for tomorrow?" Andy asks me. "I've left you a million voice mails . . ."

I hesitate as Rosie's face turns white.

"Right," she says eventually, her voice tight. "Right. Well. I-I'll leave you to it, then." She ducks her head as she stumbles away around the corner.

I glance at Andy, who's staring at his feet. We stand in silence for a moment, words difficult to find.

"I thought you'd gone," I say eventually. "I think we all did."

"I thought about it," Andy admits. "But I wanted to be here in case you decided—in case you needed someone to go with you. Tomorrow." He shuffles his feet. "And you've got my phone."

"Oh," I say, fishing in my bag. "Right. Sorry, I completely forgot."

"You forgot?" he says, surprised. "How'd you forget when it keeps ringing?"

"It hasn't," I tell him, pulling it out. "It hasn't made a sound since—"

"Pass it here," he says. "It's turned off." He smiles, pressing a button, and the screen comes to life. "You'd better check your voice mail—it's full." He shows me, passing it back. "I thought you were ignoring me."

"Why would I? *I'm* the one who—" I break off, my cheeks burning as I remember our kiss. "I'm so sorry, Andy—I don't know what came over me last week, I should never—"

He shrugs. "It happens. I'm a lovable guy." He grins.

"Whatever." I smile, rolling my eyes. "But Rosie . . ."

"Rosie and I have got our own problems," he tells me. "Don't worry about us—you've got enough on your plate." He looks at me, his eyes softening. "So are you still going? Tomorrow?"

I take a deep breath and nod. "I've decided I'm gonna get myself tested first."

"You're sure?"

I nod. "I'm not putting my baby at any unnecessary risk. If I'm negative, then there's no point." I bite my lip.

"And if you're positive?" he asks, his voice gentle as cotton candy.

I close my eyes, shivering as the wind whips past.

"I still don't know."

Rosie

The image of Andy kissing Holly burns in my memory and I feel sick.

All this time—*all this time*—I've been calling him, leaving him messages, begging him to talk to me . . . all this time he's been calling *her* . . . ?

Be careful what you wish for, I think, blinking away my tears as I hurry away down the street. All this week I've been praying for a way to make things up to Holly—swearing

I'd do anything, give up anything for her . . . but I never dreamed it would be Andy. He's my future. At least, I thought he was.

Perhaps this is destiny?

I swallow hard.

Perhaps they were always meant to meet?

If Holly and I had never been switched, I'd have been brought up here, after all, and Andy and I would never have met. Instead, Holly and Andy would both be back home in Bramberley.

And now I'm the one who's brought them together. After all, Andy wouldn't be here if it weren't for me—if I hadn't dragged him on this roller-coaster ride.

I sigh.

Yet again, I've got no one to blame but myself.

Holly

I stare out my bedroom window at the dark driveway.

Still no Rosie.

I hope she's okay. Hope she's not hiding away somewhere, upset.

Hope she's going to keep her promise . . .

I sigh. *Yeah, right.* Like she's really gonna still give me five hundred dollars, after her boyfriend just returned from out of the blue—*to see me.*

I sink onto my bed.

But my appointment's tomorrow . . .

I bite my lip. I could try asking Dad again after he finishes work, but . . .

But he wants to *sit down and talk about it properly,* I remember miserably. *This isn't something you want to rush into—there's no hurry.*

But how can I tell him there *is* a hurry, without telling him I'm *pregnant*?

I close my eyes, imagining the whole new can of worms *that* would open—something I just can't even bear thinking about to-night. Everything's hard enough already.

I flop back onto my pillow and pull Kitty's letter from my drawer:

> *Dear Holly,*
>
> > *I know nothing I say can ever make up for what*
> > *I did, or the years I've missed . . .*

No kidding.

> *And I know you probably won't believe me, but I've*
> *regretted it every single day since.*

My heart bleeds.

> *You're an adult now, Holly, and while I realize I've*
> *missed my chance to be any sort of mother to you,*
> *I hope you will accept my gift of $10,000.*

Translation: I'm so rich I can buy myself out of any situation, and usually do.

I've missed so many birthdays, so many Christ-mases, and whilst I know money can never make up for what we've lost, I hope it may be useful to you—that I can at least make your life easier in some small way as you head into adulthood—to college, or whatever path you choose.

I swallow. *Whatever path I choose . . .*

The last thing I want now is to make your life any more difficult, but I do fear that now our paths have crossed once more, the media may try to intrude on your life—as they do in almost every aspect of mine.

I shudder, imagining reporters swarming round our house, digging up all our secrets—*my secrets*—printing them for the whole world to see. . . .

Consequently, I feel it would be much better for everyone if the press does not get involved, and wonder if you would be so kind as to sign the enclosed form, fill in your bank details, and fax it back to me, so I may transfer your money directly.

Ten thousand dollars . . . I glance at the form: the space for my account details, the paragraph promising I won't speak to the press, then a box for my signature.
Ten thousand dollars . . .

Darling Holly, you may not be my biological daughter, but you are the baby I held in my arms, the child I named, the daughter I've missed all these years . . .

I swallow hard.

Please believe me when I say I will never forgive myself for leaving you. The only excuse I have is that I was seventeen, no one knew I was pregnant and I was scared out of my mind.

I bite my lip. She was like me, I realize suddenly. Except she was a year younger . . .

I feel so ashamed of what I did, and understand if you can never forgive me, if you never want to see or speak to me ever again. But I would be eternally grateful if you would accept my olive branch, and allow me to at least help you in this small way, my Holly.

Sincerely,
Kitty Clare

I stare at the letter.

Strangely, I don't feel as angry this time. What she did doesn't seem quite so awful. Despite myself, I even feel a stab of sympathy for her, this woman who deserted me, whose footsteps I'm inadvertently following.

Yes, Kitty abandoned her baby—but she was a teenager, younger than I am. And aren't I doing something similar—*worse, even*—by considering abortion? I close my eyes.

At least Kitty's trying to make up for what she did. True, money isn't a great way to do it, but as it happens, it's exactly what I need at the moment. Kitty may not have been my mother for all these years, but now, ironically, she's the one person who can help me out, give me the money I need, no questions asked.

And she's offered it to me on a plate.

In return for . . . what? Forgiveness? Closure? A guarantee that I won't run off to some tabloid and sell my story? As if I'd want to. Why would I want my life invaded, my secrets splashed all over some magazine, some paper, some Website?

And, if not quite forgiveness, I can certainly swallow my pride for the sake of my baby—for the sake of ten thousand dollars that will allow me to get tested anonymously, to protect my future—our future.

And why *shouldn't* I get something from Kitty after all these years? She owes me. And she's right, it would make my life—*my decisions*—much easier . . .

I stare at the form a moment longer, then grab a pen and fill it in, sign my name and fax it off.

Perhaps some good can finally come out of this awful situation after all.

Rosie

The frosty wind whispers around my shoulders as I gaze up at the huge two-story lobster-pot Christmas tree, its cheerful lights glowing determinedly, despite the darkening night and icy cold, despite the fact that there's hardly anyone here to see it—despite the fact that Christmas was nearly a month ago.

The pretty red ribbons flutter in the breeze as I huddle in my hoodie, chilled to the bone, but not from the wind. I can't face going back to the house yet—not if Andy might still be there. I have enough imagined pictures of him with Holly floating round my head without risking adding real ones by returning too soon.

I hug my hoodie closer, Holly's money tucked safely inside. It's still hers, after all—she deserves it, whatever's happening with Andy. From the sounds of it, she wouldn't even take his calls—his "million voice mails," I remember bitterly.

I realize I'm fiddling with the birthstone necklace and pull my hand away sharply, staring at the lights until they splinter and blur like reflections on the tide.

Suddenly they're blotted out.

"Hey," Andy says quietly.

I look away. "How'd you know I'd be here?"

"I didn't."

"Oh." I flinch, hating my heart for leaping at his arrival,

only to be crushed yet again. He hasn't come to see me. It's just a coincidence. It's only a small town, after all.

"I looked everywhere else," Andy explains, sinking down next to me on the bench. "There's not that many places to search. Especially in off-season." He smiles wryly but I don't look up.

"And I remembered how much you loved this tree when we found it."

I stare up at it, at the cheerful red plastic lobster, king for once, high above the beribboned pots, trying to ignore the heat I feel from Andy's body close to mine.

"Rosie," he sighs. "I'm sorry about what I said. I was wrong." He looks at me. "You were right to come here, to tell them . . ." He takes a deep breath. "Holly had to know."

I stare at my feet.

"What she's going through, what's happened—it's not your fault . . . None of it is." He shakes his head. "And it's really brave of you to stay, to face up to the consequences, take responsibility . . . I'm not so great at that." He smiles ruefully. "But I've come back to give it a go."

He covers my hand gently with his.

"I'm proud of you, Rose. You're so strong. When I think of everything you've been through . . . You're the strongest girl I've ever met."

He squeezes my hand tight, his warm palm enclosing mine.

I squeeze back. "Thank you, Andy."

"And Holly needs that strength—needs you—even if she doesn't always like to admit it."

I look away, suddenly cold again despite his hand clutching mine.

"Holly." I nod. "You came back to be with Holly."

"Don't be an idiot, Rose." He sighs, smoothing my hair as it tangles in the wind. "I'm just . . . helping her with something, trying to follow your example." He cups my face, his eyes deep in mine. "There's nothing between me and Holly." He brushes my cheek tenderly. "There's only you. There's only ever been you."

I look at him, his eyes fathomless in the dark, glittering with the reflections of the tiny lights.

"I thought you'd gone for good," I whisper.

"I promised I'd come back," he reminds me. "I couldn't leave things the way they ended—I had to apologize, tell you you were right." He smiles. "You seem to be making real progress with Jack—with Holly . . ."

I nod. "I hope so."

"And believe me, you didn't miss anything in Washington. I didn't even get to the Smithsonian—Aunt Patty was on overdrive, dragging me round town to meet all her friends and neighbors—you had a lucky escape." He grins.

I smile faintly.

"You were right to stay," he says gently. "You're needed here."

I search his eyes. "And you . . . ?" I ask tentatively.

"I'll stay if you want me to," he promises. "But you don't need me, Rose—look how far you've come on your own. You're really building bridges here, and I *really* don't want to get in the way of that." He strokes my face. "They're your family, Rose, there's nothing more important. They have to come first. They need you—*all* of you—as long as it takes." He squeezes my hand.

I nod slowly, staring at our hands, trying to work out whose fingers are whose.

"Where does that leave us?"

"I don't know," he sighs. "I love you, Rosie Kenning." He grips my hand tight, and my heart aches. "And I'm so glad everything's working out for you—with Kitty, with Jack, with Holly . . . I'm so happy for you." He looks at me, his eyes shining. "But right now . . . it seems like we're just on different paths." He sighs.

I swallow hard, my insides twisting as he lifts my chin.

"Once everything's settled down—when the moment's right, when we're both ready . . . that's when our paths will come together—that'll be our time . . ." His eyes swim as he cups my face. "We'll have our time. I know it." He smiles fiercely and my throat swells. "And we'll finally go traveling together. Just you, me, the beach and the sea— no stress . . . no worries . . . and it will be . . . *incredible*." He grins. "If our week in New York's anything to go by, I can't *wait*!"

His eyes sparkle and I giggle weakly.

"I love you, Rosie," he tells me, his voice husky as he kisses a tear from my cheek. "But for now—just for now— they need you more."

I nod painfully, his face blurring in the dark.

He pulls me close and I shut my eyes, trying to memorize the feel of his body against mine, every centimeter his warmth touches . . . until finally he breaks away.

"Au revoir." He smiles, kisses me softly before slowly walking away.

And although I feel cold without him, shivering violently

in the empty square, watching him disappear into the night—
though the future's dark, and I don't know when I'll see him
again—deep inside me, a flame burns on.

Holly

The burning sun is just starting to creep over the neighbors' houses,
gilding the roofs and chasing away the shadows, as I brush the dirt
off my knees and wriggle into the dusty corner. It's smaller than I
remember up here, darker, damper. But then, it would be; I haven't
been up to my tree house in about eight years.

I pull my jacket tighter against the chilly morning air as I gaze
around at the peeling pictures and discarded toys. A long-forgotten
treasure chest sits rotting in the corner, the bright paint faded, like
the old scrap of damp carpet beneath me. It's been a long time—a
lifetime—but it's still my place. The playroom Dad built for me; the
den where Melissa and I shared our secrets and spied on the neigh-
borhood boys, watching for hours as they lay bronzing in the sun,
imagining our first kisses.

I lean back and my hand rests on something soft. I pick it up
and dust it off, surprised. His fur is coarse, roughened with age and
adventures, but the teddy bear's deep chocolaty eyes smile at me
knowingly, his scent wonderfully familiar. Mr. Brown. My favorite toy
since I was a baby.

A baby. I hug my stomach, which is just beginning to swell
against my waistband.

*Will you play up here someday, baby? Will you cuddle Mr.
Brown, read these books, climb that rope-ladder . . . ?*

343

Suddenly the ladder pulls tight, and I spring back, startled, as Dad's head pops up above the floorboards.

"Hey." He smiles, wobbling on the rungs. "Sorry, didn't mean to scare you. Your mobile was ringing." He tosses me Andy's cell phone and I glance at it quickly—it could be the clinic. I forgot to check the voice mail.

"Permission to enter?" he asks.

I shrug, wiping my eyes and scooting over quickly as he crawls awkwardly into the tiny room, tucking his knees up against his chin.

"I like what you've done with the place," he jokes, looking around at the layers of dust and cobwebs.

I smile despite myself. He looks ridiculous—like a giant folded into a nutshell.

"Well I never!" He gasps, his eyes falling on the teddy bear. "Mr. Brown! How are you, old fella?" He fondles the bear's ears affection- ately. "I thought we'd lost him years ago—never dared mention it to you because one time when you lost him for just a day you were inconsolable. Even ice cream for breakfast, lunch and dinner didn't cheer you up! You cried so hard you gave yourself a headache. Just as well, really—it was only when I went to get some painkillers that I found him, hidden in the medicine chest!" He laughs.

"I'll never forget the look on your face when I brought him riding into your bedroom on my shoulders. You looked at me like I was your hero, like I could fix anything." He smiles wistfully. "I loved that. You'd come to me with your cuts and scrapes and nightmares and I'd kiss them all better, solve everything with a wave of my magic wand. It was the best feeling in the world." He beams at me for a moment; then his face clouds over.

"I'm sorry I can't fix this, Holly-berry." He sighs heavily. "I'd give anything, you know, do anything to change things—to swap places . . ."

I look at him. For the first time in my life he looks old.

"You lost your magic wand?" I joke, my voice light.

He smiles sadly. "Yes, yes, I suppose I have."

I stare at the floor, at the knotted wood swirling and splintering beneath us, yet somehow still managing to hold us up, at least for now.

"But I still have some magical powers."

"Oh, yeah?" I raise an eyebrow.

"Uh-huh. My shoulders are actually super-spongy-sturdy stress supporters, *plus* I have super-sensitive-sympathetic listening skills."

"Bonus." I grin, and he smiles.

"So . . . you and Josh . . ."

I shrug. "Didn't work out."

"I'm sorry," Dad says sincerely. "What happened?"

"It just . . . didn't work out," I repeat quietly.

"Right." He nods. "Only I hope it wasn't to do with Hunt—"

"It's for the best," I interrupt quickly.

"Right." Dad nods, and we both stare at the floor. "You know, I do also have super-sonic-shutting-up powers . . . ," he says gently. "On occasion . . ."

I grin despite myself. "Rarely used."

"Rarely used," he admits, smiling.

I sniff. "How about super-human-hugging powers?"

"Now, *those*," he says, wrapping one big arm around me and pulling me close, "are my specialty."

I close my eyes and lean into him, his arms tight around me, the musty smell of his old woolly sweater warm and familiar.

345

"Oh, Holly-berry," he sighs, rocking me like a child. "You know, it hardly seems two minutes ago that I first gave you Mr. Brown to soothe you to sleep as a baby." He looks at me. "Did you know he used to be mine, when I was a little boy?"

I stare up at him. "Really?"

He nods. "I loved him so much, I never went anywhere without him—I never thought I could ever part with him." He looks at me. "But it turned out I could—for something I loved infinitely more. My first child."

My heart sinks as rapidly as it rose.

"Then he wasn't for me, was he?" I say, looking away. "He was for her. For Rosie." *Just like everything else.*

"No, Holly-berry," Dad says gently. "He was always meant for you. You're the one who needed him, who couldn't sleep without him. Who loved him." He strokes my hair off my face. "Some things are yours because you're born with them—your DNA, the color of your eyes—and other things become yours because they're a part of *you,* who you *choose* to be—and that's so much more important." He sighs. "Huntington's . . . whether you have it or not, that's not who you are. It doesn't define you, Holly."

I look away.

"You are the decisions you make. The things you do. The people you love and who love you. They're the things that really make you who you are." He smiles. "That's why Mr. Brown here will always be yours, just like this tree house, like the scar on your knee where you fell off your trike." He links his pinkie with mine. "He's a part of who you *are.* Intertwined. Inseparable. And no one can ever take that away. Ever." His eyes linger on mine, deep and full. "He'll always be yours."

My heart swells.

"Until you decide to give him to your own child one day." He grins, handing Mr. Brown to me and pulling me closer. "It's a crazy thing, becoming a parent," he whispers into my hair. "You never realize just how much it's possible to love someone else. How another life can be so much more important than your own . . . until suddenly you do."

I stare at Mr. Brown and swallow hard. Now's the time, the moment.

"Dad . . ."

"I know, I know." He grins. "Slushy slushy, but you'll understand one day, when it's your turn."

"Dad . . ."

"And that's a long way in the future, I know!" He laughs. "Super-sonic-shutting-up powers activated."

"No, Dad . . ." I hesitate. *I have to do this.* "Dad, you know those super-sensitive listening skills?"

"Super-sensitive-*sympathetic* listening skills," he corrects me.

"Dad."

"Sorry," he says. "Activated. Shoot."

I look at him, my heart pounding in my chest. Suddenly I smile, certain that everything will be okay. "Dad, I—I'm—"

"Jack!" Megan yells from the garden.

Dad glances outside, then back at me. "Go ahead."

"I . . . ," I begin again.

"Jack!"

His gaze remains firmly on mine.

I take a deep breath.

"Jack!" Megan yells again. "Jack, where *are* you?"

I look down at her pacing the garden, and my pulse races. I can't do this in a hurry.

"You'd better answer her," I tell him, my heart sinking.

He sticks his head out of the door. "Megan!" he calls. "I'm in the tree house with Holly—can it wait?"

Megan hurries over, a large envelope in her hand. "I'm sorry, no, it can't," she says, swiping her frazzled hair from her eyes. "Jack, you have to see this," she says, her face deathly pale. "You too, Holly."

Rosie

I turn the kitchen tap on and drink straight from my hands, the water cold and refreshing after my walk along the harbor, my cheeks burning despite the morning chill.

"Well, what the hell can we *do* about it?" Jack's voice bellows from the living room, making me jump. My heart sinks. I turn the tap off carefully and hurry upstairs, anxious to be out of the way of another argument.

"Rosie." Megan steps into the hall, her hair a nest of frazzled curls. "You're back."

I nod. "But I'll get out of your way," I say quickly.

"No, Rosie." She sighs. "Sweetheart, you'd better come and see this."

I walk slowly back downstairs, a feeling of unease sinking over me.

Jack is sitting hunched over in an armchair, the contents of an envelope spread across the coffee table.

"I need some air," Holly mutters, pushing past me.

"What's going on?" I ask, watching her go, my skin

prickling with dread, the tension in the room hanging like icicles ready to strike.

"These arrived a little while ago," Megan says calmly, handing me a stack of photographs.

I stare at them, surprised. They're of me—me and Kitty in the center of Boston . . . trying on clothes . . . having manicures . . . hugging tearfully . . .

"I—I don't understand . . ." I frown. "When were these . . . How . . . ?"

"They were sent by one Janine Lithgow." Jack sighs. "Kitty's publicist."

"Janine . . ." I trail off. *Janine*, the assistant woman? Kitty's *publicist*?

"I don't understand," I say again, looking to Megan for help. "I don't know how those photos were taken—" Then suddenly I remember Janine and her huge Gucci bag . . . clutching it in the car . . . peering through the dressing room curtain at Chanel . . . thrusting the bag at Kitty desperately as we left the limo . . .

"I don't understand . . ." I sink into a chair. "Why would she . . . ?"

"This came with the pictures," Jack interrupts. "It's a draft article: 'Mamma Mia—Reunited at Last!: How I Found My Long-Lost Daughter.'"

"*What?*" I stare at the page, words and phrases leaping out at me. *Babies switched! Tearful reunion! Life of misery and heartache* . . . My stomach turns as I read my own words: *She didn't mean to be violent—it was the disease—and all that time I feared I'd inherit it too.*

349

"What *is* this?"

Jack sighs. "I'm afraid it's a publicity stunt. Kitty's reinventing herself as Mother Teresa, apparently," he says. "Or Mamma Mia, anyway—it says here she's the favorite for the new Broadway lead with—get this—rumors that her real daughter will play opposite her!" He tosses the envelope back onto the coffee table. "I should never have let you go with her," he groans. "What a bloody mess."

I stare at the article, the pictures, Kitty's smiling face. All a *publicity stunt? A career move?* I remember her tears as she left me, the love in her eyes, the regret. It seemed so real . . . It *was* real, I'd swear to it . . .

But then, she's an actress, I remind myself. She does this for a living. Fooling people, deceiving them into thinking she's someone she's not—that's her *job*. Onstage, on camera, her relationship . . . God, she'd even told me!

It's all a sham—a career move—my whole life's one big charade, Rosie—nothing's real . . .

Except when there are no lights, no cameras—hidden or otherwise—then the real Kitty emerges. *And I saw her*, I realize painfully. The real Kitty—the one I met in New York. The one who wanted nothing to do with me . . . until it worked in her interest.

God, how could I have been so *stupid?* I scan the page again, her words in the hotel room echoing in my ears: *I need a hook—you know, capture the public's imagination, attract media interest—constantly raise my profile* . . . Well, what better hook than to have a long-lost daughter turn up? A *swapped* long-lost daughter, no less—a scandal—and then to be photographed in a joyful reunion?

350

I close my eyes, sick with the realization of it, the betrayal, my stupidity . . .

It was all an act. She never loved me, never wanted me . . . Andy was right—I should've known, should've been more suspicious when she turned up, all hugs and smiles. Instead, I'd stupidly swallowed the whole act—hook, line and sinker.

But then, I'd wanted to. So desperately.

"I've been asked to give my comment on the whole sorry saga before it's submitted to the press on Monday." Jack groans. "I daresay she'll get one of those tabloids to run it, a celebrity magazine perhaps, online . . ."

"No!" I gasp, my blood running cold. "No, she can't!"

"Oh, I'm afraid she can." Jack sighs wearily. "They'll print anything with a celebrity attached."

"No!" I cry, squeezing my eyes tight shut. "*Oh, God!* Nana—*my nana*—she doesn't know . . ."

"Doesn't know what, Rosie?" Megan asks slowly.

"She doesn't know *anything!*" I tell her desperately. "She doesn't know about the swap—the mix-up—anything!" Nana's frail face swims in front of me. "It would—it would destroy her!"

Megan glances at Jack as I stare miserably at the article, wishing I could turn back the clock, wishing I'd never come here, wishing I'd never even heard of Kitty Clare.

"It might not run in the UK, right?" I ask desperately. "She's not even famous at home. These magazines and papers—this story—it's just for the U.S., right?"

"I guess . . . ," Megan says slowly. "But sweetie, what about the courts?"

351

"What?" I frown. "What courts?"

"Rosie," Jack says. "Kitty's planning to sue."

"What?" I stare at him, frozen.

"She's going to sue the hospital where you were born," he explains. "It's all part of her Mother-of-the-Year campaign. She wants the record set straight, wants your birth certificate rectified—she wants to be officially recognized as your mother, never mind the fact that for *eighteen years* she's never shown *any* interest in—"

"No!" I stare at him, horror surging through me like boiling lava. *Sarah* . . .

"It shows she wants you, at least," Megan says. "After all this time."

"It shows no such thing!" Jack argues. "It's all about publicity. She has no idea what a can of worms she's opening. Do you have any idea what this could mean—to all of us? Besides being swamped by journalists day and night, Rosie and Holly will have their whole *lives* rearranged!"

I stare at him, dumbstruck, the world tumbling down around me.

"The two of you live in different *countries*, for God's sake, you can't just swap back eighteen years down the line. You have different passports, different driver's licenses— the list is endless—and they're all going to be investigated, all 'set straight'—just so Kitty can bag the story of the year!"

"Oh, God . . ." I feel dizzy. "Kitty can't sue . . . she can't . . . I'll deny it!" I protest. "I'll say she made it all up!"

"She had a DNA test done, sweetie," Megan says gently.

"DNA? What DNA? How?"

"It says here, your nails—"

"My *nails?*" I remember Janine insisting we get manicures and pedicures together as soon as we arrived—"perfect girly bonding"—*all to collect my nails?*

"No!" I exclaim. "We have to stop this!"

"I don't see how we can, Rosie." Jack sighs. "After all, Kitty's got a case—it's a hell of a mistake to *swap* two babies."

I squeeze my eyes shut. *But it wasn't* . . . Oh, God, if they *investigate* . . . Sarah . . . God, Sarah . . . I feel sick to my stomach.

This is the worst thing I could ever imagine. If Nana finds out, she could have a heart attack; Sarah could be arrested—could go to *prison*—all because of me and my *stupidity!*

"It's my fault," I sob, my voice ragged. "It's all my fault . . ."

"No," Megan tells me firmly. "No, Rosie, it isn't. You're the victim here. You and Holly. It's all been a mistake, a terrible accident."

"Except that it wasn't." Holly's words cut through my tears like ice, freezing my breath.

"Holly," Jack sighs. "Sit down, sweetheart, you're upset."

"No, Dad," she says calmly. "I know what I'm talking about. It wasn't an accident. It was deliberate."

Through my tears, I look up at her, standing in the doorway, holding up something small and shiny in her hand. It takes me a moment to recognize it.

"We were swapped deliberately," she says again, her eyes cold and clear, Andy's phone gleaming in her fingers. "Weren't we, Rosie?"

Holly

The truth hangs like a shadow in Rosie's eyes—I can see it; so can Megan. So can Dad.

She trembles in our gaze. Little Miss Goody Two-shoes exposed in the harsh headlights of her lie.

"I don't understand," Megan begins. "What do you mean? How . . . ?"

"I think Rosie had better explain," I suggest, taking a seat. "After all"—I meet her gaze coolly—"Sarah's *your* friend, isn't she?"

She cringes at my words, closing her eyes and visibly crumpling into her chair.

"Rosie?" Megan says quietly. "Who's Sarah?"

Rosie's head hangs miserably in her hands.

"Rosie?"

She takes a deep breath. "Sarah," she says slowly, her voice croaky and unrecognizable. "Sarah is . . . my neighbor, a family friend . . ." She trails off in a heavy, trembling sigh, screws her eyes closed tight. "And a midwife."

Dad stares at her. So do I, Rosie's voice mail on Andy's cell phone ringing in my ears: *Sarah changed everything when she swapped me with Holly—whether she was right or wrong . . .*

"But . . . how? I mean, why?" Megan frowns. "Why would she swap you?"

"She thought . . ." I watch Rosie struggle for the right words, if any exist. "She thought she was doing the right thing . . ."

"How?" Dad demands. "How could she *possibly* think—" He rubs his hand over his face, flattening and creasing his features. "God!"

"Sarah said that—that Kitty didn't want her baby," Rosie explains, her voice cracking, agony etched in every word. "That she was going to abandon her . . ."

Dad looks at her, his eyes deep and fierce in their sockets. I look away. So does Rosie, her lips trembling.

"She thought that Trudie's baby was going to die," she continues, her voice quavering. "My dad had an accident on the way to the hospital . . . he died, and . . . and Sarah didn't think that Mum—that Trudie could cope with any more grief." She breaks off as tears flood her words and I look away, folding my arms tightly, determined to swallow my sympathy.

Like mother, like daughter—the article's right. She's just like Kitty—breaking out the sob story, making me feel *sorry* for her, making me think she's *like* me, that she truly wants to make *amends* . . .

When all along they were both just buying me off—Kitty with her ten thousand dollars, Rosie with the five hundred dollars she slipped under my door last night. When all along they were concealing the bitter truth.

Rosie always *knew* the swap was deliberate, and Kitty—my blood boils—Kitty *used* me. The first letter—the first *contact*—I've had from her in my entire life, and it was a *lie*! She didn't want to *apologize,* didn't want to *compensate* me for everything she'd done, didn't want to *make amends* or stop the press from *intruding* on our lives! She just wanted to buy me off, buy my silence, so she could spin her own twisted version of events, paint herself as a victim, a perfect mother—without worrying that I'd tell the world the truth, the terrible sordid truth about America's beloved sweetheart and her precious freaking family reunion.

And I fell for it.

Well, not anymore.

"So Sarah swapped you," Dad says, his words cold, devoid of emotion. His jaw tightens. "She did this for your mother. For Trudie."

Rosie nods miserably. "She was desperate—she thought Trudie's baby was going to die—"

"So she stole mine?" he demands. "Sarah's friend's child was going to die, *so she stole mine*?!"

He punches the arm of the chair, making me jump. I look away, my cheeks burning. I've never seen him so angry.

"Jack," Megan says softly.

"Jeez!" he says, rubbing his hands through his hair. "Jesus!" He shakes his head. "So when I arrived . . . it was already done." He closes his eyes. *"God!"*

"Sarah didn't mean . . . she really thought she was doing the right thing . . . ," Rosie says nervously.

Dad's eyes fly open. "You can't honestly— Rosie, she did this *deliberately*—and you want to *protect* her?" He glares at her, his eyes burning, incredulous. "After *everything* she's put us all through, you honestly want to *protect* her?!" He springs from his chair, his hands in his hair. "Jesus, Rosie!"

"I'm—I'm so sorry." Rosie crumples.

"My child was stolen from me—*you* were stolen from me—Holly will *never* know her mother, all because of this woman—your *friend*! And you didn't think we had a right to *know*?" His eyes bore into her as she shrinks in her seat.

356

"Jack." Megan touches his arm. "Jack, come on, sit down."

"I can't." He swallows, his face pale. "I'm sorry, but I can't be here right now." He opens the door and slams it behind him, the glass ornaments shuddering on the mantelpiece as he hammers down the steps outside.

The silence throbs.

I stare at my lap, Andy's phone cold and shiny in my hand, Dad's words rebounding around my head. *Swapped. Abandoned. Deliberate. Stolen.*

Rosie sniffles beside me. "Holly," she whispers, her voice broken and frail. "Holly, I'm so sorry . . ." She reaches out to me.

"Don't!" I flinch. "Don't talk to me." I hug my arms tightly and head for the door. "Don't ever talk to me again."

I walk through the kitchen, my body on autopilot. I know what I have to do now. I grab my jacket and bag and head out the back door, down the steps, along the street and straight past Andy, who smiles.

"Don't bother," I tell him, tossing him his cell phone. I don't need any more liars, any more deceit. I trusted Andy, and I was just beginning to trust Rosie. I thought she was like me—that this awful mistake had happened to *both* of us, had bound us together. But it wasn't a mistake. And all this time she *knew*!

And so did he.

I race toward the dock, tears hot on my cheeks. I need to know now. The truth. Whatever it is. The truth may hurt, but lies—they're vicious. They hide coiled up inside you, ready to strike without warning, without your even knowing they're there.

Until it's too late.

Rosie

Megan and I sit there in the aftermath, the silence unbreakable.

I feel like an empty sponge, every ounce of energy, every last drop of truth finally squeezed out of me, leaving me brittle, hollow, and exposed. This is it. It was all for nothing. I've lost Jack and Megan, I've lost Holly and Ben, and now Nana and Sarah are being sucked into the black hole too.

I should call Sarah, warn her. I should call Nana . . . but somehow I can't move, can't speak . . .

"Rosie . . . ," Megan says, then sighs. There are no words. There are too many. "Rosie, I— Shoot, is that the time?" She jumps up, then stops at the door, her voice gentle. "Rosie, look, I have to go get Ben, but . . . but when I get back—"

"Okay." I nod, understanding perfectly. *When I get back . . . don't be here.*

"Okay." She smiles awkwardly, pausing for a moment before hurrying out of the door.

I close my eyes.

It's over.

Holly

It's over.

I shiver as I pull my sleeve back down, my blood deep red in the sample tube. It's done. Everything's in the hands of the doctors and lab technicians and geneticists. It's up to them now, baby. Up to them to discover whether I'm HD-positive or not. Whether we live or die. All we have to do is wait.

Easy, huh?

It was surprisingly quick . . . not much more than a pinprick, really, when it came down to it. All that talking and stressing and wondering and worrying, and all it ultimately came down to was a few seconds with a needle.

First there were a load of questions, and then I had to follow a pen with my eyes, walk heel to toe and play a bizarre variation on the paper-rock-scissors game—I had to copy the actions the neurologist did in the order he did them. I felt like I was back at kindergarten, concentrating so hard on the simplest things. It was quite scary—are these really things I won't be able to do in the next ten to twenty years?

Then Charlotte was waiting to see me. She'd been surprised when I turned up alone, but I said Andy had been unavoidably detained. It's getting frighteningly easy to lie these days. She offered to reschedule, but I told her no—I'm already nine weeks pregnant, and I have to get the results and decide about CVS before week twelve. I gave her the five hundred dollars to remain anonymous, then the blood was drawn. Easy. All over. Out of my hands.

I feel numb as I walk toward the exit. I thought I'd be relieved—and I am, in a way. No more worrying or deliberating about the right thing to do. It's done, and now there's nothing I can do but wait. Two weeks, Charlotte said, though they'll try to be as quick as possible, given my situation. Just two weeks and my fate will be decided. *Our fate.*

With tremendous effort I push the door open onto the street, and bright sunlight hits me full in the face, its warmth dazzling, blinding, until something moves in front of it.

"Holly." Andy looks down at me, tall and shadowy.

I look up at him, the last of my strength melting away as I dissolve into his arms, dark against the light, firm against the crumbling world.

Rosie

It doesn't take long to pack. I take a last look around the bedroom—spick-and-span. Almost as if I never came. I sigh. If only it were as easy to pack up the last few weeks, to leave everyone as they were before. Happy. Intact. A family.

I glance out the window. Still no taxi. I don't know where I'll go. Home, I suppose, if I can still call it that. If it hasn't been totally annihilated by the time I get there. I sigh heavily, close the bedroom door and head downstairs.

"Jack?" Megan bursts through the back door, Ben in her arms. She looks at me, surprised. "Rosie!"

"I'm sorry—I thought the taxi would be here by now," I say in a rush, my cheeks burning. "I'll wait outside."

"Rosie, wait!" she says. "You don't have to go. We can work this out, get through this—as a family . . ."

I look at her, her hair spilling out from its elastic band, Ben sucking his thumb in her arms. I shake my head. "I've destroyed this family."

"No, you haven't," she argues. "None of this is your fault."

"Thank you, Megan." I smile weakly. "For everything."

"Rosie . . ." She trails off helplessly as I move past her through the kitchen. "Look, at least wait until Jack gets back, okay? You can't leave without saying goodbye."

I shake my head.

"Rosie, please—it's not your fault—any of it! It was Sarah and—and Kitty!" She spits the name. "Kitty's the one who started all this—she caused it and now she's the one dragging us all—" She breaks off suddenly and moves to the counter, pressing a button on the answering machine.

"First message: Friday, January fifth . . . Hello?" Kitty's irritated voice shatters the silence. *"Hello? Jack? Are you there? Jack?"*

I cringe. As if I needed any further reminder of the moment this all started, the moment I should have walked away and never come back. I shoulder my bag and open the door.

"Rosie, wait!"

Something in Megan's voice makes me turn back, though to do so is painful.

Her eyes sparkle. "I have an idea."

Holly

The same sun I watched rise this morning now bleeds slowly into the sea as I step off the ferry. But the ground's still moving.

"You're sure you're okay?" Andy asks.

I nod. "Nothing's changed, has it?" I reason. "I've always either had Huntington's or not. And I still don't know which, I'm just one step closer to learning the truth, that's all. And it's best to know the truth." I sigh heavily. "However much it hurts."

He looks at me, his eyes pained. "Holly, I'm sorry—"

"Don't." I shrug, hugging my arms. "It doesn't matter. None of it matters now."

He stares at the ground. "You know, I could always stick around a bit longer . . . be here when you get your results?"

"No." I smile. "Thank you, but I think it's time to tell them. It's time everyone knew the truth."

"Okay." He nods. "Well, you've got my number if you change your mind. I don't leave the States for a few more days."

"Thanks, Andy," I tell him. "Thanks for everything."

"Anytime," he promises. "Good luck, Holly."

He hugs me goodbye, and I wave, watching as he walks away, this one person who knows all my secrets, yet hardly knows me at all. I take a deep breath and walk slowly back to the house. My house. The same house I've lived in for as long as I can remember. The same squeaky wooden sign, the same creaky steps I've run up a thousand times.

Everything's the same as it always was.

Except for me.

Rosie

I wait in the living room, staring at my bag, packed and waiting by the door. I want to be ready—just in case this doesn't work, in case Jack doesn't change his mind, in case the world is still coming to an end.

In the kitchen Megan is playing Jack the answering-machine message, telling him her idea. I watch Ben driving his trucks around the carpet in front of me, and want to cry. I'll miss him so much. Miss them all. My eyes stray restlessly round the room, remembering the day I arrived here, less than two weeks ago; imprinting the room in my memory: the driftwood sculptures, the seascape over the fireplace, the photo collage . . .

The pictures scream at me accusingly. *Look!* they cry. *Just look what you've destroyed!* And like I'm witnessing a car crash, I can't turn away.

There's Holly as a giggling toddler, high on Jack's shoulders; Holly holding baby Ben, so nervous and excited and proud; Holly peering out of her tree house with Melissa; Holly beaming beneath a Sweet Sixteen banner while Jack holds a cake filled with candles, ready for her to make a wish . . .

I press my eyes closed tight. Wishing. Hoping. Praying. If I click my heels together three times will I be home? Will all this have simply been a dream? A Technicolor nightmare?

Something hard presses into my hand, and I open my eyes. It's a book. *The Three Little Pigs.*

Ben looks up at me expectantly.

"Storwy, Rosie?"

I smile despite myself.

"Sure," I tell him, and he climbs up onto the sofa beside me, a mountaineering expedition. I open the book, and before I know it he's crawled onto my lap. I stare at him, his warm weight heavy on my legs, his pale blue eyes clear and wide as he stares up at me. My little brother. My heart flips and sinks. I'm going to miss him so much.

"Once upon a time," he prompts.

I smile, turning back to the book, and flick to the first page.

"Once upon a time," I repeat, "there lived three little pigs."

And so I read to him, this little boy who's somehow, incredibly, a part of me. He turns the pages, and at his command I do all the different voices as the little pigs run about frantically trying to escape the Big Bad Wolf as he recklessly destroys their homes and lives.

Until finally he gets what he deserves.

Holly

I take a deep breath and push open the front door. I hear Megan reading to Ben in the living room and close my eyes, imagining my own child, allowing myself the luxury to dream . . .

I sigh. *The truth,* I think, opening my eyes. I need to tell them.

I'm going to tell them now, get it over with. Then somehow we can start trying to pick up the pieces—attempt to put them back together again—try to work out what the new picture might look like.

I swallow hard and open the door.

"And they all lived happ—"

Rosie looks up, midsentence. I stare at her, the sight of Ben sitting on her lap snatching my breath.

"What's going on?" I demand.

"We're just reading a story." Rosie smiles nervously." 'The Three Little Pigs.'"

"My favewit!" Ben beams.

"I thought your favorite was 'The Three Billy Goats Gruff'?—you know, the one with the big fat ugly troll?" I glare at Rosie.

He shakes his head fiercely. "Nope, I like the Big Bad Wolf—Rosie does good voices." He grins.

I feel sick.

"Where's Dad?" I say, my voice tight.

"He's just in the—" Rosie begins.

"Rosie!" Dad beams, bursting in, Megan following closely behind. "Rosie, it worked!"

I have ceased to exist.

"Really?" Rosie stares at him as if her life depends on it.

"Uh-huh. I rang her up—this Janet . . . Janice . . . whatsherface . . . and I said that if they run with the story then I'll go public with the tape of Kitty—and then I played it for her."

"What did she say?" Rosie asks eagerly.

"Well, she didn't say anything for a good thirty seconds, then she just swore and hung up! That's got to be a good sign, right?"

"What's going on?" I ask.

"Holly!" He smiles, turning to me for the first time. "Sweetheart, it's gonna be okay—they're gonna drop the article, the court case, everything!" He grabs me in a hug. "It's over. It's all over. We can get back to normal."

Normal.

"Are you sure?" Rosie asks. "Did Janine actually say that?"

"Well, Kitty can hardly go ahead with her World's Best Mother campaign if it gets out that she abandoned her own baby, can she? And with the tape too, it'd be the end of her career." He grins. "Apparently there *is* such a thing as bad publicity!"

He hugs her, the girl he couldn't bring himself to look at a few hours ago.

"Now, what do you say we all go out for some pizza to celebrate?" He beams. "As a family."

"That's a great idea," Megan says.

"Pepperwoni, pepperwoni!" Ben chants, and Rosie laughs.

"Holly?" Dad says. "I'll split you a stuffed-crust Mexican Meat Feast?" He winks. "Extra jalapenos . . . ?"

"You go on," I tell him. "I'm actually not feeling too great. I might go lie down."

"Really?" Dad frowns, pressing his hand to my forehead. "You okay? You want us to stay in?"

"No! Pepperwoni!" Ben protests.

"No, you all go ahead." I force a smile. "I'm fine."

"Okay, well . . . we'll bring you back some pizza, okay? I know you prefer it for brekkie, anyway."

I close my eyes, the thought of cold pizza making me queasy.

"Boots, Ben!" Megan instructs.

"No—more storwy!" Ben protests, waving his book at Rosie.

"Sorry!" she laughs, scooping him up and tickling him. "We didn't quite finish did we? Where did we get to?"

And they all lived happily ever after, I think bitterly as I turn away, closing the door firmly behind me.

Unbelievable. I grit my teeth, trying to control myself.

Every time. Every *freaking* time she somehow ends up on top— the cat that gets the cream, having her cake and eating everybody else's too! *Un-freaking-believable!*

Poor Rosie—the girl who's lied through her teeth since she got here—who's had it all—who's *got* it all—now getting all the sympathy because she doesn't want her friend to get into trouble! God forbid the woman who did this—who *ruined* my life—should be punished! And they're *helping* her! She deserves to go to prison—to hell—for all she's done. I hold my stomach tenderly. And I can't even tell them I'm pregnant because they're too busy celebrating with freaking Rosie!

She's had a mother, she's free of the disease, she's lied to us all and still *she gets the happy ending? Still she gets to play happy family?*

I hurl my jacket at the coat rack—and miss. Typical. I snatch it up and find the rest of this morning's unopened mail underneath— abandoned in the wake of Hurricane Rosie, just like everything else. A green logo catches my eye.

DNAnytime.

Great. Perfect. Just what I need—a stab in the gut with the DNA results that have ruined my life. I snatch up the envelope and stomp upstairs. Wouldn't that just make Rosie's freaking day? DNA proof—her golden ticket to a happy ending in my family, my life! I can imagine them all now, crowding into a booth at Pisa Pizza, the mom, the dad, the son and the perfect, healthy daughter. The textbook happy family. My eyes sting as I throw myself miserably onto my bed.

They're not mine, they were never mine—that's the truth. It was all a calculated move, a deliberate switch by a screwed-up midwife designed to give Rosie to her friend and leave me for dead. I'm the sick one, the doomed one. I was never meant to survive.

I reach for my pillow and my fingers find something hard beneath it. I pull it out and my heart plummets as I stare at my engagement ring. Now even that's over too. *Everything's* ruined because of Rosie and her freaking DNA!

I glare at the envelope, ripping at the seal and pulling out the folded sheet of paper. Everything else has gone to hell, why not stick the cherry on top while I'm at it? Bring it on!

I stare at the letter, numbers and scientific jargon swimming before me. Then I read it again, convinced I'm getting confused by the mumbo-jumbo, the terminology. When it still says the same thing the third time, I stop breathing.

Negative.

I stare.

There is no genetic match between the subjects.

Rosie is not Dad's daughter.

Rosie

"Don't you think we should wait till we hear from Kitty?" I ask nervously as I help Ben tidy his trucks away. "We're only assuming at the moment—we don't know for sure . . ."

"She can't possibly go ahead with the story now, Rosie." Jack laughs. "Or the case—it would be professional suicide!"

Yes, I think, but a little voice nags in my head. *But if she really loved me, if she really wanted me . . .*

I banish it guiltily—what am I thinking? That I *want* her to sue Sarah to prove she loves me after all?

"Rosie's right, though," Megan says. "We know how determined she can be. She might think of some way to get around the answering machine message—"

She's interrupted by the shrill ring of the telephone. We all stare at it.

"Well, that was quick," Jack says.

"Should we let it go to the machine?" Megan jokes. "For evidence?"

Jack picks the receiver up carefully. "Hello?"

I stare at him. *Is it her?*

"Oh, hi, Pete."

I sink into a chair, not even realizing I've been holding my breath till it comes rushing out.

"No, no, that's fine," Jack tells the phone. "Yep. Friday's great. Okay, glad you're feeling better. Bye."

He replaces the receiver and almost immediately the phone rings again. Jack stares at it, startled.

"Place your bets now," he jokes.

"Jack, just answer it, for goodness' sake," Megan urges.

"Hello?" he says, lifting the receiver. "Oh, hello." I stare at him as he touches his finger to his lips, all humor wiped from his face as he takes the phone into the kitchen.

It's Kitty.

I hold my breath consciously this time, my fingers crossed so tightly they hurt.

Please, I beg, *please let her drop the case! Please let this all be over!* I close my eyes and wish hard—trying to block out the little voice in the back of my head, still pleading just as much for the opposite.

Holly

She's not his daughter.

I stare at the page, hardly able to believe it.

This whole nightmare . . . this whole awful, horrific fortnight has been some mistake—some monumental mistake! Rosie's not his daughter!

Which means I am!

I laugh incredulously. I feel like Scrooge waking up on Christmas morning to find that Tiny Tim's still alive, that the spirits have given him a second chance, given him back his life, and it was all just a dream . . . *It wasn't real!* The baby swap, the Huntington's—I don't have it and never will—never *can*—because *Rosie got it wrong!* Somehow she got it all wrong—the wrong mother, the wrong father . . . It was all just one big, bad, terrible nightmare . . .

And now it's time to wake up.

I feel dizzy with delirium, laughter bubbling uncontrollably inside me—Dad's still *really* my dad, I'm not ill, my *baby's* not ill, and Josh . . . I stare at the plastic ring in my hand, my heart soaring as I remember his words: *I love you, Holly Marie Woods—I will love you till my dying day . . .* And now there's nothing in the way—no illness, no reason to hide . . . it's time. I have to call him—right now—have to tell him he's going to be a dad!

Trembling with excitement, I grab the phone extension by my bed, my finger poised to dial—but am stopped short by a voice on the other end.

"Jack, please," Kitty begs. "Let me talk to Rosie. She has to know I never meant—I didn't realize—It wasn't my idea. Janine—"

"Did what?" Dad asks coolly. "*Forced* you?"

I grin, savoring the moment. She's my mother now, and I can tell her just where she can stick her bogus lawsuit, just how stupid she'd look if she went to press with a humongous lie, just how little I think of her as a mother . . .

"No, she—I just wanted to find Rosie—to have another chance." Kitty sighs. "The article was Janine's idea."

I take a deep breath, adrenaline surging.

"And the court case?" Dad asks coldly. "The DNA test?"

I freeze.

The DNA test.

Kitty had a DNA test done too . . .

And it came out positive.

"Just . . . tell Rosie I'm sorry, will you?" Kitty sighs. "I've had to drop the case."

Positive . . .

"And the story?" Dad asks.

"The story's toast, Jack, you know that," she says bitterly. "I can't take the risk. The negative exposure . . ."

I screw my eyes shut, trying to make sense of it all.

"Thank you, Kitty," Dad says.

"Don't *thank* me," Kitty says hotly. "It's not like I had a choice. Rosie's my daughter, after all—I have a right. And I don't appreciate being blackmailed, Jack."

Rosie is Kitty's daughter . . .

"I understand," he says. "But I've got to look out for *my* daughter—this wasn't the right way, Kitty."

But she's not Dad's . . . ?

"Oh, really? God, you're so high and mighty—you think you know everything, don't you, Jack? But you don't."

"Really?" Dad says patiently.

But if Rosie is Kitty's and isn't Dad's—and we were born the same night, how . . . ?

"Uh-huh. Because I've got news for you, Jack Woods." Kitty sneers. "That precious daughter of yours? The one you say you're protecting? Rosie? She's not your daughter, Jack. When I met you I was already pregnant."

My eyes fly open and I stare at the phone, stunned to the core. Suddenly the test results fall into place.

He wasn't the father . . .

"Oh, Kitty," Dad says eventually, his voice cool, calm. "You think I didn't know? I've always known."

I gasp.

"Kitty?" Dad says suddenly.

I hang up quickly, my head rushing. I close my eyes, their words tumbling in tangled circles around my head.

Rosie is Kitty's baby, which means she was swapped at birth— with me. Then I was given to Kitty and Dad took me because he thought I was Kitty's child—but he was never the father, never the father of Kitty's baby—never Rosie's father . . . I open my eyes suddenly.

Which means he was never my father either . . .

And he always knew.

Rosie

"Well?" Megan urges as Jack slowly hangs up the phone. "What did she say?"

My heart sinks as he slowly turns, his face pale.

"She's dropping the case." He smiles weakly. "The article too. I was right—professional suicide."

"That's wonderful!" Megan cries, grabbing me in a hug. I hold her tight, that little voice in my head finally extinguished in the flood of relief. I don't need Kitty. I never did. And now I know I'm better off without her. I can't believe I risked so much to find her, came so close to losing everything . . . I close my eyes, breathless with the thought of it. It's a miracle. She's dropping the case. She's not going to print the story, she's not going to sue. Sarah's safe and Nana need never know—*thank God!*

"We should tell Holly!" Megan says suddenly. "She'll be anxious to know—"

"I'll go!" Jack says quickly. "In fact, you three go ahead to the restaurant and order me the spiciest pizza they've got— I'll see if a bit of good news can't tempt her to come with us." He heads upstairs.

"We'll wait." Megan smiles.

"No need. We'll catch you up. You lot are slow coaches, anyway." He grins at Ben. "We'll race you—last one there doesn't get any ice cream!"

"Go, go, go!" Ben screams, grabbing my hand and racing for the door as Jack disappears upstairs.

Holly

He was never my Dad . . .

I stare blankly at the phone. Which means . . .

I close my eyes as the sky falls in all over again.

It wasn't a dream—or a mistake . . . It's true—it's all true—the baby swap, the Huntington's . . .

I crumple to the floor as my world crashes down once more, twice as hard this time, a million times more excruciating after a brief glimpse of hope.

And he *knew*?

All this time—my whole life—he brought me up, raised me . . . *knowing he wasn't my dad?*

I struggle to breathe.

Then when Rosie arrived, claiming to be me, claiming she was Kitty's daughter, that he was her father—*he let her!* He let her take my family, my life, my dad—*and she's not even his daughter!*

And *he knew!*

The door flies open and Dad bursts in.

"Holly!" he says urgently. "Holly, were you on the phone just now—on the extension?"

I bite my lip.

"Holly!" He stares at me, his eyes wide, anxious.

I nod, looking away, the tears spilling over.

"Sweetheart!" He engulfs me in his arms, this man who isn't, who never was, my dad.

"You knew?" I whisper incredulously. "You knew all along?"

"No!" He cups my face, his eyes deep in mine. "Oh, sweetheart, no, I only said that because Kitty . . ." He hesitates, swallows. "I didn't know," he repeats, his eyes full of sorrow. "But there were times when . . . I wondered. . . ." He falters.

"Everything happened so soon after Kitty and I met—and we weren't together very long." He looks at me, pleading with me to understand. "But Kitty told me you were mine and I believed her. I wanted you to be! I love you so much—you've always been my daughter, you know that. Blood doesn't matter to us. We've proved that already, right?" He looks at me fearfully. "Right?"

"Blood doesn't matter?" I ask, my voice wobbling.

"No," he promises, pulling me close. "No, it's never mattered. Blood isn't anything when it's you and me."

"Okay." I nod, my thoughts racing. "Okay, if that's true . . ."

"It is—sweetie, you know it is."

"Okay. Then tell Rosie."

He goes very still. "What?"

"If blood doesn't matter . . . if it makes no difference . . ." I look at him, my heart pounding. "Then you should tell her."

"Holly . . ." He pulls back and looks at me. "Why?"

"You're not her blood father," I say, meeting his gaze. "Just like you're not mine. If it doesn't matter, you should tell her. And if it does matter . . ." I search his eyes. "She has a right to know."

Dad closes his eyes, rubs his hand across his face. "Holly, I—"

"She has a right to know the truth, Dad," I tell him.

He shakes his head, looks away.

"Holly, we don't—we don't even know if it *is* the truth. Kitty might be lying now—in fact, she probably is! She's angry and spiteful, and she just wanted to hurt us, sweetheart. She just wanted to hurt *me—that's* why I told her I already knew—that's the *only*

375

reason. There's no evidence that she's telling the truth, and absolutely no reason to believe her now!"

"Yes, there is."

"What?" He frowns, confused, as my eyes fall to the letter, discarded on the floor. Slowly, I hand it to him.

"What's this?" His eyes scan the page and I watch as the color drains from his face.

"You have to tell her," I say quietly. "But if you don't . . ." I take a deep breath. "I will."

"Holly, no." He grabs my hands. "Please. You can't!"

"Why not?" I cry angrily. "Why shouldn't I?"

"Do you have any idea how she would feel—to find out something like this?"

"Yes, actually!" I choke on the words. "I know *exactly* how she would feel!"

"Holly . . ." He looks at me, torn. "Holly, I'm sorry, but that was different."

"How?!"

"She only told you because she didn't have a choice—you needed to know about the disease!"

"Lucky me!" I laugh bitterly.

"Holly, if you told her the truth . . ." He trails off, shakes his head. "Sweetheart, please, think about it. Your biological parents loved you—*I* love you. Imagine how Rosie would feel to learn that *neither* of her real parents wanted to know her—that they both abandoned her. Look what she's been through with Kitty!"

"I don't care!" I exclaim. "It's the truth!"

"Holly!" He stands up, paces the room, hands in his hair. "What is it—you want to hurt Rosie? It would make you feel better if she knew I wasn't her father either?"

"Yes!" I explode, the truth bursting from me like a jack-in-the-box—bright and bold, and ugly. "Yes! Why should she get you as a dad if I don't—*if she's not even really yours*? It's not fair!"

"*Life* isn't fair, Holly!" Dad yells suddenly, his face pale. "You think it was fair that the woman I loved was already pregnant with another man's child? You think it was fair that I loved her so much I didn't care, I didn't question, I took them both on? That she then left me to come flitting over here like a moth to the spotlight? That I *followed* her, for Chrissakes, taking care of her child, loving her, and she didn't even *care*?"

I stare at him.

"You think any of this is fair, Holly?" he asks wearily. "On any of us?"

I bite my lip hard.

"But it stops here. Now. No more revelations that are going to hurt this family—I don't care if it's the truth. We're saturated. We're done."

I look away, the tears springing afresh, my hand moving instinctively to my stomach.

No more revelations . . .

"I'm not going to tell Rosie, Holly." He sighs. "And neither are you."

I stare at my feet, my heart beating fast, my eyes stinging. "Then I can't stay here."

"Holly-berry."

"No, Dad," I tell him. "I'm sorry. I can't stay if she's here." I look at him. "Not if you don't tell her."

"Holly!" He shakes his head. "Holly, please, telling her would just be spiteful, vindictive—you're not like that, I didn't bring you up that way—"

377

"You shouldn't have brought me up at all," I retort. "You're not my father!"

He sighs. "Holly . . ."

"Just like you're not her father," I say. "But you won't let *her* go. You'd *rather* have her as your daughter. Is it because she looks like Kitty?"

"Holly, don't be ridiculous!"

"Or is it because she's healthy—*normal*?"

"Holly!" He stares at me, shocked. "I would *never* choose her over you."

"Then prove it," I demand. "Tell her the truth."

He looks at me for a long moment, then rubs his hands roughly across his face.

"No," he sighs heavily, his voice cracking. "Holly, sweetheart, I can't."

"Then you've made your choice," I say, opening the door, the blood pumping in my ears. "Now go."

"Holly!"

"Go, Dad! Go on—go to her!"

"Holly-berry, please, let's talk about this."

"Are you going to tell her?"

"Holly . . ."

"*Are* you?"

He searches my face desperately, a deep frown furrowing his forehead, his eyes tortured, watery—but I don't care. He's choosing her over me—the healthy daughter over the sick, the brand-new daughter who looks like his first love over the girl who's loved him her entire life.

"Go," I order.

"We'll . . . we'll talk about this more later." He sighs, reaching for me as I turn away. "Holly, I promise, we'll—"

"I won't be here." I slam the door behind him, cutting him off as the world blurs around me.

Rosie . . . I can't believe he chose Rosie . . .

I look around the room, my pulse stabbing my temples as my eyes skim over the wallpaper Dad put up for me, the keyboard I begged him for when I was twelve, Mr. Brown . . . Everywhere I look, presents and photos and memories . . .

A scream rips from my throat as I fly at them savagely, shoving and clawing, ripping at the pictures on the wall, the photos, the posters—tearing at the lies, the souvenirs of a life I should never have had. I lob books and shred photos and kick at a pile of clothes, when something small and pink tumbles out of a pocket.

I snatch it up, about to rip it—when suddenly I realize what it is.

Rosie's address book.

I'd forgotten all about it. I open it up, its neat pink square small and hard in my hand as I flip through it. All these people I've never met. Who might have been my friends, my family . . . My thumb stops suddenly as a name jumps out from the thin pages.

Nana Fisher.

I stare at it, rubbing my thumb gently over the black ink as if I could touch her, see her. This woman who would have been *my* nana, my *family,* but for the mistake that's kept us apart.

My whole life's one huge, horrible mistake.

Or rather, it wasn't a mistake, at all . . .

Suddenly my fingers scrabble in the pages, flipping through quickly to the *S* section. I scan the lines urgently, but it's all surnames. I take a deep breath and start at the beginning, forcing myself to go slowly, be thorough, my pulse racing as my eyes dart over the pages, searching, searching . . .

Until I find her.

Rosie

We're tucking into our sundaes by the time Jack arrives at Pisa Pizza.

"Hi, where've you been?" Megan stands to kiss him as Ben covers his bowl protectively.

"You can't have any, Daddy!" he sings. "You're the last!"

"Meany." Jack smiles halfheartedly.

"We saved you both some pizza, though." Megan smiles. "Where's Holly?"

"She's not coming." He slumps into the booth and runs his hands through his hair. "She's moving out."

"What?" Megan drops her spoon.

I stare at him.

"Why?" she asks. "I thought everything was okay now—Kitty dropped the case!"

"I know," he sighs. "I think she just needs . . . some time alone for a while."

"Where's Holly?" Ben asks in a small voice.

Jack and Megan exchange looks.

"She's gone on a little vacation," Megan says quickly.

"To the beach?" Ben asks hopefully. "Can we go too?"

"Not this time." Megan smiles. "She's gone somewhere very boring and cold."

"The North Pole?" Ben asks. "With the penguins?"

Megan laughs. "Something like that. Brrr!" She tickles him and he laughs.

"I like penguins," Ben says.

"Well, you obviously don't like ice cream!" Megan says, picking up her spoon. "So I'll just have to eat yours up!"

"No!" Ben squeals, digging in.

"Good boy." She ruffles his hair, then looks at Jack anxiously.

I stare at my ice cream melting in my dish, my wafer sliding over onto its side. I push it up again with my spoon, but no matter how many times I keep trying to prop it up, it always slides back down, the pool of slush getting bigger every time.

Holly

"Whoa," Melissa gasps after I've told her everything—almost everything. She may be my best friend, but as she's also Josh's sister, I still can't tell her I'm pregnant. Not before Josh. Not until I know if the baby's at risk.

If there's even going to be a baby.

"Jeez." Melissa shakes her head. "Holy crap, Holly."

I nod. That pretty much sums it up.

"I can't believe it—your dad . . . Huntington's disease . . . *Kitty Clare!*"

I look up quickly. "You can't tell anyone, Melissa. Swear it."

"I swear!" she promises earnestly. "Jeez, Holls, why didn't you call me? I must've tried your cell a million times."

"Sorry, it's broken."

"I thought you were avoiding me coz of what happened with Josh—I was ready to kill him for wrecking our friendship!"

I squeeze her hand. "Never."

"And then your dad said you were sick when I came around, and you've been out of school so long I thought you had mono—or worse!"

I nod. *Worse.* Much, *much* worse.

"Don't worry, you can copy all my notes." Melissa smiles. "Not that you've really missed much. Except Natalie Van Pelt came back from vacation with the *worst* nose job I've ever *seen,* though she claims she just had a skiing accident, but—yeah, right!" She looks up suddenly, contrite. "Not that you really care when your life's going down the crapper, huh? Sorry." She squeezes my knee.

"No, it's okay." I smile. It's actually good to think about something else for a change. "What other gossip have I missed?"

Melissa grins, her eyes sparkling as she spends the next hour filling me in on school scandals, from fashion faux pas and disastrous dates to a hilarious horror story about a girl who cut off the school diva's ponytail because she flirted with her boyfriend, which has me in hysterics, imagining the look of horror on Kimberley's perfect face when her golden curls plummeted to the floor—priceless!

"Which just goes to show"—Melissa winks—"don't get mad. Get even."

I giggle, wiping tears from my eyes, and I suddenly realize how long it's been since I laughed, since I thought of anything but Huntington's or Rosie or the baby.

Thank God for Melissa.

Just then there's a knock on her bedroom door, and her mom steps inside.

"Hi, girls." She smiles awkwardly. "Listen, I know I said you could stay over, Holly—and you know you're always welcome . . ." She squeezes my hand and my heart sinks. "But I just got a call from your dad, honey. He's really worried about you. I think you should go home."

"Mom!" Melissa exclaims. "You can't kick Holly out—she's my best friend!"

"And her dad's worried sick. I'm sorry, Holly, I can't let you stay here. Your dad wasn't exactly thrilled the last time you stayed over without his consent . . ."

"Mom, she's *eighteen.*"

"It doesn't matter, he's still her dad."

No, he's not, I think. *He never was.*

"You just need to talk to him, sweetie, work this out." Melissa's mom smiles gently. "You need to go home."

"Sorry," Melissa sighs as her mom shuts the door. "This sucks."

Once again, her analysis is flawless.

Crap. I sigh.

If I can't stay here, there's only one place I *can* go . . .

Rosie

"There's no place like home," Dorothy chants on the screen, clicking her ruby heels, eyes closed tight as Ben copies her. "No place like home, no place like home . . ."

I close my eyes. *There's no place like home . . .*

In the week since Holly left, the house hasn't felt much like a home. It's been like living in a shell, everybody wandering round like zombies, waiting for the phone to ring, for her to come back. Jack's still kicking himself for asking Melissa's mum to send her home—at least she was nearby before. But while he's not exactly thrilled she's staying at Harvard, at least she's safe, and as he doesn't want to scare her off again, he's got no choice but to wait, hoping she'll come back or call when she's ready.

The shrill ring of my mobile makes me jump. Jack and I stare at it, and Megan comes racing in from the kitchen.

I pick up quickly. "Hello?"

"Rosie?" Sarah's voice sounds unfamiliar, strained.

"Oh—hi!" I say, surprised. "Just a sec."

Jack looks at me anxiously, hopeful, but I shake my head.

"Just a friend from home," I whisper, watching his shoulders droop as I head upstairs. He's been like this ever since Holly left, jumping up at every knock on the door, every telephone ring. It's killing him that she's gone. Mentioning Sarah might not go down so well just at the moment either.

"Hi," I say again, closing the bedroom door behind me. "Is everything okay? It must be the middle of the night with you!"

"It is," she says quietly. "I just got in."

"Sarah?" Something in her voice makes me sit up. "What is it? Is Nana—"

"Your nana's fine," she sighs. "At least for now . . ."

"What do you mean?" I ask, my skin prickling. "What is it?"

"Rosie . . ." She hesitates. "Look, I don't blame you. I really don't, I just wish . . . I just wish you could've given me some warning, that you could have told me yourself." She sighs heavily, and I imagine her running a hand over her frazzled hair. "Rosie, someone's found out—about the swap— I'm being sued."

"What? No!" I tell her, relief flooding through me. "No, it's all right. There was . . . there *was* a problem, but it's over. The case was dropped." I didn't know Kitty'd even *opened* the case.

"Really?" Sarah's voice is hesitant, hopeful. "So this email I've got—I don't need to worry?"

"No, it's all over," I promise. "Kitty called it off."

"Who's Kitty?"

"My—my real mother . . ." I trail off awkwardly. "I'm sorry, Sarah, I came over here to find her—I had to . . . But she called a week ago. The charges were all dropped, don't worry."

There's a short pause.

"Rosie . . . ," she says slowly. "The email was sent today."

"*What?*" I stare at the phone. "That's impossible." *She can't have changed her mind, she can't . . .*

"I check my emails every day," Sarah says. "It just arrived."

"It was sent to you *personally?*" I gasp, my breath tight in my throat.

"Yes."

"Sarah . . . ," I say carefully, dread trickling through me like ice. "Who is the email from?"

Holly

I smile as I stare at the little pink address book for the hundredth time.

I don't know why I didn't think of it before. After all, why should Rosie get everything while I'm left with nothing?

And Sarah—well, she's going to get what's coming to her, I'll see to that. Kitty had the right idea. Make her pay. Make her pay for causing this whole mess. But Kitty didn't care enough. Her precious career was more important than the truth. Well, now I'm going to tell the truth—just like Rosie did when she arrived on my doorstep, ate my birthday cake and stole my life.

How does the saying go? The truth will set you free? Let's see if Sarah sees it that way.

After all, Melissa was right:

Don't get mad.

Get even.

Rosie

This can't be happening, I tell myself as Jack swings the car onto the main road and slams his foot on the accelerator.

She can't do this—she can't sue Sarah—not now . . . not after all we went through with Kitty . . . But of course, she can. And why shouldn't she? It's Holly's right, after all . . . it's her right more than anyone's.

But I can't let her. I have to stop this—I have to stop this now—but how?

I hang up miserably. She still won't answer her mobile.

"Keep trying!" Jack urges, the passing headlights picking out his frown lines in the dark. "We *have* to find her, make her see that suing won't help anything, help *anybody.*"

He thumps the dashboard and I quickly redial, getting through to voice mail over and over all the way to Boston as Holly and Josh refuse to answer.

Finally Jack swings the car to the curb outside a vast redbrick building and jumps out. I hurry after him across a neatly manicured quad crisscrossed with pathways and lined with naked, shivering trees.

He hammers on the locked door until finally someone answers.

"Where can I find Josh Samuels?" he barks.

The girl shrugs, startled. "I'm sorry, I don't—"

"Which room is he in?" Jack pushes past her. "Where's my daughter?"

387

"Hey." A muscly guy strides forward. "You can't just barge in here."

"I'm looking for my daughter!" Jack says firmly. "She's with Josh Samuels, and I need to see her *now!*"

"I'm sorry, sir, you'll have to leave." The guy walks right up to Jack, his hands balled fists at his sides. "Now."

Shit. "Jack . . ." I tug on his sleeve.

"I'm not leaving," Jack growls, eyeballing the guy, "till I find Josh Samuels."

"Really?" The human wall raises an eyebrow.

"Jack, maybe we should—"

"I saw Josh."

Jack spins and pins the second guy with his anxious stare. "When? Where?"

"Uh, about a half hour ago—"

"*Where?!*"

"He was getting into his car with a red-haired chick."

"Where were they going?" Jack urges.

"No idea." He shrugs.

"Shit." Jack sighs.

"But he had a suitcase."

Jack looks up quickly. "A suitcase?" His face relaxes. "She's coming home . . ."

"You leaving now?" Mr. Muscle grunts.

"Down, boy. We're going," Jack mutters, sighing with relief as we head back toward the car. "My little girl's coming home."

I follow silently, an uneasy feeling niggling in my gut.

Holly

Home. There's no place like it.

I watch the city lights fly past the car window and know I'm doing the right thing.

Whatever's happened—whatever happens—it's still my home.

Where the heart is.

Where my family is.

Where I belong.

I smile.

I can't wait.

Rosie

I hear the familiar ringtone before we even reach the car, and hurry to open the door.

"Rosie, finally!" Andy cries as I answer my phone. "I've been calling for, like, an hour!"

"Sorry, I've been trying to call Holly, she—"

"Has she got a new mobile?"

"What?"

"She broke hers—did she get a new one? I need to contact her."

"I dunno, we're trying to find her, she's staying with Josh—"

"No, she's not."

I blink. "She's not?"

Jack looks up sharply as he starts the car.

"No, just . . . if any of you hear from her, tell her to call me, okay?"

"Wait—Andy, how do you know?"

"I'm sorry, I can't tell you—I promised."

"*Andy, Holly's moved out. Jack's beside himself! If you know where she is . . .*"

"I don't . . ." Andy hesitates. "But I know where she's headed."

"*Where?*"

Andy sighs. "Rosie, she's going to England."

"*England?*"

Jack stares at me. "Shit! The airport."

My head slams against the window, the phone tumbling to the floor as Jack swings the car in a sharp U-turn and hits the accelerator.

Panic races through my veins.

England . . . Sarah . . .

Nana . . .

Holly

"Hey." Josh appears beside me in the line for check-in with a bag of candy. "I thought you might need these for the plane—for when your ears pop." He grins as he chews. "And maybe a few for now?"

I smile as he offers me the already-opened bag. It wasn't until I spent time with him this week that I realized just how much

I'd missed him—his warmth, his laughter, his reassuring presence beside me. It's been weird staying in his dorm, though. It's like he's got this whole other life, filled with friends I don't know and experiences I can't share. He's on the debate team, the university newspaper—he's even in the choir! My Josh, who I've never even heard *sing* before. He's thriving—changing and growing before my eyes, embracing each new challenge and adventure, gaining more and more confidence in himself. He *fits* here. He belongs in this world, this new life.

But that hasn't stopped him from being there for me when I needed him most. I smile. Maybe we will find a way through this— maybe it doesn't have to be all or nothing, college or us, engagement or breakup. We can bridge this gap, we can make it work if we try hard enough. I've met all his new friends now, after all, and he's been incredible this week—lending me his phone to call Charlotte, who'll contact a clinic in England when my results are ready, and listening without judging as I finally told him everything.

Well, almost everything.

I bite my lip. I feel awful not telling him about the baby, but with things still so undecided between us after our engagement fiasco, I don't want him to commit to me again just because I'm pregnant— especially when the baby and I might both have inherited a debilitating disease. When I still don't know whether I should keep it anyway . . .

Just one more secret. Just for now.

Until I know.

"You okay?" Josh asks gently. "D'you want me to come with you? Get a flight?"

I stare at him. He'd do that? For me? The girl who ditched him? He'd leave his studies and come with me halfway around the world to find my family?

I smile and squeeze his hand. Of course he would. That's exactly why I can't tell him about the baby. Can't let him sacrifice everything for me.

"Thanks." I smile. "But this is something I need to do myself."

"Okay." He nods, a frown flickering across his features. "But if you need anything at all—I'm here. Always. This isn't leaving my sight. Okay?" He holds up his cell phone and I want to cry.

As if to prove his point, the phone buzzes as he receives yet another voice mail.

"My dad again?" I sigh.

He nods, listening to the message, wincing at the raised voice, almost audible from here. "Crap."

"What now?" I frown.

Josh looks at me. "He's on his way."

Rosie

"Come on, come *on*!" Jack hisses, thumping the dashboard as we stop at yet another red light. "Which terminal does the Website say?"

I check his mobile. "Terminal E," I tell him, fidgeting in my seat, all my fingers and toes crossed as I stare at the lights, willing them to change.

We have to stop Holly, we *have* to—this is worse than Kitty. She was just looking for publicity, but Holly's out for revenge. On me, on Sarah . . . I press my eyes closed. I *have* to stop her.

Before it's too late.

Finally the airport looms up beside us, and I unbuckle my seat belt.

"Rosie, I can't leave the car here—"

"You park," I tell him, opening the door. "I'll find Holly."

I slam the door behind me and sprint toward the terminal building. *I have to find her.* I burst through the doors, my breath tight in my lungs, running, searching, scanning the concourse like my whole life depends on it.

Because it does.

Holly

Come on, come *on*! I tap my foot nervously as the check-in guy scans my passport.

"Never been abroad before, huh?" He grins. "Hope you don't get airsick!"

I smile tightly, glancing anxiously at the entrance. Still no sign of Dad, thank God—this'll be so much easier without a scene.

"Aisle or window?" the guy asks.

"Whatever!" I shrug, my eyes glued to the doors, scanning everyone who comes in. Josh squeezes my hand and I remember to breathe.

Finally the guy gives me my boarding pass, and I watch my bag disappear on the conveyor belt. No going back . . .

A niggle of doubt squirms inside me, but I ignore it. I'm doing the right thing, I *know* I'm doing the right thing—she's *my* nana, it's *my family*—I deserve some answers too.

And as for Sarah . . . My skin turns cold. She deserves

everything that's coming to her. It's time she faced the consequences of what she did—faced me.

"Hey." Josh grabs me in a warm hug and I begin to soften. "You take care of yourself, okay?"

"You too," I whisper, his strong arms wrapped around me like he'll never let go.

"Bring me back a gnome."

I laugh despite myself. "A gnome?"

"Yeah." He grins. "I always wanted a gnome. Named Yoda."

I grin. "It's a promise." I kiss his cheek softly.

Then my smile fades.

Rosie

"Holly!" I yell at the top of my lungs.

She turns and hurries away, and I sprint faster, grab her arm. "Holly, wait!"

"Hey!" Josh warns as she wrenches away.

"Holly, please—just listen. Please don't do this."

"Why not?" she challenges, her eyes cold. "Why *shouldn't* I?"

"Holly, *please*," I beg. "Sarah will go to prison! She never meant you any harm—it was a mistake. You'll ruin her life!"

"*She's* ruined *my* life!" Holly rounds on me. "Why shouldn't she be punished? Why shouldn't I go claim my family, Rosie? You did. She's *my* nana, after all!"

"Because . . ." I stare at her helplessly, a million reasons flooding to my lips. *Because she's an old lady. Because it would destroy her world. Because she's mine . . .*

"Because she doesn't know," I tell her, my words sounding feeble, even to me.

"Neither did I." She turns away, dragging Josh across the concourse.

"Holly, please." I chase after her, desperate now. "You have a right to be angry—we both do—but this won't solve anything! You can't turn back the clock!"

"You tried to!" Holly counters.

"Yes, and look where it got me with Kitty!" I reason. "You were better off without her!"

"That's easy for you to say!" she retorts. "I wouldn't know. My mother's dead!"

"I know, Holly—I'm the one who had to watch her die!" She flinches.

"You really think my life's been so easy—that I'm the *lucky* one in all this?!" I stare at her incredulously, blood blazing in my veins. "She was my *mother*, my *whole world* . . . and there was nothing I could do. I just had to watch . . ."

She looks away.

"You've had eighteen years, Holly—eighteen happy, blissful years with a dad who loves you more than anything else on this planet, a wonderful stepmother and a gorgeous little brother—and you think *I'm* the lucky one?" Tears scorch my eyes.

She bites her lip.

"Don't you see, there are no winners here, Holly. We're the same—I never had a dad, you never had a mother. This accident, this mistake, it happened to *both* of us."

"We're *not* the same!" she yells. "My parents are dead! I'll *never* know them!" She glares at me, her voice trembling.

"*They'll* never know *me*—because of Sarah, they never had the chance!"

"Holly." I lower my voice as people begin to stare. "I know. I'm sorry, I didn't mean—"

"And no, it wasn't an accident," she spits, eyes blazing. "It wasn't a mistake—*your* mother didn't *want* you. She left you, she *ran away. That's* how this all happened! If Kitty hadn't abandoned you we wouldn't be in this mess!"

I freeze as she glares at me, eyes shimmering.

"My mother was desperate for me—you said it yourself—she wanted me more than anything else in the whole world, but I was taken from her—your friend *stole* me—*that's* the difference!"

I stare at her, stunned, as Josh wraps his arm around her shoulders, tries to calm her down.

"It wasn't an accident," she repeats, her eyes burning into mine, clear as glass. "You were abandoned," she clarifies coldly. "I was stolen."

I stare at her as the room spins sickeningly. She's right. Kitty didn't want me—she never wanted me—she left me. *Twice* . . .

"No one was abandoned," Jack says quietly, walking up behind me.

Holly looks up at him, her jaw clenched tight.

"Holly," he says gently. "Rosie, both of you have been loved. *Are* loved. None of this makes a difference, DNA doesn't matter—"

"Ha!" Holly laughs coldly. "Well, you would say that, wouldn't you?"

Jack stares at her, his face draining of color.

"You're not my father, are you?" she says coldly. "You never were." To my surprise, she looks at me. "And you're not—"

"Holly—don't," Jack interrupts, grabbing her shoulders, his back to me. "Please . . ."

She stares up at him, her face stricken with pain. She shakes her head, disbelieving.

"Even now," she whispers. "Even *now?*"

"Holly—"

"Get *off* me!" she yells, shrugging him away. "Don't you *dare!*" Her voice is broken, splintered by tears. "Don't you *dare* tell me what to do—you're not my father—you were *never* my father!"

"Holly—" Jack tries again.

"Don't *touch* me!" She recoils, stepping behind Josh, who looks awkwardly at Jack.

People are staring openly now, and a security guard is heading our way, but Holly seems oblivious, her face raw with emotion as she glares at Jack.

She turns to me, opens her mouth to speak, then closes it again, a hardness descending over her features. She picks up her bag, her back straight, her shoulders square, and without another word, she grabs Josh's hand and walks away.

Holly

"Holly!" Dad cries, following me, but I keep walking, concentrating on putting one foot in front of another, heading for passport control. Hot tears spring, and I swipe at them angrily, Josh's hand tight around mine.

"Holly!" Dad grabs my arm.

"Jack," Josh says gently. "Sir, you can't stop her."

Dad shakes his head, his voice quiet, lost. "I'm not trying to."

He looks at me, so sad.

"Holly, if this is what you want, if this is really what you want . . ."

"It is," I tell him firmly, my jaw set.

"Then I'll come with you."

I stare at him in surprise.

"You're my little girl, Holly-berry," he whispers. "No matter what you say, you'll always be my little girl." He looks at me, his eyes full. "I just want you to be happy."

I stare at him. He'd come with me? To find my family? My real family?

"No." I shake my head, my voice trembling. "Thank you, but no—I have to . . . I have to do this by myself."

He looks at me, his eyes mournful, like we're saying goodbye for the last time.

"I understand." He nods, blinking quickly. He rubs his hand over his face roughly, then opens his wallet and presses a wad of bills into my palm.

"Good luck, baby," he whispers, leaning forward and kissing my forehead gently, the familiar scent of his jacket washing over me and stinging my eyes. "I love you."

I look up at him, my heart wrenching in my chest.

How did it come to this?

I gaze at him for what seems like forever, until his face swims in front of mine and I can't breathe . . . then I close my eyes tight, take a huge breath and force myself to turn away—away from everything I've ever known, everything I've ever loved—toward a future blurring before me . . .

Rosie

"This is crazy!" I yell at the airline rep. "There must be a flight—a stand-by seat or *something?*"

"Not tonight, I'm sorry, ma'am," she says calmly. "Would you like me to book that flight for you on the thirtieth? That's the earliest available seat right now."

"Fine!" I say, tearing at my hair. "Fine—yes. Yes, please."

I watch miserably as she makes the booking.

The thirtieth—four whole days away. I've got to wait *four whole days* before I can fly. Four whole days during which Holly could destroy my world, my life, my nana . . . and there's absolutely nothing I can do about it.

"Come on, Rosie," Jack says gently. "Let's go home."

Home. If such a place even exists anymore . . .

I follow him gloomily back to the car.

I can't believe he let her go—he just let her go . . .

But then, how could he stop her? I sigh. She's just doing what I did. I close my eyes, thinking of Nana, so frail, so fragile; of Sarah, so warm and loving. Neither of them deserves this.

And it's all my fault. I opened this can of worms, and now they're everywhere, squirming wildly, ripping apart everything I love, totally out of my control. I sigh heavily.

But not yet—Holly's not there yet, I reason. There's still time. She won't land for another six hours. Maybe she'll change her mind . . .

Yeah, I sigh. And maybe the moon really is made of cheese.

Holly

I wake with a jolt as the seat belt sign pings on. I pull off my eye mask and squint around the cabin. Morning light streams through the tiny windows, and there, below, is London. I rub my eyes, staring at the famous landmarks unfolding beneath me—the London Eye, Big Ben, Buckingham Palace—it's like a dream.

This *is* my dream, I think wistfully. Here I am, traveling at last. I rest my hand on my stomach. Though not quite the way I planned . . .

By the time I check into a hotel, I'm exhausted—jet lag, I suppose. I've made it as far as Maybridge, the nearest big town to Bramberley, but thought it might be better to leave the meet-and-greet until I've freshened up. One glance at the hotel mirror, and I'm glad I did: I'm a total mess.

I flop down on the bed and stare at the little address book.

Nana. The word tingles on my tongue. She's so close now—just the next village, just the other end of that phone . . .

I could call her, I think, the idea dancing in my mind. Just to make sure I have the right address . . . I pick up the receiver, pushing the buttons tentatively—the code that will unlock my history—then hold my breath as it rings.

"Hello?" a pleasant voice sings. "Laura Fisher's residence."

I can't breathe, paralyzed by the sound of her voice.

"Hello?" she says again. "Is anyone there?"

I put the phone down quickly, my heart racing. It's her.

She's real. My nana . . . And I'm going to find her. *Tomorrow,* I'll find her.

I bite my lip, fear mingling with my excitement.

Or maybe the day after.

Rosie

I stare at my mobile as sunlight begins to creep across the ceiling: *5:05 a.m.*

Holly will be in England by now. She's five hours ahead—she might even be in Bramberley.

My skin prickles.

I stare at the phone, trying to guess what's going on on the other side of the Atlantic.

I could call Andy for the fiftieth time, check again if he's managed to get hold of Holly yet, to talk her out of telling Nana . . .

Yeah, right. Like anyone could talk her out of it. I've never seen anyone more determined. And he'd have called me if he had. I sigh.

I could always call Nana myself . . . It would be better coming from me, better at least than hearing it from Holly, a stranger . . . even if that stranger is her *granddaughter.*

I pick up the phone, my hand shaking as I dial the familiar number, holding my breath as it rings.

Maybe she's out. Maybe she'll be out when Holly—

"Hello?" she says, her warm voice achingly familiar. "Hello, Laura Fisher's residence."

I can do this. I close my eyes, the phone trembling in my hand. *I have to do this.*

I open my mouth, but nothing comes out.

"Hello?" she says impatiently. "Hello? Who *is* this?"

My throat constricts as I struggle desperately, but there are no words—how do I start? How can I even begin to explain this whole horrible mess?

"Hello?"

I drop the phone like a hot coal, burying my head deep in my pillow.

I can't . . . I can't do it . . . How can I possibly tell her?

Holly

I stare at the sign as we drive past.

WELCOME TO BRAMBERLEY, TWINNED WITH CHARMOINES-SUR-MER

A shiver thrills through me. This is it. My hometown—village, rather. I gaze out the cab window as the rolling green hills give way to rows of huddling houses, then a duck pond and—no way!—a real live castle! I grin. Melissa would love this. It's like traveling back in time into a whole other world, filled with fields of sheep and cows, thatched cottages, rustic pubs, a large stone church . . .

"Wait!" I cry suddenly, turning to the cabdriver. "Stop here, please!"

I step out of the car and stare up at the tall gray stone building with its enormous stained-glass windows and large black clock face. I follow the gravel path up to the large iron gate and beyond, into a graveyard scattered with headstones.

My breath catches at every new stone as I scan each inscription nervously . . .

And then, suddenly, there she is.

I stare, mesmerized, at the stone, the letters fresh and clear.

GERTRUDE KENNING

BELOVED DAUGHTER, WIFE, AND MOTHER

Mother . . .

"Mom . . . ?" My heart suddenly constricts, crippled by the crushing realization that no matter what I do or where I go, this, here—a stone, a patch of mud—is the closest I'll ever get to her.

I stroke my fingers over the frozen soil, my tears glistening on the infant grass.

She was my mother and we never even met. She never knew me . . . She'll *never* know me . . .

"I'm here, Mom," I whisper. "I came back."

Too late.

The stone swims before me as I lean forward to touch it—so smooth, so hard, so cold.

Just a few weeks . . . I realize wretchedly. *I missed her by just a few miserable weeks.*

"I miss you, Mom," I tell her, my voice shuddering in the empty graveyard. "I miss you so much."

The words blur as I trace them with shaking fingertips.

D—A—V

Surprised, I blink, focus.

DAVID KENNING

LOVING SON, HUSBAND, FATHER

Father . . .

My dad's headstone as well as my mother's—my *birth* dad.

January 5th . . .

My birthday. The year I was born.

Guilt hits me without warning. Rosie never knew her dad. She never had a dad . . .

The image of Dad at the airport burns in my head and my heart twists painfully. I've had a dad all this time, my whole life, as real and as wonderful as any dad could be, and I would have never known my birth father, whatever happened. He died the night I was born . . .

The night we were born.

I shiver as I imagine what it must have been like—what it would be like if I was giving birth now and I discovered that Josh had been killed—if my baby was ill . . . if it died . . .

A wave of overwhelming sadness floods through me as I gaze at the stone.

This—*this* is what started it all. Not greed, not selfishness, not neglect—this tragedy. *This* is why Sarah switched us. This man—my dad—he died. If he hadn't—if there hadn't been a storm . . . I close my eyes, imagining how she must've felt—my mom—how helpless, how hopeless . . . worrying for her sick baby, grieving for her dead husband . . .

And now she's dead too. They're both dead. Here we are, fighting over them, while they're dead and gone.

We've *both* lost them. Forever.

And nothing can ever bring them back.

Rosie

This is ridiculous. I check my phone for the hundredth time this weekend. No news is good news, right? If Nana knew by now, surely she'd have rung me?

Or maybe not . . . Maybe she'll never want to speak to me again . . .

My insides twist as I stare fearfully at the silent phone.

This is torture! I've tried not to think about it, tried to get on with other things, but I can't concentrate, can't sleep, can't live like this—not knowing, fearing, waiting for the phone to ring, yet dreading it so much—it's driving me mad!

I take a deep breath and pick it up determinedly.

I'm going to do it this time, I tell myself. *I'm going to tell her.* I have to. She has to know.

If she doesn't already.

I hesitate, then punch in the last number, steeling myself as it rings at the other end.

I'm not going to hang up—I'm not going to hang up—I'm not going to—

"Hello—"

"Nana!" I cry quickly, before I have the chance to chicken out again. "Nana, I—"

"You have reached Laura Fisher's phone—I'm not here at the moment. Please leave a message after the tone."

Shit! I can't tell her on a *machine!*

I snap my phone shut and hurl it onto the bed, pacing the

room like a trapped animal, tearing at my hair. This is hope-less! I can't just sit here waiting, wondering, worrying . . . My eyes fall on my rucksack.

I grab my stuff and start shoving it in.

I can at least wait somewhere useful.

Holly

The silence is broken by a peal of jangling bells, the sudden noise startling me and sending a flock of chattering sparrows scattering into the sky like confetti. A group of giggling girls spills out the church doors, followed by a fleet of young mothers with strollers, their children racing and chasing around the headstones.

More people stream out of the church, flowing along the path behind me, chatting loudly, their footsteps noisy on the crunchy gravel. I duck my head as they pass, hurrying away from the crowd, the noise, my eyes glued to the ground as I quickly cross the street.

"Mrs. Fisher! Laura!"

I spin around, my heart pounding. I scan the crowd quickly, ur-gently, my eyes flicking quickly over each person, afraid I'll miss her, though I don't even know what she looks like.

Until I see her.

I know it's her. I just know. Her white hair is a fluffy cloud around her heart-shaped face, her lilac coat and skirt flattering on her small frame, her laughter warm and bright as she turns to gratefully re-ceive her forgotten scarf from a little boy.

My nana. I stare at her, absorbing every detail. She's got my nose, I realize suddenly, tingling. Or rather, I've got hers. I wander along the street, trying to keep track of her as she moves, craning my neck to see past the churchgoers who keep wandering into my way. Frustrated, I cross back over the road, anxious for a better view.

Suddenly, she looks my way, and I freeze, my heart in my mouth.

I stare at her, my eyes locked tightly on hers, my breath caught in my throat.

I don't even see the car skidding to avoid me.

Until suddenly I do.

Rosie

I take a deep breath, hitch my bag onto my shoulder, and walk into the living room.

Megan's reading, and Jack's doing a jigsaw with Ben, so it takes a moment for them to notice me. I watch them silently, imprinting the scene on my memory, my heart heavy.

Finally Jack looks up, taking in my coat, my backpack. He puts down his jigsaw piece. "I thought your flight wasn't for a couple of days?"

"It's not," I admit. "But I want to go and wait at the airport. There might be a stand-by seat, and if I'm there . . ."

"You know, you don't have to go," he says quietly.

"I do," I sigh. "I really do. I need to be there—to tell Nana myself." I blink fiercely. "If I'm not too late."

Jack pulls me to him, strokes my hair, and I close my eyes tight, trying to remember this moment forever, his warmth and love equally comforting and heartbreaking.

My dad.

With great effort, I pull myself away, swallow hard.

"Can I use your phone to call a cab?"

He shakes his head. "I'll drive you."

"I think I'd rather get a cab," I say gently. "It could take hours to get a flight, and—" I look away. "I'm no good at goodbyes."

Jack swallows hard, rubs his brow, then nods.

And if you're there, I think, moving past him toward the phone, *I might not ever get on the plane.*

Holly

I open my eyes and have no idea where I am. I blink a couple of times, struggling to focus. People in white coats drift past, and I'm lying down, my body heavy, with an odd feeling of having been abducted by aliens.

I try to move, and pain spears my temples, stopping me short. I screw my eyes shut, and, in a flash, I remember the car.

The baby.

Suddenly I can't breathe.

I try to sit up, my hands flying to my stomach.

I've lost it, I know I have . . .

"Holly?" A nurse appears next to me, taking my hand. "Holly— good, you're awake." I look at her desperately and she smiles. "It's okay, the doctor's just going to check you over—can you tell me where it hurts?"

"My baby," I tell her. "Oh, God, my baby . . ."

"You're pregnant?" she says, a frown flickering over her face. She smiles again quickly. "Don't worry, we'll do a complete check on you and your baby." She squeezes my hand. "You're in the best place now."

I nod weakly, the fear inside me so deep, so real, it takes my breath away. My baby, my precious baby . . . it's my fault, I didn't deserve it—I was going to have an abortion . . . an *abortion!* Bile floods my mouth and I close my eyes. *I'm sorry,* I tell it, too late. *I'm so sorry . . .*

"Is there anyone you'd like me to call for you?" the nurse asks. "To let them know you're all right?"

I shake my head, and she turns to leave. I watch her go, feeling small and helpless.

"Dad," I say suddenly, my voice thin and childlike. "My daddy."

Rosie

The phone rings just as I'm about to call the cab. I stare at it, startled, then lift the receiver. "Hello?"

"Hello," a distant voice says. "Hello, can I speak to Mr. Jack Woods?"

"Just a minute." I hand the receiver to Jack. "It's for you."

"Hello?" Jack says as I sit down again, my backpack between my knees. Megan hugs me tight as Ben climbs into my lap.

"We'll miss you," she whispers, kissing my head.

"You too." I hug them close. I'll miss all of them so much—Megan and little Ben—and especially Jack. I look at him, talking on the phone, and my heart aches. My *dad* . . .

But this is something I have to do.

Jack hangs up, and I move to take the phone, but he stops me.

"You won't need a cab, Rosie," he says, rubbing his face. "I'm coming with you."

"Jack—"

"To England."

Megan stares at him. "*What?*"

"That was a hospital over there," he says, his face ashen, drawn. "Holly's been in an accident."

My head snaps up.

"*What?!*" Megan gasps. "What happened—is she okay?"

"She's fine." He nods absently, still staring at the phone. "The nurse said she's just fine . . ."

"Oh, thank goodness!" Megan sighs, relief flooding her features.

Thank God!

Jack looks up, his face pale. "And so is her baby."

Holly

"Everything's okay?" I stare at the midwife incredulously. "Are you sure the baby's okay?"

"The baby's fine." She smiles, wiping the ultrasound jelly from my stomach. "Perfect. You're a lucky girl to have got away with just cuts and bruises—if that car had been going any faster it would've been a completely different story."

"Thank God." I rest my head back against the pillows, my hand warm against my cool belly. *Thank God.* I can't believe it. Can't believe I've been so lucky.

"You should get some rest," she advises me. "You've been through a lot, young lady, and it would do the baby good too."

I nod, suddenly exhausted. "Okay."

"And if you're good, I'll see if I can get you some chocolate mousse with your lunch—we only get it on Mondays, and there's always a bit of a scrum for it, but I'm friendly with the kitchen staff, so I'll see what I can do." She winks. "It's heavenly."

"Thank you," I tell her, my throat swelling with gratitude. "Thank you so much."

"You're welcome. Now rest, okay? They'll be kicking you out of here in the morning, so make the most of it." She grins at me, and I smile back.

"Sarah!" another nurse calls. "Sarah, have you got a minute?"

The smile freezes on my face.

"No rest for the wicked." She winks. "Don't go anywhere, I'll be back with that mousse."

I stare at her as she walks away, the feeling of disbelief stronger than ever.

Sarah?

Rosie

She's *pregnant?* Holly's *pregnant?*

Oh, God, all this stress, and she's *pregnant?*

I gaze out the window as we rumble along the runway, the past couple of hours a blur, my head still whirling with the news, trying to spot the signs I missed—in her moods, her actions, her words . . .

The test, I realize suddenly. She was asking me about getting tested . . .

I close my eyes. I can't even imagine what I'd do in her situation, what she must've been going through all this time. God, it's bad enough having to deal with Huntington's, but knowing you could be passing it on to your *child?* And she didn't tell anyone. I glance at Jack, who's staring blankly out of the plane window. He's been in a state of shock ever since we got the news. At least we managed to get stand-by seats—at least we're on our way. But he didn't know. She didn't tell him. She didn't tell anyone. Unless . . .

Andy. Andy gave her his phone, kept coming to visit her, spent the day with her . . . He knew! Holly must've confided in him. I smile. I only wish I'd done the same.

I glance at my watch. Six and a half hours. Six and a half more hours and we'll be there. Jack will be with Holly and I'll be home. My stomach lurches.

Who knows what'll be waiting for us.

Holly

I step outside the hospital door, and the sun is blinding. It's a new day, and it's beautiful—crisp and fresh and clean. A clean slate, I think, taking a deep breath, the fresh cold air alive in my lungs. A second chance. *For both of us.*

I spot a pay phone and fish some coins from my purse, crossing my fingers as I dial Dad's cell. *Please pick up . . .*

Hello, this is Jack's phone . . .

My heart aches to hear his voice—even his voice mail—and again I can't believe I ever left.

"Dad—I—it's me . . . I'm coming home." My heart swells. "I love you."

I smile as I hang up, rushing to catch a cab that's just dropping a family off.

"Where to, love?"

"Just a second." I reach into my bag for the hotel address—I need to pick up my stuff before heading to the airport. I can't wait to get home, to feel Dad's arms around me, have him tell me that everything will be okay—that he's excited about becoming a grand-dad! To be back with my family.

My eyes fall on the little pink address book nestled in the corner of my bag, glinting in the sunlight.

My family . . .

Rosie

"Welcome to London. You may now unfasten your seat belts and turn on your mobile phones," the flight attendant announces as Jack and I scramble into the aisle, only to get stuck behind people slowly retrieving their luggage from the overhead bins.

"Come on, come on!" Jack mutters as the queue inches its way off the plane.

We hurry into the airport, only to be stuck in yet more queues for passport control, baggage collection, customs . . . I watch Jack, his eyes closed in exasperation, the strain etched in the lines on his face.

I almost leave my luggage behind.

Finally we're outside and into a taxi, speeding away from the airport, heading south. Jack stares out the window, his face blank, his fingers tapping impatiently on the door handle. It seems to take forever. I stare out at the green fields, the patchwork landscape, heading home.

It's weird hurtling through the familiar countryside, the familiar towns, with Jack by my side. It's like we're out of place, like he's been inserted here from another world—his world—though of course this is his home country too, he's even been to this town . . .

"Oh, my God," he says suddenly, and I look at him. He's as white as a sheet.

"What?" I ask anxiously. "What's wrong?" Then I realize.

Outside, the enormous white walls of the hospital loom ahead, tall and foreboding.

"Oh, God," I say quietly as the taxi pulls up outside. "*This is the hospital she's in?*" I stare at him incredulously. "*Here?*"

He nods, the lines on his face catching the shadows.

"I should've realized, I—" He shakes his head as we pass the familiar sign and pull into the car park.

ST. ANNE'S HOSPITAL, MAYBRIDGE

Where it all began.

Holly

I stare at the house and check the address again. This is it.

Behind me, the cab pulls away and disappears around the corner. No going back.

I gaze down the street at the neat little cottages crammed together like sardines, with their identical walled-in front yards. A plastic gnome sits fishing in a frozen pond, his painted smile wide and jolly despite the cold, and I grin, thinking of Josh. *Yoda.*

I take a deep breath and walk carefully up the driveway, my feet crunching treacherously in the gravel. I bite my lip as I reach the door, raise my hand to knock.

What if this is a mistake? I hesitate, shoving my hand back into my pocket and looking up at the door. There is an iron horseshoe hanging above the doorframe, and a little handwritten sign tacked inside the glass window: *No junk mail please* with a smiley face. This is real. This is my nana's house.

I close my eyes and touch my fingers to the horseshoe for luck, and before I know it I've rung the bell. I stare at the door, my heart hammering.

Nothing.

I wait for a minute, holding my breath. Braver now, and slightly hopeful that there's no one in, I ring the doorbell again like a kid playing chicken—peering through the window as the bells resound through the empty house. I close my eyes, swallowing my disappointment, dizzy with sudden relief.

It's a sign. I'm not meant to find her. She's not meant to know.

I take a last long tender look at the house, smile, and turn away—just as a car sweeps into the driveway.

I stare at it, totally exposed, frozen to the spot. The door opens and a small white-haired woman steps out, shrugging her handbag onto her shoulder. The lady from the church. My nana.

"Hello." She smiles, locking the door and walking toward me. "Can I help you?"

"H-hi," I stammer, my feet as immobile as the plastic gnome's. "I'm . . ."

I'm what? *Hey, surprise, I'm your long-lost granddaughter?* She'd probably have a heart attack right here on the driveway!

"Sorry, do you live here?" I check. "You're Laura Fisher?" I don't wanna give the *wrong* old lady a heart attack!

"I am." She smiles. "Forgive me, you look familiar, but . . . do I know you?"

"I'm . . ." I stare at her, lost for words, dumbstruck by her sparkling blue eyes, her easy smile. She's old—so old—and yet there's something youthful in her eyes.

"I'm Holly," I say finally.

She looks at me afresh, recognition sparking in her eyes.

"Of course you are!" She beams, her whole face lighting up.

"Hello, Holly!" she smiles, her eyes twinkling at me. "I've been expecting you."

Rosie

The sliding doors hiss open with a blast of warm air, but Jack just stares at them, unable to move, his face unreadable.

"Jack?" I say gently. "Jack, are you okay?"

I touch his arm and he looks up, startled.

"Yes," he says, "yes, I'm fine—it's just . . ." He hesitates, his eyes sweeping over the door, the entrance, the reception within. "Jeez, the last time I was here . . ."

I nod. "I know," I say quietly.

Memories slide across his face, clear as our reflections in the glass as we step inside. The warm air breezes through my hair as our footsteps squeak on the shiny lino and I'm bombarded with smells—cleaning fluids and disinfectant and mashed potato . . . and a million memories hurtle back at me: broken arms and ankles as a child . . . that awful night of the prom . . . visiting Mum . . . my encounter with Jamila just a few weeks ago . . . I glance at Jack, unable to even imagine what he's going through.

Somehow we arrive at the reception desk.

"I'm here to see my daughter," Jack tells the receptionist. "Holly Woods? She had an accident."

The receptionist checks her computer screen.

"Woods?" she says. "I'm sorry, Ms. Woods was discharged earlier this morning."

Jack stares at her. "She's not here?"

She shakes her head. "I'm sorry."

"Well, do you know where she went?"

She looks up at Jack, then glances at me. "No, sorry, I don't."

Jack looks as if he's about to burst.

"Hang on—Nurse Willows!" My heart jumps as she calls over our shoulders toward the entrance. "Miss Woods was your patient, wasn't she? Do you know where she was heading to?"

We both turn as a blond woman looks round, pulling her coat on over her uniform.

She starts to speak, then stares at me.

"Rosie! What are you—"

"Hi, Sarah," I say, my cheeks burning as I glance anxiously at Jack, whose face is draining of color.

"Sarah?"

Holly

I stare at Laura, dumbfounded. She's been *expecting* me?

"Andrew rang a couple of days ago." She smiles, unlocking the door and ushering me inside. "He said you might pop round. I understand you know Rosie?"

"Yes—yes, I do." I stare at her uncertainly. *What has Andy told her?*

"Come in, come in!" She beams. "It's freezing out there!"

I follow her nervously into the house. It is warm and homey and smells of toast.

"Now, you make yourself comfy in the lounge." Laura smiles. "And I'll pop the kettle on."

I step gingerly into the living room, my feet sinking in the deep red plush carpet, my jaw dropping as I gaze at the dozens of photographs covering the wall. These must all be my ancestors— my great-grandparents . . . my grandfather . . . my dad . . . My heart stops.

There she is.

I move forward slowly, my breath trapped in my lungs, my eyes flicking from one photo to the next, the same hazel eyes shining out from each one.

Trudie.

I'd only ever seen the one photo Rosie gave me—had only imagined her at one age, in one setting—but here she is as a child, a teenager, a young woman . . . grinning and posing, beaming proudly at her graduation, laughing happily at her wedding. And there she is on a park swing, glowing with pride as she cuddles the tiny dark-haired girl in her arms.

That should have been me.

I finger my own hair, the hair I've always hated, till now. Now it's our bond, my inheritance, the exact same shade. Gingery-chestnut.

"Ginger nut?"

"What?" I turn, startled.

Laura is holding out a tin of cookies. She smiles. "I'm afraid there's not much choice—it's ginger nuts or chocolate digestives."

"Oh—thanks." I smile, taking a chocolate cookie.

"I rang Andrew, but I got one of those awful messagey things," she says, following my gaze to the wall. "That's a lovely photo, isn't it?" She beams, passing me a steaming cup and a saucer. "Rosie wasn't even two there, but she was already a right little minx—into

419

everything—you couldn't take your eye off her for a second! But then she'd grin at you with those big green eyes and you'd forgive her anything. Butter wouldn't melt."

I smile uncertainly.

"And that's her mother, Trudie. My own little girl," she says tenderly.

"She's beautiful," I breathe.

"Yes." Laura smiles. "She was."

"What was she like?" I ask quietly, holding my breath.

"She *was* beautiful." She sighs. "Inside as well as out. She was the kindest, most loving girl you could ever meet. An amazing mother to Rosie."

My heart aches. "Rosie said she'd died recently?"

"Yes." Laura's face clouds over. "She was very ill. She had Huntington's disease." She glances at me. "Rosie told you?" she asks slowly.

I nod. "I'm so sorry. It must've been awful."

"It was," she says. "It's a hideous disease. It was horrible seeing her suffer, watching her slip away. And the awful thing was we hadn't even known she was at risk—I'd never heard of Huntington's before, and Charles . . ." She nods at a photo of a handsome police officer. "My husband, Charles, died before his time, so we never knew it was in the family." She sighs. "No one should have to suffer like that, especially your own child."

No, I think, my hand reaching automatically for my belly. *No, they shouldn't.*

"Still, she made the best of it. Typical Trudie. No point moaning, she'd say, always turning her signs and symptoms into little jokes." Laura smiles. "She said it was the best weight-loss regime ever—she just loved stuffing her face with chocolate and cakes, flaunting the fact that she had to eat high-calorie foods to make up for the weight loss. Rosie and I were just relieved that she was officially banned from the kitchen!" She laughs. "She finally had an excuse for being such a terrible cook—and for being so untidy! 'Don't blame me!' she'd sing merrily. 'It's the Huntington's!'" Laura chuckles. "Always making the best of things . . . as far as she could, anyway." Her face clouds again.

"But the real curse was that the disease didn't only affect her. Trudie was so worried she could have passed it on to her own child. If she'd only known . . ." She sighs and I hold my breath.

"But you can't change the past any more than you can change the future." She smiles suddenly. "And knowing Trudie, she would've gone ahead anyway—she was so desperate for a child. And I have to admit she would probably have been right. I don't think you can live your life like that, fencing yourself in to be on the safe side. Worry is like a rocking chair—it keeps you busy but gets you nowhere. I wouldn't have swapped her for the world, even if I'd known. She was my Trudie, and even if I'd only had her for a few years, I'd still thank my lucky stars."

I stare at her, soaking her words up like a sponge.

"She felt that way too—was always saying how lucky she was, even when she was diagnosed. That was typical Trudie—anyone else would have been cursing the fates that now she'd finally got a child her time was going to be cut short. But not her. She might only have a few years left, she said, but how blessed she was to have been given a child, to share them with."

She gazes wistfully at the photograph.

"Children are the most important thing in the world," she says softly. "Don't you think?"

I bite my lip.

She turns to me, her eyes sparkling. "When's it due?"

I stare at her, my hand flying to my middle.

"Oh, don't worry, you're not showing," she laughs. "Just female intuition."

She smiles, and I find myself smiling too.

"When he or she enters this world, when you hold him or her in your arms for the first time, you'll understand. You'll know. This tiny being waiting to meet you will turn your life upside down and inside out, and you won't remember what it was ever like beforehand. You'll never want to." She beams. "You'll love them and take care of them as best you can, and that's all you can do. *Que sera, sera.*"

I smile. "Doris Day?"

"Yes!" She laughs. "Oh, I love her films!"

"Me too." I smile.

"Really?" she says, surprised. "I didn't think young people liked films without gallons of blood and gore in them these days. Rosie watches Cary Grant with me, bless her, but I don't think he's really her thing. Can't quite see him out 'clubbing,' can you?"

I laugh. "No, not really."

"And your young man?" she asks, her eyes twinkling. "Is he a Cary Grant?"

"He's . . ." My cheeks burn, my heart twisting as I think of Josh— our uncertain future—our baby . . .

She takes my hand, squeezes gently.

"My dear, men come and go." She smiles. "But you seem like a wonderful young woman." I look up at her as she strokes my hair behind my ear, her eyes bright. "And I'm sure you're going to be a wonderful mother. My Trudie did just fine on her own."

I look up at the photo again, the love in her eyes.

"True love is a marvelous thing." Laura beams. "But the love between a parent and a child—that's the most magical thing in the world."

I look at her. My nana. So loving, so wise.

I squeeze her hand, warm in mine.

Suddenly the sharp ring of the telephone pierces the silence, making us both jump.

"Oh, goodness—that scared me to death!" she laughs, moving to pick up the receiver. "Hello? Laura Fisher's residence?" She glances at me. "Of course." She covers the mouthpiece and hands it to me. "It's for you."

Rosie

"I still can't believe it!" Jack paces up and down the car park as Sarah nervously hugs her coat. "*You're* Sarah?" Jack stares at her, his eyes popping from their sockets. "You're— You *did* this?"

She stares at her feet. She looks wrecked, like she hasn't slept in days.

"I can't believe it." Jack shakes his head incredulously, hands in his hair. "How can you still work in a— How can you still be trusted with *babies*, after . . ." He glares at her, his eyes wild. "How many times? How many babies have you stolen? How many lives have you destroyed?"

"I—I'm so sorry." Sarah crumples before him. "It was only once—only Rosie . . ." She glances at me.

"Well, aren't we the lucky ones!" Jack explodes. "And how dare you come near my daughter again? How *dare* you!"

"I—I didn't know it was her," Sarah says helplessly. "I didn't know—"

"What have you done to her this time? Given her MRSA? Taken a kidney?"

"Jack!" I protest.

"Holly's fine," Sarah assures him. "She's completely recovered."

"No thanks to you—you left her for dead!"

Sarah flinches. Then she takes a deep breath, her voice shaking.

"Mr. Woods, you have every right to be angry—"

"Damn right!"

"But you have to understand—I didn't . . ." She falters. "I thought I was doing the right thing—I had *no idea* Holly was going to survive—"

"That's even worse!"

"Or that anyone was going to come back for her," Sarah insists. "I was told she was being put up for adoption—her mother had abandoned her—I didn't think it would hurt anyone."

"Well, it has—*you* have—have you any *idea* what you've done to my family? To my *daughter?*"

"Yes." She nods wretchedly. "Yes, I have—it's all I've thought about since I got Holly's email." She presses her eyes closed, her face tortured. "And she's got every right to sue me, to tell the police—whatever she wants to do—whatever *you* want to do . . ." She trails off, looking at Jack miserably. "I am so, so sorry."

"Yes, well!" Jack looks at her, then looks away agitatedly. He rubs his forehead.

"Look," she sighs sadly. "We can stand here all day

agreeing that what I did was wrong—it was terrible—and I deserve a multitude of punishments for the pain I've caused you all . . ." She looks from me to Jack, who stares at her, his jaw tensing and untensing. "Or we can do that later—and go and find Holly, make sure she's okay now."

Jack looks away, glaring at a parking meter. I glance at Sarah, so worried, so drained, then watch as Jack rubs his hands over and over his face. Finally he looks up.

"You got a car?"

Holly

I look at her in surprise. "For me?"

"It's Andrew." She smiles, and my heart sinks. "I'll just go and make another brew," she whispers, closing the door behind her.

Andy. Great. No doubt Rosie's put him on my case.

I sigh as I put the phone to my ear. "Hi, Andy."

"Holly, thank God—I didn't know how to get hold of you."

"Look, Andy, you don't have to worry," I tell him irritably. "I haven't said anything, and anyway it's really none of your—"

"Holly," he interrupts. "It's not about that."

I falter. "It's not?"

"Holly, the clinic rang—they still have my mobile number for you."

I freeze. The *clinic? So soon?*

"You need to call the clinic in Westhampton," Andy tells me. "They want to see you. Today."

"Why?" I ask, the phone trembling in my hand. "Is there a problem?"

"No," Andy says carefully. "Not that I know of."

"Then . . ." I can hardly hear, my heart's pounding so loud. "Then what?"

"Holly," he says gently. "Your results are in."

Rosie

As soon as Sarah slows down, I spill out of the car and race up Nana's driveway, skidding on the gravel as I run to her front door, ringing the doorbell and knocking madly on the glass.

Please, I beg. *Please tell me it's not too late!*

"Rosie!" Nana's eyes widen as she opens the door. Her hands fly to her mouth and I stare at her, paralyzed. *Does she know?*

"Oh, Rosie!" she cries, engulfing me in a hug. "I can't believe it! What are you doing here? Holly didn't say anything about you coming back so soon!"

I freeze. *Holly.* So I am too late. I close my eyes, limp in her arms.

"Nana," I begin. "Oh, Nana, I'm so sorry, I can explain . . ."

"Tush!" Nana chides, stroking my hair. "There's nothing to explain—it's a lovely surprise."

"What?" I pull back and look at her, confusion and fear jostling in my head.

"We had a lovely chat, Holly and I—she's a charming girl, isn't she?"

I stare at her, searching her eyes, tortured.

"Oh, it's just so good to have you home!" She grabs me in another hug and I feel myself relax slowly. She doesn't know. Holly didn't tell her. She was here, but she didn't tell her.

"I'm sorry—and you are?" Nana smiles, turning to Jack.

"Jack Woods," Jack says, extending his hand. "Holly's dad. I mean—"

"Oh, how wonderful!" Nana says, "But I'm afraid you've just missed her—Andrew rang and she had to dash off in a taxi."

Andy? Andy rang Nana's house? He stopped Holly telling her?

"Do you know where she went?" Jack asks.

She frowns. "Yes, Westhampton, I think she said."

Westhampton . . . the genetics clinic!

"Thanks, Nana—I'll be straight back, okay? We just have to find Holly."

"Oh, okay then, dear. Doesn't she know you've come to see her?" Nana smiles at Jack. "What a day of surprises!"

I kiss her cheek, then hurry back to Sarah's waiting car.

She can say that again.

Holly

I pay the cabdriver and stand for a moment, staring up at the red-brick building, unable to move. Across the street is a playground. How ironic. I look away, the sound of children's laughter playing like torturous music in my ears, and just concentrate on breathing—*in, out, in, out*—watching my breath rise in wisps and float away to nothing.

I've longed for this moment, for the waiting, the endless waiting to be over. And now it is . . . finally.

You don't have to know, Charlotte said. *You don't have to collect your results—lots of people pull out partway through.* I gaze up

427

at the clinic. *You have to be ready to live with the result, whatever it is. Positive or negative . . .*

I thought I was ready. I've imagined this moment so many times—both bad news and good news—I thought I was prepared . . .

But here I am. Now. Today. I look at the clinic, my heart hammering madly, all my hopes and dreams and wishes whirling with my fears and doubts and anxieties, about to hear the news of my life. Literally.

I close my eyes, trying to preserve this moment, to predict what the outcome will be. For both of us. Our future. Or not. *Fifty percent.* Heads or tails. Place your bets now.

I take a deep breath and force my legs to move, slowly, one after the other; force myself to breathe—*in, out, in, out*—and suddenly I'm at the door, my breath fogging the glass. My last clinic visit? Or the beginning of a lifetime membership?

With the last of my strength I push inside, the rush of warm air making me dizzy.

"Holly Woods," I tell the receptionist. "I'm here to get my results."

Rosie

"Come on, come on," Jack urges as Sarah speeds through Bramberley, through Maybridge, and on toward Westhampton, to the clinic.

I stare out the window, willing the roads to clear, the lights to turn green.

We have to get there in time—she can't go through this alone, it's too hard.

"It'll be okay," Sarah says quietly, catching Jack's eye in the rearview mirror. "Whatever the outcome, I promise it'll be okay."

He looks away.

We finally arrive at the clinic, and I race into the waiting room, an awful feeling of déjà vu hitting me like a sledgehammer as I scan the patients waiting anxiously on the hard plastic seats, reading the same magazines I flicked through just weeks ago. I feel sick.

"Holly?" Jack cries, bursting through the door.

"She's not here," I tell him miserably. "She must've already gone in." *All on her own.*

"Can I help you?" the receptionist asks.

"I'm looking for my daughter," Jack tells her breathlessly. "Holly Woods. Is she here? Has she gone in yet?"

The receptionist glances at me, then back at Jack. "I'm afraid I can't give you that information, sir," she says awkwardly. "Patient confidentiality."

"Screw patient confidentiality!" Jack bangs his fist on the counter, sending leaflets scattering to the floor. "She's my daughter—my little girl!"

The receptionist backs away, startled. "I'm sorry, sir."

"I'm her midwife."

I turn, surprised, as Sarah walks confidently up to the counter, showing her ID.

"I need to see my patient urgently. Could you tell her I'm here, please?" She eyeballs the receptionist, who hesitates.

"Look," she says slowly. "I'll let the counselors know you're here, all right? Then *if* Holly's here, she'll be told. Okay?"

Jack hangs his head, exhausted. "Thank you," he sighs as she picks up the phone. He glances at Sarah. "Thank you."

"Don't mention it." She smiles.

"Take a seat," the receptionist says, and Jack slumps into a chair. I follow silently. There are no words. No comfort. Only the wait. Always the wait. The weight.

I sigh, my eyes wandering aimlessly around the room, feeling uncomfortable and restless in this too-familiar place. This was me. I've lived this. This is where I sat while Mum had her tests, got her results, where I sat to get my own. The familiar wallpaper, the saccharine-smelling air freshener. But this time it's worse. This time there's so much more at stake.

My gaze trails to the window, the winter sunlight struggling through the stubborn clouds. Across the street, children squeal and giggle as they chase each other merrily round a colorful payground. My eyes follow a little girl as she races from the climbing-frame to the swings, her daddy pushing her higher and higher as she shrieks in delight, until suddenly she jumps off, sprinting toward the seesaw, the slide, her next adventure. The swing jangles wildly in her wake, careering forward and backward, joyful still, despite her absence.

On the swing next to it, someone else sways listlessly, barely moving at all.

Holly

I kick at the leaves as I swing slowly by, watching as they scuffle and scatter, living for a moment in the breeze, before dropping, lifeless, into the mud.

One leaf still clings to its branch, high above me. It quivers, fluttering and flickering as the wind tugs at it again and again—and yet still it stubbornly holds on, glistening in the sunlight.

In all likelihood it too will eventually fall and become mucky, trampled into the sodden ground. But maybe a merciful breeze will spare it—carry it safely to alight on a rooftop or a nest. Maybe, somehow, it will cling to its branch forever. But for now it glimmers, golden in the winter sunshine. Untouched. Its destiny undecided.

I watch the children race around me, laughing and shrieking, their chubby cheeks rosy with adventure, their eyes sparkling with possibilities, and I close my eyes, the hot tears spilling down my cheeks. I hug my coat tighter, as if I can protect my child with this cocoon, keeping out the cold and the danger, holding on to my burning heart, my aching hope.

"Holly!" The word whispers on the wind and tickles my ear. "Holly!"

I open my eyes.

"Holly!" the voice calls, louder now. *"Holly!"*

Dad? I look up slowly, my face numb with tears.

"Oh, Holly!" Dad runs across the grass toward me. "Holly, thank God!"

"Daddy?" My voice cracks as he drops to his knees in front of me, engulfing me in his arms.

"Dad . . . ," I cry, drowning in his embrace, unable to believe he's real. "Dad, what are you doing here?"

He pulls back and cups my face in his hands, his eyes deep green overflowing pools. "You're here," he says simply, stroking my hair from my face, kissing away my tears, which are mingling with his own. "You're here, Holly-berry. Where else would I be?"

I crumple into his arms, the pain suddenly overwhelming.

"Oh, sweetheart," he soothes, holding me tight. "I can't imagine

what you've gone through—what you've been going through all this
time—all on your own . . ." He trails off, his eyes bright. "But I'm here
now. It's all right."

"It's not all right!" I cry miserably, tears flooding my words.
"Daddy, I'm pregnant—the baby—"

"Shhh." He pulls me close, holding me together as I fall apart.
"It'll be okay, I promise—whatever happens, whatever you decide."

My insides twist painfully.

Whatever I decide . . .

"I'm here for you," he says gently. "I'll come into the clinic with
you, hold your hand—if that's still what you want?"

I stare up at him, sobs clogging my throat, tears filling my eyes.
*I want to be strong, to be brave enough to face the truth—the con-
sequences, but . . .* I clutch my stomach desperately. *But I can't . . .*

Dad strokes a tear from my cheek.

"If not—if you've changed your mind and you don't want to
know yet—that's okay too," he promises, kissing my forehead. "It's
not too late."

I screw my eyes shut, helpless to stop the tears as they stream
like acid down my cheeks, my head throbbing mercilessly, my heart
on fire.

"It's your child, Holly," he says gently, his voice like cool water.
"Your choice. I'll support you either way, you know that." He strokes his
thumb gently along my jawline and I bite my lip. "You're my little girl."

I look up at him, his face shining with love. Words stick in my
throat and I hold on tighter, his arms warm and strong around me.

My dad, I think, melting into him. No matter what the truth is—the
blood, the DNA. He always has been. Even though he knew he might
not be. But I didn't know, and I was happy. I bury my head deeper
into his jacket, into the familiar smell I've known since I was a little girl.

Sometimes it's not the lies that hurt you, I realize. *It's the truth.*

I close my eyes. "Daddy . . . ," I whisper, my skull throbbing. "I want my baby."

"Okay," he sighs, engulfing me in his warmth. "Oh, sweetheart, that's okay." He folds himself around me, shielding me from the cold winter wind, the world, the truth.

"You've made a lot of tough decisions lately, huh?" He glances over at the parking lot, where Rosie is standing with Sarah, then back at me, his eyes full. "I'm so proud of you, Holly-berry," he whispers, his voice cracking as he holds me tighter than ever. "You're gonna be a wonderful mum."

Rosie

The sun finally breaks through the clouds as we round the corner away from the clinic. I watch it disappear in the rearview mirror, behind the trees, the lampposts, the houses; then I sink back in my seat, my eyes closed, glad to leave it behind for the very last time.

So this is how it ends, I think, glancing at Jack, his arm around Holly in the backseat. My dad. I smile. I found him, and he's terrific. We're reunited. A family. And now . . . now we're all going home.

My gaze falls on Holly, her eyes closed, exhausted, the opposite side of my coin in so many ways. She made the choice I couldn't. She decided not to know. She'd rather live life hoping for the best than risk discovering a dark cloud looming over her future. Maybe she'll be lucky, maybe she'll

433

be clear, maybe she'll never develop symptoms. Even if she does, it won't be for many years. Perhaps there'll even be a cure by then. Maybe she'll live a long and healthy life with her child and I'll get hit by a bus next week. Who knows?

I glance at Sarah in the driver's seat, her face aged a decade since I saw her last, haunted by the repercussions of one split-second decision she made eighteen years ago . . . Her eyes meet Jack's in the rearview mirror again. This time he smiles peacefully as he strokes Holly's hair.

The past has passed, after all. It's time for us all to move on, look to the future.

Time to say goodbye.

I sigh as I climb out of the car and look up at Nana's house. The front door opens and I freeze as I recognize the familiar face.

Andy.

"Hey, stranger," he says, walking down the drive toward me. "Fancy seeing you here."

I beam at him, my heart racing. What's he doing here? He should be on the other side of the world—shouldn't he?

He glances at the car.

"I came to give Holly a lift to . . ." He hesitates. "Has she—is she . . . ?"

"No." I shake my head. "She chose not to know."

He looks relieved.

"But what are you—how did you—aren't you meant to be in . . . Cambodia or something?" I stammer.

"Vietnam." Andy nods. "Yep. Yep, I am."

"So you came all the way back home . . . for Holly?" I ask.

"Well, no . . . ," he confesses sheepishly, hands deep in his pockets. "Not *exactly* . . ."

"Then . . . ?"

"Well . . ." He sighs, shuffling his feet through the leaves as he shuffles closer. "I realized I'd left something behind . . ."

"Oh?" The scent of his aftershave drifts on the breeze as he moves closer.

"The same thing I keep leaving—the most important thing of all."

"Your passport?" I whisper, his breath warm on my face.

"No, idiot. Much more important than that." He grins, brushing my hair behind my ear. "I keep leaving *you*."

My heart flips, my skin tingling at his touch.

"I thought I was missing out, being stuck in tiny Province-town, that I was getting in the way and missing my trip—the adventure I'd looked forward to and worked for and planned for so long . . ." He sighs. "I didn't get it. *You're* the adven-ture, Rose—*you're* the trip! You're a bloody roller coaster!" He grins. "You're what made New York so incredible—you're what made me want to go traveling in the first place. This is *our* dream. Vietnam, Cambodia, Thailand . . . it doesn't mean anything unless you're there."

He looks deep into my eyes and my pulse races.

"I can't go without you, Rose." He shakes his head. "There's no point—I'd rather not go at all. I'll wait for you, we'll travel together." He cups my face gently, smiles. "When you're ready . . . I'm gonna be right here waiting for you,"

435

he promises, pulling me close, searching my eyes. "However long it takes."

I look at him and can hardly breathe, my heart thumping like crazy against his, my necklace nestled between.

"I love you, Rosie Kenning, and I want to be with you. Full stop."

"I love you too." I smile, and he kisses me, a long, deep, lingering kiss that thrills through my veins and makes my head spin dizzily, as only Andy can. I kiss him back, holding him as tight as possible—like I'll never let him go again.

"Oi, no snogging on the driveway, young lady!" Jack shouts.

I laugh, my cheeks hot as I turn to grin at him standing by the doorway with Nana, Holly and Sarah.

"Can we cadge a lift to the airport, young man?" he calls.

"Certainly, sir!" Andy salutes, kissing me again before going to unlock his car.

I take a deep breath and steel myself, my insides twisting. I hate goodbyes.

I walk up the driveway, gazing fondly at the little bungalow, at Nana in the doorway, and my heart aches. I know I'm doing the right thing. It's time to go home. For all of us. Them to New England. Me to my old England.

More or less.

It's so weird—it's only been a few weeks, just over a month, really, since I left, but it seems like a lifetime. So much has happened, so much has changed. Yet here nothing has so much as shifted position. Nana's garden gnome is still fishing determinedly in the frozen pond, the hall clock still runs two minutes fast, the old family-photo collage still hangs at a jaunty angle beneath—I even bet Cary Grant's still in the DVD player. Everything the same as it always was, as it always has been—ever since Mum was a little girl.

Mum. My heart floods with love for her. My mother, my mum. She always was. She always will be. She beams down at me from a multitude of photos, her chestnut hair gleaming in the afternoon sunlight. *Trudie.*

"Oh, Rosie, I'm so happy you're home." Nana smiles, and suddenly I see Mum there too—in Nana's sparkling eyes, her bright smile, the warmth of her hug as she holds me tight, her hair soft as candy-floss against my cheek, her love spreading through me like melted chocolate.

"Me too, Nana." I hold her close, her small frame dwarfed by mine, the familiar smell of hot tea and toast wrapping round me like a cozy blanket, engulfing me with memories. I press my eyes closed, imagining—fearing—just how awful all this could so easily have turned out, and my skin prickles.

"You've got goose bumps!" she laughs, rubbing my arms. "Are you all right?"

"Yes," I say. *Just one more secret, one more lie . . .* "Just chilly."

"You need a nice hot chocolate!" Nana grins. "Warms you from the inside out, you know?" She winks.

I look at her—so happy, so fragile, so precious . . .

"That'd be lovely." I smile tightly, locking the truth inside forever, realizing fully for the first time how Sarah felt, why she kept her secret for so long.

Some things are more precious than the truth . . .

Holly

"Goodbye, Holly," Sarah says softly, almost afraid to look me in the eye now that she knows who I am. "Take care."

"Goodbye, Sarah," I sigh, gazing at the woman who changed my life. The woman I thought I'd hate—this tired-looking woman with sorrow in her eyes and lines etched across her face, who brought me chocolate mousse and cared for my baby—who took me from my real mother and gave me to my wonderful dad.

For that, I could never hate her, not really.

Laura hugs me goodbye, and I smile. She was right. *Que sera, sera.* I squeeze her tightly, breathing in her faint perfume. You can't predict how life's gonna work out . . . *For better, or worse*—I smile, thinking of Josh waiting for me at home. *For richer, for poorer*—I think of Kitty . . .

Usually life's a bit of all those things. But it's what you do with it that counts. And I intend to make the most of every single moment.

I take a deep breath as Rosie walks me to the car.

"Well," I say. "I guess this is it."

She nods. We look at each other for an awkward moment; then I stick out my hand.

"Well, goodbye."

"Goodbye," she says quietly, taking my hand, then holding on. "I know it's not enough—it never will be . . . ," she whispers, takes a deep breath. "But Holly, I really am so sorry," she says, her eyes deep in mine. "About everything."

I look at her, my cheeks growing warm in the frosty air, then

438

shake my head. "It wasn't your fault, Rosie." I sigh. "It wasn't anyone's. Not really."

"I'm still sorry," she says softly.

I look at her for a moment. "Me too," I admit. "I've been a bit of a bitch lately."

She laughs, shakes her head.

"Blame the hormones." I grin.

"Congratulations." She beams. "You're going to be such a great mum!" She holds me close, and I return her hug, feeling all my resentment and hurt finally ebbing away.

"And for what it's worth," she whispers, "I think you made the right decision." She pulls back, her eyes earnest. "I think some things you're better off not knowing."

I nod slowly, then glance at Laura standing by the door. I squeeze Rosie's hand, a lump forming in my throat. "I think you're right." I smile.

She follows my gaze, her eyes shimmering as she pulls me into another tight hug. "Thank you," she whispers, squeezing me tight. *"Thank you so much."*

I smile.

"Now, don't be a stranger," she commands. "Come and visit whenever you want—you know where we are now."

"Speaking of which . . ." I pull out the little pink address book and give it to her guiltily. "I believe this is yours—I, er, guess I got a bit confused about what belonged to who . . ."

Rosie smiles, then tears a page out. "Keep this," she says, handing me their contact details. "Then you'll always know how to find us—*Mi casa et su casa.*" She laughs at the irony. "Literally."

"You too," I tell her. "You'll have to come meet this little one when he or she arrives."

"Try and stop me!" She grins, squeezing my hands. "Thank you, Holly."

Yes, I think, smiling as she walks away. *She's right.*

I look at her as Dad hugs her goodbye. *Father and daughter.*

I watch Laura's face light up as Rosie hurries back down the driveway. *To her nana.*

I smile at Dad as he slides into Andy's car next to me and squeezes my hand as we glide away from the curb, heading for home. He pulls me close and kisses my head.

His daughter.

I close my eyes, the blood hot in my veins. *Undiagnosed . . .*

Yes, I think as Dad's palm gently settles on top of mine on my stomach, his large hand feather-soft, stroking the resting place of my unborn child, who's sleeping soundly—its fate, its future unknown, a new leaf springing up on this bizarre family tree.

Yes, some things people are better off not knowing . . .

Epilogue

Sunlight dances over the little girl's red curls as she gazes at the camera, her brown eyes wide as she suddenly lunges chocolaty fingers toward the screen.

The picture immediately jolts and twists, continuing at a skewed angle as her chestnut-haired mother struggles to wrestle the webcam from her iron grip.

"She's gorgeous!" I tell Holly, laughing as she adjusts the camera.

"Just like her mom." Josh smiles, resting his head on Holly's shoulder as she beams at him. She's glowing. They both are.

"Well, she definitely got my hair, anyway," she concedes. "Born with a whole head of it, poor thing!" She grins. "So, Rosie, when're you gonna come visit? Tru can't wait to meet her godmother."

I beam, my heart swelling at the name, and the honor. I can't believe they've made me godmother!

"Red alert, red alert—she's trying to suck you into

babysitting duties!" Jack appears behind Holly, grimacing. "Holly seems to have an aversion to changing nappies!"

"They stink worse than you!" she retorts.

"Hey, Granddad." I grin.

"Watch it!" Jack laughs. "I'm feeling ancient enough as it is. So, you coming over or what?"

"I'd love to, but I start back at Sixth Form in two weeks, and I've got heaps of catching up to do."

"Ugh! Tell me about it!" Holly rolls her eyes. "I've got so much reading to do before I even *start* college!"

"Maybe Christmas, though?" I say. "Or Easter? Of course, I'd *have* to come over for a wedding . . ." I grin at Holly and Josh. "Any sign of a diamond yet, Holls?"

"Not yet." She smiles at Josh, her fingers intertwined with his like a candy cane. "But you never know what the future holds . . ."

I look at them; they're so happy. *You never know . . .*

She's right. A year ago I could never have imagined that this was what the future had in store—that Mum wasn't really my mum; that her real daughter was on the other side of the Atlantic; that I'd discover my real mother was a TV star, and that I'd be reunited with my wonderful dad, my gorgeous half brother, and to all intents and purposes a sister too . . . I smile. We've come a long way. And Holly's so right. Who knows what'll be around the next corner—a wedding, a tsunami, a cure . . . All any of us can really do is make the most of the time we've got, seize the day, treasure every moment with the people we love.

My screen bleeps.

"Oh! I've got another call," I tell them. "It's Nana."

"Give her my love." Holly smiles. "Speak soon."

I say goodbye, then connect to Nana. It still amazes me how she's got the hang of all this technology. She's a whiz at Skype now, bought her own webcam and even has her own Facebook account to keep up with my photos!

"Hello, sweetheart, just a quickie, as I saw you were online." She smiles. "I wanted to check you're still coming home next week?"

"Next Saturday, two-fifteen p.m."

"Wonderful! I can't wait."

I smile. "Me neither."

There's no place like home, especially as it was so nearly ripped apart. I still shudder to think how things might've been if Nana had found out the truth—have to watch myself every time I mention Holly or Jack. I guess it's something I'll just have to live with—the last secret I have to keep.

"Holly sends her love," I say carefully.

"How lovely, and isn't she doing well? I get her updates on Facebook—isn't her baby adorable?"

"Beautiful." I smile wistfully. *Your great-granddaughter.* My heart aches to tell her, but I never can. "She's perfect."

"All that gorgeous hair! Almost the same shade as Trudie's."

I bite my tongue and nod, the irony of her comparison almost unbearable. "She was born with it, Holly said."

"Yes." Nana beams. "It was the same with her. Beautiful fluffy ginger wisps, and that funny little kinky ear—like a little pixie." She chuckles. "Just like her mother."

I frown suddenly. "Nana, you don't have a kink . . ."

"And look at her now."

My breath sticks in my throat as I stare at her, her eyes twinkling as goose bumps prickle down my arms.

"Nana . . ."

"Oh, Rosie, I've got to dash—the girls have arrived. We're going bowling."

"What? Nana, wait—"

"I'm a big girl, Rosie, you don't have to worry about me— on the bowling green, or off." She winks. "I'm not daft."

I stare at her.

"Listen, I've got to go—we'll catch up properly when you're back, okay? It'll be much better in person." She beams. "You can tell me everything I've missed. Now stop worrying, and go and have fun!"

"Okay, but—"

"I love you, darling—byee!"

"Love you . . ." The call disconnects and her name fades on the screen. I stare at it numbly for a moment.

She knows . . .

My heart hammers wildly.

Has she always known . . . ?

I scour my memory quickly, remembering how Nana was there the night I was born, how she was with Sarah when they discovered Kitty had run away, how she always referred to me as a miracle, how she didn't think Trudie would've coped without me . . . how insistent she was that I take the test as soon as possible, *even though there isn't a cure . . .*

I step outside into the blinding sun, the air dense and hard to breathe.

How she knew that Holly was born with ginger hair and a kinky ear . . .

The sand shifts beneath my feet.

Did she always know I wasn't Trudie's baby?

Or has she just worked it out . . . ?

Andy looks up from his tatty guidebook. "Everything all right?"

I look at him, my head spinning.

"Yes." A smile blossoms slowly across my mouth. It is. *It finally is.*

Whether she always knew, or whether she just figured it out—she knows. Nana knows—and it's okay . . . everything's okay . . .

She can finally know Holly—and Jack—and little Tru . . . We can finally be a family—a real family.

No more secrets, no more lies . . .

I beam at Andy—my Andy—relaxed and bronzed and happier than I've ever seen him, lying on the golden Thai beach waiting for me, the sun warm on my face, my heart soaring with the birds wheeling freely high above, feeling simultaneously like I'm dreaming and like I've just woken up. "Everything's perfect."

"Good." He grins, dropping his book on his towel. "Ready to dive in?"

The waves wink at me, glittering with promise as far as the eye can see—as boundless, beautiful and fathomless as the future.

"Definitely." I beam, sprinting across the beach, the wind dancing in my hair, sand flying, shrieking with laughter as Andy chases me toward the sparkling water, the crashing waves, the infinite horizon, our footprints mingling in the sand behind us . . .

Author's Note

Huntington's disease (HD) is a terminal hereditary disorder of the central nervous system, caused by a faulty (enlarged) gene on chromosome 4. Named after Dr. George Huntington, who first described the hereditary disorder in 1872, HD affects as many people as hemophilia, cystic fibrosis or muscular dystrophy.

Every child of a parent with Huntington's disease is born with a 50 percent chance of inheriting it. If the child does not inherit the gene, he or she cannot pass it on—it cannot skip generations. If the child does inherit the gene, he or she will, at some stage, develop the disease, if he or she lives long enough. In 1993, the HD gene was isolated and a direct predictive genetic test was developed. The test can accurately determine whether a person carries the HD gene, but not the age at which symptoms will begin.

Symptoms of HD usually develop between the ages of thirty and fifty years old, although they can start much earlier (there is a rare juvenile form) or later and can differ from person to person, even within families. Likewise, symptoms can vary from person to person, but include physical, emotional and cognitive changes.

Physical changes often include involuntary movements (chorea), stumbling and clumsiness, difficulty in speech and swallowing, and weight loss.

Emotional changes can result in stubbornness, frustration, lack of inhibition, mood swings, paranoia, aggression or depression.

Cognitive changes can include short-term memory lapses, loss of organizational skills, difficulty multitasking, and loss of drive and initiative—which may be misinterpreted as laziness.

Symptoms progress slowly over ten to twenty years, with death usually resulting from complications such as choking, infections, aspiration pneumonia (caused by difficulties in swallowing) or heart failure.

Although there are currently about 6,700 reported cases in England and Wales—and 30,000 in the United States— probably over twice as many people are affected. This is because people with HD often hide the condition due to social stigma, or insurance or family issues, and because many cases are never diagnosed. Many people with a family history of HD decide not to be tested, since there is currently no cure, and people with no known family history of the disease are also often misdiagnosed with other conditions, such as dementia or depression.

Though no cure has yet been found, since the discovery of the gene that causes HD, scientific research has accelerated, and much has been added to our understanding of Huntington's disease and its effects.

There are many ways to manage the symptoms effectively.

Medication can be used to treat symptoms such as involuntary movements, depression and mood swings, while speech therapy can significantly improve speech and swallowing problems, and a high-calorie diet can prevent weight loss and lessen symptoms such as involuntary movements or behavioral problems.

Useful Websites

Huntington's Disease Advocacy Center:
hdac.org

HDSA National Youth Alliance:
huntingtondisease.tripod.com/nya

Huntington's Disease Society of America:
hdsa.org

Huntington Society of Canada:
hsc-ca.org
Young People Affected by
Huntington's Disease, Canada:
ypahd.ca

International Huntington Association:
huntington-assoc.com

Acknowledgments

Many thanks . . .

To everyone whose lives have been touched by Huntington's disease, either personally or professionally, who have helped me in so many ways, sharing their knowledge, advice, and personal stories, particularly Matt Bower, MS, CGC; Susan Walther, MS, CGC; Phillip Hardt; Stacey Barton, MSW, LCSW; Professor Joseph Boyd Martin, MD, PhD; Andrea Gainey, MS, CGC; Bonnie L. Hennig, MSW, LCSW; Dave Stickles; Christina Barnes; David Harbourne; Bill Crowder; Karen Crowder and everyone in the HDA; Jean E. Miller; Frank Medina's wife, Gloria; Dave Hodgson; Hugh Marriott; Peter Webb and everyone in the Sussex branch of the HDA; Tracie Tuhill; Jean Morack; Fred Taubman; Jennifer Williamson, MS; Adam Coovadia, MLT (CSMLS), MB, CG (ASCP); Kristin Kitzmiller; Shelby Duffer, MS, CGC; Kendell Aitchison; and especially to the exceptional and inspirational Pat Leslie-Penny and Matt Ellison.

To Colleen Begg for her advice about maternity wards.

To Miss Higgins for encouraging my writing after reading my "Owl" poem.

To Ruth Moose for her wonderful writing classes at UNC, where this story was born, and for introducing me to the great SCBWI.

To the Society of Children's Book Writers and Illustrators, particularly the fabulous Sara Grant and Sara O'Connor, for running the incredible Undiscovered Voices competition with Working Partners, giving unpublished, unagented writers a chance to climb out of the slush pile and make their dreams come true.

To my lovely editors, Michelle Poploff, Venetia Gosling, Jane Griffiths, Amy Black, and Rebecca Short, for making this dream come true.

To my brilliant and very lovely agent, Jenny Savill at Andrew Nurnberg Associates Ltd., for believing in *Someone Else's Life* from the moment she first read it—and then helping me to ditch forty thousand words.

To Chris, for his constant love and support for my pursuit of this dream, no matter how penniless I've been or how hopeless it's seemed, and for putting up with me scribbling away beside him at ridiculous hours, and in the craziest places.

To my granddad Charles, a true gentleman, for his selfless love of all his family and for always being so proud of us.

To my lovely sister Caroline, for showing me that joy and laughter can be found in every single day.

To my equally lovely sister Jenny, for her incredible humor, courage, and selflessness whilst proving that while life may not follow the route you planned, it's what you do with it that counts, for sometimes the greatest happiness lies down those unexpected avenues.

To my gorgeous niece Summer, my little clown, with whom the world is an infinitely magical, hilarious, and wondrous place.

To my wonderful dad, for his endless love, support, wisdom, and humor, and for his ingenious "Moley" stories.

And finally to my amazing mum, for always believing in me, encouraging me, and inspiring me every day of my life.

Thank you all so much, from the bottom of my heart.